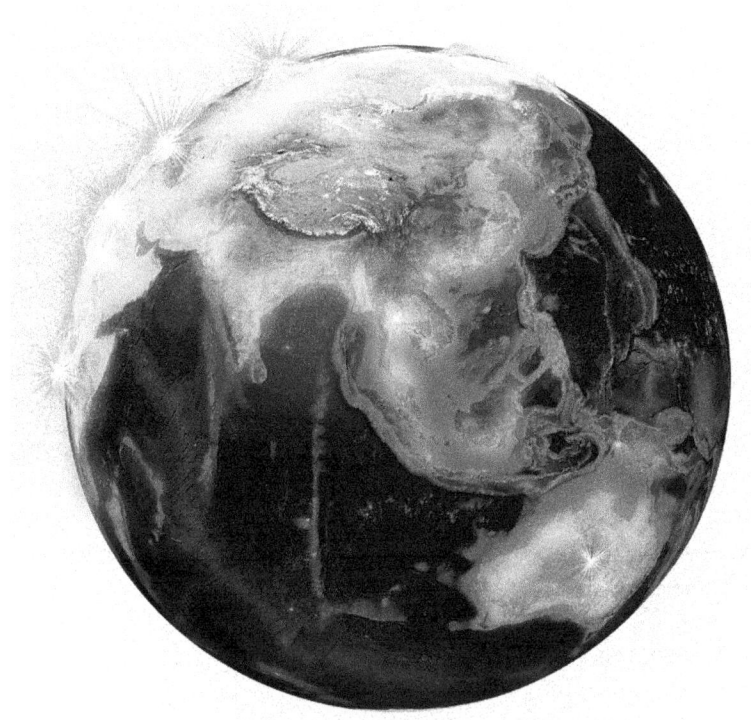

THE SECOND OF SEVEN

A NOVEL

JEREMIE GUY

ANAPHORA LITERARY PRESS

QUANAH, TEXAS

ANAPHORA LITERARY PRESS
1108 W 3rd Street
Quanah, TX 79252
https://anaphoraliterary.com

Book design by Anna Faktorovich, Ph.D.

Copyright © 2018 by Jeremie Guy

Printed in the United States of America, United Kingdom and in Australia on acid-free paper.

Edited by Alicia Jacques and Joseph Foster.

The second installment in *The Seven Series*.

Published in 2018 by Anaphora Literary Press

The Second of Seven: A Novel
Jeremie Guy—1st edition.

Library of Congress Control Number: 2018904275

Library Cataloging Information
Guy, Jeremie, 1988-, author.
    The second of seven : A novel / Jeremie Guy
    310 p. ; 9 in.
    ISBN 978-1-68114-421-4 (softcover : alk. paper)
    ISBN 978-1-68114-422-1 (hardcover : alk. paper)
    ISBN 978-1-68114-423-8 (e-book)
1. Fiction—Science Fiction—Apocalyptic & Post-Apocalyptic.
2. Fiction—Science Fiction—General.
3. Fiction—Fantasy—Action & Adventure.
PN3311-3503: Literature: Prose fiction
813: American fiction in English

THE SECOND OF SEVEN

A NOVEL

JEREMIE GUY

OTHER
ANAPHORA LITERARY
PRESS TITLES

PLJ: Interviews with Gene Ambaum and Corban Addison: VII:3, Fall 2015
Editor: Anna Faktorovich

Architecture of Being
By: Bruce Colbert

The Encyclopedic Philosophy of Michel Serres
By: Keith Moser

Forever Gentleman
By: Roland Colton

Janet Yellen
By: Marie Bussing-Burks

Diseases, Disorders, and Diagnoses of Historical Individuals
By: William J. Maloney

Armageddon at Maidan
By: Vasyl Baziv

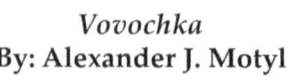

Vovochka
By: Alexander J. Motyl

CHAPTER 1

"I'm sorry, Mr. Jacobson, but we're going to have to amputate your arm," Doctor Riscala said, wrinkling his brow to show his compassion.

Abram's jaw dropped. The words were like a baseball bat to the gut. He felt as if he was dreaming. He'd imagined the doctor's visit being a standard follow up. They'd already run the tests and he'd expected to receive a few antibiotic prescriptions, maybe a pain killer or two.

He peeled back the bandage and gauze covering the spot on his shoulder, wincing slightly from the pain. The doctor stood silent, watching with an understanding face that was furrowed from years of being the bearer of bad news. Glaring at the wound forced the words to sink in a little. The white streaks branched out from the tiny wound like the roots of a pulled weed, traveling to just below his shoulder socket, stretching down nearly to his wrist. The wound itself oozed yellow and black pus constantly, and he'd gone through an entire bottle of rubbing alcohol trying to keep it clean.

He shook his head in disbelief. "Isn't that a bit extreme? Can't you just cut out the bad parts or something?"

Doctor Riscala pursed his lips. "Unfortunately, the infection is spreading. It has entered your bone, and if it travels to your heart it could take your life."

Abram thought of how hard it had been to raise his arm recently and frowned. "There's got to be another way!" Abram checked his voice, lowering it as he continued. "Medication? Something?"

With a sigh the doctor shook his head. "We've never even seen this bacterium before. There's nothing we know of to treat it. We plan to continue studying it to find a cure for future patients, but immediately there's nothing. We have to act now or your life will be in jeopardy."

Abram pulled his eyebrows together, hating how the doctor spoke the sentence as if the arm was unimportant. Abram's heart beat faster, and he stared at the ground for a moment. Doctor Riscala never stopped eying his patient.

"I've scheduled emergency surgery for you tonight."

Abram looked up, lifting his brows in concern. "Tonight?"

Doctor Riscala nodded and jotted something on his clipboard before clicking the top of his pen and sticking it into his shirt pocket. "I'll show you to the room where you'll wait while we prepare."

Abram slid from the examination table and the paper sheet crinkled and ripped. There had been a push a few years back to stop using paper in an effort to help preserve the environment. Hospitals simply stopped using the paper sheets for a while, and Abram hated having his skin touch the same surface as other patients, even with the knowledge that the staff cleaned the tables between occupants. The outcry against the sudden halt of paper was too loud for the decision to stick, but now the paper sheets were recycled paper. He grabbed his folded civilian clothes from the back of the table and cradled them to his chest.

Doctor Riscala led the way and Abram moseyed behind, slow enough that the doctor had to pause a few times to make sure Abram could keep up. The doctor opened his mouth to speak a few times, but decided against pushing Abram any further. They walked in silence through the halls of the base hospital. Men and women in both uniforms and civilian clothes walked about minding their own business. Some looked troubled and sad, others looked distracted. None paid Abram any attention.

As they walked he wondered how many other people had come to the hospital thinking things would be favorable, only to discover something life changing. How many of these men and women were visiting loved ones or friends whom possessed life-threatening illnesses or whom had been seriously injured? A uniformed soldier wheeled past. He was missing both legs up to the knee, and Abram felt a wave of sadness rush through his heart. He'd never paid much attention to amputees, even the ones that had been injured in combat, but their struggles were brought into a new light.

A nurse passed the doctor and they chatted briefly about another appointment he had. Habitually, Abram used a squirt from a hand sanitizer station before they continued down the halls.

Hospitals always smelled strongly of antiseptic and cloth, and he usually enjoyed smells that reminded him of being clean, but the thought of so many germs in one place made him antsy. Thankfully, usually, few people in hospitals bumped into him or offered to shake his hand, and he usually only had issues with doorknobs he had to touch. Sometimes doctors thought it was okay to touch his back or shoulder after greeting him. Doctor Riscala was one that never did, and that was the reason Abram made him his primary doctor.

They arrived at the room, and Doctor Riscala stayed by the door. Abram went to the bed and examined it briefly before setting his clothes on it. He tried not to think about how clean the nurse's hands were when she made the bed. The guardrails were up on both sides and he lowered one before scooting onto the mattress.

"A nurse should stop by around 2200 hours to bring you to surgery. When was the last time you ate?"

"Around noon. I'm actually getting pretty hungry".

"Sorry, but don't eat anything under any circumstances. It may cause complications during surgery."

Abram nodded and the good doctor left, leaving Abram alone with his thoughts. The room was situated for two people, but he was the only one present at the moment, and the dividing curtain was drawn around the second bed. He had always wondered why the gowns and linen and curtains were always some variation of pastel pink, blue or white, but staring at them on this day reminded him of vomit.

CHAPTER 2

We're going to have to amputate your arm.

The words echoed in Abram's skull, and he looked at the affected limb. Since coming back from the Third, the wound had only gotten worse, but he'd never guessed that there was some deadly bacteria swimming around inside his cut. He'd cleaned it the minute he made it back to his house, scrubbing the scab that was forming until the wound was open and throbbing, but the infection must have set in long before he'd made it back to his home dimension.

He checked the clock on the wall and stared at it for a few ticks until the sound of the second hand was loud enough to become an annoyance. Three hours to kill before surgery. He dug through his clothes and took out his phone before sliding off the mattress. It creaked from the change in weight.

Walking over to the window, he dialed Ruth's number and waited for her to pick up. She'd told him she had an urgent meeting to attend, but he hoped the meeting was over so they could talk.

Ruth's tinny voice came through the earpiece, and he sighed, waiting out the recorded message to the beep.

"Hey, honey," he started. The pet name still sounded weird to him. "Just wanted to tell you some pretty crazy news." Abram bit his lip and thought about running his free hand over top of his shaved head, ultimately deciding his hands weren't clean enough. He balled up his fist and wrapped his knuckles against the window pane. With a sigh, he continued struggling with how to break the news. "I'm not quite sure how to say this so I'll just say it. The doctor's visit went a little differently than we had expected." He sighed again and looked at his arm. "They say they have—they have to amputate my arm." After another pause, "I would rather you be here so that we could talk about this a bit before it happens, but I guess your meeting is still going on. There are still a few hours between now and the surgery, so when you get this call me back." Then, after a few more raps on the window pane, "It'd be great to have you here."

Abram hung up and tossed the phone over onto the bed, sighing again and looking at the window. The horizontal blinds were pulled across the glass but in the open position. It was too dark to see out into the yard, or the parking lot depending on which side of the building he was in, so he stared at his reflection.

The whole evening had felt surreal, but as he stared at himself in the mirror, the news suddenly took on a heavy weight that pulled down his shoulders and stuffed up his throat. Tears welled into his eyes and spilled down his cheeks before he could wipe them away with his forearm, and when he finally caught them he started thinking of how he'd never be able to use both arms for anything ever again.

Simple tasks like taking a thorough shower and tying shoes would now be impossibly difficult. As he thought of countless other tasks that required two arms, the tears streamed down his cheeks faster. He caught a sob that tried to come out, sniffling it away and coughing a few times, happy that the image of himself was too blurred to see anymore.

Being in the room started to make him claustrophobic. He felt hot and his breathing turned to shallow heaves. He debated changing back into civilian clothes but opted against it. His skin had already touched the germ-laden hospital examination table, and he wanted to avoid putting the germs into his clothes for as long as possible.

After swiping at his face a few times with his wrists, he nabbed his phone. He hated feeling sorry for himself and decided he needed a distraction. He exited the room and headed down the halls. The foot traffic was slowly dying down as the night pressed on, but the variety of people pushing gurneys increased. They weren't rushing like they might in the ER, but it was still odd to see a steady stream of them.

"Ma'am! Lookout!" came an unknown voice.

The scream alerted Abram as well, and he looked up in time to see a large metal rack tipping over a foot or so ahead of him. A nurse was flipping through a chart below the tipping rack, oblivious to the looming danger and the warning shout.

Abram acted fast and reached out with his right arm, wincing from the pain but still managing to grab the nurse and yank her backward. The shelf banged and clanked onto the ground. Glass shattered and crashed to the tile floor.

The nurse placed a hand to her chest as she stared at the mess on the ground where she once stood. She turned to Abram with wide eyes.

"Thank you so much, sir." She looked back at the mess, slowly shaking her head. "I must have been in my own little world."

"Don't mention it," Abram said.

A few civilians started trying to help with the mess, but they were waved off by the nurses who claimed maintenance would be called to come mop it all up.

Now cut off from progressing down the hall, he turned and went the opposite direction. He found a waiting room and watched a television for a little while, but the people inside noticed his attire and started asking him questions about why he was in the hospital. It was a little difficult to talk about, so he said he was in to hear his lab result. It was only a partial lie, since he had come in to hear his lab results, but he still felt guilty. He gave up on trying to wander to pass the time and headed back to his room for the peace and quiet.

CHAPTER 3

Back in his room his phone chirped, and he picked it up without checking the caller ID.

"Ruth?" Abram said, clearing his throat, thankful she was unable to see him.

"No, General Alvarez." Abram instantly stiffened out of habit even though the general was on the phone. "Doctor Riscala informed me of your impending surgery."

Abram swallowed and shook his head, moving the phone to the other ear to wipe away a stray tear. "I imagine you'll have to give me a medical discharge, sir?"

"Would be debatable under usual circumstances, as you're not active duty and you're technically not even a part of the military anymore. You don't need all your limbs to—" the general paused as if hunting for the proper word. "—engineer things."

"Under usual circumstances, sir?"

"Right. This is one of those *unusual* circumstances. I have a proposition for you."

Abram remained mute. In the background Abram could hear distant chatter, but he was unable to determine voices.

"I'm getting pressure from every angle to have a team of rangers trained in inter-dimensional travel. Project Hide and Seek is still on the table. The Pentagon still wants to utilize any potential military advantages inter-dimensional travel could give us, and they are looking to me as the one who can provide them with the access to that advantage."

"Sir, considering my impending…condition," Abram frowned at the word but was unsure what to say to describe himself. "If you're thinking of asking me to be a part of that team, I don't think I'm really qualified."

"Don't jump the gun. I wouldn't think you were qualified with or without your condition," the general said matter-of-factly. It burned Abram's ego. "That's not what I want you for. You're going back to the other side. You're going to reconnoiter, but we also need you to learn more about these *arts* that you gave such great detail about in your report. The Pentagon is especially interested in that."

"Sir, I don't think I'll have the capability to deal with conflict, should situations so arise in the Third, and—"

"This call is not meant to be a discussion!" Alvarez roared. Abram swallowed hard again, thinking back to his disciplinary hearing and how lucky he'd been to not be court-martialed. Instead, he and Ruth were allowed to resign and the general hired them as contractors. Still, for Abram not much had changed and he still felt like he was a bona fide member of the military.

"Sir, sorry, sir."

"That's more like it. Now, before you get your panties in a bunch, you aren't going back alone. I'll be sending a protection detail of five combat contractors to lend a hand with *situations*, should any so arise. The Pentagon isn't willing to risk rangers on this escapade until they receive more intel. Ruth is also going, and will do most of the reconnaissance study. I need to know everything I can about this place before I start pumping rangers through it, and the lot of you will find out what I need to know. They also babbled about the cave Ruth mentioned in her report, saying something about discovering a way to grow plants in the dark and possibly even a new energy source, so she'll be tasked with going back there."

"Sir, yes, sir."

"Now, about your…condition." The general's voice was almost playful, as if he'd been waiting to talk about it the whole conversation, and now that he had adequately built up to a reveal he could deliver it. "There's a prosthetic prototype that our boys have been dying to test." The general paused and said something to someone else in the room. "If the surgery is a success, you'll lose your gimp arm and get a brand new one that's fully functional. I know they've had some success with robotic implants and automated prosthesis, but this thing takes the cake. A magnesium, silicon carbide alloy will act as your bone, and it's so light you'll forget you even have an arm. Two types of graphene composites will make up your muscles and ligaments, and when I say you'll have strength like you wouldn't believe, I'm barely scratching the surface."

Abram whistled. He'd heard of graphene before, but it had never been used to work in tandem, like with a muscle and a ligament. Graphene was virtually indestructible. Scientists had long believed that the strength potential in human muscle was only limited by the connection between ligaments and bones. Muscles made of graphene would provide him near limitless lift capacity, while ligaments made of the same would remove the fear of tearing a ligament free from the bone due to something the muscle could handle but the ligament could not.

"We coated the thing with warming gel packs and a nice layer of fabriskin, patent pending, so no one will know your limb's a prosthetic unless you tell them."

"Sir, permission to speak freely?"

"Granted."

"I'm grateful to be given this opportunity, but why give it to me?"

"Didn't your mother ever tell you not to bite the hand that feeds you?"

Abram swallowed hard again. The thought of his mother saddened him, but he focused on the conversation.

"You're the perfect candidate because you're already losing your arm. Of course, this prosthetic will come with the ability to communicate with us, and it'll also have a camera that can be activated. We still believe that electronics are partially destroyed during the transition process, so it may not remain intact, but your engineer buddies tell me the graphene material will be able to withstand the journey if anything can. If all goes well with your mission, we'll be able to coat whatever we need to transport in graphene and we'll be back to being the unquestionable superpower of the world." The general paused and chuckled. "Maybe even all the worlds."

"I'm honored, sir, thank you again."

"That's not all, Jacobson." Abram knit his eyebrows together. "You spoke of warring sides in the Third, and we need you to infiltrate the Gray Lord's ranks and find out any secrets he's hiding."

"You want me to be a spy?" Abram frowned again. He thought of the Shaman and how kind he had been. Even though the Gray Lord did seem to have ulterior motives, he was uncomfortable with spying on anyone, much less a person he knew.

"That's exactly what I want you to be. And find out what you can about this shaman guy. From what your report says, he has way too much power for any one person. We need to verify he will be an asset and not a liability. Neutrality is too dangerous. You mentioned he was going to take you under his wing, so this should be easy for you, seeing as how you'll be close to him all the time."

"What of the protection detail assigned to me? I'm not sure I'll be able to train with the Shaman and still have them around."

"Then they'll go with Ruth. She won't have a separate team, so if you're okay without them, good."

"Understood, sir. When will all this happen?"

"As soon as you're healed. I'll have someone you're familiar with go over the basics of the prosthetic, but it's fairly self-explanatory. All the complicated parts are for remote use."

Abram acknowledged the general and they hung up. Abram tossed the phone on the bed and went back to the window. He turned on the television to add some background noise and glared at his reflection again.

CHAPTER 4

Lightning flashed in the distance and he sighed as a rumble of thunder vibrated the windowpane. A few minutes later the sound of rain crackled against the glass and he smiled. The last time he'd seen or heard rain was before he'd crossed over into the Third. He'd been back for a month and some change, but it was as dry as usual. Rain had been too acidic and polluted to be potable or usable for crops without a filter for a long time, but it was still pleasant to see and hear fall.

Even with all the advances in the scientific field, they still had no viable solution for the environmental problems. They'd tried all the things that various authority figures had claimed would work, but as of yet nothing had halted the process of environmental degradation. The harm had gone too far already. Their dimension was dying.

For a brief moment he wondered if the general and the Pentagon ever thought of crossing everyone to another side to escape the fate they would all suffer one day at the hand of Mother Nature. Perhaps just the country. But as the thoughts slid through Abram's mind he prayed they ultimately decided against invading another dimension. Even if they were able to transport that many people, chances were the people would all pollute and destroy the other sides as well. Abram thought of all the wonder he'd seen in the Third, and could only imagine all the wonders he was yet to behold. The thought of destroying that sickened him, but at the same time guilt plagued him. Why should he and a select few others be the only ones to enjoy the Third?

"Mr. Jacobson?" a high-pitched voice said at his back.

He turned and another clap of thunder rumbled through the hospital. The nurse that had spoken was young and had hair dyed similarly to the pastel colors in every fabric in the building. She was smiling and had both hands on a gurney. A sturdy male nurse accompanied her.

"Yes. You two here to ferry me to my doom?" Abram said with a smile.

The nurse politely nodded and motioned for him to get onto the gurney. He complied in silence and the male nurse offered to help.

Abram refused, hoping to never need another person's assistance with doing things as easy as getting onto a gurney.

He sat up until the female nurse insisted that he lie back. The pillow was soft enough, and he hoped he was the first user. She pushed him along and the ride was less than pleasant. The back wheel squeaked and stuck every so often, creating vibrations that annoyed him. The nurse provided little comfort, trying to make small talk about how it was his lucky day since it was raining.

To distract himself he thought of his upcoming mission. The prosthetic he would be receiving popped into his head, and he started thinking it would be uneven with his other arm. Images of Jax Briggs from Mortal Kombat popped into his head and he almost laughed at the notion of him with a single bodybuilder arm.

At least 80,000 people died every year from hospital negligence, and he wondered what his odds were for this surgery. Thankfully, they weren't operating on a vital organ. Still, the chance of his already overworked immune system being penetrated by an additional infection was in the forefront of his mind. All it would take was a single doctor forgetting to clean his hands long enough and he would die a senseless death. He always wanted to die in a heroic way.

In addition to the risk of infection, there was the chance he'd suffer from an allergic reaction to anesthesia, or any of an infinite amount of unknown variables. He sighed as they pushed through two double doors.

The lighting changed and the white ceiling took on a teal color. He wondered if they were close to where he'd have the surgery, and his question was answered when they stopped. He was situated under a bright light that forced him to turn away. Around him were an assortment of trays and instruments. Machines hummed somewhere in the background.

A nurse in teal scrubs, a face mask, and gloves came over holding a clear, plastic oxygen mask attached to a tube.

"Are you Abram Jacobson, with an address of 638 Prime Street?" she said, her voice muffled. Abram nodded. "Here for surgery on the right arm?" He nodded again. "Perfect. Count backward from 100 for me."

Abram ignored her and knew what was coming. He allowed her to press the mask against his face. Before the anesthesia was able to take effect he wondered if he would be one of those rare cases of people that were rendered immobile by the drug, yet still able to feel every cut and incision from the surgery. He shuddered from the notion, but a warm darkness floated down on him and his eyes drifted closed.

CHAPTER 5

Abram eased his eyes open. Things were blurry at first, and a head-shaped blob leaned over him. He blinked a few times and wanted to rub his eyes, but when his arms twitched a searing pain burned through his whole right side.

"Take it easy, sweetie," the head-shaped blob said with a gentle voice.

Abram recognized the voice as Ruth's. "Hey, where ya been?"

He smiled but wanted to groan. Everything was dulled as if cotton balls had been jammed into his senses. The only sharp edge was the pain, but it only surfaced when he moved so he lay as still as he could.

"How did it go?" Abram started, his vision finally adjusting after more blinking.

He was back in the room where he had waited for surgery. Ruth was stooping over him, but two chairs had been pulled up beside the bed. He looked down at his arm. It was wrapped in gauze even though it was artificial. The white wrap had been wound around his upper right torso as well. As he examined himself he felt an ache rising in him.

"Good. No complications were reported," Ruth said, her face hinting she was struggling with finding the right words.

Abram tried to sit up but the pain kept him in place. "No, I meant your meeting."

Ruth brushed a hand over his head and smiled at him. "We can discuss that after you have recovered a little more."

Abram started shrugging but the pain halted him before his shoulders moved very far. He tried to hide the pain and stay strong for her, but she was able to read him.

"Would you like me to hail the nurse?"

Abram shook his head. "No, thanks. I'm fine." He smiled despite her frown, glancing down at his arm. "Did they tell you what they did?"

She nodded, saying: "General Alvarez is here. Said something about signing a consent form, but he went to get coffee."

Abram glanced at the clock. It was 0800 hours but he felt like it was still night. Abram recalled her words and answered. "If it's for the arm, shouldn't I have signed that before they—" Abram glanced at his arm and struggled with what to call the addition. "—attached this thing to me?"

Ruth looked at the prosthetic, apprehension flashing across her face. "Go back to sleep before he comes back and talks your ear off. Bet he would try to give you a new one of those too, one that could hear him from anywhere in the world." They both shared a laugh, but Ruth's seemed forced. "I am surprised you slept through his voice. He has been extra chatty since he arrived."

"You'll have to forgive my garrulousness, Johnson," the general said from the doorway. "I only speak so much because I'm so excited."

Ruth stiffened and stood up, saluting him. She knew she only had to salute when she was still a part of the armed forces, and now that she was just a contract engineer for the military, the salute was unnecessary. Though, the general was one who was all about respect, and he had pull on each side of the civilian-soldier line.

Abram lifted his head but it was still too painful to move much more than that, so he did his best to look reverent.

"No need to ask for forgiveness," the general said to Ruth, but she remained stiff. "Coffee?" He held out a steaming cup that Ruth denied. Abram was more of a water drinker, but the smell of the coffee made his mouth water. The general shrugged. "More for me." He sat in the second chair and motioned with his chin for Ruth to do the same in hers. "How are you feeling?" The general asked Abram, taking a loud sip from the cup in his right hand.

Abram nodded slowly, again fighting the urge to shrug. "A little sore but grateful for this opportunity."

The general broke into laughter, holding his curved arms up like he was trying to hug a beach ball. "That's rich! A little sore, ha. I bet we take away some of that morphine and you'll feel a little more sore." Ruth let out an awkward chuckle. "Well, if we're passed all the laughs, let's get down to business. I have this form that needs signed, saying that you gave us the okay to give you that special arm. It also reminds you that while you aren't the property of the U.S. Army unless you return to active duty, your arm *is* my property."

A lump of cold uncertainty pressed against Abram's face. Knowing that the general owned a part of him was unsettling. If Abram ever decided to quit, the general would have the right to take back the arm.

"Sir, I'm unable to move my arms comfortably at the moment, sir," Abram said, happy to be able to hold off for a little while longer.

The general broke into laughter again, this time spilling a little coffee from the still full left cup. It dribbled down and dripped onto the tile floor. His laughter died down and he took a sip from the full cup, noticing his spill.

"Right you are! Well, it seems I made the trip down here for nothing," the general said.

"I am sure Abram appreciated the company, sir."

Abram faked a grin as the general stood. All the laughing made the general seem sinister, and Abram second guessed keeping the prosthetic. Abram wondered if all the happiness came from being able to try out new technology or knowing that Abram was at his mercy as long as he wanted to enjoy two arms.

The general took long gulps from the right cup and tossed it into the waste basket before going over to the television stand. An envelope was resting on it, and he opened it with one hand, pulling out a stapled document. He also pulled a pen out of his pocket and clicked the back, flipping through the pages of the document and scratching marks every so often. When he was finished he came back to the bed but remained standing.

"Go ahead and sign when you gain full use of that special arm." The general smiled and took another sip of his coffee. "But try not to break the pen."

He laughed some more, turned and headed for the exit. When he was gone Abram turned to Ruth.

"Well that was weird," he started. "I don't think I've ever seen him in such a light mood. Come to think of it, I don't think I've ever seen someone laugh that much. Even when I tell one of my famous jokes, most people laugh just to ease the tension. Not him though. He usually just stares at me with a blank face. But today..."

Abram's voice trailed off at the end and they shared a moment of quiet reflection. "He is so lighthearted because of your arm." Her expression was pulled down as she continued. "I read the report on it, and it is indeed impressive." She looked at it with concern. "Did he mention anything to you about being able to control it? Will it be safe?"

Abram swallowed. "I think. When he first brought it up he mentioned I would be able to use it like any other arm. I think it'll only be dangerous if I want it to be."

Ruth stood again and bent over to kiss him on the mouth. His senses were continuing to sharpen, and he noticed her perfume was of flowers. He remembered the scent and always questioned it every time she wore it. The only real flowers left in the world had to be grown in labs, and Abram had never smelled one. The scent was simply dubbed *flowers*, but for all he knew, it could really be baked banana pudding. The thought of food made his mouth water, and he hoped they would bring him something to eat soon.

"You should rest. The heal-gauze only works if your body is strong enough to work with it." Abram looked at the gauze and sighed. He was starting to get his energy back, and as his mind continued to awaken, he was able to focus on more than the aches of his body. But he knew she was right and he relaxed against the pillow.

She started humming and he closed his eyes. Then, surprising him, Koñél's face popped into his head and he swallowed. It felt like forever since he had first met the beautiful woman from the third dimension, and he wondered if she ever thought of him.

The present rushed into his mind and he felt as though Ruth could read his thoughts, but he relaxed when she kept humming. He wondered where Koñél was now and what she was up to. The possibility of seeing her again during his mission made his heart flutter. Perhaps she had switched sides and now fought for the Gray Lord.

The single kiss they shared sent a fire through his veins as he reminisced. Due to amnesia, he was yet to remember that he was engaged to Ruth when he kissed Koñél, but it was the most amazing experience. How warm and soft were her lips. How entrancing were the strands of her hair. How pleasantly comforting was her natural aroma. How dazzlingly attractive were her face and body. How confident and strong was her personality. She was as perfect a woman as Abram could ever have imagined.

Every interaction he had with Ruth since that fateful kiss felt like acting. It was as if the contact with Koñél had rewired his brain, and now he was forced to think about her forever.

Kisses with Ruth were mundane and he had to force himself to keep them going. He thought of their wedding date and wondered how he would make a marriage work when he was in love with another person. Koñél may have been a person he was forbidden from being with, but what he felt for her was love nonetheless.

CHAPTER 6

Days slipped from the calendar and Abram recovered quickly. The gauze helped, and when he was strong enough to stand on his own, the nurses removed the white wrap and insisted that he attend physical therapy.

But the general was right. The arm integrated fully into his nervous system, and if someone told him that it had always been his arm he would have believed them. After lifting the heaviest weight they had in the therapy room, Abram laughed at how light it was. He tested his strength on the metal rail used to assist people with walking, denting it with a pluck from his finger. After that, the nurses approved of him checking out.

While he waited to be picked up he mulled over the therapy session. He had decided to keep quiet about the fact that every authentic bit of muscle and flesh near the prosthetic felt sore, but he doubted that was the right call. The weight might have been easy for the arm, but the rest of him paid the price of being normal. He questioned how successful he would actually be if he had to lift something massive like a car. Would the weight tear the arm right off his body? More testing was needed.

When Ruth picked him up he shook off the doubts as he scooted into the car, persuading himself that the general had to have more testing in mind. Everything would be okay.

"Let me get a good look at it," Ruth said, and Abram held up the limb with a smile. "Wow, it even looks like your other arm."

She started the car and pulled out of the hospital parking lot. She merged onto the road leading toward their home.

"I know, it's uncanny. If I didn't know better, I would think the general had been planning this all along."

"That would be a little scary," Ruth said with a reassuring smile, but Abram started wondering if that was what had happened.

The phone call about the prosthetic had occurred the exact same night the doctor gave Abram the amputation news, as if the general had been waiting. What were the odds they had an experimental prosthetic ready to be utilized the same night they found out they had an eligible participant?

Abram had brought the document he needed to sign, and he glanced back to where it rested on the back seat. The whole situation made uneasiness churn his stomach, but he sighed. He'd already accepted the limb, so refusing to sign would render him limbless. Plus, the general would undoubtedly fire him if he refused to stay on board with the mission.

He glanced at the appendage, taking solace in the fact that it was at least a fine piece of craftsmanship. He thankfully did not look like a lopsided Jax Briggs, and the architects of the arm had gone so far as to add veins. He flexed and extended his fingers and Ruth noticed.

"The report said the heating pads serve to make the limb more life-like, but they also help regulate the temperature of the internal hardware."

"Did the report mention how it's powered? I mean, something tells me it can't have unlimited juice."

Ruth changed lanes and Abram watched the cars go past. He wondered how many other people had been given experimental second chances, and how many of those same people had regretted taking the opportunity.

The grass on the side of the road was gray green and half-wilted. Abram still saw a stark contrast between it and the grass in the Third. The bees had died out in the Second some years back, and with them all of the aromatic flowers. A few species of weeds still survived, but they rarely smelled like more than trash. Artificial pollination reigned as the main way to produce vegetation.

"Well, actually," Ruth started, smiling wide. "It is powered by the heat your body generates. Your blood flows into the limb. Most of the components are on standby, so they use minimal energy. In theory, if you used the arm nonstop and exceeded the stored energy your body contained, it could run out of juice, but as long as your heart beats the limb is continuously receiving energy."

Abram whistled and looked at the arm. He pressed against his forearm but felt only the pressure. He scratched at the artificial skin a little but still only felt pressure. The nerves they'd attached were only to allow him to know when he was being touched, instead of knowing the meaning of the contact. Since his arm was all but indestructible, the need for pain registering would have been pointless. In fact, if he could feel pain his experience with the arm might be hampered.

Ruth pulled onto their street and eased the car to a stop in the driveway. He thought back to the first day he'd returned, and how odd cars had seemed to the Shaman. He chuckled to himself and wondered what the distant friend was up to now. The Shaman had been sent home shortly after answering all the general's questions.

Ruth opened the door and held it for Abram. He inhaled deeply. His home always smelled clean, and the welcoming aroma of a freshly shampooed carpet put a smile on his face. He usually took care of all the cleaning, as he was never truly satisfied with anyone else's abilities, but since he had to be absent for a short time Ruth had agreed to pick up the slack. He walked into the kitchen and browsed the refrigerator shelves.

"We need to go to the grocery store," Abram said, frowning at the contents.

"I know, I apologize," Ruth said, putting her keys in the key bowl before sauntering to the sofa and turning on the T.V. She enjoyed the background noise more than watching the programming, and as per her habit, picked her sketchpad up from the coffee table. She used a pencil and started sketching a picture. "I have been swamped with all the wedding planning, it just slipped my mind."

Only a pack of ground beef was sitting on the middle shelf. The expiration date was the following day so he pulled it out. "Guess I'll make burgers?"

"There are no buns."

Abram chuckled. "Guess I'm making beef patties. Want one?"

"Not really hungry, but you go ahead and eat. We can stop by the store tonight."

Abram debated getting out the grill, but thoughts of the Third and the pollution at home in the Second caused him to decide against it. He'd heard somewhere that the meat industry was the biggest cause of most of their problems. He shrugged and made a mental note to stop buying meat if he could. The country had also attempted to regulate the population's meat intake by passing bills that restricted the number of animals any one farm could produce. The result was higher prices on animal products and weeks of rioting. The bill was also overturned.

Abram fired up the gas stove and pan fried the burger, careful to cook the beef until it was a black hockey puck of meat. Satisfied all the germs had been extinguished, he cooked two more in the same fashion and tossed them on a plate before joining Ruth on the sofa.

Fresh linen scent puffed up when he sat, and he was happy for the change from the constant smell of antiseptic at the hospital. He dug in, and Ruth started talking.

"I finally found a baker to do the cake, but they tell me an ice cream cake the size and shape I want is next to impossible." Ruth frowned.

"I'm sorry," Abram said, trying to talk through the food in his mouth. "Why don't you keep looking? I bet someone could pull it off."

Ruth sighed. "Maybe, but the longer I wait the harder it will be to find a decent price."

There was a long pause. Abram enjoyed the show that was playing and Ruth continued sketching. Abram finished his pucks and tossed the plate in the sink before returning to Ruth on the sofa. Thoughts of seeing Koñél experiencing his dimension bombarded his brain. Seeing her watch television for the first time would be a fun experience.

"What has you smiling so wide?" Ruth said, grinning and glancing up from her sketch.

"What? Oh, nothing. I was just thinking of all the food we're going to get at the grocery store."

"Okay, silly man." She put her drawing down and nuzzled closer to him, placing his prosthetic over her shoulder. "The arm feels real enough," she said, running her fingers down his skin. He wondered if she meant to tickle him.

His conscious plagued him as he again thought back to the kiss with Koñél. So far, he had still kept that fact from Ruth, uncertain of how she would react. He thought about the wedding and wondered if he should tell her now or after. Was it a secret that would destroy them? Would it even be right for him to get hitched knowing that Koñél truly had his heart, even if he knew he would never be able to be with her?

The situation was odd. His heart was with someone else, but at the same time he felt like he was meant to be with Ruth. There was still a chance he would grow to love her, as only a relatively short time had passed since his kiss with Koñél, so was it worth throwing that chance away? Honesty was important to him, and even though she'd never asked, hiding it from her was a form of deceit.

Credits rolled down the screen and indicated the show had ended. Ruth tapped him on the leg and hopped up.

"Ready to get some food?" she said in a playful, deep voice.

He grinned and stood as well. They left for the grocery store and Abram purposed in his heart to tell her about the kiss before they left for the mission.

CHAPTER 7

"The maximum time you should be in the parallel dimension is thirty days. We have only produced enough of this pill to last you that time," said Ronald Sundback, the lead engineer. He held up a white oval between his fingers so the whole team could see. "The data culled from Mr. Jacobson's report informed us of the memory loss, and after a few tests, we determined the loss was not due to anything more than body vibrations."

"What do body vibrations have to do with losing your memory?" The head mercenary said.

The mercs were all ex-soldiers and their leader was once a sergeant. Fond of his military days, he still went by "sergeant" even though his service days were far behind him.

He stood next to Abram and smelled of musk and cherry bubblegum. He popped the gum in his mouth every few minutes but never stopped chewing. Abram had been unable to sleep more than a few hours at a time for the remainder of the week leading up to their dispatch day, and the constant popping sounds were starting to grind his nerves. A migraine pulsed a constant pain behind his eyes.

"Sergeant Bethune, if you would let me finish I would be more than happy to explain," Sundback said with an annoyed look. "The parallel dimension, named 'The Third' in Mr. Jacobson's report, vibrates at a different frequency than our dimension. Everything has a natural vibration, though we don't normally notice except in extreme cases or study. Because the dimension's natural vibrations are different, they affect the brain and subsequently lead to memory loss. The longer the exposure, the more the body is able to adjust. We also suspect this vibration difference affects the body's strength and ability to fight off infection."

Abram was still groggy and only half-heard what the lead was saying. The rest of the team shifted their weight and looked on with interest. Ruth jotted something down on her notepad before pocketing it.

"The report details a number of hostiles, and you should expect many more upon your return." Then, looking at the five mercenaries, he said, "Your only objective is the preservation of Ms. Johnson and Mr. Jacobson." He paused and looked between Abram and Ruth. "*Your* primary objectives are research, specifically, growing plants in the dark, and uncovering a new energy source. If we are to forge an even greater nation, it is imperative you learn everything you can."

Abram thought most of the speech was unnecessary, but protocol demanded they review objectives prior to the start of a mission. The general stood at the back of the room and eyed the bunch with a smirk on his face. Abram wondered how many others had secret objectives, or if they knew he was tasked with doubling as a spy. The idea still bothered him, and he took a deep breath.

Sundback walked in front of the team, stopping in front of each person and handing over one orange pill bottle. When Abram received his he noticed there was no drug name on the label. Instead, *take me upon arrival* had been scribbled across an otherwise blank white sticker. There was a brief mention of side effects on the back, though there had been little time to test the pills. Most things had long term effects. What would these do to him in the long run?

As the portal's machinery hummed to life, one mercenary shook his bottle. He held it to his ear as if it contained some secret utterance waiting to be revealed with a few more shakes. Abram bit his lip and kept quiet, though he started to question the intellect of his protection detail.

Like their first visit, Abram and Ruth were in their combat uniforms, though this time they also had additional equipment. They had each been given M9A sidearm pistols, which came standard with anti-matter-laced particle rounds. It was a small pistol but packed a reliable punch except when submerged in water for extended periods of time. Abram was a terrible shot, but if he saw the Red Mage again he'd empty his clip and pray for the best.

Solar-powered, compact tents were given to everyone, but Abram doubted they would even work. It was almost a waste, but he chocked up the decision to another test the engineers and scientist seemed keen on running. They were given extended-burn emergency flares that fastened to hooks on their waists.

Three of the five mercenaries in the escort had M16A5 assault rifles and loads of extra clips. One soldier had an M25 hyper-rotation round sniper rifle, while the biggest of the bunch had an M249A LMG with a 200 round ammo box compliment and collapsible stock. Surprisingly, he was also the only one without any facial hair. In fact, his entire head was hairless, save for two fox moth caterpillars that acted as his eyebrows.

The lead engineer went to a computer and tapped away on the virtual keyboard. The general walked over and stood in front of them. The mercenaries saluted with vigor, while Abram and Ruth halfheartedly did so. Alvarez bid them good luck before returning to his place in the corner by the door. There were a few soldiers by the door with him.

During the break, Abram went over to Ruth. As he approached, she cut him off with a smile.

"This mission better not last longer than the designated month. We have to get back and have our wedding," she said.

She smiled as she spoke and it made what he wanted to say that much harder. "Can I speak to you for a second? There's something I want to tell you."

Ruth's big, green eyes widened as if he bore good news, but his heart started racing. Thoughts of Koñél and their kiss flashed into his mind and he swallowed. He couldn't believe he was finally going to tell her, but he knew it was the right thing to do. He swallowed again and looked at the ground, and Ruth started noticing that he was distraught. They moved a little ways away from the group, and their voices dropped to whispers.

"What is it? Something wrong?" she said, brushing a lock of her red hair behind her ear.

Abram looked her in the eyes and could see the trust and love she felt for him. She relied on him and everything he represented. Now it was possible he was going to shatter that with the secret he'd kept hidden since she'd reminded him they were engaged after the "different vibrations" caused him to forget. In case he ever forgot again, she'd gotten him a ring, and she insisted that he had to wear it at all times. Wearing it started feeling like a lie, and he spun it around on his finger as he struggled to say the right words.

"We aren't going to have to wedge a 2x4 between you two to keep you separated, are we?" one of the mercs with an M16A5 said. He had a nasally voice and bad breath, and Abram cringed when the guy threw an arm around his shoulder. He introduced himself as Grodin.

Abram knocked the arm down as politely as he could, but his migraine prevented his face from hiding how annoyed he was that the man thought it was okay to touch him. He felt his pocket for the bottle of Purell and made a mental note to sanitize his neck when Grodin was occupied with other things. Abram was thankful to have remembered to bring the precious commodity this time around. Finding a shower may take a while in the Third, but at least he could remove germs properly.

"No, but thanks for checking," Abram said, flashing a polite smile but unashamed to lace his words with the annoyance he felt. "We're both aware of appropriate work conduct, but last time I checked, speaking was classified as appropriate."

Grodin held up two hands in surrender, his crooked smile still on his face. He fell back into the line, but the others made whistling noises. Being the brunt of jokes and jeering was one of the main reasons Abram had never wanted to reveal their engagement. Work was work and home life was personal. There was no need for the two to bleed together, but now it was too late. Apparently even the mercs had been told.

"Please, fall back into line," Sundback said.

Abram frowned and looked Ruth in the eyes, mouthing *later* before getting back into line. He was bothered by still being unable to tell her, but at the same time enjoyed the relief of being able to keep his secret for a little while longer.

Coming back to the group, Sundback stopped in front of Abram. He held a holocube in his palm at waist level. Activating it by touching the top, a three dimensional image appeared. Abram lifted an eyebrow.

"That supposed to be anything specific?" Abram said.

"Absolutely. Raise your right fist and move it around the room." Abram complied and the image changed, displaying wherever he pointed his hand. "Looks like the video software is working fine. As you can see, the lens is in the top of your hand. It's just below the pseudo-dermis, between your second and third knuckle."

Abram looked at the holocube image a bit more, shadow boxing a bit with a smirk. Everyone else looked on, but the mercenaries showed no indication they were impressed.

"What happens if I get in a bar fight and knock the guy out? Will the camera get broken?"

"Unless you get in a bar fight with 6000 pounds of pressure per square inch, you will not break the camera." The engineer touched the top again and the picture dissolved. "However, we have no way of knowing if the transition to the other side will permit preservation of functionality until you return."

"Should have outfitted that thing with rockets and an antimatter rifle. Maybe a retractable shield?" the biggest mercenary said with a grunt.

The idea had gone through Abram's head, but the thought of having that much destruction attached to the palm of his hand was terrifying. What if the warheads went off without warning, or what if the antimatter particles leaked into his body?

"Mr. Stribling," the lead said to the big merc, his voice taking on a layer of condescension. "Mr. Jacobson is not an experimental soldier. The HFT40-Cyborg had all of the above, and you saw where that got the country."

"That was because the stupid thing didn't have an off switch. It's not my fault the boys behind the scenes weren't bright enough to program it for peace time." Stribling glanced at his LMG and grunted again, mumbling under his breath. "It'd be nice to have some heavy support every once and a while."

"Zip it, Stribbles," the sergeant said.

Stribling looked hurt but kept quiet, clenching his jaw and gripping his LMG tighter.

"In either case, Mr. Jacobson has only a few toys installed on his arm, as this was mainly awarded to him for its potential communications capabilities. All other attempts to take battery operated equipment over has been unsuccessful, but we're hoping the interface with his brain and body will allow it to remain intact," the lead started. "As you may have noticed, much of your usual equipment has been stripped. This parallel dimension is still too novel to fully understand, but Mr. Jacobson's report mentioned elements of the supernatural, and according to said report, the supernatural has prevented mechanized technology on that side—well, it has *potentially* prevented mechanized technology on that side." Sundback sighed deeply. "It is a shoddy explanation at best, but it is the hypotheses we will rely on until more information is gathered. We are still uncertain if armaments will function, but we will see."

The mercenary with the M25 reached to his arm and unfastened a combat knife. He pulled it out with an expressionless face, examined it briefly before sticking it back into its sheath.

"Whatever is preventing technology from operating, we surmise the arm will function because it is powered by the human heart. Since humans can cross, it logically follows that things physically connected to humans may also cross successfully," Sundback finished.

"Shouldn't we get machetes or something in case our guns don't work?" Grodin said and Abram agreed.

"Perhaps," the lead said, glancing at the general and saying nothing else.

Abram thought of Ruth and her quest to study. How she was supposed to record and observe with only a notepad was beyond him, but he still envied her. At least she was allowed to be honest with everyone. He looked at his knuckle to try and see the camera, but it was too tiny. He shrugged and figured if his camera still worked he'd be able to record data for her.

After a few final preparations they were given the green light. Though it was unnecessary, Sundback went to where the general and the other soldiers were standing as if an energy discharge would hit him if he stood too close to the portal when it opened.

The familiar black mass of the portal appeared and Abram felt a nervous happiness. He looked at Ruth, wondering how excited she was to be returning. She had been the main one to talk about going back one day, and now that they had been granted the opportunity he wondered what they would discover.

The engineers had lengthened the time the portal could remain open to a full thirty minutes, though the building's lights still flickered as the tiny device sucked up massive amounts of power. The sergeant led the way, running through the portal in silence. The other mercenaries followed suit, and Abram and Ruth hopped through together.

CHAPTER 8

As the dark mists dispersed from his mind, he opened his eyes with a start and sat up. He darted his eyes around, noticing a gaggle of others with him. They were scattered in an assortment of positions: most were facedown or face-up, but one was twisted on his side with his legs bent in a running position.

Who am I? Abram thought, trying to force his mind to cut through the black fog that gummed up his memories. *Where am I?*

After a few seconds he recalled his name, wondering why he was in a desert and why he had been unconscious. He stood and looked around. The sun blared in the corner of the sky. Tendrils of heat drifted off the rolling sand dunes that rose and fell for miles around him. He shielded his eyes with his hand but could see nothing but sand and mirages—not even a lone cactus broke up all the bland tan.

A gust of hot wind tossed sand granules against his face, and he held up an arm. He coughed and turned away. As he hacked the others started stirring, sitting up and looking around as well. Five of the six were armed with large guns, and they immediately held up their respective weapons, pointing them around but slowly lowering them when they realized everyone was wearing a black shirt beneath a camouflage jacket and a pair of camouflage pants.

His memory was still spotty, but he could recall that the clothing pattern matched the United States of America's armed forces uniform. He was wearing the same thing as the only female in the group: the US Army Combat Uniform. The wind picked up and whipped at his back.

"Who are you and why are we here?" one of the men said, holding up a palm to shield his face from the sun.

Abram shrugged. "Beats me, but we seem to all be on the same side, so at least that's good."

Everyone was on their feet and wiping sand from their clothes. Abram wiped his brow with the back of his hand, almost gagging at the scratchy, mud-like substance that the sand and his sweat had created.

A few more seconds passed and people started recalling their names. Each person took a turn introducing themselves and trying to remember the connections. Everyone spoke except Brooks, but he pointed to his name badge as an introduction.

For some reason sergeant Bethune was adamant that no one say any curse words, and the mercenaries that had already casually cursed apologized, saying they vaguely remembered him being weird about foul language.

"I bet we're in Iraq," the biggest of the bunch, Stribling, said as he looked out over the dunes and nodded his head as if one of the dunes were familiar to him. "Definitely in Iraq."

"What makes you think that?" Grodin said, standing next to Stribling. Grodin was a full two heads shorter. "We could be in the Sahara. Even Death Valley. Or any desert really."

"Death Valley don't look like this, dude. There are barely even dunes there. Look at the angle of the dunes around us." Stribling pointed and bent over until he was eye level with Grodin. "If you squint you can barely see a mountain range in the distance. Iraq is all mountains, dude. Definitely Iraq."

"Have you even been to Iraq?" the guy whose name strip read Feldman said. He shook an orange bottle of pills into his hand and popped two into his mouth, chewing them up without a thought.

"Four tours. Would have been five but most of my squad got injured during a training exercise." Stribling turned to Grodin and pointed a thick finger at him. "Have you ever been to the Sahara? Or Death Valley? We've established that we're all ex-military, but I don't remember any operations being carried out either place."

Grodin shrugged. "I was already out of the service, but I've been to both. Tons of times. My point is that they're all deserts though. Not like they have sign cacti every mile saying which desert it is."

"I call BS. You've been zero times."

"Nah, man, more like nineteen."

Grodin laughed and the other mercenaries did as well. Feldman eyed the bottle and shook it a few times.

"These don't look like no Tylenol pills man."

Ruth walked over to him and looked at the bottle. "What made you think it was Tylenol?"

"I don't remember much but I remember getting headaches. Got an axer right now that's splitting my skull in half. All I ever take is Tylenol."

Ruth rotated the bottle in her fingertips and hummed. "Definitely not Tylenol. But even the knockoffs have labels. This just says *take me upon arrival.*"

Feldman's eyes widened and he snatched back the bottle, examining it for himself as if anything other than aspirin spelled certain doom.

"Then what is it? I can't just go popping pills. That's how people die!"

Grodin started chuckling. "Why would you have a bottle of death pills in your pocket?"

Feldman shrugged but started patting his pockets. "Dunno, but I found my Tylenol."

Calmer now, he pulled out the medicine and shook two capsules from the bottle. He popped them into his mouth, chewing them again. He sighed and swallowed.

"That's the good stuff. I can feel my headache starting to—" He froze mid-sentence and knit his eyebrows together. He looked at everyone as if seeing them for the first time and he started breathing a little harder.

"Uh-oh, looks like they were death pills," Grodin chuckled.

"Zip it, Grodin!" the sergeant said, and everyone huddled closer as Feldman continued to look confused. "What is it? How are you feeling?"

Then Feldman started laughing and everyone relaxed. "These pills are for our memory," he said, laughter still trailing out after his sentence. "Everyone should have them." He sucked his teeth after his last word. "But we're only supposed to take one. It'll last us the full thirty days that we're supposed to be here."

Everyone started patting their pockets until they found their own bottles. Abram read the sticker but questioned how trustworthy the source was. Lacking a viable alternative, he shook one out and downed it. It had a bitter, plastic taste that Abram was able to detect even though he swallowed it whole, and he wondered how Feldman was able to chew his.

The others matched his example and after a few minutes everyone was back to their usual selves. Abram glanced out over the horizon and wondered how he would find the Shaman, or anyone else in the desert. He recalled his first visit to the Third and how he'd also landed in the desert. He was grateful another slave caravan hadn't found him, though he was itching to try out the strength in his new arm. He reminisced of the tent peg he had been unable to remove from the ground and frowned. Though Sundback had explained that the differing vibrations in the Third had likely contributed to his weakness in the tent, part of him hoped the peg was just surprisingly difficult to take out of the ground. Now he could have another chance. It was an odd thing to want another chance with, but it had bugged him. He flexed his experimental limb.

Activating the radio in his arm, he tried checking in with General Alvarez. He did exactly what he had been told would open a channel, but all he received was static. He sighed and decided to try again later.

"Told you we weren't in Iraq!" Grodin said, pointing at Stribling this time. "You owe me a ration."

"I owe you squat!" Stribling said. "You weren't right either."

The two argued for a bit before the sergeant stepped in.

"Zip it! Both of you! We're in enemy territory with limited resources and ammunition. There's no telling what's lurking out here in the sand, so until we verify the safety of our surroundings, keep a lid on it."

"Sir, yes, sir," the two chimed.

Abram still found it odd that they all acted like they were still active duty, but none of them had served recently.

"So what do you two think? You're the resident experts," the sergeant said, placing one hand on his hip but keeping the other on the handle of his M16.

Ruth looked at Abram, and he shrugged. "Last time I was here I was with a group of slavers." He looked over at the sun and thought back to the direction the caravan had been heading. Koñél had said they were taking him to the Gray Lord, so it made sense to try and follow that route. Abram pointed away from the sun.

"The Red Mage's mountain lair was back toward the sun, so we want to head away from it. Last time we had lizards to ride, so this may take a few days to cross on foot."

"We'll keep our eyes peeled for any means of transportation," the sergeant said, pulling out a miniature pair of binoculars and scanning the area where Abram had pointed.

"You and the fiancé going to hold hands and frolic through the sand?" Grodin asked, coming up behind Abram and draping his arm around Abram's neck.

Abram quickly removed the limb and looked Grodin in the eyes. "Please, I'd prefer it if you only touched me if doing so was required to save my life, and even then, ask first."

"Touchy, touchy," Grodin said, holding up his hands again.

Ruth looked at Grodin and smiled to reassure him. "Abram hates germs, not you."

"Right. Well why didn't you just say that? Being germaphobic is a perfectly good reason not to want to be touched."

"I'm not germaphobic, just germ-aware. I'm not afraid of germs, I just don't like them."

"Whatever floats your little germ-free boat."

Grodin continued snickering and Abram already wanted to punch him. He balled up the fist on his strong arm and debated giving the disrespectful soldier a light jab to the gut.

"Alright, troops. We're heading out," the sergeant said, spinning his finger in a circle. No one had really taken much out of their pockets aside from their pills, but they all moved closer together and followed the sergeant as he headed forward.

Abram lingered for a few moments with Ruth, and she put on an *I'm-sorry* face. As they walked, Abram remembered how tedious it was to trudge through the desert coated in sand and sweat and wearing combat boots.

CHAPTER 9

"This desert never ends," Grodin said, dragging uneven lines in the sand with his feet as he walked.

A few people grunted but no one responded. The mercenaries' footfalls were slow but rhythmic, like they'd marched together a number of times and now did so without thinking. Everyone's clothing was darkened with sweat at the pits and neck and back, and the pungent odor of the same was thick in the air. They'd only been walking for a few hours, but their water was already running low.

Ruth and Abram hung a ways back, but neither felt like holding hands. It would just make their palms sweatier than they already were. He'd pulled his ACU top over his head to protect his neck from the blaring sun. Ruth had let down her hair to do the same, and in the sunlight the locks were brilliant, fiery strands.

"Back before we left, when you pulled me aside," Ruth started, glancing at Abram every so often. "What did you want to talk about?"

Abram gulped. The heat and fatigue had allowed him to focus his brain on things other than Koñél and their kiss. He took a deep breath and kept his eyes on the backs of the mercenaries. Thinking of his secret made him wonder how long it would be before he saw Koñél again. Would she try to kill them?

"Yeah, I've been meaning to talk to you about this for a while now." He chewed on the right words to say, playing with his engagement ring. "Remember Koñél?"

"That hot-tempered firecracker that tricked us into thinking the Red Mage was a good guy?"

Abram swallowed. The heat in Ruth's voice indicated she harbored less than positive feelings toward Koñél, which could certainly make the reveal that much more difficult. Alternatively, since she already saw Koñél as manipulating she might absolve him of wrongdoing since his memory was gone at the time of the kiss.

"Exactly. Her." Abram made eye contact with her for an instant but had to look at the ground before continuing. "Well you know how our memory wasn't that great when we first crossed? Well, I—"

A scream from ahead jerked their eyes forward and they froze in place. Four of the mercenaries jogged forward a few paces before pointing their weapons at the sand. Feldman was gone. Ruth and Abram both ran to catch up to them, confusion wrinkling their brows.

"What is it? What happened!" Abram said, looking at the ground and all around.

"Hang in there, Felds! We'll figure out how to get you out!" Grodin said, tossing his rifle over his shoulder and dropping to his knees.

The sand in front of Grodin was lowering at a point as if draining. Abram grabbed Grodin by the arm and yanked him back as the sand below his knees started to funnel toward the drain point.

"Everybody back! It's quicksand or something!" the sergeant yelled, taking a few steps back and pushing Brooks and Stribling back as well.

The sand continued funneling, and the area of effect continued to grow. Ruth pulled out her notepad and started jotting something down, glancing up every so often as the events unfolded.

"Definitely not quicksand," she said. "Quicksand usually has liquid, and it makes sounds, and if he had stepped onto a patch of some he would have sank down instead of vanishing."

A faint cracking sound could be heard and Abram held up a finger, cocking his head to the side. Ruth turned to him and did the same.

Then a louder crack sounded and Ruth disappeared, falling straight through the sand as if she'd been standing on a frozen lake.

"Ruth!" Abram yelled, wanting to jump but knowing he would just fall through as well.

The faint sound of cracking continued to reach Abram's ears and he tried to still his breathing. Everyone else caught on to what was happening, and they spread out to try and relieve the pressure. With more distance between them, they froze . The cracking sound intensified and Abram gulped.

Then he was falling.

CHAPTER 10

By the time Abram realized he'd broken through a surface of some sort he had already landed on the ground with a thump. Sand puffed into his face and he coughed, blinded and disoriented. Pain ricocheted up his body, and he groaned. Something hard and sharp rained down on top of him but didn't penetrate his skin.

A cloud of dust dissipated around him and he coughed a few more times. His eyes started watering and cleared out the sand that had managed to sneak in, but he attempted to wipe out the last few granules with his undershirt, thinking it would be the only thing without grime.

After some serious blinking he was able to clear the blur and scratchy sensation. He was in a vast room with a low ceiling. Examining the ceiling he could see that it was glass, and the sand had been packed on top of it. A few of the holes had already brought in all the sand over top of them, and stabs of light beamed in and revealed the floating particles in the air. Other holes were still streaming sand down into neat little heaps on the ground.

Everyone had fallen through now, and they groaned as they recovered. Thankfully, the sand in the face had been the worst of it, and the drop was only about ten feet.

"Everybody okay?" the sergeant asked, still coughing a little and knuckling the remaining irritants from his right eye.

"No, I think I twisted my ankle," came Grodin's nasally voice. He limped over to Sergeant Bethune.

"Walk it off, soldier!" the sergeant bellowed, and Grodin straightened almost instantly. "Where's Feldman?" Everyone was still recovering, and no one gave the question any real attention.

Ruth hobbled over to Abram and hugged him. She was shaking. After a tight return squeeze, he let her go and picked up her notepad and pen that were lying on the ground a few feet away.

"None of your test tubes or vials broke, did they?" Abram asked.

"No, thankfully they gave me the field-ready set that can allegedly take a bullet without breaking."

Grodin and Stribling had both dropped their weapons during the fall, and they picked them both up and checked the chambers.

"Mine's all full of sand," Stribling said, shaking the gun a little. "Not sure if it'll fire consistently until it's had a good clean."

"Same here," Grodin said with a sigh.

Brooks's gun had never left his hand. He slung his rifle over his shoulder without checking it. He had a few bits of dust on his clothes, which he calmly brushed off before looking around the group in silence.

The room they'd fallen into was square and big enough that they could only see a few feet around them. Some of the holes with light filtering through were near one of the walls. If they'd walked a few more feet away they would have made it off the building. The walls were too sandy to make out anything other than a solid surface, and the same was true for the ground. A few broken pieces of wooden furniture and clay pots were scattered about.

"I wonder if this place was built on top the sand but has since slowly been buried by the ever shifting surface?" Abram said.

No one responded. The feeling of being watched settled over him and he started to question if the place was really abandoned.

Sergeant Bethune pulled out a stick of cherry bubblegum and popped it into his mouth, chewing furiously.

"You always have to chew that stuff?" Abram said, trying to sound as polite as possible.

"Helps me not think about smoking."

"Then do you have to chew that loud?"

The sergeant shot Abram a dirty look, pausing for a moment before chewing again, a hair quieter.

"Appreciate it," Abram said, still wanting to be polite but fed up with annoyances. A migraine still thumped behind his eyes, and falling through an old structure buried beneath the sand pushed him near his tolerance limit.

A gagging sound turned everyone around. Feldman was toward the back of the structure, shrouded in a dusty shadow. His head was shaking and his throat was making gurgling sounds. The group ran over to him.

Abram's eyes widened when he reached Feldman, and Ruth turned away, grabbing at Abram for support. He embraced her, and the sergeant started yelling orders to his men. A three inch sliver of glass was wedged in the side of Feldman's neck.

CHAPTER 11

Blood squirted from the wound and puddled on the ground. The artery had been hit, and there was no hope he would survive, but the sergeant still ordered his men to help. Stribling ripped a hunk of Feldman's sleeve off and tried to clean the dusty cloth as best as he could using water from his own canteen. Sergeant Bethune fumbled with one of the pouches at his waist, finally pulling out a small package of alcohol swabs and a laser cauterizer.

"It's too late," Ruth said, noticing the sergeant as he moved to try and seal the wound. "Even if you remove that shard without doing more damage, the cauterizer only reaches a couple inches deep."

"We have to try!" he yelled back, his hands shaking and his face turned downward. "We have to try!"

Grodin held Feldman's head steady. The sergeant did a brief countdown before yanking out the glass and dabbing the wound with the alcohol swabs. Stribling used the bit of cloth to put pressure on Feldman's neck when the sergeant stopped, but the blood seeped through, bubbling and oozing around his fingers. The sergeant activated the laser, and for a while only it and Feldman's gagging could be heard. The acrid smell of burnt blood filled the air.

Feldman lost consciousness and his body stopped moving.

"You stay with me, Felds! You hear me!" the sergeant said, still trying to seal the wound. His hands shook too much, there was too much blood, and the wound was too deep.

Stribling and Grodin's shoulders sagged, and they stood up. The sergeant continued on for another thirty seconds, still shaking too much to be effective.

"Sarge, you've done all you can do," Stribling said, kneeling down and touching the sergeant on the shoulder.

"No! We have to keep trying!" he said, using the cauterizer for a few more seconds before finally giving up. He snorted loudly and punched the ground, and even Grodin and Stribling had a tear sparkle in their eyes before they could blink them away. They'd all probably seen their fair share of death on the battlefield, but losing a friend was hard no matter how many times it happened.

Abram hung his head. He had nothing to do with the accident, but he still felt partially at fault. The mercs were there to protect him, and now one of them had died before they'd even made it through a full day.

"I've known Felds for dang near eight years," the sergeant said, finally standing to his feet. His face was set and stern again. He spit the gum in his mouth over his shoulder. He popped in a fresh piece after wiping his hands with an alcohol swab.

"He was a good man," Stribling said, his features set again as well.

"The best," Grodin added, throwing an arm over Stribling's shoulder.

There was a moment of silence before the sergeant pulled out a flare, lit it, and held it up to illuminate the room. Everything took on a red hue.

"We have to get him out of here and give him a proper burial." He glanced up at the ceiling. "Looks like it'll hold since we aren't on it anymore, but I don't want to take any chances. If anyone hears a crack we're bolting out of here. Last thing we need is the whole thing coming down on our heads.

The new light revealed the mouth of a tunnel on the other side of the room and the sergeant tossed his flare toward it. The sand on top of the glass roof had finished filtering through and now seven beams of light cut through the darkness.

"Come on, help me grab him," the sergeant said, motioning to Grodin and Stribling.

Abram wanted to say that they should come back after they found a way out, as dragging the poor fellow behind them now would only hinder their progress, but he couldn't bring himself to say a thing. In his mind, everyone blamed him and if he spoke they would verbalize how they felt.

"Here, cover his face," Ruth said, taking the bloody strip that Stribling had discarded and laying it over Feldman's face. Stribling also took off Feldman's M16 and slung it over his own shoulder.

The three dragged their fallen comrade toward the tunnel entrance, trailing a bloody path in the sandy floor as they went. Abram and Ruth followed close behind. Abram pulled out a flare and struck it to life. He used it to scan the room.

"Fascinating," Ruth said, scribbling on her pad. "I wonder if we're in the ruins of a lost civilization." She jogged over to the wall and wiped her hand against it, revealing faded paintings. She jogged back and continued writing and sketching her best rendition of the space.

A flash of concern rippled through her face.

"What was that look for?" Abram said, still casting his light in various places. He felt it was a little wrong of her to go right into research when Feldman's blood was still warm, but he kept quiet.

"Nothing, just a memory from my time inside that awful cave. This reminds me a little bit of the tribe that lived there." Ruth pocketed her pad and looked around for a bit before pulling out her sidearm. "I think they were stuck in that cave, but if they are here too I am ready this time."

Abram almost chuckled. Ruth and violence were as opposing as oil and water. He pulled out his own sidearm and checked it for sand, happy to see that the holster had protected it for the most part. He kept it in one hand just in case. Now that the mercenaries were occupied with Feldman, the duty of protection fell on the two engineers.

They closed the distance to the tunnel opening and paused. Abram looked at Ruth but she was already sketching the opening and jotting down notes.

"Should we still go through?" Grodin said, voicing the question everyone was thinking.

"Well we can't go back through the roof," Sergeant Bethune said.

The hole was not a part of the structure like they'd originally thought. Pieces of the wall were strewn on the floor. Something had broken through from the other side. The apex of the tunnel stretched about two feet above their heads.

Though cut through the sand, the tunnel had been sealed by some sort of casing. The material was a foggy light brown and coated the walls of the tunnel and the rim of the opening. Layers of the gook had dripped down before hardening, fanning out on the floor like molasses from a jar.

The trio of mercenaries started pulling again and Brooks chambered a round.

"That thing any good at close range?" Abram said, wondering if Brooks and Stribling should switch.

Brooks ignored the question. Abram entered the tunnel first, but Ruth was close behind him, scribbling on her pad often enough now that she stopped putting it away. Every so often she would rub the wall, commenting on grooves or pocks, trying to recreate the creature or machine that had created them on her pad.

The path was serpentine and took them on for hours, forcing them to take breaks and rotate flare and carrying duty. The path eventually forked. Abram led them to the right, and they walked on, soon coming to another structure. Like with the first, this wall also had the foggy brown stuff coated around the rim, but the wall bits were inside the tunnel this time around.

"Does this ever lead back out into the desert?" Stribling said as they took a break. He took a gulp from his canteen before screwing on the lid with a squeak.

"I kind of like it in here. Less heat and less sand. I swear that garbage was seeping into my pores. I still feel gritty all over." Grodin also took a swig of water after finishing his sentence.

"Check it out." Ruth held out her notepad for Abram to take.

He accepted it and examined the sketch. She had drawn a crude mutant earthworm with spikes on its head and rear. She'd even drawn a slime it secreted that looked like the foggy brown substance.

"You think that brown stuff is slime from a worm? What makes you think it's not a machine digging these tunnels?" Abram said, handing back the pad.

Ruth shook her head. "If it were a machine I would surmise the operator would attempt to travel the shortest distance between structures. Thus far, we have weaved around and this indicates a searching pattern as opposed to a guided pattern. Whatever made these tunnels had no specific knowledge of where the structures where. Unless the inhabitants of the structures had no affiliation with the operator of the machine, a machine driving in such sporadic and uncertain patterns would be a waste of resources." She smiled as she continued. "A living, hunting creature may make a tunnel like this, but it could just be my imagination."

Abram shrugged.

"What created these tunnels is irrelevant as long as it's gone," the sergeant said. "These tunnel formations give you any indication of how long it'll be before we get out?"

Ruth shook her head. "No, but it may be a good idea to try breaking through the side and burrowing through the sand ourselves."

"Not a chance. No telling how deep we are or if we'll be able to tell up from down. We could burrow to the center of the Earth before realizing we're headed the wrong way."

"Water is unique, at least while on a planet's surface, in its ability to disorient—relating to you thinking we will not know up from down. Gravity would hint which way is up, but we may suffocate before reaching the surface." Ruth sighed. "I suppose we are at the mercy of this worm's whim, but if it is anything like the worms back home, it will only surface when in danger. Out here in this desert, a worm's skin would dry out in the sun, so it is highly unlikely that the worm would go to the surface."

"Either way, we aren't going through the side of a tunnel. If we can find something to stand on, maybe we can try breaking through a roof and crawling back on top. There was only a couple feet of sand above us when we fell through."

Ruth nodded in agreement and they searched the room they were in. Nothing was fully intact, but they decided to pile a bunch of broken furniture and pots together and try to stand on that. They would try to escape through the tunnels since the roof in the structure had collapsed on them before. There was no way to know if the tunnels would support their weight, but they decided to try anyway.

Momentarily leaving Feldman's body in the structure, they culled everything from inside the room except for the bones they found. Grodin joked that the worm ate the people that lived in the building and pooped out their bones.

While everyone pulled the materials out into the tunnel, the sergeant started building a foundation as sturdy as he could manage. When he was done, the pile barely rose a few feet.

"So how do we poke a hole in this casing?" Abram said, staring at the apex.

No one said a word. A gun discharged and everyone ducked. Brooks had been the one to fire. The antimatter round had blasted a three foot hole in the casing, and sand poured in, creating a growing pile on the floor.

When the sand had stopped the blue moon's light speared through the hole.

"Well that's different. It's way more eerie than your report," The sergeant said, looking at the blue light.

The other mercenaries nodded in agreement, and Abram smiled. He still found the blue hue entrancing.

"We could probably use that sand that fell through to get some extra height," the sergeant said, transferring his pile of items over to the sand.

Everyone helped, but the sand flattened and only added an inch or two.

"Here, I can still make it up if someone gives me a boost," Stribling said, stepping up to the top of the pile.

"You weigh a million pounds. Who in the world is going to boost you?" Grodin said.

Stribling gave Grodin a dumbfounded look but hopped down. "Fine, I'll boost, but who's strong enough to lift us up through the hole? Sure as snow in the Arctic, you ain't."

"Am too!" Grodin said, folding his arms.

"I'll do it," Abram said, stepping up onto the pile. "Just give me a boost."

Stribling complied while Grodin pouted. Stribling knelt on the pile, creating a step with his hands and knee. Abram tossed his flare on the ground before stepping to Stribling.

"There will only be snow in the Arctic for like another thirty years! So ha!" Grodin yelled as Abram started climbing.

Stribling hoisted Abram up, holding onto one leg's thigh and ankle when Abram was up. Stribling was as strong as he looked, and Abram almost banged his head against the rim of the opening. He guided himself through until he was high enough to pull his body up.

The desert was cool in the moon's light, and he felt at peace in the blue. The rolling sand dunes still stretched on for miles, but in the distance he swore he could see some green. All he could do was hope it was tangible instead of a mirage.

"Whenever you're ready. We aren't in a rush or anything," Grodin said from below and Abram focused.

He cleared the sand a few feet around the hole and tested the surface's strength by jumping a few times. He heard no cracks or breaks so he dropped to his belly, lowering an arm through the hole. Now that he was through, he realized no one would really need help aside from Stribling, as the big man could do for everyone what he'd done for Abram.

Ruth was next to come up, and Abram helped her through. While she was being pushed up, Grodin, the sergeant, and Brooks went to bring out Feldman's body.

"Wait, guys, feel that?" The sergeant said, pausing and holding up both hands. A few moments after he spoke a squeal echoed through the tunnel. "Double time!"

They retrieved Feldman's body and hoisted it up next, but it took a few tries for Abram and Ruth to grab hold of it. When they finally did, they pulled it through and Abram felt sick. The strip of cloth had fallen off, and Feldman's poor head was caked in red and rolled about on his neck. Guilt twisted in Abram's gut like a corkscrew. Upon pulling Feldman's body through, they gingerly set him in the sand a few feet from the hole. Abram thought of sanitizing, but decided to wait.

Grodin came up next, followed by Brooks. By the time the sergeant was through, the ground above the tunnel was vibrating. Another squeal echoed through and Stribling passed all the weapons up before standing on the pile. He was too short to reach by a few inches, even when Abram lowered a hand through to get him.

Jumping, he finally connected with Abram's arm, but he was heavy and started pulling Abram through the hole. Brooks acted fastest and jumped over onto Abram's legs, stopping him so that only his waist was through. The hole was sharp and dug into his stomach and he winced, trying his best to hold on.

Everyone else grabbed on as well, pulling Brooks and Abram back until only Abram's arm and shoulder were dangling over the edge.

"Guys, can we hurry it up. I think the ground is moving up, like something big is rising," Stribling said, slowly swinging on Abram's arm.

Brooks stayed put on Abram's legs and everyone else braced Abram's body so he could heave the big man up. Abram lifted Stribling up and everyone helped get him through the opening.

The group took a few deep breaths, but Stribling was on his feet in an instant, scrambling to find his LMG. The ground vibrated violently now, and Brooks stood up so Abram could as well. Brooks grabbed his rifle, but before the sergeant and Grodin could gather their guns, the ground beneath their feet rose a few feet into the air before instantly falling. They were all suspended briefly with the sand before dropping back to the ground with a thud.

No one had time to get to their feet before they were bounced again. The tunnel was not firmly planted in the ground, and whatever was inside was bumping against it, trying to break free. This time they landed and everyone but Stribling started rolling down the dune they were on. Abram spun head over heels. He gave up on trying to see.

Sand and limbs were everywhere.

Finally coming to a stop, Abram heard another squeal and looked up the dune. They had been on top of one of the higher mounds, and Stribling was sprinting down with his LMG. He kept looking over his shoulder. Terror was etched into his face and Abram stood to his feet, blinking to clear the grains of sand that tried to find their way into his eyes.

Then a loud crash sounded and a monstrosity burst into the air behind Stribling. It erupted at an angle and spiraled down toward Stribling's body.

CHAPTER 12

Stribling leapt forward as the creature crashed into the ground at his rear. A giant cloud of dust and sand puffed up from the impact and consumed him, and Sergeant Bethune sprinted forward toward the rolling cloud. Abram was stunned, but the sergeant's screams steeled his nerves. He un-holstered his M9A, heading toward the danger.

The sand made a terrible running surface. Making matters worse, the ground rumbled and vibrated hindering his ability to move quickly.

Stribling burst through the cloud of sand and dust with his eyes closed. He was clutching his LMG still, running as if he could see where he was going. Sergeant Bethune caught him and Stribling fought for a few seconds, his eyes still closed.

When he rubbed at his eyes and blinked them open he had to keep blinking as he was unable to fully clear the sand and dust.

"Move!" the sergeant bellowed, breaking into a sprint toward Ruth and the other two mercenaries. They had all started running on instinct, but once they noticed Stribling's peril they stopped and cheered for the three men to hurry.

A squeal yanked Abram's head over his shoulder. The monstrosity broke through the top of the dust cloud, slowly rotating, trailing shards of the casing from the tunnel as well as sand behind its tail as it went. Ruth was right about the tunnel maker being a worm.

It had a head like a lamprey, but instead of stationary teeth, this creature's teeth swirled clockwise on their own. It passed the apex of its jump and started descending toward them. Two black bulges rested on the top of its head, and Abram caught a thin lid swiping across. The rest of its body was as smooth as glass, though it was much shorter than he had imagined. It barely reached the length of a school bus, and had skin the same color as the sand. Though smooth, Abram could tell the body was stacked with muscles. He wondered if it was able to leap by coiling first. The body thinned toward the rear, but a thick venom sack balanced it out. A needle-sharp stinger curved forward from the venom sack.

Brooks took aim and fired. The venom sac exploded, showering down a yellow liquid that sizzled and bubbled against the sand. Abram hoped he never discovered what it felt like. The beast continued descending.

They were moving fast enough that the creature would miss them. Moments before impact, the creature's skin revealed hundreds of holes, and goo squirted from the openings and covered the body. It slammed into the ground and Abram stumbled, catching himself with one hand but continuing to run. Seeing their companions running, Ruth and the other two mercenaries started running as well. Abram was faster than Stribling and Sergeant Bethune, and started closing the distance to Ruth and the others. The ground continued to rumble.

Stopping Ruth and the other two mercenaries in their tracks, another worm erupted from the ground, kicking up sand and dirt and tunnel casing but staying in the sand. It bent toward them and squealed, shooting out globs of saliva and wet sand. The trio was knocked onto their backs.

Brooks whipped his weapon around as the creature's head lowered toward them. He fired two rounds in less than a second. Both hit their mark, blowing a chunk out of the back of the worm's head. In reflex, the worm's skin opened and oozed goo.

The worm drooped toward them, and the three scrambled to get out of the way. Abram screamed for Ruth as the worm impacted the ground, shielding her condition with another cloud. The remaining worm erupted from the ground again and Abram tracked its arc as it fell. If they stayed on their current path it would devour them. Abram looked over his shoulder and signaled for the two mercenaries to veer off to the left. Abram headed to the left as well and squeezed the trigger on his weapon. A click sounded and his heart sank.

Then the worm opened the holes on its right side only, expelling air and goo and guiding itself back down toward them.

"Split up," Abram yelled, a little stunned the creature was intelligent enough to guide its glide. The two mercenaries followed orders without hesitation. Stribling went to his right and Bethune to his left.

The worm fell toward Abram and made no indication of confusion or further redirection. Abram squeezed the trigger, but it kept clicking so he tossed the gun as hard as his prosthetic would allow. The gun struck the worm but its soft body absorbed the force and the gun dropped toward the ground.

As it squealed and spit out sand and saliva, time slowed to a crawl. Abram glanced to the side and saw Stribling attempt to fire his gun. It clicked as well, and no bullets were released. After a moment or two of squeezes with no result, he lowered the weapon and looked at it, confused and upset.

Abram glanced at his arm and wondered how effective it would be against the monstrous creature. His heart hammered nails of adrenaline through his veins that tingled through his fingers and limbs. He squatted down a little in preparation, and fear clutched his chest.

Before the creature could land, he reacted, jumping away but swinging back to punch the side of the creature's head with all his might. The goo had been secreted and had already hardened, but his prosthetic knuckle shattered through with no trouble. He closed his eyes from his fist's impact. The force of the punch pushed him further from the creature. When he landed dust whooshed into his face, and he was unable to see how successful he had been.

CHAPTER 13

By the time Abram recovered, Stribling and Sergeant Bethune had reached him. He used his forearm to try to clear his eyes, but his whole face felt like one giant scratch. His chest squeezed in protest of all the particles he'd inhaled.

Unable to see, he kept his eyes closed and allowed his tears to do their duty.

"You so happy to see me, you're crying?" Grodin said, out of breath. "I know it's been a rough day, but don't cry. I'm here!"

His voice was as annoying as ever, but surviving the life-threatening situation eased the annoyance Abram felt toward the man. He felt a few pats on his back and welcomed the relieved chuckles. Since no one sounded terrified, he assumed the worm was dead.

Everyone made it over to the same spot, and he finally managed to breathe easy. His eyes cleared and he found the dead worm. The side he'd punched was buried in the ground, and the remainder of its body was motionless. Cracks zigzagged around the whole beast's body, and he wondered what the punch area looked like.

Abram happily sighed and looked at his arm. It looked as it always did. Unlike his flesh arm there was little to no sand and no sweat clinging to it. The rest of his body still tingled with adrenaline and fatigue. He wondered if his arm would feel any different if he did manage to expend all the energy in the battery cells.

"Let's finish what we started with Felds," Sergeant Bethune said, hanging his head briefly before looking up the large sand dune they'd descended.

Everyone agreed and trekked back to the summit. Abram found his gun and holstered it as they went. The worm's original explosion from the tunnels had blasted Feldman's body a ways from where they started, and all the disturbed sand had covered most of him. Despite the hindrance that the dark brought, Ruth was able to spot the toe of his boot poking through the surface.

After a minor debate about moving him, the majority agreed that they intended to bury him and he was already mostly buried. They dug enough of him out so his belongings could be retrieved. The sergeant collected the dog tags, took the extra clips of ammunition, removed the canteen, and swiped the Tylenol and memory pills in case they would need them.

The group assisted in scooping another foot or so of sand onto his corpse. Sergeant Bethune gave a brief eulogy, while Stribling and Grodin said a few kind words. They reminisced of old missions and special ops training, while Abram and Ruth wandered off. They were close enough to hear but far enough away to avoid invading the mercenaries' privacy. They felt they were foreigners to the moment, as they'd barely known the deceased. The last thing either of them wanted was to cause offense.

It came time for Brooks to speak, but instead he pointed his rifle into the sky and fired. The report echoed across the dunes. He picked up the spent shell casing, knelt down, and placed it atop where Feldman's chest was. He made the sign of the cross and stood.

The group stood around in silence, and only the scratching sound of the wind against the sand surrounded them. After a few moments the ground started to rumble again. Urgency swept through them and they jogged back down the dune, hoping any additional gigantic worms decided to stay underground in their tunnels.

As they passed the worm that Brooks had shot, he hopped onto the lip and knocked out one of the few small teeth with the butt of his rifle. When it was free, he studied it for a moment before pocketing it with a smile. When the sergeant shot him a look Brooks just shrugged and kept grinning.

The ground rumbled for another quarter mile and Ruth furiously jotted down notes of the encounter and of the seismic activity.

Fatigue set in before long and they were forced to stop. No shelter was visible; just sand for miles in every direction. They stopped and made camp at the base of a tall dune. No fire but they rested on their backs in close proximity.

None of the field tents worked. So far pretty much everything had failed, and Abram questioned if they had provided the supplies more to test their theories instead of actually sending the group off with useable equipment. Regular, manual-assembly tents would have been perfect.

The group lay on their backs in the blue moonlight. The temperature had dropped to a merciful fifty degrees, and paired with their sweat-dampened uniforms, several of them began to shiver.

Ruth talked with Abram of what they would bring on their next trip, and Abram agreed on most of the supplies she mentioned.

"You're already talking about another visit?" Stribling said, raising an eyebrow. "Can we at least get halfway through this one?"

"Y'all are crazy! I wouldn't come back to this place even if you threw me in an air conditioned tank with a built-in fridge," Grodin said, covering his face with his arms.

"Stock the tank with a couple packs of gum and a beer and I'd do it any time." Sergeant Bethune smiled for the first time since before they fell in the tunnels.

"Maybe if the tank was full of beer. But it'd have to be good beer. Not that shoddy mainstream garbage. I'm talking the crafty type, from one of them breweries that don't skimp on the percent by volume. Nine and ten percent or higher alcohol by volume is what I could use right about now," Grodin responded.

Stribling chuckled. "You'd barely be able to handle one bottle before blacking out."

Grodin sat straight up. "Wrong. Wrong," he said, smirking. "I'd take on at least three."

Stribling laughed and slapped his thigh.

"Can we all just cut the chatter and go to sleep? We've been on our feet for like eighteen hours today, and I'm not trying to do that again tomorrow without at least getting some sleep," Abram said.

"I'm sowee. Is the widdle baby tired?" Grodin said, jutting out his lip and doing his best infant impression.

"Zip it, Grodes. Jacobson's right. We need to rest if we're to get anything accomplished tomorrow. I'll take first watch. I'll wake up whoever's next when it's time."

Grodin continued grinning but lay back down and covered his face again. Abram sighed and tried think of anything but all the dirt that was covering his body. He filled his mind with the smell of fresh linen and Clorox wipes. He pulled out his hand sanitizer and looked around. Everyone was either staring at the sky or trying to fall asleep. He sniffed the open bottle and smiled. The last time he'd visited the Third he'd been alone, and though companionship had its perks, he started to miss the solitude.

He missed home as well, and being generally free of filth, and he started to wish none of the previous events had happened to him. He pocketed the Purell and looked at his arm. It was a powerful tool, but he'd trade it all away to go back in time to before the first trip. He'd still have his arm, and he'd never know what a giant, flesh-eating worm looked like. Or what sound a man makes when he chokes on his own blood.

Abram pushed the thoughts from his mind and instead thought of hot showers, clean towels, and fresh clothes until he fell asleep.

CHAPTER 14

The familiar scratch of sand and heat roused Abram from sleep. Ruth was up and sitting cross-legged, drawing in the sand with her finger. Grodin had taken the last watch shift, and was also awake, staring off toward the mountains.

"How'd you sleep?" Abram said, standing and stretching, surveying the expanse of sand before them.

"Bad. Sand is rather comfortable." Ruth glanced up at him and flashed a smile. "Beats sleeping on a rock though."

Abram chuckled. After a few minutes of stretching and good mornings, the group was ready to head out. They each took their vibration pills before leaving. They trudged on through the unforgiving terrain in relative silence.

"What's that?" Stribling said, pointing to their right. "Three o'clock."

Everyone followed his finger and Abram perked up, heading toward the object of interest.

"Looks alive," Sergeant Bethune said. "Fingers at the ready."

"No need. I've seen those before. Some of the slavers that originally captured me rode on them."

They closed the distance and Ruth started drawing again. It was one of the camel lizards, and the familiar sound of sloshing water reached Abram's ears as the creature started to meander away from them. It remained calm but stomped its way east. Abram hadn't noticed during his first trip, but the lizard stank.

"That thing full of what I hope it's full of?" Sergeant Bethune said, pointing to the hump on the creature's belly.

"Beer! The giant lizards here are full of beer!" Grodin said.

"Zip it!"

Bethune glanced at Abram, and he nodded before answering: "Though, I'm not sure if it would be drinkable. Might be bloody and stuff."

"Camel humps don't contain water," Ruth started, finishing her sketch of the creature. "The humps are to store fat."

"Why are we talking about drinking this beast's belly dry? Can we ride it out of here first? Or maybe even ride it to a water supply?"

The group looked at Stribling. Abram shrugged, thumbing at Stribling. "I'm with him. If we can get out of this place faster I'm all for it."

"Do the math. There are six of us and one of it. How are we going to ride it unless we can all get on?" Grodin pointed an accusatory finger at Abram, though Abram remained silent. "And don't even think about saying you and the missus can ride it and leave us here to dry up and blow away."

"Wasn't going to, but thanks for making that clear."

"Everyone just stop for a minute. Let me think," Sergeant Bethune said, rubbing his forehead. He popped in a stick of gum and chewed loudly for a few seconds. "Riding it is out of the question, since only one or two people would fit on its back. Eating it is a good option, as it'll save us some rations. The only other alternative I can think of is to load it up with all of our gear and have it haul for us."

"I can haul my own stuff once I've had me a camel lizard steak," Grodin said.

"Well, what if—" Ruth's sentence was cut off by a scratching sound and everyone froze.

Circles of sand in various places around them started to rise and shift. Brooks cocked his weapon and aimed at the nearest rising mound, but soon everyone else followed. Since assault weapons were still crammed with sand, the other mercs pulled out their sidearm pistols and aimed, darting their weapons between the hills.

As the sand fell back to the ground, unknown faces with familiar eyes appeared. All appeared to be male, and each bore a scowl. The spears primed and pointed at the group indicated hostile intentions.

"Drop your weapons and identify yourselves!" Sergeant Bethune roared, lowering his weapon to the nearest head.

The newcomers looked around as if confused at first, and one stepped forward. They were all wearing loose garments with hoods, and the one that moved forward flung back his head. They were all around four feet tall, but the one that had moved was the tallest.

"Outsiders. Ours now," the tall one said with a sneer.

The voice had the same underwater quality that Abram remembered on his first visit. The slavers had been rough with him, though at the time he'd thought they were stronger. Now he had his arm and almost laughed at the idea of getting into a fight with them now.

"Yours? Explain?" the sergeant said, keeping his gun trained between the tall one's eyes.

"These are slavers like the one I encountered during my first visit here."

The tall one made an odd, bird-like sound and movement over a nearby sand dune pulled everyone's attention. Coming over top of the dune, more slavers riding lizards poured into the area. Some hooped and jeered and others just ran down the slope toward the troop. Most bore spears, but their numbers alone made Abram question how smart it would be to fight. Even if they surrendered they could just break free at night, sneaking out quietly like he'd done with Koñél. She popped into his head briefly but faded away as the cavalry arrived. Their camel lizards grunted and shifted their weight from side to side.

"Did we just walk into a trap?" Grodin said, his gun still aimed at one of the slavers.

"Sure seems that way," the sergeant said. "Jacobson? Should we engage or withdraw?"

"Probably could just scare them."

Bethune glanced at Brooks and nodded. Brooks discharged his weapon at the feet of the tall one. The blast blew a crater in the sand and made the whole group of slavers jump. Some started screaming while others appeared to debate if throwing their spears was a smart move.

Priming another shot, Brooks pointed his weapon at the tall one.

"We are not your property. You can leave us be or suffer the consequences," Abram said.

"Great power!" the tall one said, looking around at all the weapons pointed at him before glancing at the spear in his own hands. He tossed it on the ground and glared at Abram. "Give!"

The other slavers tossed their spears down and echoed the command.

"Lead us out of here and you can have one gun."

"Gun? Lead out where?"

Abram sighed and held up a hand to the group. They all lowered their weapons and Abram tried again, holding up the M9A. "Gun." He paused and looked around, picking up a handful of sand. "Go from sand." He tossed the handful and it dispersed on a breeze. "Find solid ground." Abram stomped and the tall slaver seemed to catch on. "Find Gray Lord."

"All gun. Take to solid ground," the tall one said, mimicking Abram's stomp. "To Gray Lord."

"One gun," Abram repeated. He turned to the sergeant. "Give me Feldman's rifle."

The sergeant frowned but slid the additional firearm from his shoulder, handing it to Abram. Abram turned back to the slaver and held it out.

"Powerful gun. We give. No more."

After a few seconds of thought, the tall one stomped again and shook his head, saying *yes* in his odd voice. The rest of the slavers cheered, pumping their spears in the air as if they'd just won a victory. Abram turned over the gun to the tall one and the slaver imitated the sergeant in the way he placed it on his shoulder. He played with it a little but seemed too fascinated with the outside to bother asking how the firing part worked. It would probably need to be cleaned anyway, but Abram was careful to stay out of the path of the weapon, just in case, and the rest of the group followed suit.

"Good job," Sergeant Bethune said patting Abram on the back, though his voice indicated he was still unhappy with the trade. "We need to conserve our ammunition for the real threats."

Hearing the sergeant's words, Brooks checked his rifle's clip and his spare ammunition. He had two fresh clips and each clip held nine rounds. He spent six bullets so far so he had three left in the used clip.

The caravan headed west, falling into a loosely organized line. With no slaves in their company, Abram wondered if the trick his group had just fallen for was how the caravan found their captives. How many people wandered through the desert? He thought back to the tunnels and wondered if there were less abandoned but hidden cities beneath their feet.

They trudged on through the remainder of the day and were given a tent to sleep in at night. The slavers were even generous enough to provide some insect snacks and water. They adamantly refused to slaughter a camel lizard for steaks, though Grodin begged them three times.

Abram was a little disappointed that they weren't chained to a peg in the tent. He wanted to test his real arm against the peg this time around and see if he could remove it.

CHAPTER 15

Sleeping under the cover of the tent helped Abram get a few good hours of rest, and he woke up relatively refreshed in the morning.

The caravan allowed the Outsiders to ride on the camel lizards on the second day, and everything seemed to go so much faster. They reached the end of the desert and the ground slowly changed from sand to dirt to dirt with sporadic grass patches. Bushes and small trees could be seen in the distance, but the caravan stopped before things got too lush.

Walking up to Abram still bearing the rifle, the tall one said that the slave caravan would go no further. On the downswing of getting their bounties, they had no reason to waste a full journey through to the greens. Still, he informed Abram that traveling in a straight line in the same direction would get them to their destination.

With little choice in the matter, Abram bid them goodbye and good riddance.

"So now we just walk the rest of the way? How long are we talking?" Stribling said as they took their first few steps.

"Not entirely sure, but last time I was airborne and it still took two or three days."

Grodin was the only one to groan but Abram could feel the spirits of the group fall. The trip was shaping up to be far worse than he imagined, and there was no telling what additional problems awaited them in the meadows. He thought of the *muva* phenomenon and hoped clear skies instead of rain was in the forecast.

Abram missed the camel lizard cushion. At least they were off the sand, but it was still hot. The rolling green swards stretched to the horizon in every direction, and it was a welcome change from the unsteady surface of the desert. Aside from pulling boots in a few inches with every step, the sand had also concealed more than Abram was comfortable with. The worms were bad enough, but there was no telling if something more sinister would have popped up and attacked them.

Ruth continued sketching as they walked, guessing that the temperature in the desert was between ninety and ninety-five degrees. She surmised that the further they walked west, the cooler it would become, though she mentioned the temperature was currently about the same as the desert.

As they pushed on for miles with no end in sight, Abram got the idea of contacting home in the off chance his radio had started working. He still only received static, so decided to try recording the endless green. He had no way of knowing if the camera actually recorded, but he tried anyway. Perhaps picture could get through even if sound couldn't.

"Please tell me we can eat that thing without worrying about it being a trap?" Grodin said, spotting one of the amphibious yaks.

Unlike the first time he'd witnessed them, this yak's fur was black. It had the same furry protrusions dangling from the side of its head, and it chewed cud without a care in the world. As they neared it, its eyes widened but it kept chewing, releasing a wet gust of air from its gills.

"This thing didn't even try to run away." Grodin patted the amphibian on the side and it blew out another gust. "What's that furry cow? You want me to eat you?" Grodin smiled from ear to ear.

Abram shrugged. "I think I had a chance to taste it my first time around, and it wasn't great but it beats nothing."

Sergeant Bethune was the one to slaughter the animal, humanely inserting his combat knife through the temple.

"Alright, little lady," the sergeant started, looking at Ruth. "How's about you try to get a fire started while we take care of skinning and gutting this thing."

Ruth rolled her eyes but started searching for dry grass.

The mercenaries pulled out their combat knives and started slicing off the layer of skin below the fur while Abram watched. Ruth meandered a good distance away.

"Well don't just stand there," Grodin said, pointing his knife at Abram as he talked. "Whip out your blade and give us a hand."

"You guys look like you're handling it pretty well," Abram said, earning raised eyebrows from the mercenaries. "Not a fan of touching raw meat without a nearby sink."

"Oh right, scared of the *germs* and such," Grodin said, holding up his hands and waving them in mockery.

"Aware!" Abram said, more offended than he should have been.

"You don't know how many forms of bacteria are swimming around in that blood that you're bathing in up to your elbows." Abram glanced at his prosthetic, wanting to yell that it was germs that had caused him to lose his arm. Instead, he said, "I'll look for dry stuff to help with the fire."

Grodin snickered but kept digging in and Abram searched the area, intentionally avoiding going near Ruth to avoid hearing the group jeer at them being alone together. The ground was too alive and wet, and grass was all there was. There weren't even any dead stalks or flowers, and Abram wondered what home would look like with this much life and green still in the grass. Giving up, he yanked out handfuls and brought them back to the mercenaries.

"I doubt this stuff will catch, and the fur probably won't be much better, but it's all we have," Abram said, piling his grass in front of them.

Ruth returned and they all agreed that their chances were slim, but fur and grass would be their only shot. Clearing out a patch of grass down to the dirt, they organized as many tufts of fur as they could into one spot and used Brooks's flare to start it up. The fur caught fire much better than they anticipated, almost burning as quickly as flash cotton.

"Well that was a fail," Stribling said. "I'm no germaphobe, but I dunno if I can eat this stuff raw."

"Here," Ruth said, taking Stribling's knife from him.

The group had tied their camo jackets around their waists back when they were in the desert, and since it was still hot they had kept them at their hips. Ruth pulled Abram's and held it up to him to verify the right side before slicing into his right sleeve.

"Hey, I might need that at some point," Abram said, frowning.

"Unlikely. It has been hot everywhere we have been, but just in case I am removing the sleeve from your prosthetic side. Since you lack feeling in that arm, the temperature will be irrelevant."

The sergeant whistled. "Good luck winning any arguments in your future."

Ruth just smiled and finished removing the sleeve, tossing the jacket back to Abram. He caught it but, unable to retie it around his waist, slung it around his shoulder. She grabbed some fur and grass and mixed the two together before stuffing enough of it into the sleeve to make it appear to be filled with an arm.

"With any luck," Ruth said, organizing the sleeve on the dirt. "The sleeve will burn for a while, and the grass will dry out inside, hopefully burning too."

She lit the fabric and the fur flashed brightly for a moment. The sleeve did catch and started creating a horrible smell, but the mercenaries immediately tossed their meet on the fire. They'd cut the meat thin so it would cook faster, and they were successful. Abram felt a little bad about avoiding helping them cut, so he helped maintain the fire by tossing grass on it every so often. He tried not to think of how dirty his sleeve and the grass were, reminding himself that heat was the ultimate purifier.

The meat was very similar to what he'd eaten at the Gray Lord's. It was a bit juicier this time around, but still a bit like watered down beef. His broke apart easier than the others, since he'd cooked it for so long, but everyone's appeared chewy.

"You guys feel that?" Sergeant Bethune said, swallowing a bite before speaking again. "Feels like another earthquake." He looked at Abram with concern. "There aren't grass worms too, are there?"

"No clue," Abram said, biting into his meat again, thankful it had gotten burnt and the chance for germs was minimal. "But I didn't know about the sand worms either."

The intensity of the ground vibrations increased.

"What's that?" Grodin said, pointing behind Abram.

Abram looked over his shoulder and his eyes widened. His heartbeat picked up pace and he stuffed the remaining meat into his mouth.

"We gotta go. Now!" Abram said, standing and staring.

"Go where? What is that?" the sergeant said, also stuffing the remainder of his meat into his mouth.

"*Muva.*"

"Move a what?"

"It's how rain happens here. Only instead of hundreds of droplets across miles, all the drops are combined into one giant ball of water and it rolls across the ground. Did you notice how that furry cow had gills? They were so it could breathe in that."

The giant ball of water roared toward them and shook the ground. It was wider than they would be able to outrun, but Abram ran anyway. The rest of the group followed suit, leaving the remaining meat where it was and sprinting as fast as they could. Abram ran diagonally away from the approaching water, hoping it would have started fizzling out by the time it reached them.

Hiding flocks of camouflaged birds erupted from the path of the moving water and some passed overhead. Abram's heart beat so hard he thought it would give out, but they kept going. When the tidal wave was close enough to see inside, Abram knew all hope was lost. Grass, unknown animals, a few birds and amphibious yaks were roiling around behind the wall of blue, and seeing them gave him an idea.

"Just before it hits, everybody jump so you aren't crushed beneath it! Maybe we can swim to the top or something once we're inside!" Abram screamed as loud as he could, but he feared the roar of the water drowned him out.

The water crashed down around them and Abram took a deep breath, jumping up just before the liquid touched him.

CHAPTER 16

Abram's jumping idea was successful, but the water was far more turbulent than he had imagined. He felt like he was trapped inside of a washing machine, and he was spun and twirled head over heels. His arms and legs bumped into things, and the pressure of the water forced him to close his eyes. He tried his hardest to swim in the direction he thought was up, but his normal arm was a useless noodle in the might of the water. Sticking out his prosthetic only caused him to catch the current and spin even more cause him to spin more.

He forced his eyes open every so often but saw nothing. The water was deceptively clear from the outside, but inside all was black. The current dragged him along and he felt like his body was being ripped apart. The sound of the water was like a muffled train shooting past his ear.

As the lack of oxygen started to settle in his chest squeezed and begged him to inhale. He fought with all his might, determined to find a way out but failing with every attempt he made.

Drowning had always been a death he'd hoped to avoid. The idea of being trapped in a place with no oxygen was as terrifying as he thought it would be. His diaphragm continually heaved, trying to force in oxygen, but he kept his mouth shut.

Then brightness caused him to open his eyes. Light was all around him, and heading to heaven was his first guess.

But the light focused and cut through the water and he fell straight down, landing harshly on the wet ground. Instantly he gasped and sucked in air until his lungs were sore. He coughed and panted, marveling at the sight around him.

The water had been split in half, and he could see inside each of the walls. The amphibious yaks were the most prevalent, though the occasional bird swirled passed before being sucked back toward the center. The water formed an arch above him and he could see more life within, rushing past as the water continued to move.

Then Stribling fell through the arch and landed beside him, coughing and gagging on the water but managing to finally breathe normally. Seconds later, the sergeant, Ruth, Brooks, and Grodin fell out, all landing on the ground with soggy thuds.

Everyone inhaled deep, and a few coughed and vomited water. Everyone except Grodin. He was crumpled on his side, unmoving and unbreathing.

"Grodin!" Sergeant Bethune bellowed, scrambling to his fallen soldier. There was a moment of sickening silence. Everyone just stared at the two men. Debris-laced water was dripping down Bethune's face, and he had to rub his forearm across his eyes every so often to clear them. "I'm not losing you too!"

The sergeant attempted CPR. "Come on, soldier! Wake up!" the sergeant mumbled some unintelligible words and continued trying as the others gathered around.

After nearly a minute the sergeant began to fatigue and Abram felt guilty enough to offer help. Though the things that had happened were circumstances of their environment, everyone was still in the dimension because of him.

"Here, let me," Abram said, dropping to his knees. "I know CPR too."

Abram gulped and grimaced at the idea of touching another human's mouth with his own lips. He thought of all the mouth-borne bacteria, of all the diseases that could be transferred via lip contact and started second guessing his decision. What if Grodin was one of the millions of people suffering from cold sores? The likelihood of transfer was lowered by the fact that there were no visible sores, but there was no telling if viral shedding was occurring, which would increase the chance of the virus spreading. He barely even liked Grodin during the brief moments his mouth was mute, much less all the times he actually spoke. All of that only made him feel more guilt.

"Either do something or get out the way!" Sergeant Bethune said, dropping down beside Abram again after seeing Abram's inertia.

Abram glared at Grodin and took a deep breath. He clasped one hand over the other and locked his elbows, pumping down on Grodin's chest. An uncertain silence settled into the group and Ruth folded her arms and fidgeted with her sleeve, nervous.

Abram's heart picked up pace as he worried about his success. If he failed, he knew he would blame himself for Grodin's death, even though, technically, Grodin was already dead. CPR was about resuscitation, but Abram knew how his brain worked. He tried calming his nerves by recalling the pace-setting songs the CPR instructor had told him to sing in his head to make sure he got the right number of chest compressions. The words of the classic song, *Staying Alive* by the Bee Gees rang through his head, but the tune switched to Queen's *Another One Bites the Dust*.

He made it through the chorus and tilted Grodin's chin up. He pinched the nose and made a mouth-to-mouth seal before emptying his lungs into Grodin, making sure the mercenary's chest rose.

Looking over and taking a single breath for himself, he breathed into Grodin again and started up the chest compressions. He tried his hardest to avoid swallowing, hoping to spit if Grodin ever woke up. He knew he wouldn't be able to spit out all the germs, but he would do his best to expel the highest number. After another chorus of *Staying Alive*, he forced himself down for another set of breaths before continuing the compressions.

It felt like forever before Grodin finally heaved and coughed out water and air. He gagged and coughed again, and Abram rolled the mercenary onto his side. Abram wanted to vomit but saved face. Though he did hock up a number of loogies and spit them on the ground. Every time his mouth built up enough saliva to swallow, he spit.

The mercenaries were consumed with helping Grodin, and even Ruth was bent over trying to make sure he could breathe okay. Grodin continued to cough, but soon started to quiet down, and the sergeant and Stribling made jokes of how stupid he was for being unable to hold his breath. While no one was looking, Abram squirted some hand sanitizer on his lips and rubbed it in. After a moment of debate, he squirted some in his mouth and swished it around before spitting it out, rinsing his mouth with water from his canteen.

"So, Jacobson, you couldn't resist these rosy red smackers?" Grodin said, still on the ground but sitting up. He smirked up at Abram. "They tell me you did the honors."

Abram rejoined the fold and sighed, wanting to kick Grodin in the teeth for cracking jokes instead of saying how grateful he was to be alive.

It took the group a few moments to snap out of the shock and become aware of their present predicament. The *muva* waters continued shifting and roiling overhead. They marveled in nervous curiosity. What if whatever held the waters back was removed?

"Anybody care to explain how we're underneath this monsoon without a drop dripping on us? Last time I checked, Moses was a made-up character from the Bible," Stribling said, slowly rotating.

"He wasn't made up, he's historical fact," Abram said. "But I have no clue who or what's causing this to happen."

Abram was still wondering how long they had before the water crashed back down. The sunlight barely made it through the *muva*, and the area was cast in an unsettling blue darkness that was reminiscent of night.

"Did you guys see that light too?" Abram said. "Before we fell out."

Most of the others shook their heads, but Stribling responded, "My eyes were closed. I hate opening my eyes in pools and oceans. That burn is annoying."

"That is either from chlorine or saltwater. This undoubtedly contained neither," Ruth said, starting to sketch a picture of their surroundings but stopping when her wet paper ripped. She frowned and sighed. "Still, there was enough debris in there to irritate your eyes. I saw no light."

"I think we can all guess that mine were closed," Grodin said, finally standing to his feet and brushing the wet grass and soil from his backside. "You know, being dead and all. I totally wish I had gone to heaven. Or hell, or wherever I'm going when I die. But there was nothing. I guess it's possible I just don't remember what there was, but all I remember is getting hit by that water, taking a breath full of it, and then passing out. I woke up to Abram's beautiful brights."

"Dude, hasn't anyone ever told you that you talk way too much?" Stribling said.

"Great," the sergeant started, holding up the empty hook at his waste. "My flare is gone."

The group checked and realized they had all suffered the same fate. The water had claimed their best source of light or chance to start another fire.

The sound of splashing water pulled all of their attention to the wall at their rear. A figure stepped through the liquid.

CHAPTER 17

Though the figure had walked through the water, none of it actually touched his clothing. A hood covered his head and helped veil his face. He held a glass rod with a stationary snake inside that glared at them with an eeriness that was reminiscent of the "eyes that follow" in oil paintings. His clothes were all white, faintly glowing in the darkened environment. He was barefoot, yet even in the mud his feet were immaculate.

The mercenaries, save for Grodin, pulled their weapons forward and the figure froze.

"Identify yourself and your intent?" Sergeant Bethune said, his voice shaky.

"Welcome, Outsiders," the figure started, and Abram recognized the voice, smiling at the memories. "And, Abram, welcome back."

Abram walked forward and almost fell into the Shaman's open arms. The two embraced, chuckling with joy. Ruth followed suit, joining in the hug and giggling along with them, and the mercenaries lowered their weapons.

"Wouldn't have fired anyway," the sergeant said, checking his weapon briefly before letting it hang by its strap. He pulled out a stick of gum and popped it in, chewing it vigorously. "Dang things are all soggy now."

Introductions were in order, so Abram moved with the Shaman back to the mercenaries.

"Everyone, this is the Shaman. Probably the only guy from this side that I trust."

"Hearing your view of me is most warming, Abram," the Shaman said.

Hearing the accented English again made Abram smile. The Shaman's voice was as charming as it always was.

"You already know Ruth, but this is our escort team. They're all mercenaries—previously soldiers from our armed forces back home." Abram held a hand to each of them as he said their names.

Brooks still had his rifle in his hand as if he was ready to shoot at a moment's notice. He jokingly saluted the Shaman but remained as mute as he always did.

Even though the air remained calm and peaceful, Abram could see the glint of sadness in each soldier's eye. The introduction was short the man they had lost, and they'd almost lost another. Abram hoped they placed the blame on the dimension instead of him. He was the reason they were there, but he hoped they continued to see him as an ally. He hoped they saw him different than the way he saw himself.

"Pleased to have warriors escorting you. We are in perilous times."

"Are we?" Abram said, wrinkling his brow. "More so than usual?"

"Yes, but all will be explained in its due time."

The *muva* finally passed over top of them. The bubble or whatever had been shielding them collapsed, and the roar of the water filled the air once again. The water phenomenon continued moving on, slowly losing momentum and mass.

"It is a treat to see you again, but we must flee from here. It is unsafe," the Shaman said, looking to the skies.

He started whispering into the air and a flock of *wam-baika* descended from the clouds like angels. Their white wings were silhouetted by the sunshine at their back. Even their chimpanzee-like heads appeared angelic in the light, and Abram smiled.

The mercenaries instinctively brought up their weapons again.

"Fear not," the Shaman started. "They will carry you with care, warriors of the armed forces. Allow their grasp."

The mercenaries relaxed and the *wam-baika* took hold, screeching and grunting in their usual fashion. Abram welcomed the grab, happy to be airborne again. His feet were killing him, and riding with the beasts could be soothing at times.

The rolling green hills were a peaceful sight, and Abram found himself marveling at all that he saw. Even though he'd ventured a similar path before, the beauty of nature rarely got old. Herds of the amphibious yaks roamed and stampeded across the plains, sometimes even intentionally running into *muva* that rumbled below every so often. Flocks of a variety of species of birds, some brightly colored but most camouflaged with shades of green and brown, flew and weaved around the *wam-baika*. The *baika* snacked on the birds as they desired, and Abram wondered why the silly, small birds kept flying near the predatory flyers.

"Am I the only one who's afraid of heights?" Grodin said, moving his legs and twisting in the air as if he wanted the *baika* to drop him.

"No, but you're the only one who seems to think talking about it will make it better."

"Screw you, Stribbles, talking always makes me feel better!"

"You must stay on cloud nine then."

Grodin mocked Stribling's dialogue but continued to struggle. His *baika* squawked and dipped him toward a *muva* blob that was just starting to accumulate speed as it rolled down a hill. Grodin's terrified screams made everyone laugh, and Stribling made a few jokes. The other *baika* dipped their cargo down as well, taking them close enough to the water's surface to mist them with the droplets.

"That feels amazing," Ruth said, closing her eyes with a smile as water droplets splashed and flew into her face.

"It does indeed," Abram said, doing the same. "The Shaman tells me they do this because they see us as their young."

"Comforting," Ruth said, her eyes still closed.

CHAPTER 18

They traveled a full day before resting. Instead of landing near the fields of corn-like, but pumpkin-tasting fruits that they had landed near during Abram's first visit, the *baika* touched down in the middle of the plains. They were in an area un-trampled and un-eaten by the amphibious yaks, and much of the grass was as tall as the group. The Shaman was a bit shorter than the mercenaries and Abram, but he seemed the most comfortable in the concealing grass. They stomped a circle around the area so that the grass wasn't constantly pressing against their skin. Ruth spoke up about their being soaked, her primary concern over being hindered from taking notes on her pad, and the Shaman was gracious enough to whisper a desiccation utterance.

"I could go for another one of those yaks," Grodin said, sitting with his legs in front and rubbing his belly.

"The *Kondor* do not travel this far north in *Anga*," the Shaman started, sliding his glass staff back and forth against the tall stalks of grass. He barely bent the stalks as he moved the rod. Abram had no idea what he was doing and felt it was rude to ask, so he remained quiet. "*Mamba* hunt the brush in these parts."

"*Mamba*?" Grodin asked, an uneasy look settling onto his face. "Wouldn't happen to be related to 'Black Mambas'? Would they?" The Shaman responded with a blank stare, looking between Grodin and Abram. "The snakes? Those nasty buggers that bite for sport or something. I hear there's less than 100 left in the wild, but it only takes one to kill you."

The Shaman chuckled. "No, *mamba* are not serpents, though a great many serpents do slither through these stalks."

"You look like the snake-loving type," Grodin said with a hint of distaste, nodding at the staff.

The Shaman ignored the comment, but continued on about the *mamba*. "*Mamba* are the size of *paka*, but with scales for skin. While they're unable to achieve true flight, they have powerful leaps and wing-like flaps that enable them to glide for great distances."

"*Paka* sounds like alpaca, and if you're telling me there are flying alligators the size of alpacas, I think it's time we moved on. I'm not trying to sit around and wait to get eaten, especially not by an alligator alpaca." Grodin stood up, his face twisted halfway in fear and humor. "Where's my rock-winged angel thing?"

Stribling snuck up on Grodin as he tried to stand on his tiptoes and locate his *wam-baika*. Getting right next to Grodin's ear, Stribling hissed and grabbed his shoulders, and Grodin jumped and fell.

"Cut it out you two!" Sergeant Bethune roared. "I swear, you guys are a bunch of two year olds. Pull it together or I'll fire you both and see to it you never work as a mercenary again!"

"Sir, yes, sir!" Grodin said from the ground, stiffening. Stribling repeated the same thing, stiffening on his feet.

"*Mamba* hunt in packs, but they move forward fastest by gliding. If we keep attentive, we will see them heading toward us."

Grodin was too shamed to speak and kept quiet, glaring at the ground. Abram smiled, wishing the sergeant would yell at Grodin more often. Abram turned his attention to the tops of the grass, but nothing was visible but seed pods. Hopping insects created a cacophony all around them, but it eventually became soothing. The bugs were everywhere, hopping from the edge of the clearing the humans had created and crawling all across the dirt and bent stalks.

"We should keep up our strength," Ruth said, nabbing one of the hoppers by its back legs and holding it up. She bit everything down to the back legs, chewing and swallowing, pulling stares from everyone.

"Ruth is correct," the Shaman said, grabbing his own and downing it.

Abram swallowed, thinking of how many germs the insects were harboring. He looked at Grodin, who looked as grossed out at the idea as he was, and he was grateful no sick jokes were made about eating the bugs. Despite the look, Grodin grabbed one with his hand and tossed it down like a kernel of popcorn. He coughed and gagged and his face flushed red.

"Make sure you chew. Those things don't do well in the throat," Grodin said, coughing a few more times.

"It hasn't been that long since we ate, has it?" Stribling said with a sigh, eventually yielding along with the others as they started tossing down the bugs.

Eventually the disgusted looks turned to contentment. Abram

grabbed one and it squirmed in his hand. He swallowed hard again, thinking of the creature in his mouth and he felt nauseous. Stribling was right. Why were they resorting to insect eating already? They still had rations left, and even though it was better to save them for an emergency, eating bugs was just nasty. He took a deep breath, squeezed and smashed the bug, thinking it would be easier if it was already dead. When he opened his hand it made him gag even more. The blood was brown and viscous. Most of the body parts were still visible in the brown goo. He swiped his hand on the nearest stalk of grass and grabbed another, tossing it to the side of his mouth and trying to avoid tasting it. He bit once and the brown goo exploded in his mouth and made him gag, but he forced it down with a swig of water from his canteen.

"Well, I'm full," Abram said, forcing a grin and hoping no one had paid attention to him.

The rest of the day slipped by and the moon cast blue shade on their camp. The bent stalks made an excellent mattress, and he was able to ignore most of the grumbling coming from his stomach. Ignoring the insects that curiously crawled across his exposed skin was a different story.

He fantasized of returning to the Gray Lord's fortress and dining at the great table again, partaking in the treats he'd eaten before. With thoughts of real food he fell into a deep sleep before anyone else.

CHAPTER 19

Abram's eyes shot open to the sound of yelling. The blue of night was still present, and the Shaman was shaking the two still-slumbering mercenaries. Sergeant Bethune and Ruth were gathering their supplies, their faces rigid with worry. Abram stood to his full height and looked around. Figures glided down toward them like giant kites guided by a strong wind: *mambas*.

The *wam-baika* stretched their wings uneasily and the Shaman whispered something to them. The *baika* seemed to understand his words, and they began to act. They grabbed everyone and flapped up high enough to hover. The *mamba* closed the gap to a few feet as the *baika* started to ascend. Each flap they took carried them closer to safety as the *mamba* neared the ground.

The *mamba* landed and their flaps retracted, and Abram caught a glimpse of them before his *baika* gained more altitude. They were a little bigger than the *paka*, and closer to the size of a male lion from back home. They had snouts like an alligator with just as many teeth, but they had hind legs swollen with muscles. They had tales as thin as whips when the flaps weren't opened. There were seven altogether and they snarled and barked like big dogs.

Then each of the *mamba* was back in the air and Abram's heart leapt into his throat. The Shaman had failed to mention just how high the creatures could jump, and they were higher than the *baika* in a few seconds. Their flaps sprouted quickly and caught the air, making the sound a parachute makes when it's deployed. They almost looked co-medic when fully gliding. The thin skin stretched from their front paws to their back legs and made them look like greenish black Frisbees. Their tails also sprouted flaps that rose or fell on one side, steering their flight. They angled downward toward the *baika*, and the closest one to Abram snapped at his heels but Abram lifted up his legs and avoided danger. He looked around and saw that almost everyone else was able to do the same.

But Stribling was the biggest of the bunch, and his *baika* struggled to get to the same height as the others as quickly. It squawked and continued struggling to climb. A *mamba* glided onto its back and clamped down on the *baika's* head, and in an instant the *baika* and Stribling dropped like a bag of rocks.

"Stribling's down!" Abram screamed, and the others tried to maneuver to see.

"We can't leave him! We have to go back,"

The other six *mamba* narrowed their flaps and glided toward where Stribling had landed. The *mamba* that had killed the *baika* disappeared beneath the tall stalks along with Stribling and his *baika*. Rustling and jostling grass could be seen, but nothing else. Barks and grunts and a single cry reported before Abram saw a darkened line moving away from the crash site and his spirits rose. Stribling must have got out from under the *baika* and ran.

A few seconds later the other *mamba* landed and vanished beneath the green.

Come on, pay attention to the downed baika *and ignore Stribling,* Abram thought.

The *wam-baika* veered back and the Shaman's led the way. Like most predators, the *mamba* gave chase to the moving object and Abram's heart sank. They erupted from the grass, opened their flaps, spotted Stribling, and surrounding him, gliding down in seconds.

CHAPTER 20

The Shaman touched down a few feet away from where the six *mamba* had disappeared, but he sprinted into the brush. Abram landed next but felt light headed as he too broke into a run. The sounds of the *mamba* snarling and barking were muffled by the grass, but grew louder as he headed forward.

Pulling out his M9A he primed a shot, trying his best to push through the thick grass with one hand. The stalks beat and slapped at his face but he persevered, the thought of having another man die because of him urging him faster and faster until he passed the Shaman.

He burst into the clearing and ran into one of the *mamba*, tumbling over onto the ground. The beast whimpered and snapped at him but missed, opening its mouth for another try. He spun his weapon around and pulled the trigger, but only a *click* reported. The *mamba* was still on its side and took another bite at him but missed. Abram kicked the *mamba* off and it whimpered but recovered after a second. It leapt for him, flaring its skin flaps as it flew, but he sent an uppercut into its chin before it could bite him. He used the prosthetic and the beast went flying, motionless and soundless, landing out of sight in the grass. The other *mamba* were distracted with Stribling, and Abram froze.

It was a terrible sight. Blood was everywhere. Stribling was screaming, doing his best to keep teeth from sinking into his neck. One lunged and he moved just enough to stay alive, pulling around his free arm and squeezing the trigger on his M9A. It too clicked so he whacked the *mamba* with it. The blow was strong enough to disorient the creature, and when he whacked it again it whimpered before slipping out of consciousness.

Attempting to swing the weapon around and take out the next opponent failed, as one of the *mamba* sank its teeth into his wrist. He yelped again as the Shaman broke through the clearing. Abram charged forward and backhanded the next *mamba*, sending it flying to the side into the grass. It made no motion of return.

One *mamba* was gnawing at Stribling's thigh while the other two tore into each of his arms. He used his free leg to kick at the *mamba* below his waist but it kept coming. Displaying amazing strength despite his wounds, he brought his arms together with the *mamba* still attached. He clonked them against one another and dropped his arms to his sides, and the creatures whimpered and crumpled to the ground. After a moment of recovery, they shook it off and were back on their feet, lunging for Stribling's neck.

Abram charged forward, hoping to have time to stop each assailant before either could bite Stribling's neck and end his life, but before he could reach them the Shaman whispered something and tapped his staff on the ground. A shockwave flew forward and the attackers froze.

The *mamba* had stopped moving, though they retained their look of ferocity and intensity. Their eyes were locked onto Stribling and blazed with primal hunger and instinct. The one by his thigh had its teeth still buried in his flesh, and red squirts of blood were frozen in mid-air around its face. The one on the right had its mouth splayed beside Stribling's neck. If it had closed, Stribling would be dead. The one on his left had just shut its mouth beside Stribling's head but he had moved. Droplets of saliva carried by the gust of air were like painted pearls caught in an artist's sadistic masterpiece.

"Quickly, you must leave at once," the Shaman said, looking to the sky and whispering.

Stribling groaned on the ground and barely moved. The adrenaline- and desperation-fueled effort to lift the two creatures, compounded with all the blood he continually lost, had left him barely able to move. A *wam-baika* landed on the clearing, and the force of its flapping wings tipped over the frozen *mamba* by his head.

Abram grabbed the one on his thigh and lifted, and fresh droplets of blood squirted out but moved freely. He shoved the *mamba* off to the side. Stribling's pant leg had been shredded, and his flesh was no better. His forearms and wrists leaked crimson rivulets, and a tear on his side revealed a nasty bite there as well.

The Shaman whispered something over Stribling's body before the *wam-baika* grabbed him by his good leg and one of his arms. Stribling grunted from the pain but passed out as the *baika* took flight. His LMG was left on the ground where he had dropped it.

"I have stopped the bleeding, but he may be mortally wounded," the Shaman said, looking into Abram's eyes.

Abram realized he was taking deep, labored breaths as he tried to speak. "How much further? Will he make it to the fortress? What can be done for him there?"

Abram saw the others hovering nearby, but he avoided the grip of the *baika* that came for him until the Shaman answered.

"Another full day's journey is between you and the fortress, but this is good. The fortress is in peril." The Shaman thought for a while. "Yes, a nocturnal arrival will be much safer than that of one during the day."

"In peril? What does that mean? What's going on?"

"When you arrive, the Gray Lord will have healers that can examine him." The Shaman paused and stepped forward, adding emphasis to his words. "But it may be too late."

"Use the arts and heal him or something. There has to be something you can do."

Abram felt the grip of the *wam-baika* and he fought against it. He lost and started rising, but the Shaman yelled up at him.

"I have done what I can. The Lords of Luck shall dictate the rest. Now fly."

"Safi! Wait. Come with us! We need you!"

The *wam-baika* took Abram too high for the Shaman to hear, or he simply ignored the words, but the Shaman turned and disappeared into the tall grass. Abram cursed but averted his attention to the others. They were calling out to him about Stribling's status, but as Abram tried to respond the words stuck in his throat. He felt sick and wondered how long it would be before the mercenaries deserted him, or worse. They had to blame him for the constant disaster that had taken the group by storm. It seemed every mercenary would have his turn at dying. How long before the sergeant used the Gray Lord's door to go back home and claim the mission was an utter failure? How long before he turned on Abram? Perhaps he would even kill Abram and Ruth and claim a native did the deed.

The group called out to him a few more times before catching on that he would not respond. They flew through the rest of the night in silence and Abram wished it had been him that had been taken down by the *mamba*.

CHAPTER 21

The day was hot, and only grew hotter the longer Abram baked in the sun. Sunburns had only affected him once in his life, and he recalled that even though he'd been out in the desert for at least a full day during his first visit, he'd never been burnt. The second trip had been hotter so far, but his skin felt fine.

The rest of the group was nowhere near as lucky as him. Brooks had it the worst. His face and neck were a bright shade of red and the skin was cracked, though as usual he was the quietest. The other three mercenaries grumbled every so often, exchanging stories of other bad burns and attributing their current burns to the altitude and wind.

Ruth was quiet but studied Stribling more than the others. Her burn mainly affected her nose. He noticed the wind rippling her hair and making it appear to move on its own. Seeing the movement reminded him of Koñél and he sighed. The end result between them was still fogged in negativity, but being back in Koñél's dimension sent his imagination reeling through possibilities. He still had to tell Ruth, and a part of him hoped she blew up with anger and severed ties so he would be free to work out his issue in peace. Another part of him felt bad for even thinking of ending it with Ruth. She was blameless, and their breakup would hurt her the most.

A dot finally appeared on the horizon with the blue moon rising above it as a backdrop. Abram smiled, happy to have a reason to escape his thoughts.

"Guys, we're almost there," he yelled.

"So you *do* still have a voice," Grodin yelled back. "I talked more than you when I was drowned."

Abram gagged at the thought of Grodin's germs lingering in his mouth and throat. Normally Stribling would have a snarky reply to Grodin, and Abram averted his attention to the wounded soldier.

Thankfully, the *wam-baika* carried him on his side. If he'd been transported upside down the whole way he'd be dead for sure. Though, as Abram examined the wounds as best as he could from his current position, the injuries looked far more fatal now. The bleeding had stopped like the Shaman had said, but reddish black openings riddled Stribling's skin. His clothing was ragged and bloodied as well, and his face seemed swollen, taking on a bluish tint.

Abram had managed to avoid looking at Stribling for much of the day, and seeing him again washed him in more remorse.

Mercifully distracting Abram, something black in the distance caught his attention. As they continued to rush toward their destination, the black object continued to grow as well, turning into a black wave that rose and fell with the hills, smothering all green in its path.

When they were directly above the black, Abram realized it was a mass of soldiers. They all seemed thicker than the Gray Lord's men, and their armor was banded with red lines on their arms.

Being nighttime, a number of fires had been started and were peppered among the ranks. Plumes of black smoke swirled and hovered around the army, giving many pockets of soldiers the appearance of shadows.

A few black tents had also been erected, but they looked to be more for meetings and strategy than for barracks. Catapults were also scattered throughout, all loaded with triangular black rocks. Bigger soldiers were also present, and Abram assumed they were *Magnums*. His heart started to sink.

Large pits had also been dug in a few locations, and the holes went down deeper than Abram could see. Ladders and ropes had been tied to the edges, and Abram wondered what they were burrowing for, or too.

"Friends of your Gray Lord?" Sergeant Bethune yelled as they continued on, passing the middle of the group of soldiers below.

Shot directly at Bethune's question mark, an arrow zipped through the midst of the group.

CHAPTER 22

The *baika* squawked and flapped harder as more arrows were released.

"We're under fire!" Bethune yelled, stating the obvious.

Only Stribling had a free hand, but he was still unconscious, so returning fire was out of the question—though only Brooks seemed to have a working weapon, anyway. They were at the mercy of the *baika*'s ability to dodge. Their white wings were clear targets.

Arrows flitted past and the *baika* banked and rose, trying to avoid the projectiles. As if his body remembered his first real battle, his thigh grew sore. The infection in his arm had distracted him from most of his other injuries, but being under attack in a similar location caused him to reminisce, and he wondered if his leg would get infected this time around. All he needed was to lose a few other limbs to infection, and he'd barely be human anymore.

Countering the course of bad luck they'd plotted since their arrival, they cleared the mass of black and soared over friendly territory. A few arrows trailed behind them but fell harmlessly into the grass in no man's-land.

The gray army was outside, but were mere raindrops compared to the ocean of darkness bearing down on them. Flocks of *wam-baika* had been roused on their approach, and the friendlies circled and squawked at the new arrivals.

As the group approached their destination, Abram realized the black wave was sealing them in on all sides. The gray army was spread thin in a pathetic defense circle, backed only by the flocks of *wam-baika* and a handful of *Magnums*.

The *wam-baika* released the group thirty feet or so from the fortress, and Stribling's *baika* was gentle enough to set him down without dropping him. The grass was wilted and browning as if it were parched. Civilians from the Gray Lord's town came running out to meet them.

"*Kuja, kuja, kuja,*" the civilians said, waving the group to follow them.

"*Kuja?*" Bethune said to Abram, bringing together his brow.

Abram shrugged, but Ruth started walking after the townspeople.

"*Kuja* means come," Ruth said, jotting notes on her pad. "I recall that word from my first visit."

Brooks and Grodin picked up Stribling as circumspectly as they could. Then they all followed the townspeople. The gate was raised by a team of *Magnums*.

Inside the fortress things were different than Abram's first visit. The civilians took them through the courtyard with the fountain, but it was no longer filled with water. The bone-dry, white stone was like a gravestone. The bazaar was devoid of any movement. The empty but familiar booths and furniture were like ghosts from his past. He shivered.

Another two civilians rushed over and motioned toward Stribling, repeating a number of phrases in their tongue before motioning for the two mercenaries to follow them. They glanced at Bethune and he nodded. They carried Stribling off with the new townspeople through a door and out of sight.

Abram thought their civilians would lead him to the dining room, as that was where everyone had gone the last time they'd come under attack, but instead they headed to the Gray Lord's overlook. They traversed the more than a thousand velvet steps and Abram was relieved to see that at least they appeared the same.

They reached the top and walked down the velvet hallway. Ruth and Bethune glanced at the paintings lining the wall, but Ruth made no move to jot or redraw them.

No guards were at the end of the hall waiting for them this time, but the townspeople refused to go through the door leading to the Gray Lord's overlook. Instead, they said a few others words in their language that Ruth jotted down. Being the most experienced with the Gray Lord, Abram decided to open the door, and the team followed closely behind him.

"Welcome back, Outsider." The Gray Lord said without moving from in front of the glass overlook. "I received news of your return. Your companion has been taken to the healers."

Abram played with his engagement ring, nervously spinning it around his finger. "Thank you. How long before we can tell if he'll be okay?"

The Gray Lord finally turned around, his eyes dull and his face sullen. His rod plinked against the ground as he walked forward and he sighed, collapsing into his throne and leaning to the side.

"As long as is needed. We have many wounded as of late, but our healers are skilled."

Abram nodded and swallowed. "What's going on around here? Whose army is that at your door?"

"Is your eye so blinded by optimism that the obvious is shielded from it?" the Gray Lord said, rubbing the longer-than-usual stubble on his chin.

Embarrassed by the response and unsure how he should counter, he remained mute and the only sound was the scratching of the Gray Lord's fingernails against his hair and skin.

"The great threat of the Seven has returned with the full force of *Ghafaria* to drain the blood from our veins. Their hunt transpired successfully, and the warriors have returned. The Red One has laid us under siege and our resources are dwindling."

"But why?" Abram said, walking to the glass and looking out. "There are enough of those barbarians out there to trample you on every side. I apologize for being so dismal, but why are they waiting?"

The Gray Lord continued to scratch his beard. "Unknown, but I can only attribute this anomaly to the *wam-baika*. We have many, and the *wam-baika* would be able to eliminate a great deal of their numbers. But, this plague *would* still overrun us." Standing, the Gray Lord joined Abram by the window. "We are hard pressed on every side. They have dammed the subterranean springs that nourish this fortress, and our resources are mere crumbs and droplets. Unless Safi breaks through with the might of all of *Magnus* of the Great Mountain, I fear Shetani will achieve victory without swinging a single sword."

Abram's rage for the Red Mage was kindled again, and he wondered if the evil man was among the ranks.

"Then attack him," Sergeant Bethune said, turning both Abram and the Gray Lord. "If you're going to die either way, shouldn't you at least go out with a fight? And what about that magic? The arts or whatever Abram spoke about in his report? Can't you use that too?"

The Gray Lord sighed, and his shoulders stayed bowed. "There is another force among the ranks that I dread will be awakened if I intervene prematurely."

"What? What force could stop the arts?" Abram said, confusion pulling his eyebrows together.

"Another artist."

"What? But I thought the Red Mage was the bad guy. If you have the Shaman, there is no one else. Right?"

"Shetani was never the only artist to oppose the White Lord's teaching, nor was Safi my only ally. Another dark force, Zanda, has been in hiding until shortly after your departure. He commands this veil of evil that blankets my lands. The Lords of Luck have frowned upon us."

Abram's mind raced with questions. Was Koñél still fighting for the Red Mage? Why was the Gray Lord terrified of this Zanda character? If he was unafraid of the Red Mage, how much worse was the new guy? Or, how weak was the Gray Lord? Abram felt the vibe that the Gray Lord had battled the forces of evil before and lost.

"I don't mean to keep butting in, but this is a little ridiculous. You're saying you won't attack because doing so might incite *someone else* to fight back. But, this *someone else* is already waiting you out. What possible hope could you have in sitting here as if everything is just going to turn into cupcakes and jellybeans? Fight!"

The Gray Lord shot Bethune a look and returned to his throne. "Outsiders have no ability to fathom the reality of the arts. You are an ignoramus that willingly voices the inadequacy of his intelligence before introductions or proper acquaintances have been achieved. You shall still your tongue or I shall still it in your failure."

Fury rippled across Bethune's face and his hand hovered over his sidearm. He glanced at Abram and Abram shook his head, trying to will Bethune to understand that the fight that mattered was outside. Ruth was as still as a statue, save for her eyes, which darted back and forth between the three men.

"What can we do to help?" Abram said, breaking the tension.

"I hear you and your men are warriors. You can help by adding numbers to our ranks."

"What good will that do if you're unwilling to fight," Bethune said.

The Gray Lord rose to his feet and gripped his staff, his eyes turgid with anger.

"Wait, wait, hold on," Abram said, moving between the Gray Lord and Bethune before anything could happen. "I apologize for the sergeant," Abram continued, shooting Bethune an angry look. "What he meant to say was that we have other missions here that go beyond this fight. We still have duties to our side, though we will help however we can."

"Every arm able to swing a sword or axe is needed. But I understand your duties. What do you need to accomplish?"

"Well, if the Shaman ever returns, I need to train with him to become an artist. I don't know how long the process normally takes, but it's what the leaders of my home want. Plus having another artist on your side would definitely help."

"Truer words are rarely spoken, but it will undoubtedly take longer than we have to live."

"Fair enough, but that is still my mission. I can stay here until the Shaman returns and do whatever I can in the meantime."

Ruth stepped forward. "I need to gather data." Her face was drawn down as she formulated her next words. "I have been instructed to travel to the *Giza Sana*." Ruth paused, glancing out the window as if acknowledging the desperation of the situation. "Please allow us to use the *wam-baika* that carried us here to carry us to the cave."

The Gray Lord glared at her for a few moments but finally nodded. "Doom is in all of our futures, so your desires are unable to worsen our predicament. It will be as you say."

There were no smiles shared and the Gray Lord continued to glare at the ground. "But please, leave now and return as swiftly as possible. If we are still here, you can aid in the battle at that time." The Gray Lord looked at Bethune and scowled. "Even buried in the words of fools can wisdom be found. Something must indeed be done before we starve to death."

CHAPTER 23

"Time is of the essence. Tarry only when you must," the Gray Lord said, turning back to the window.

Four *wam-baika* flew up and hovered in front of the overlook, their majestic wings brilliant in the blue light. Their transparent tummies held no food, and even their stomach acid seemed low.

The Gray Lord whispered toward the *baika*, and after a few moments they descended out of sight.

"I have bonded the *wam-baika* to you and your companions. They will adhere to all of your instructions until their death."

"Thank you," Ruth said. She took out her notepad and scribbled some notes down before pocketing it again.

"May the Lords of Luck cast success in your path." The Gray Lord patted his side, saluting in the way of his army. "Now fly and return with haste."

Bethune nodded to Abram, and Ruth gave Abram a hug before turning and heading toward the exit with the sergeant. The notion of telling her about Koñél flashed inside his head, and he realized now it would take even longer to tell her.

"Try to get some sleep during the journey," Abram called out, stopping the two as they opened the door. "It's not easy, but it's possible." Then, after a brief pause. "And pray they stop somewhere to eat."

They nodded and left. With them gone, Abram felt lonely for the first time since his return. During his first visit he almost always felt lonely. Though he was rarely truly alone, there was somehow a difference between being with people that you shared a common ancestry with and just being with people.

Abram moved to the window, and after looking out for a few minutes he saw his companions exit the fortress. Grodin and Brooks had joined Bethune and Ruth, and the overlook's height made them as ants in his sight. The four *baika* flapped and carried them higher than they had on their arrival. They vanished into the clouds and Abram sighed.

"There is no reason for sadness. They are safer than we," the Gray Lord said, joining Abram by the window.

"Maybe, but only for a while. If this fight starts and we lose, no one will be safe. The teleportation device is still here, and they will gain control of it."

"Then it shall be my duty to destroy it in the event of a breach."

Abram gave no verbal response, but turned from the window. He half felt he needed to ask for permission to leave, but decided the Gray Lord and he shared enough respect that such a formality was unnecessary. He traveled back down to the ground floor and maneuvered through the empty courtyard. He reminisced about his first visit and headed toward the dining hall, expecting to find the townspeople waiting in there.

Along the way he saw the door that the townspeople had gone through with Stribling, and Abram took a detour. He entered a hallway, lit at each end by candles with wax tears caked down to their stands. Paintings similar to the ones in the velvet hallway covered this hall as well, but the flickering light source gave the faces a ghastly appearance.

One painting was of the Gray Lord, the Red Mage, and the Shaman, but there were also three others in the picture and Abram wondered who they were. Each of the men he recognized looked younger. The Red Mage's contrasts were the starkest, but the only real indication it was them were the snake staffs they wielded. The Red Mage had no beard in the picture, and his clothing was disparate—less evil in a way, despite the effect of the candles.

The group looked happy, but why? Why would the Gray Lord display a picture that depicted him with his enemy? Was the artist laying siege to the fortress one of the others depicted?

Abram kept moving and made a mental note to ask the Shaman about it later. The Gray Lord would probably be just as good to get an answer from, but Abram still felt a tinge of uneasiness around the lord. The Shaman never made him feel that way.

The door at the end of the hall was thick but easy to open. The other side was a dark room filled with incense. The incense shrouded the room in a gray veil that smelled vaguely of cinnamon, but lingering beneath the aroma was the smell of sweat and body odor. The room had a shelf that wound around the entire perimeter, and candles burned atop it. The room was still rather dark, but light enough to make out faces and bodies and colors. Groans and coughing noises sounded off around the room sporadically.

Rows of beds created a maze. Most of the beds were full of soldiers with dressed wounds. Some were fresher than others, but all were similar. Male and female townspeople were moving between the beds performing various tasks. Some were spoon feeding, others were redressing wounds, and a few were even giving sponge baths.

Abram went to one of the beds and examined the soldier atop it. He had gray eyes like everyone else in the fortress, and his skin mirrored a corpse. He was breathing shallowly, but his eyes were attentive and stared at Abram. He had three bandages covering wounds on his abdomen. The square bandages all sported a spot at the center with a circumference of a few inches, bearing a resemblance to the Japanese flag.

Moving on to another bed, Abram found a similar man with similar injuries. Three sword strikes like that would leave a man mortally wounded, but three arrows may or may not kill depending on what they struck upon penetration.

"Excuse me," Abram said, catching a nurse between beds. "Do you know where my friend is?" The woman stared blankly at him and Abram remembered the language barrier. "Other Outsider?"

The woman shook her head and looked a little afraid, as if her inability to respond would result in punishment. Abram frowned but thought for a moment before grabbing a portion of his ACU. He shook it and she understood, pointing to the back wall. Abram smiled and nodded at her and hoped she understood his appreciation.

He maneuvered through the maze of beds and nurse obstacles until he found Stribling. The mercenary was in bad shape. His wounds had been dressed, but the utterance the Shaman had cast on him had worn off. The bleeding had returned, and the nurse by his side was in the middle of changing one of the bandages.

Abram was surprised to see an IV drip set up next to his bed. He wondered whether the solution feeding his veins was medicinal or if it was just a saline solution to keep him hydrated after all the blood loss. Stribling was still unconscious and his skin had a blue tint as if he wasn't breathing properly. His chest barely rose and fell, but the nurse attending to him sported a calm demeanor.

"Hang in there, buddy," Abram said, placing a hand on Stribling's shoulder.

He watched for a few more minutes before he felt he was just getting in the way. Leaving the room and exiting the hallway, he headed for the dining hall. Like with his first visit, the door was propped open and no guards were standing in front of it. Abram had given it little thought before, but now he wondered if they gathered in the great hall for protection. Perhaps the doors were propped until danger arose, and then they would seal themselves inside and hope for the best. Abram thought of *Magnums* and *Ghafarians* trying to get in, and he felt the barricade would only last a few minutes.

Inside, smells made Abram wish he'd stayed in the cover of the cinnamon incense. Body odor and the smell of old garbage crammed into his nostrils and made his head spin. He hoped they still possessed enough civility to use the bathroom in a different room, even if the siege had gummed up their plumbing.

Some of the townspeople stood around the table while others sat. There were fruit cores and seeds scattered across the table, but there were also piles of refuse in the corner. Small buzzing insects surrounded the trash heap and whirred around the faces of some of the people. Most ignored the bugs, but Abram swatted them away whenever they neared him.

The stench was too much for Abram to bear and he exited. With no one to talk to and no old friends in there, he had no real reason to stay anyway. There was no way these people—much less the soldiers expected to fight with little to no nourishment—would survive more than another few days.

Abram decided to check out the room he'd stayed in during his first visit. The door still lacked a nob, so he easily pushed inside and saw that it was just as he'd left it. No candles were lit this time around, but some of the light from the courtyard illuminated all but the corners of the room.

After plopping down on the bed and seeing the cloud of dust puff outward, he sighed. His excitement had enabled him to forget about all the germs that were probably on the cloth. After sitting for a few moments and watching the particles caught in the moonlight, he shut the door to a crack and closed his eyes. At least he was still filthy, so any germs he encountered on the sheets would have to fight all the germs he already had on his body.

Imagining giant germs and murderous viruses, Abram drifted off to sleep.

CHAPTER 24

Ruth watched the horizon as they traveled, and she found herself marveling at the beauty of the foreign world once again. The moon was setting, tickling the bellies of clouds in a hodgepodge of blues.

The flight was peaceful. Brooks was his usual, silent self, but Grodin and the sergeant were uncharacteristically mute.

Sleeping was more difficult than Abram had let on. The *wam-baika* were pretty smooth in flight, but when she closed her eyes, the flap of their wings was exacerbated. They squawked loudly every so often, and the sound of wind constantly rushing over her ears was quite annoying. Every once in a while they would drop suddenly and her heart would fly into her throat. Times when the other distractions fell away, thoughts of their mission and the fates of their worlds plagued her mind.

In the middle of the second day, the *wam-baika* set down in a heavily wooded area. The trees were clustered in groves and separated by lush green hills. A strident buzzing like the song of cicadas droned a terrible tune all around them.

"Anyone want to shoot me now?" Grodin said, trying to plug his ears with his fingers. "I swear it sounds like those stupid bugs are in my head."

"Reminds me of my grandmother's farm," Sergeant Bethune started. "Place was 100 or so acres of nothing but overgrown weeds and buzzing insects. I was the outdoorsy type until one too many creepy crawlies found their pinchy or bity or stingy way into my shorts."

"That why you never married?" Grodin said, propping his torso against one of the straighter trunks.

Even Brooks laughed, but Ruth felt bad for him. He had to be in his late thirties to early forties, and the thought of being that old and never experiencing the joys of being married was crazy in her mind.

"I am going to take a walk," Ruth said, trying to keep a straight face and avoid any stray fiery darts the sergeant shot toward Grodin. "That hill looks like it has some interesting flower species I can document."

Even though she was surrounded by people, she still felt ostracized.

"Isn't it enough that we're going to the cave?"

"You can never compile too much research," Ruth said, starting to walk toward the hill.

"Brooks, stay with jabber jaw here. I'll escort her," Sergeant Bethune said.

Brooks nodded and sat down next to Grodin. In his perpetual silence, he started cleaning his weapon, keeping a watchful eye on the nearby groves for signs of danger.

"Can you get some target practice on those awful bugs?" Grodin said as Ruth and the sergeant walked away. Ruth was happy his voice was a little more bearable now that there was some distance between them. "All I want to do is take a nap," he said, still in earshot of Ruth.

She continued on and they found a path. A herd of something heavy had trampled down the overgrown grass and other plants, and they followed the trail, taking care to step around the patties of dried manure that dappled their road. The path wound around and up the hill, and the overgrowth bowed toward them. Ruth thought of ticks and did her best to avoid the bent over vegetation.

Flowers of all kinds were poking through the overgrowth, but the most prominent one was a saggy, purple flower. It resembled a lilac in color only, and reminded her of a small, colorful version of a weeping willow. The purple strands that dangled swayed in the breeze, and Ruth sketched a few pictures.

"Why do you draw everything?" the sergeant said, squinting and shielding his face from the sun.

"I have always been better at drawing than writing." Ruth bent down and smelled the purple flower, jotting down notes when she was finished. "Usually, it's a way for me to express how I'm feeling. Here, I figure the pictures might help in case my words don't cut it."

Sergeant Bethune shrugged. "Guess that's as good a reason as any. What made you want to be a scientist, or whatever you are?"

"Just always enjoyed learning about the planet. When I was a kid my parents bought me one of those toy science kits. My father would always say how proud he was of me for being so smart when I came to him rambling on about experiments or insect dissections. Thinking of that always makes me smile."

The sergeant grunted. They kept walking up the path until they neared the top of the hill, and their cronies were out of sight. Ruth sighed and took in the view. In the valley before them were more groves of trees, accented by blankets of yellow and purple and red flowers that were intent on only growing with their own kind. Past the valley were more hills, though none were as high as the one they were on. Even further away were the peaks of mountains, shrouded in a bluish-gray veil.

At their back, the top of the hill was crowned in swirls of the droopy purple flower and Ruth tried to sketch it as best she could.

The sergeant whistled. "Some view, huh?" Ruth nodded but the sergeant never took his eyes off the distant mountains. "You ever do any hiking?"

"Here and there." They turned and started descending the same way they'd come, and Ruth looked forward to ending their alone time. Nothing against the sergeant, but she felt like they had to talk or things would be awkward, and that made her feel uncomfortable. "I have to ask. What is Brooks's story? Does he ever talk?"

The sergeant grinned and glanced at the ground as if it was an embarrassing question he'd been waiting for her to ask.

"He has before, but there's no telling if he ever will again."

"Do you mean he has spoken in his past, but stopped and may not start again?"

"Yeah, well, I sort of meant he's said a few words to me, but I don't know if he'll ever say more. When there's something worth saying, he'll speak up."

"Mmhmm. Did something traumatic happen?"

"Could be, but he was this way before he joined my crew." They walked in silence for a bit, and the sergeant avoided an insect with a stinger as it buzzed past him to cross the path and reach more flowers. "Maybe even before he joined the army. I've heard a few rumors, though."

"Well, you know what they say about rumors," Ruth said, grinning.

"Yeah, but these were pretty good explanations, even though only one can be true. Some say he saw his uncle in law cheating with his mother, and when he told his dad, his dad killed them both and he's been quiet since."

"I feel as though that was a plot in a bad movie from a long time ago."

Sergeant Bethune shrugged. "Maybe, but maybe it happened to him."

"And the other rumors?"

"Well there's only one other good one." He popped in a stick of gum before continuing. "It's that he's killed so many people, or at least seen so much death that he refuses to talk for fear that someone may ask him about the experience. And it'll, you know, push him to a bad place."

"That is worse than the first one," Ruth said with a chuckle, and the sergeant shrugged again.

"You're welcome to ask him yourself, though don't get mad if he refuses to answer."

They moseyed down the path until they could see their company again.

"Can you just order him to speak," Ruth said, batting down one of the noisy insects with her notepad as it screeched around her face. When it was on the ground she stomped it and squatted down, scribbling what was left of it and trying to recreate it, pre-squash.

"I could do that, but we aren't Army anymore, so he wouldn't have to comply," the sergeant started, putting his hands on his hips and looking down at the grove of trees that Brooks and Grodin were under. "Even if he would though, somehow it just wouldn't seem right. He ain't hurting no one with his silence. Heck, Grodin talks enough for all of us."

"Preach," Ruth said, feigning her best church voice. "Why do you think he talks so much?"

"Just the way he is. Probably wasn't held enough as a child or something."

"No rumors about him?"

Sergeant Bethune laughed. "Just that he once literally talked a man to death."

"Seems like a pretty terrible way to go."

"Well, if it happens to anyone else it'll probably be me. So I'll let you know how it feels. I'm just happy he's respectful of my language rules."

Ruth thought of asking why he was against foul language. The notion opposed every stereotype and experience she'd had with soldiers or most men in general, and Bethune struck her as unreligious. Ultimately, she decided to just wonder.

The *wam-baika* were clumsily crawling around in the grove near Grodin and Brooks. The creatures were drawn to the buzzing bugs, and whenever one flew near their faces they chomped it down.

When Brooks noticed their approach he stood to his feet and slung his rifle over his shoulder again. Grodin was still napping.

"These look like walnut trees from back home," Ruth said, noticing some of the thicker trees mixed in with the others at Grodin's back.

She studied the branches for a while before stepping into the outgrowth. A few of the branches were bent down from the weight of brown clusters that were very similar to ripe walnuts.

"Either of you gentleman have a med kit?" Ruth said, plucking a few of the brown clusters free. "It would be good to have a potential remedy on hand in case I am allergic to this."

Neither one nodded, and she hesitated. She was hungry, and she'd researched survivalist strategies in the past. They indicated ways of testing unknown food before eating large amounts, but there was always a chance it would kill her without revealing any telltale symptoms of poisonous food. She examined it with her fingers and figured the hard shell would need to come off first. Finding a medium-sized rock, she went to the trunk of the tree Grodin was sleeping against and wacked the fruit with the rock. Grodin woke up and groaned, but Ruth ignored him and focused on her fruit.

"Your hungry tail couldn't crack those against another tree?" Grodin said, and Ruth responded by tossing the shells at him.

Grodin yawned and stood up, staring at Ruth as she continued to examine the food. He glanced around before snatching the fruit from her hand and tossing it whole into his mouth.

"Wait! No, it could be poisonous," Ruth said, holding up a hand even though Grodin continued to chew. "You should have taken a nibble first."

He shrugged and swallowed. "Tastes fine to me."

Ruth scoffed at his rashness, almost verbalizing the foolishness in weighing taste when determining whether something was poisonous. She watched him intently for the next few minutes, searching for a reaction. He grabbed a few more of the fruit from the tree and used her method to crack them open before tossing them down.

When he showed no signs of having an adverse reaction, she sampled the fruit herself. After a minute or so with no numbness or other reaction in her mouth, she took in a whole piece. It had a nutty flavor, though it was closer to almonds than it was walnuts and she smiled, cracking open another and gobbling it down.

The rest of the group joined in and the *wam-baika* continued to feed on the insects whenever they revealed themselves. After they'd had their fill, they decided to partake in Grodin's idea, and they slept for a few hours before roars awoke them all. No one wanted to wait around and discover what had produced the roars except for Ruth, but they persuaded her that it was a bad idea. They took to the skies again.

CHAPTER 25

Light filtered in through the crack between the door and post, warming Abram's face. He woke up and stretched, taking his vibration pill. He felt refreshed and well-rested, but when he walked out into the courtyard and saw that it was still abandoned, he felt a heavy weight latch onto his shoulders.

Meandering through the empty booths, he found that all of the food was gone or moved elsewhere. Empty cages were everywhere, and even the hay that had padded many of them was gone. Had the people been reduced to feeding like animals or were they generous enough to feed the livestock before slaughtering it for food? He thought of his amphibious yak steak and his stomach grumbled.

He ambled over to the dining hall and found that everyone was still inside. The room still reeked, but he suffered through the smell to see if any new food was out and being eaten. He walked around the table and people glanced at him but no one spoke. It was as if speaking burned calories they didn't have, so silence was the only option, though the groaning and coughing must have been mandatory. Their faces and bodies were gaunt. Bones bulged against skin. Eyes were sunken and eyelids were darkened. Flesh was pale and pasty. A few had bulging bellies but most just looked like the living dead. The gray color of their hair added to their haggard appearance.

Abram saw someone gnawing on a bone and his heart sank. He really hoped something would be done and soon. The smell started to get under his skin and he exited, checking a few other rooms for food before giving up. He found no morsels but did find the latrine before deciding his hunt was pointless.

He headed back up to the Gray Lord's overlook and let himself in. The lord was sitting in his chair and barely looked up when Abram came in. Abram headed to the window first and looked out, playing with his engagement ring. He could barely make out some of the soldiers eating the dying grass.

"This is bad," Abram said, going to stand in front of the lord.

The Gray Lord grunted and Abram searched for a chair. It struck him as odd that there were no seating arrangements aside from the throne, but he sat down cross-legged on the floor and stared at the lord. The lord stared at the ground.

Thoughts of General Alvarez's words floated into his head and he bit his lip. The Gray Lord's true intentions always made Abram uneasy, and he thought of the prophetic paintings he had seen before. The espionage the general wanted still seemed wrong, but he had his duties to his country and his dimension.

"So are you still planning a trip to my side?" Abram said.

The Gray Lord glanced up before responding. "Perhaps, but the urgency has dissipated. Problems here must first be addressed."

"Makes sense. Leaving probably wouldn't go over well with your people."

"Indeed, though it is a viable option in the wake of utter failure."

There was a brief silence before the Gray Lord stood up and Abram joined him. The sun was bright but high enough that it allowed them to see without having to squint. Many of the soldiers were sitting. Some were still munching on dry grass, others just baked inside their armor with their heads hung between their shoulders. The ones eating grass seemed to do so out of boredom instead of for taste or nutrition.

"I don't know how they do it," Abram said, thinking of the unforgiving heat compounding by the second inside their armor.

"Nor do I." The Gray Lord sighed. "But their sacrifice will blot all other words from the scrolls of history. Many will sing of their valor, no matter the outcome."

Unless the Red Mage is the one writing, Abram thought, keeping the perception to himself.

"Did the Shaman tell you about what happened back on my side? The strides we're making to be better stewards of the planet?"

"He spoke briefly, but was convinced more is needed to be done."

Abram looked down. "Yeah, I'm not exactly convinced either. This is the first time another dimension has said anything about it to us, but we've definitely heard this warning before. It seems like every year there is a new leading scientist or news story talking of how we keep edging ourselves further over the precipice of extinction."

"Yet no changes have been made? Ignorance such as you speak of is unfathomable."

"I wouldn't say *no* changes have been made. It's just that people get irate when things change, and sometimes the powers that be bend under the pressure. There are only a few things I remember from my childhood, but people fighting about the survival of the future has always been constant. It snowed when I was little, but only every few years. By the time I was a teenager, it had stopped completely." Abram smiled as thoughts of his mother washed warmly against his memory banks. "Now it only snows at the caps, and even there it's rare. When it does snow it's more like raining ash, but we still call it snow."

"Safi told me that *muva* falls in droplets from the sky there. He called it wondrous, but it seems it would be an annoyance to be unable to avoid the falling water. He said miles around are affected and everything is soaked. Is your *snow* like the falling *muva*?"

"It's really not bad once you've had it happen a few times. I mean, give me an umbrella and I'll stand in the rain all day if it means I never have to deal with *muva* rolling over my head. I feel like there would be so many deaths every year just from people drowning in that stuff."

"Only the ignorant get caught in it. We have ways of foretelling its appearance, and we avoid areas foretold to have it."

Abram chuckled. "Yeah, we have that ability too, though it's only half-reliable. Guess if our rain was as deadly as it is here we'd work on predicting it more accurately. We call it forecasting though."

"Strangely termed. The name indicates you initiate what is cast as opposed to simply predicting it."

Abram laughed this time. It was oddly pleasant to discuss the differences in their two sides, and for brief moments Abram was able to forget that his world was dying and bringing the aggregate other worlds down with it. He looked out over the fields again and his smile dissolved back to a frown.

"So what will you do if my side doesn't listen? What happens if we keep edging over that precipice?"

The Gray Lord sighed and rubbed his stubble. "I fear participating in an action that will upset the balance of the Seven will result in catastrophe either way. But, when faced with catastrophe at every avenue, I would elect the path least likely to negatively affect my interests." The Gray Lord turned to Abram. "A choice I'm sure any in such a position would settle upon."

They both stared at the window in silence. Abram knew what the Gray Lord was saying. If the way to save the Third meant destroying the Second, Abram's home, the Gray Lord would destroy it. General Alvarez would take action on that without question. He would organize a raiding party and force the Gray Lord's abdication via death or imprisonment. After putting a person from the Second in power, the general would undoubtedly start to colonize the Third. Chances were he would see the Third as the contingency plan should home become irreparable or inhospitable. If they kept pushing and things looked bleak, the general would abandon ship and hop to the next one until that ship sunk too. It took hundreds of years to destroy the second, and by the time the Third was destroyed it would be more hundreds of years. Abram imagined the general consulting all the powers that be, maybe even uniting the world against the Second and invading. In the hundreds of years it would take, perhaps new technology would arise and they'd be able to go back and save the Second, or at the very least prevent destruction of the Third.

The idea sickened Abram, but at the same time he felt as though the plan might be the only option. But would he be able to live with himself after telling the general what the Gray Lord had said, knowing that in doing so he would be condemning many of the inhabitants of the Third? If history said anything on the topic, many people in the Third would perish during the invasion. And the survivors would be forced to assimilate, probably even drop their cultures and customs. Would they be persecuted just for being different?

"Let us hope that the rulers of your side take drastic action, and at the very least the destruction of your side is halted, if reversal is impossible."

"Let us hope," Abram repeated, glaring at the black mass and envisioning it as troops from his own side. "Let us hope and hope hard."

The Gray Lord walked back to his throne and Abram stood in front of it this time, thinking of taking his leave.

"So the Shaman said he planned to train me. Anything I should know about it before I start?"

"Focus only on the end, even in the beginning."

"That it? Nothing better than think about it being over as soon as it begins?" Abram chuckled.

"Every artist endures a different challenge. If you tarry too long in the present, you may lose sight of your goals and failure will claim you as an ally."

Abram shrugged. "Well hopefully whatever I have to do is done quick. And I hope the Shaman returns soon. There's no way we can hold out for much longer."

The Gray Lord grunted and Abram headed out and back down the steps. He wandered around the fortress, hoping the Shaman would burst onto the scene at any moment.

CHAPTER 26

Another full day passed and Abram thought he would die. Going without water for more than a day was bad enough, but suffering through the day with nothing but his hunger and thirst to occupy his mind was maddening. His throat was dry and his stomach ached, but he refused to groan like the others. He lay on his back in front of the entrance gate, anticipating the Shaman's return at any minute, but it was others that became his saving grace.

Four soldiers dressed in navy cloaks instead of armor appeared from somewhere beyond the courtyard, bearing gifts more valuable than any treasure. They were loaded down with wineskins that sloshed with water instead of wine, and Abram had never been happier in all his life. They tossed him one as they passed and headed to the dining hall, and he downed his entire skin in a few minutes. Doing so almost made him vomit, but he felt too refreshed to care.

The initial team only had enough for some people, but they came back with more and Abram's curiosity was aroused. He asked where they were getting their supply from since the fortress was still under siege. They reported digging a tunnel under the black army and finding another well, sneaking the precious commodity back and distributing it.

They kept coming and going, and Abram was able to snag a second container. The water had an earthy taste, but he forced his mind to forget about all the germs that undoubtedly swam around in his hydration. It was either drink up or die a slow death.

The time passed a little better, but he was still hungry and his stomach growled constantly. He debated going outside and eating grass with some of the soldiers, but something told him if it was a feasible option the townspeople would have been participating as well. Maybe eating the meager stalks would cause more hunger, or maybe there was a sickness to be contracted by eating. Whatever it was, Abram held off and stuck to his water, hoping amphibious yaks were brought in next.

No yaks came, and Abram again went to bed with a hungry stomach.

He only made it halfway through the night before a gong boomed through the fortress and rumbled through the floor. It echoed and sounded again and Abram thought of his first visit. Something important was happening.

CHAPTER 27

Abram hopped out of bed and opened the door as the gong continued to boom. Sprinting back through the abandoned marketplace and up the velvet steps, Abram burst through the Gray Lord's overlook door. He took a moment to catch his breath. The Gray Lord had his nose to the glass. A smile crept up the corner of his mouth and Abram joined him.

The blue moon was still sitting in the corner of the sky, staining the area shades of cerulean, but a white light pierced through the darkness to the left of the fortress. A number of large figures were stampeding through the Red Mage's black force, leaving some *Ghafarians* trampled underfoot and sending others flying. The large figures were *Magnums* cutting a fissure through the enemy lines, and leading them had to be none other than the Shaman. His light was a beacon and the *Magnums* charged after it, demolishing everything in their path.

Trailing behind the group of *Magnums* was a flock of fresh *wambaika* outfitted in armor. They assumed a layered V shape as they flew, and Abram imagined them moving as one, like a fluid spearhead penetrating all in their path.

There had to have been at least 500 *Magnums*, and though there were far more *Ghafarians*, there were definitely less enemy *Magnums*. Nothing could withstand the might of a *Magnum*, not even the best of *Ghafaria*.

The remainder of the black force began to turn inward toward the *Magnums*, but Abram continued smiling. Unless these were the weakest *Magnums* in existence, there was little the black force could do. Even if these *were* the weakest *Magnums*, they would still probably be strong enough to win.

Abram felt a tingling sensation in his chest and he knew he had to help. Last time he was inexperienced but willing to fight. This time he was mildly more experienced and just as ready. Thoughts and sounds of his old battle echoed in his head and he looked at his arm. He made a fist and knew exactly the weapon he wanted to use this time.

"I have to help," Abram said, still glancing at his arm before looking over at the Gray Lord.

The Gray Lord was still grinning and shot him an unconcerned glance. "I doubt that there is much I can do to sway you to stay, and there is even less reason for you to do so. Go. Even with this *Magnum* cavalry, we need all the help we can muster."

Abram nodded and bit his lip. "Will you come as well? I'm sure that you and the Shaman could take out this Zanda person with no problem."

The Gray Lord saluted in his way. "I will act when the questions of destiny align with the answers of the present."

Abram shrugged, unsure of exactly what was said before exiting the chamber. He felt weird running in the room, but as soon as the door closed he bounded down the steps two at a time, keeping a hand on the wall to prevent himself from falling. At the bottom he was even more out of breath than after the ascension, but he kept running until he reached the weapon room.

"Please still be in here," Abram whispered, looking around through the candlelight.

A glint of green sparkled toward the back and he smirked, closing the distance to it. When he arrived, his mouth grew sore from all the smiling but he kept it up. He reached out and grabbed the weapon with his flesh arm. It was heavy, and he was barely able to lift it. He chuckled and tried again with his prosthetic, breaking into a full laugh with how easy it was now.

He glared at the war hammer and admired the craftsmanship as he had the first time he saw it. It was the same height as a sword. The head was a clear, curved horn that resembled a ram's, but on the cheek of the head was an open eye. The pupil was a green jewel that glowed faintly, and it appeared to follow him as he maneuvered the weapon to be horizontal in both of his hands. The handle was a glistening glass with streaks of green swirling throughout it. Abram held the head in his prosthetic and supported it with his flesh. The hints of green swirling around the shaft twinkled in the candlelight and if Abram wasn't holding it, confirming it was stationary with his own hand, he would have thought the spirals were a fluid, green rivulet.

He readjusted and held the grip with his prosthetic, testing the feel of the weapon. He spun it a few times and gave a heaving swing. If he had his weight on one leg the weight of the weapon would have carried him forward and onto the ground. He swung again, adjusting his stance to flow with the momentum a little better.

"It is as if it has a mind of its own, eh?"

Abram brought the weapon to his side and spun. The Gray Lord was smiling at Abram. He nodded to the hammer. Abram grinned and looked at the weapon as well, feeling his body trying to compensate for its weight by tensing his abdomen.

"I was just thinking that," Abram said. "Where did this thing come from? It's nothing like any of the other weapons.

"Nor was it meant to be used like any of the others."

"Something tells me there's a story behind it."

The Gray Lord grunted before speaking. "Its crafting was actually devised by a previous ally of mine, Vidogo. Vidogo showed promise, though his potential was cut short by the Red Mage."

"Sorry to hear that." Abram glared at the hammer and frowned. "I'd be honored to avenge your fallen friend by sinking this into the Red Mage's chest."

The Gray Lord grunted again and started stroking his chin stubble. "That would make the whole world smile, but your power is far beneath his. The ally whom that belonged to intended to entrap his *noko-fimbo* within. He was close to achieving mastery before his resolution."

"A noko-what?"

The Gray Lord held up his staff. "The creature within my staff, and the staff of any master of the arts."

Abram whistled. "And I thought those rods were strong enough. Can you imagine hitting someone with this thing after it was inspired by the dust stuff?"

"Indeed I can, and many nights I have."

Abram glared at the weapon and envisioned his own snake inside, empowering him to squash the forces of evil one climactic smash at a time.

Another gong reverberated through the fortress and Abram was brought back to the present. He'd been so engulfed with nabbing the weapon to fight with that he forgot he still had to fight.

He and the Gray Lord shared a brief, understanding look. Abram nodded and jogged to the entrance alone. The *Magnums* guarding the gate looked at him in silence. He motioned to them to open the door and they shared a look of confusion.

"Open up, please," Abram said, hoping they spoke English.

The *Magnums* grabbed their respective chains and heaved until the door was high enough for him to sneak beneath.

"Careful," one of the *Magnums* said in a slow, deep tone, his face indicating he wanted to say more but lacked the words.

The door slammed shut behind him and Abram's heart started pounding in his chest. The battle had begun to spill back toward the fortress, and small, loud, bloody skirmishes were everywhere.

Arrows flew in every direction but often missed their targets. Abram was unable to tell friendly projectiles from foes' until one landed at his feet. The arrow was a solid piece of metal painted all black. Instead of feathers at the back, wings had been fashioned from the metal. The tip smoldered and smoked against the ground. At first he assumed it had been ablaze, but the distinct vinegar-and-jalapeño smell of *sodarma* permeated the air and he shivered.

"That's just wrong," Abram said, though no one was close enough to hear him.

He kicked the acid-tipped arrow over before turning toward where the *Magnums* had broken through the black ranks. He spun his hammer in his prosthetic hand and looked at the mayhem in front of him. The danger from his first battle echoed in his head and he swallowed his doubts, hoping God would keep him safe.

I've got more than hope this time, Abram said, spinning his hammer again and thinking of the words he'd gone into battle with the first time. He continued spinning his hammer and ran forward.

CHAPTER 28

Abram charged into the mayhem. Though he was of the utmost importance during his last visit and this time he was merely another soldier, he still basked in the inspiration of fighting for a good cause. It tingled his fingertips and toes and gave him enough courage to quiet the voice begging him to hide. But even with the inspiration he started feeling tired before he got very far or did any fighting. The hammer was wieldable only because of his prosthetic, but the strain the weight put on his other muscles fatigued him.

Cacophonous cries commingled with the clang of a variety of metals. He bumped into a few people as he ran, but it was only when he saw a *Ghafarian* charging straight for him that adrenaline entered his veins and his fatigue faded to an afterthought.

The *Ghafarian* was as muscular, albeit also as short, as any other *Ghafarian*, and he wielded a curved sword that he held above his head. Abram spun his hammer a few more times.

His weapon was longer than the *Ghafarian*'s sword, and Abram swung with all his might. His arm moved faster than he was used to, and faster than the *Ghafarian* appeared used to. It connected with the *Ghafarian*'s waist before the poor fellow had a chance to react, and he went sideways, summersaulting through the air. His cries of pain trailed behind him. Abram paused and looked at his arm, and a smirk crept across his face. Another *Ghafarian* charged at him and he swung again, cutting the power of the swing in half but still sending the enemy flying.

Enemy after enemy was sent flying in Abram's wake until he closed the distance to the *Magnums*. They were stomping and swinging their way through the ranks as well, led by the Shaman. These *Magnums* were darker than the tawny lot he'd seen from the Great River *Magnus*, but this bunch sported similar black war paint. They were armed with clubs and maces, and one or two also had swords. None had arrows.

New to Abram's eyes, these *Magnums* also rode on giant beasts that trampled many enemies underfoot. The creatures were twice the size of the *Magnums* with skin that appeared tougher than stone. They had flat feet and a stubbly tail that resembled a club. Their heads were plated with a natural armor that spiked and jutted out around their eyes and down the front of their face. Where a nose would have been on any regular animal from back home, a stubby horn was instead. Nostrils flared beside the eyes instead of near the horn.

These creatures were a force to be reckoned with. They used their tails to smash and clobber, and their faces like battering rams and spears.

No words were exchanged between Abram and the Shaman when their eyes met, and Abram joined them in clearing out the plague of *Ghafarians*. But the tides only flowed in their favor for a brief while.

Unlike the *Ghafarians* he had encountered during his first battle, these barbarians had some brains. While some were crushed or sent flying by *Magnum* clubs, others started strategizing and bringing down the giants. They formed loose circles around the *Magnums*, and when a *Magnum* attacked one, the others would take action. Some fired acid-tipped arrows into the *Magnum's* back—where the armor was the lightest—while others climbed onto the giant and hacked into its skin at close range. Their strikes were precise and forceful.

For the first time in his life, Abram saw a giant brought down by smaller soldiers. Watching the first one drop to one knee before being carried over onto his side and decapitated was like watching an elephant taken down by hyenas. The sight was unreal and stopped Abram cold until the Shaman grabbed his shoulder and pushed him back to fighting.

But the *Ghafarians* continued their strategy and thinned out the cavalry. Abram did his best to keep fighting, but it was distracting to watch the giants fall one by one. The whisper of fear that gnawed on his sanity since his entrance onto the battlefield started to yell doubts into his head.

The beasts the *Magnums* rode on were tougher to take down, and they were able to kill many more *Ghafarians* before a workable strategy was created. Since the creatures were moving forward, the *Ghafarians* cleared a path to their front and found the creatures had vulnerable skin at the backs of their knees. They ran beside the creatures, slashing at the vulnerable spots or shooting arrows into them until the creatures could no longer run. After killing or distracting the rider, the *Ghafarians* either left the creatures crippled on the ground, or they teamed up to flip the beasts over where a soft stomach was exposed and exploited.

A *wam-baika* crashed in front of him and knocked him to the ground. The creature was riddled with arrows and Abram's heart dropped. His eyes turned to the sky and he saw that even the *wam-baika* were being whittled down one by one. Unlike when he first traveled outside, the arrows were now focused. Throughout the battlefield, swarms of the acid-tipped arrows converged on the *baika* and plucked them from the sky.

Abram kept swinging alongside the Shaman, but the forces all around them continued to get cut down. The *Ghafarians* seemed a limitless black mass that hungrily ate everything in their path.

"Come!" the Shaman said, slashing down a *Ghafarian* before breaking into a sprint.

Abram obeyed, sending enemies flying to his left and right. Fear continued to rise in him and he doubted the chances they had at winning the fight. The hordes of *Ghafarians* just kept coming.

The Shaman weaved back to the front of the fortress, but stopped short of the gate, still facing it.

"What, what's wrong? Are we retreating?" Abram said, taking deep breaths between words.

"Yes, *Safi*, are we retreating?" came a mocking voice behind them both.

Abram spun around and saw a man outfitted in a robe that was a deep, dark purple. It was dark enough to be confused for black, but when he moved and parts of it caught the blue moonlight differently, the true color could be seen. The newcomer wielded a *nokofimbo* staff as well, though his snake was purple. He had curly, dark hair that stretched to his shoulders. A short beard hid the shape of his jaw, and his eyes were piercing and determined. He was taller than most inhabitants of the Third, but only by a little.

Though they had run to the fortress with full view of their surroundings, somehow this guy had managed to get behind them. There was scarcely seven feet between them.

The Shaman slowly turned around with a scowl that furrowed his face. As usual, he had run without growing weary, but now, in the presence of the newcomer, his shoulders started to heave and he took in great breaths. His fists clutched the hilt of his sword and his staff tighter, and he glared at the newcomer with a fiery ire in his eyes.

"Zanda," the Shaman said, his voice dripping with contempt.

CHAPTER 29

"Zanda?" Abram said, looking at the new artist. He thought back to the Gray Lord and how he had said he refused to fight before the right time because doing so would cause this guy to attack.

"We meet again," Zanda said, the smirk still on his face. He held up his arms and looked around. "And on such similar grounds. Your companion's garb indicates he is a foreigner from the Second, so I will speak in English for his benefit."

The Shaman was mute, giving only his heavy breathing as a response. His shoulders continued to rise and fall with his breaths, and he lowered his head as he continued to watch the enemy.

"Though, I suppose, our last altercation was reversed, and you had come to destroy my home. With such haste has the time elapsed. It feels as though it were just the yester."

Zanda started laughing but the Shaman remained silent.

"Where is Kweli? I would very much like to kill him."

Abram glanced at the hammer gleaming in his hand. He looked at Zanda and envisioned him flying away head over heels. The Shaman wasn't talking, so he figured it was time to take action. Unable to squash the urge to scream, Abram bellowed and charged, swinging the hammer at the guy's waist.

Shock rippled through Abram's face when he connected with nothing but air. The speed his arm provided had prevented even the skill of the *Ghafarians* from dodging his attacks, but not Zanda. The momentum carried Abram to the side and Zanda continued smirking, taking another step back.

Abram turned and started swinging again, but moments before impact he saw Zanda's lips moving, whispering something inaudible.

Abram and Zanda made eye contact, and for a split second a fragment of fear sparkled in Zanda's piercing eyes. Abram connected, but instead of striking soft flesh and sending his opponent flying, he slammed into something that stopped his swing. A loud boom erupted and he feared he'd shattered the weapon but it held strong. Hitting a solid barrier caused all the power and energy from the swing to travel back up the hammer and it vibrated Abram's entire body. If his swinging arm had been flesh and bone he was convinced the entirety of his skeleton would have shattered, but the material in the prosthetic diffused much of the power before it reached his natural body. Still, his head started ringing and he dropped the weapon out of instinct.

"You're quicker than you look," Zanda said, still smirking, the fear gone. "And stronger too. I sense you are the acclaimed Abram that many clairvoyant tongues have dubbed the savior of the aggregate dimensions?"

Abram gulped and the feelings of endangering something important rushed through him. Since he'd returned and informed his side of the impending danger, he'd always thought the critical portion of his part in the story was over. Hearing Zanda mention his potential role again made him remember the prophetic scrolls, and he wondered what else he should be doing to save people.

"I will snuff the last breath from your lungs when I have finished with your companions."

Zanda took a few steps forward and Abram let him pass, frightened to make any further attacks. He grabbed his hammer and limped back to the Shaman's side. Safi's face had barely twitched since he'd started staring at Zanda. After seeing how ineffective he had been, Abram wished the Shaman had taken advantage of their enemy's momentary distraction. Perhaps it was honor that kept him in place, but whatever it was, Abram hoped it was the right choice.

"Where were we? Ah, I was just about to ask if you preferred to die before your master, or after?" More silence was the response, and Zanda pulled back the side of his robe, revealing a number of burlap bags of powder. "You are right, Safi, and I apologize. The time for words has long since expired. We are in the time of action, and act we shall."

The Shaman agreed in silence and pulled back his own robe. His staff had been glowing earlier, so Abram assumed it had been previously inspired. The Shaman threw down his sword, took out a bag and dumped it atop his head. Blue dust twinkled down around him. Zanda did the same, only instead of blue his dust was purple. The dust settled and the two artists assumed their assault stances; the Shaman lowered down against his left heel, outstretching his right leg and holding his rod above his head, while Zanda spread his legs and angled his right side forward, holding his rod above his head. Abram stepped back, wondering if he'd have the opportunity to try another strike while the enemy was distracted.

The two artists charged forward. Neither made a sound with their mouths, and their robes barely swished as they rushed together. As Abram looked on, the cacophony and madness of the battlefield around them faded away. All he could see and hear were the two artists.

CHAPTER 30

Moments before the two artists ran into one another, the Shaman jumped and twirled his rod while Zanda swung forward. Zanda hit only air, while the Shaman used Zanda's shoulder as a stepping stool. As he passed Zanda, the Shaman also cracked the end of his rod against the back of his enemy's skull. Pushing off from Zanda's shoulder, he flipped once and landed on his feet. Zanda stumbled forward before falling to one knee.

The Shaman turned after landing but stayed in place. Zanda stood up and rubbed his head, smirking. The two assumed assault positions again and waited a beat before charging toward one another.

This time as they neared, Zanda brought his rod down from over his head like an axe. The Shaman fell into a roll. As he spun he tossed his rod up. The rod spun over Zanda while the Shaman rolled through his legs. Timed perfectly, the Shaman caught his staff after passing below Zanda. The Shaman swung behind his back and hit his opponent in the spine. Zanda fell on his face this time, grunting as he landed. The Shaman popped up and turned, again standing still and awaiting his opponent's return to his feet.

Abram was now only a few feet behind Zanda. If he took a few quiet steps he could end the fight without the Shaman even having to get hurt. Perhaps even the whole battle would cease if Zanda fell. Abram toyed with the idea as the two again took on fighting stances, but decided he would intervene only if the Shaman started losing.

The two charged again, but this time Zanda was whispering something. The Shaman started whispering as well and the two swung toward each other. Their rods clapped together and produced a shockwave but both were still standing. Zanda swung again and the Shaman blocked, holding his rod with both hands. He shoved Zanda back and flung one end of the rod forward, connecting with Zanda's nose. He flung the other side forward but Zanda ducked, sending his rod toward the Shaman's side. The Shaman blocked again and thrust his knee into Zanda's stomach. Zanda bent over and the Shaman sent another knee forward. Zanda shoved the Shaman back and jabbed with the bulbous end of his staff, connecting with the Shaman's nose. The Shaman's head bounced back on his neck, and Zanda jabbed again but the Shaman slapped away the attack with his hand. Blue dust leaked from his nose. He shoved Zanda back and swung, his face appearing angrier and more intense than before he was struck. He connected with Zanda's chest and the evil artist flew back, landing and skidding on the ground a ways before stopping.

Abram smiled and had to fight the urge to start clapping, ecstatic to see the Shaman doing so well. Zanda rose to his feet and the two rushed toward one another again, their robes rippling in the air and their faces twisted with anger. Both swung again, and their staffs clanked together, but this time the shockwave was loud enough to ripple through Abram's ACU. A shimmering cloud of blue and purple dust was also produced from the impact, and it concealed them for a few moments. When the dust settled the two were both still standing, their rods locked together, their teeth bared and gritted.

The Shaman slid to the left a little and turned enough so that Zanda stumbled. While his opponent was off balance he brought the end of his rod around and clonked it against the base of Zanda's skull. Zanda fell face down, groaning, and the Shaman followed up the attack with another blow.

Zanda still groaned, but the Shaman removed the staff from his enemy's clutches and tossed it on the grass. The snake within wriggled in its confines even after the Shaman had let it go. The Shaman rolled his enemy over and knelt down beside him. After a moment of looking, he went back to where he'd discarded his sword and returned to Zanda's side. Zanda continued groaning but eventually opened his eyes.

"I see you've been training since we last met," Zanda spat, a grin sliding across his face.

The Shaman sighed. "Have you any final words? I shall avenge Zuri and end your life, as you ended hers."

Abram wondered who Zuri was. Maybe it was the Shaman's old fling, and the wrath he had displayed was because Zanda killed her in cold blood. Abram's mind started running with fantasies, but Zanda's voice brought him back to the present.

"She deserved her death, as do you." Zanda turned his head and spit on the ground, and Abram was surprised the Shaman allowed the evil man to continue speaking. "If you only knew the dangers that await you, you would dig a hole and hide in it forever." Zanda's spirits seemed to lift at the thought, and his eyes widened. He started laughing. "Strike me down if you must, but find your shovel and a suitable tombstone. I am merely the sheath. The blade can now be revealed! Soon it will swing for your knees, for a neck strike would be too merciful! Soon you shall watch your whole world crumble to dust at your fingertips! Soon—"

The Shaman slid the sword into Zanda's neck and cut off his words. Because of the dust he'd covered his body with, Zanda survived the blow but gagged and coughed as the dust filled his throat instead of blood. Abram started wondering how the Shaman would kill the artist while his body was protected by the dust.

As if reading his thoughts, the Shaman brought the sword around and decapitated Zanda. A wam-baika flew down a few seconds later and grabbed the head, carrying it away. Abram figured if the body and the head remained apart, the dust could never heal Zanda.

"For Zuri," the Shaman whispered, glaring at Zanda's headless corpse for a few more moments before walking past Abram and toward the fortress.

Abram stared at Zanda's body for a few minutes, wondering what his words had meant. Only two bad people he had seen could be more powerful than Zanda. The Red Mage or Koñél, or both of them together. The last he'd seen Koñél, she was barely an artist. She was yet to claim her *nokofimbo* rod, and he felt having a rod made you more powerful, so the thought of Koñél being worse was odd. Still, someone other than the Red Mage had to be who Zanda was referring to because the Gray Lord and the Shaman had dealt with Red before. They could probably defeat the evil mage if they worked together, and the Shaman seemed to have improved his skills as well. Perhaps he could even win alone.

Abram's thoughts drifted back to romance with Koñél, and he fantasized of saving her. If Zanda was referring to her, she sounded like she had continued down the dark path, but there was still hope. There was always hope until the end.

Cries and clashing metal brought him back from his thoughts and he was reminded of the battle still raging. He turned and ran to the gate, which the *Magnums* opened up for him.

CHAPTER 31

nside the fortress, things were as dreary as they were before, though soft sobbing could be heard in the distance now. Abram spotted the Shaman heading toward the steps that led to the Gray Lord's overlook, and he jogged to catch up. Once he did, they walked up side by side in silence.

At the top they entered the Gray Lord's room and joined him by the window.

"It is a hopeless battle," the Gray Lord whispered, and Abram knitted his eyebrows together.

"Hopeless? You guys can just go down there and cast a spell or whatever on everyone. With two of you, I'm pretty sure you could turn this around in an instant."

"No," the Shaman said, shocking Abram further. "Their armor has been inspired to repel artistry. I noticed it when I arrived. The inspirer was powerful, even more so than Zanda, and I have been unsuccessful in countering it."

The Shaman glanced at Abram for a moment before returning his gaze to the field. Gray soldier, *Magnum*, and *wam-baika* alike fell near rhythmically at the hand of the *Ghafarians*.

"I have brought allies to their slaughter," the Shaman said, his voice laced with pain.

There was a long pause before the Gray Lord spoke, and when he did he leaned his rod against the glass and folded his hands behind his back. "I fear we have all been brought to the slaughter," he said, sighing after the sentence.

"Are you kidding me!" Abram said, his face twisted in disgust and confusion. "You two are giving up? We can't just leave those soldiers out there to die." Neither man responded as Abram looked between them. Anger welled in Abram like a volcano but he swallowed it down and gripped his hammer tighter. He looked at it and turned, heading for the door. "You two can stand up here and watch them die if you want, but I'm going down to do whatever I can."

"No," the Gray Lord said, halting Abram. "I will sound the retreat."

"So everyone can starve to death inside your fortress? What good will that do?" Abram said, setting his hammer down and holding both arms up. "We need to fight. To the death if that's what it comes to."

"Abram is partially right," the Shaman said, turning from the window as well. He started rubbing his knuckle as he continued speaking. "We must flee this place and regroup with any remaining allies and wait to attack when the *Ghafarians* are no longer inspired." There was a pause as the Gray Lord seemed to think the idea over. "Fighting is not wise at this time, but having them retreat here will merely prolong their suffering. We three must flee with haste."

"I feel it cowardice to simply flee from my men."

Abram agreed, but what choices did he really have? He thought about how skillfully the *Ghafarians* had overcome every obstacle in their path. Sure, he could swing and smash a few more, maybe even a few hundred more, but how many would fall at his hand before they figured out a strategy to defeat him as well? He thought of the *Magnums* and their steeds that had died. Even if they never figured him out, he had limited energy.

"Perhaps," the Shaman said. "But I need an ally as powerful as I until Abram has been trained. After that, you can die in the way you see fit."

Abram felt a bubble of excitement from the idea of getting trained to be an artist again. He wanted to smile, but their present dilemma dimmed his eagerness. Thoughts of all the death and impending doom made him swallow hard instead.

"To tarry is to die," the Gray Lord said. "I have seen that the *malaika* are on their way here. I feel as though the *Ghafarians* were awaiting their arrival to begin their assault. Safi's coming prompted early action." When the Gray Lord finished his sentence he whispered something and the sound of a high-pitched gong started ringing through the walls. "But I will not leave the soldiers outside to be slaughtered. I will have them retreat. At the least there is hope that our success will save them before the siege claims their lives."

"What are the *malaika*?" Abram said.

"Winged demons like the *fleigh*, but more powerful with a greater lust for destruction."

Abram gulped.

"Come, while there are still *wam-baika* to fly us," the Shaman said. The Gray Lord grabbed his staff and the trio headed back down the steps. As they neared the gate, the Gray Lord paused. He ran back toward the other side and disappeared into a room. When he exited, he was cradling three parchments like a newborn baby. He entered another room and came out with a sack. He gingerly placed the parchment inside before nodding to the Shaman.

Abram was unable to see the text on the scrolls, but the paper looked like the prophetic manuscripts he had been shown on his first visit. He'd only been able to see two, but the one scroll he had not seen must have been included with these three, and he wondered if he'd be shown the text this time around.

"Wait, we must find an alternative route," the Gray Lord said, pausing before they reached the *Magnums* at the gate. "The retreat has been sounded and a rush of soldiers will be entering shortly."

Without more words they turned and headed to the courtyard. The Shaman whispered something quickly before raising his staff vertically into the air and slamming the end down into the ground. The glass above them shattered, but as it fell it dissolved into blue dust and showered around them. The area was shrouded in a blue cloud, but a loud flapping sound filled the air and the dust was dispersed.

Three *wam-baika* descended and grabbed the trio, flapping again and lifting them toward the ceiling. Abram's *wam-baika* struggled and squawked, and he figured the added weight from the hammer was slowing them down. He sighed and dropped it, hoping to one day return and claim it as his own.

As they cleared the roof of the courtyard and flew above the fortress, Abram's heart sank as he watched the gray soldiers fleeing. Many were pursued and stabbed in the back. Only a handful of *Magnums* were still alive, and the same was true for the *wam-baika*. Abram felt guilty for leaving, and he wished they had stayed to fight. Inspired armor or not, he felt they could still clear out a good number of the enemy soldiers before they were defeated. But the fantasy slipped away as they continue to rise above it all. He hoped that the men that had managed to tunnel and find water would at least be able to continue doing so. Maybe they could even find food. But how long would it be before the *malaika* arrived and came in through the same exit they had just taken? How long before the *Ghafarians* simply scaled the fortress wall and killed everyone within?

The thought depressed Abram further and he tried to focus on other things. He thought about Ruth and her mission, hoping at least that would be a success, but his mind drifted to Koñél. Thinking of her only made him think of the potential evil she now harbored, and how the world would be destroyed like Zanda had claimed in his last breath. Could the US military do anything to stop them? Abram thought of the portal and wondered if the *Ghafarians* would use it.

The *baika* flapped their way vertically until they were above the clouds. Only then did they start to head north.

Abram still felt like a coward for leaving, but in his heart he knew it was their only choice. With thoughts of regret he let his eyes fall shut and decided to rest as best as he could, but as soon as his eyes closed, Stribling popped into his head.

"Wait, we have to go back and take the injured man from my side with us," Abram said, feeling like he at least had an obligation to keep the people he'd come with alive. Contrition from losing Feldman compounded the idea.

"I am sorry, Abram, but we are unable to return now," the Gray Lord said, yelling to be heard above the flap of the *baika* wings and rush of the air.

"But we can't just leave him! We can't—"

"Quiet your fears," the Gray Lord said. "I laid a protection utterance on the fortress before we left, and penetration by any other than an artist is impossible. Only those who have been within my fortress before can enter or exit. Your companion's wounds were severe, and moving him again could prove fatal. His highest chance for a successful recovery lies where he is now. At the least, the healers will do whatever they can. The rest relies on the Lords of Luck."

"What about the portal? If the *Ghafarians* have an artist with them and get inside, will they be able to use the doorway to cross to my side?"

"No," the Shaman said. "I have the infinity sphere, and without it the device will not work."

Abram swallowed but wanted to say more. Regardless of the reassurances they provided, he feared the worst. Furthermore, at least being on site with Stribling meant he cared, but leaving him to fend for himself was no better than throwing him into a den of lions. But there was nothing Abram could do, short of breaking free from the *baika* and plunging to his own death. With a belabored sigh he closed his eyes again and inundated himself with thoughts of what a royal screw up he and the entire trip had been.

CHAPTER 32

Ruth was relieved to finally land. The *wam-baika* had been spooked by the roaring creature. Though the mercenaries never saw anything, the *wam-baika* refused to land until they arrived at the cave.

Ruth had reminisced about her first journey to the cave as the landscape changed over the course of the days, and she noted on her pad how drastic the changes were at times. They went from prairie, to wooded hills, to a desert, to a mountainous area with sporadic and varied vegetation. Her thoughts had been filled with her previous companion, Heloderma, and she hoped the giant lizard was alive and well.

"Those things murdered my guns," Grodin said, massaging his biceps.

"Maybe if your guns were worked as much as your mouth you'd be alright," Sergeant Bethune said, popping in a stick of gum and chewing loudly.

Ruth shook her head but remained silent and glowered at the opening to the *Giza Sana* cave. It seemed different this time around. Though she had more company, she still felt ostracized. Even when she had been active duty she'd felt like an outsider among all the grunts. There was something egotistical and rough about soldiers that she never quite adjusted to, and even though she'd been through a lot more with the mercenaries than with her previous company, she still felt like an outsider.

Grodin burped with unabashed volume that only added to the feeling squeezing her gut. She continued to stare at the opening and sighed, wishing she had a flashlight. For a few minutes, they all just stared ahead as if they knew there was something waiting for them on the inside, and they were debating if they were ready to face it. The *wam-baika* squawked and chomped at one another playfully. Ruth took a deep breath, un-holstered her weapon and led the way.

Bethune cocked his weapon, pausing before they made it too deep for light to reach. He examined his gun briefly before pseudo-cursing and letting his arms fall to his sides. "All weapons come standard with smart triggers that only fire with the registered users." He released a strew of more almost-curse words. "That glorious piece of safety precaution has been what's stopping our guns from firing." The group let out a sigh and everyone's spirits dropped. "Here we are thinking they just needed a good clean. We're all a bunch of idiots!"

Ruth felt a little nervous as Bethune continued chewing and yelling about the guns. His eyes were wider than usual like he was angry, and he started fidgeting with his weapon. She checked the ammo display on the back of her sidearm. The counter was dark.

"Fire a test shot out the mouth of the cave?" Grodin said, aiming his weapon. "Just in case it works." The sergeant nodded.

Grodin pulled the trigger and the familiar click echoed off the cave walls. The sound sucked the remaining encouragement and excitement out of the mission in an instant, and things turned deadly worrisome for Ruth. She unsheathed her combat knife and glints of light from the entrance sparkled off it as she turned it in her hand.

"Good idea," Grodin said with a sigh, gesturing toward Ruth's blade. "Maybe we can tickle all the monsters you mentioned in your report with that thing."

"Zip it, Grodin!" Bethune said, his voice more commanding than his face appeared. His eyes were still wild and his hands quaked against his weapon until he let it dangle by its strap on his back. "At least it's better than nothing."

Images of the *Midomo* and the sea dragon flashed inside her head. She holstered her gun and held her knife at her side. She was almost as unprepared as before, but at least this time she had allies that were her size. Still, the ghastly, self-mutilated faces of the *Midomo* sent shivers through her spine and she just wanted to hurry up and finish her research.

"But wait, hasn't Brooksie boy's gun fired? Remember?" Grodin said, and the group looked at Brooks.

Brooks shrugged and Bethune went to examine the weapon. After a few moments he patted Brooks on the cheek.

"Snipers can only be purchased special order, at least legally. They only come with the smart triggers if its requested." He paused and looked at Ruth as if she was a child. "You know, since by nature snipers are used away from other people, so the chances of their weapon being picked up and used by the wrong person are slim."

"Well, good, then we have at least one gun."

The thought of having one firearm sent a wave of hope through the group and frowns turned to uneasy grins. Brooks made an overt point of counting his ammunition, and they all agreed it would be best if he only fired in an emergency. Plus, shooting in the close quarters of the cavern presented the danger of deadly ricochets.

Grodin took point while the rest were sprinkled in around Ruth. Bethune removed his own knife. Grodin did the same. Brooks kept his weapon trained forward. They all looked down the tunnel but no one moved.

"Wish we still had those flares. Insulting our many injuries, Stribbles is the only one who smokes," Sergeant Bethune said, pseudo-cursing loudly. "He prefers matches too! Ain't that a riot? There's a small chance a lighter wouldn't work, but he had freakin matches! I knew I should have never quit."

"Sergeant Bethune," Ruth said in a firm voice, the sergeant's constantly raised voice starting to worry her to the point of action. "Please get a hold of yourself. It is bad for morale, but more importantly, the louder you are the more likely something dangerous will come looking for us." Ruth pointed down the corridor but kept eye contact with him.

The sergeant looked upset but kept his mouth shut. General Alvarez was technically all of their bosses, but during the mission he had been clear that Ruth and Abram were in charge. Failing to submit could mean the mercenaries didn't get paid, but also she was right and he knew it.

"Sarge, sir?"

"What!" Bethune said, glancing at Ruth and rolling his eyes. "What?" he repeated, quieter this time.

"I thought it would be funny to play a prank on Stribbles for when he got better. I figured the first thing he would want to do was smoke when he came to, seeing as how he hasn't had one since we arrived. He said he forgot to bring a fresh pack, and only had a couple left. Wanted to save them for something special."

"The point, Grodin?"

"Sorry, sir." Grodin fumbled with his pants pocket until he fished out what he was looking for. "I took Stribbles's matches to prank him."

The sergeant smirked and snatched the matches from Grodin.

"Bout time you started showing your use around here," Sergeant Bethune said. The sergeant opened the matches and counted three sticks. He looked around and frowned again. "But what do we light?"

"I'm tired of having this jacket wrapped around my waist. Feel free to burn it," Grodin said with a smile. "Come to think of it, I have some camo paint that might help it burn a little better. It's basically made of oil." Grodin pulled out the container and everyone's face indicated they were experiencing a palm-to-forehead moment, realizing they could have used the camo paint for fuel the last time they needed a fire. "See, sir, I think right now I'm the most useful person here."

"Okay, okay, but I'm not going to just hold an oiled up jacket and light it on fire."

Grodin looked stumped but Brooks moved down the corridor a few feet. He came back empty handed, looked around before finally pointing to Grodin's rifle.

"Good thinking!" the sergeant bellowed, glancing at Ruth again. "Sorry, I meant, good thinking."

Brooks shrugged and Grodin handed over the rifle. The sergeant tied the jacket around the butt, and smeared on a coat of camouflage paint. Ruth stopped him before he could strike a match.

"Hold on. We have no clue how long that will burn. We have three matches, so we should cut the jacket into three sections. Just in case this one burns up we will have some backups."

"Gee whiz. Everyone is just full of bright ideas today," the sergeant said with a wide grin. Ruth cut up the jacket into three relatively even sections and the sergeant wrapped one around the tip, tying it as best he could. He wiped the excess oil from his hands on the cave wall before pulling out a match and holding it up. "And here's mine," he said, using the strike strip on the matchbook to set the tip ablaze.

"Sergeant Bethune, that was the first joke I've heard you crack in all the years I've known you," Grodin said with a smile.

"Don't get used to it. This cave has me out of my element, but I'll adjust."

The oiled jacket resisted the flame for a few seconds but eventually smoldered and crackled with fire. Ruth had to hold in a burst of glee that made her stomach flutter with butterflies. But the daunting words of the Red Mage crept up on her and she swallowed. *The Giza Sana is a dark place, and the inhabitants find light alluring. They will be drawn to you.* Ruth decided to keep his words to herself. They still had a mission to complete, and revealing to them what the Red Mage had said would only ruin the morale that was just starting to pick up. They were going in either way, and they would be careful, so there was no point dampening the one thing they had that had worked so far.

"Lead on," the sergeant said, handing the torch to Ruth.

She took it even though she had no clue where she was going. The last time she was guided by the Red Mage's servant, so all she could do was hope her subconscious remembered the path. She would follow her gut and if it led them someplace other than where they wanted to be, they would tackle that challenge when it arose.

Grodin was still on point and slightly in front of her, and the other mercenaries remained sprinkled around her. Her leading them held a more figurative meaning, as they could only follow the path of the tunnel. Her role was more to tell them which way to go if the tunnel changed direction.

She thought of Vidogo and the sea dragon and felt a tinge of sadness at his sacrifice. If he had been a coward, there's no telling what would have happened. Her life could have ended right then, and thinking of it made her realize that she owed the little man. If he was willing to give his life to preserve hers, she had to survive. She clutched her knife and torch tighter and pressed on into the bleak unknown of the *Giza Sana*.

CHAPTER 33

The orange light from the torch somehow gave the cave a different personality, a different aura. The light was brighter than Vidogo's had been—at least when it was hidden beneath the curtain. The brightness frightened her at first, but being able to see so much further ahead started to bring her comfort. Save for the evil *Midomo*, the sea dragon, and the occasional small rodent, her fearful encounters from the first time had been with shadows and her imagination.

"How far do we have to go before we get to this potential new energy source, or dark plants, or whatever we're hunting for," Sergeant Bethune said.

His eyes had returned to normal and he'd stopped shaking. He was back to his usual self for the most part, but Ruth still wondered how he would react to seeing a *Midomo*. She was certain he would respond with little to no hesitation when they were outside, but as he'd already demonstrated, the cave turned him into a different man. What if that difference resurfaced when confronted by evil?

Ruth shrugged to answer his question. "However far it is. If we still haven't found it and use half of the second torch, I will collect whatever samples I can from wherever we are and we will leave."

"Fair enough."

A scratching sound at the back pulled everyone's head over their shoulder. Ruth was relieved to see that it was just Brooks, using his combat knife to carve arrows in the direction they were coming from.

They pressed on through the cave. The sound of dripping water provided background noise. After their first few turns Ruth felt lost. Since everything was in a new light, with different shadows and colors, Ruth was unsure how similar their path was.

"We've already made four right turns," Sergeant Bethune started, his eyes reclaiming their worry. "Doesn't that mean we're heading back the direction we came?"

"If these were perfect, or near perfect right angles," Ruth said, continuing on without turning around. "But these are slants and the corridors zigzag." There was a brief silence and Brooks scratched another arrow. "Plus, Brooks is providing directions, and there have been no arrows in front of us thus far."

Sergeant Bethune nodded and they pressed on, but Ruth wondered if her strategy was correct. She figured if they took the same turn at every option, they could always go back and try the opposite turn if they had enough time.

They were accompanied by an unsettling silence throughout their journey, save for the dripping water, occasional scratch from Brooks, or the slosh of someone drinking from a half-empty canteen. Once, they found a stream of clean-looking water running quickly down the rocks and they filled up their bottles before continuing on.

When they entered the first open space Ruth couldn't stop her heart from thumping up into her throat. Her demeanor went unchanged, and she hoped the flicker of the fire hid the shake of her hand. They passed one of the *Midomo* torture spoons and she was sure they were in the same cavern from her first visit. Thankfully, there were no dead snakes or smoldering black goop to indicate someone had been in the passage recently. Still, there was the smell of body odor and sweat. She hoped it was the mercenaries.

"Keep your eyes peeled and your knives ready," Ruth said. "This is where I saw the *Midomo*. If you see one, kill it."

No one in the group responded, but they held their knives up in a combat position. The darkness in the room started growing darker, like a black hand slowly making a fist around them. Her heart picked up pace and she started breathing faster. It was an eerie feeling having her eyes wide open yet seeing the light slowly being squeezed away from them. She thought she was lightheaded, but soon her mind wandered to more imaginative alternatives. Perhaps the *Midomo* had devised a knockout gas that was slowly rendering them unconscious. Now the group would be captured without a fight, and everyone would be tortured until death seemed a pleasant alternative.

"Ma'am, the torch is about burned out," Sergeant Bethune said, snapping Ruth from her imagination.

She blinked a few times and looked at the dwindling fire, happy the growing darkness hid her cheeks as they flushed with embarrassment. He pulled out the matches and she slid the smoldering shirt from the rifle, hoping the fire tarried long enough for them to set up the next torch. The embers created a dull, pulsing, orange circle on the ground and she bent over to it as far as she could. She pulled out the next piece of cloth and started wrapping it around the end of the rifle.

"What was that?" Grodin said, his face cut with shadow and appearing ghostly. His eyes darted back and forth and he held up his knife.

"Zip it, Grodin! We don't have the time or the patience for your jokes right now!"

"Honest, Sarge, I heard something. Like bare feet against rock."

"If I have to tell you to zip it one more time, I'm stuffing that shirt in your mouth and taping it shut."

Ruth put her finger to her lips and the sergeant fell surprisingly quiet. Ruth continued working, but her hand was slow and the light continued to dwindle. The men's eyes darted around and their knives followed, their breathing audible and elevated like hers.

"Hurry," Ruth whispered, waving for the sergeant to join her near the ground. "The match."

He lit one and Ruth glanced up, noticing the silhouette of a fifth head behind Brooks.

"Brooks! Lookout!" Ruth screamed.

She jumped backward and landed on her butt, crab-walking backward a little. She dropped her knife and it clanked against the ground along with the rifle torch. Everyone whipped around and jumped as well. Bethune dropped the match and it winked out, leaving only the embers in the shirt for light.

Accented by the low lighting, the *Midomo's* face was as terrible as Ruth remembered. The lips and skin along the jaw had been intentionally removed. The teeth had been filed to imitate a predator. The ears were elongated and ridged to better receive the echo-location clicks the tribe could produce. Instead of a spear like the *Midomo* she had encountered, this one gripped a club that was jagged and pocked. In the low light she was unable to tell if it was rock or wood, but it would deal a good bit of damage either way.

The three men started backing up toward Ruth. They held their knives in front of them with firm grips, but their faces—save for Brooks's—were wrinkled in terror. The *Midomo* smiled with his eyes in the uncannily evil way of the tribe, glancing between them as if deciding who to attack first. He nonchalantly held the club at his side and inched in their direction.

"Hold it right there!" Sergeant Bethune said, his voice quavering along with his hand. "Hold it or I swear Brooks will blow your head clean off."

Brooks took aim, but stayed his finger, waiting for the order. The *Midomo* continued. Even if he understood English, which Ruth doubted, there was no fear in his eyes, only the lust to cause harm.

Ruth's back bumped into something stiff and she gasped, relaxing a hair when she realized it was a rock. The three mercenaries soon bumped into the same obstruction, checking the surface with their hands but keeping their eyes ahead and their knives trained on the threat. With the wall at their back and the *Midomo* at their front, there was nothing left to do but fight.

The *Midomo* was in front of the light now, and his shadow stretched to them. His face and body were masked in darkness.

Brooks fired and the man fell backward. The light from the jacket died and darkness engulfed them. Their breathing echoed off the walls and Ruth felt it was loud enough to be heard throughout the cave. She started whimpering.

Echo location clicks started sounding off around them as more tribesmen entered the area, searching for them like feral dolphins hunting in the depths. The anticipation of being found was nerve wracking. Then the sound of hyena-like laughter echoed all around them, and Ruth heard a soft thud. Someone had been hit with a club.

CHAPTER 34

A commotion broke out and the mercenaries started yelling. Grunting and thuds were thick in the air and someone fell against her. They pushed off and went back to fighting. She continued whimpering, on the verge of tears, and started crawling on her hands and knees. A heel backed onto her hand and she yelped. Someone fell over backward, tripping over her back.

"Sergeant Bethune! Grodin! Brooks!"

There was no response, but when the figure that had fallen stood and felt for her, stepping over her before returning to the scuffle she assumed it was one of her men. More hyena-laughter echoed through the cavern and the rush of more bare feet could be heard closing in from every direction.

Her hand touched the book of matches and she snagged it from the ground, trying to focus as one of the mercs cried out in agony.

Picture it in your mind, Ruth. Think! How far was the wall from where you dropped the torch? Ruth's mind raced, trying to piece together a mental image of the room. *Did I go left or right after crawling from the wall?*

More thuds and the sound of blades clanking against stone echoed behind her. Grunts and cries were constant, but she crawled forward. In the darkness her sense of smell heightened, and she could barely detect the scent of the burnt jacket. Happy for a disgustingly pungent odor for the first time in her life, she whispered a prayer of gratitude to no particular god and headed toward the aroma.

When her hands touched the torch rifle she felt lightheaded, in disbelief with her good fortune. She fumbled the rifle and the side of it clinked against the ground. She fingered the book of matches until she found the flap. She opened it, took out the last match and struck the tip ablaze. A *Midomo* was in midair with arms outstretched in her direction, and as the match produced a flash of light, time seemed to halt.

The *Midomo* heading for her had his mouth open wide as if he would bite her when he reached her. His teeth were speckled with brown and yellow and his tongue was the same. His fingers were splayed, and his nails were packed with dirt. Even the nail beds appeared brown and dirty.

Through her peripheral vision, she could see the skirmish of the mercenaries and near seven other *Midomo*. Grodin was on the ground with a bruise above his temple and a bloodied lip, but he was conscious. A *Midomo* had both hands wrapped around his throat, forcing his eyes to bulge. Sergeant Bethune's face was bloodied, but he'd sunk his knife into a *Midomo*'s shoulder, where it remained while he and the tribesman struggled with their arms locked together. Brooks still had his knife in his hand, and a *Midomo* lay at his feet, covered in crimson slashes. Another was charging for him and he was bracing himself. A few stalagmites were on the ground around them, and shadows reached for Brooks like the fingers of his attacker.

Time crashed back to movement and the *Midomo* was on her before she could properly react. The match was snuffed out and darkness rejoined them. Her attacker pinned her arms to the ground forcefully, roaring a hot gust of pungent breath into her face. She screamed and he almost instantly covered her mouth with his sordid hand. She fought his grip but he was much stronger and heavier than her, even though he was a full foot shorter. She felt the sting of a palm across her face and her ears rang.

The cold fingers of the tribesman wrapped around her throat, lifting her head off the ground and slamming it back down. Her strength left her, and her arms felt like wet sandbags. They fell limp to her sides. She heard the *Midomo* whoop in satisfaction, but everything sounded muffled, like cotton balls had been rammed into her ears. She limply lifted an arm and felt for the *Midomo*'s face. She moved her fingers up to his eyes and pressed. He reacted and tried to shove her away by shaking his head, but when she persisted he chomped onto the meat between her index finger and thumb.

The fresh pain was like a jolt to her system, and she would have sat up straight if she could have. Her strength returned and she started slapping at his face. She felt her own blood drip against her cheeks and forehead and she wondered how bad the wound was.

A green glow started growing and her eyes widened, clasping onto the little bit of light. It was a distraction for the tribesman, and he looked up. Ruth took advantage of the opportunity. He had mounted her, so a knee to the groin was out of the question, but raising his chin to see the light left his neck exposed. She karate-chopped his Adam's apple and he gagged, clutching his own neck for a change. She shoved him off and scrambled to her feet. A stiff kick to his ribs caused the tribesman to howl and curl up on the ground. He recovered and stood but continued to pay attention to the green as if Ruth was the distraction and the light was the main focus. She wanted to kick him again, but turned to the light as well.

The scuffle had stopped mid-action at the onset of the new glow. The *Midomo* that had just started dragging an unconscious Grodin just stood there, keeping a hold on one leg but staring. Sergeant Bethune was pushed against the wall, but the *Midomo*'s arms had slackened, and they were both looking at the light. Brooks had striped another *Midomo*, leaving the enemy at his feet. A third had started attacking him but they were still a few feet apart.

Brightening further, the glow stretched to every corner of the room, sending skewed shadows reaching in every direction like a mass of black branches. A shout came from the same direction as the glow, and the *Midomo* all ducked, keeping their attention on the light and soon returning to their normal posture. A clanking started echoing off the walls and the tribesmen covered their ears, ducking and retreating to another passage toward the back of the room.

After a few more seconds, the origin of the green light and the clanking manifested in the form of a tiny, glowing green man. He entered the room and, upon seeing that the *Midomo* had fled, dropped the noisemaker at his feet and bent over, taking in gulps of air and holding his knees. The noisemaker was almost the same size as the little man, and Ruth smiled, realizing it was the crudely made one from stones and metal: the same one that the Red Mage had given her on her first visit.

Brooks and Bethune furrowed their brows and gawked at the newcomer, and Ruth folded her arms, keeping the smile on her face.

"Well, this is a pleasant surprise," she said.

The tiny, green man took a deep breath and fully erected himself. He looked around the room, grinning from ear to ear. He kicked the noisemaker and left it on the ground before walking forward.

"That thing is deceptively heavy," he said.

When he was close to Ruth she squatted down and made a platform with her hands. He hopped on. "I'm not counting or anything, but I'm pretty sure you owe me two of your lives. If I make it a hat trick you're totally catching me two snakes and I'm eating them both while you watch. You get none." He paused and snickered. "Every day I watch food slither past, and I feel like a poor man who has been glued to the outside of a window of a restaurant for days." He continued grinning, noticing the stares of the sergeant and Brooks. "Starving, you see."

There was a brief silence before Ruth cleared her throat. "Everyone, this is Vidogo."

CHAPTER 35

Before the pleasantries continued, Bethune knelt down and shook Grodin until he sat up with a start. After reminding Grodin where he was and what had happened, Bethune stood and folded his arms, staring at Ruth and Vidogo.

"How in the blue blazes do you know him?" Sergeant Bethune said.

"Or green blazes," Grodin mumbled under his breath, pushing up from the ground.

Sergeant Bethune's voice was a little rattled but a smile pulled across his face. Every once in a while he glanced at the cavern entrance that the *Midomo* had all fled through, as did Brooks.

"He guided me through this place before. If I had been alone, I would have died." Ruth looked down at him and felt warm. "As he said, he saved my life. Now he has saved it again."

Vidogo stood tall in Ruth's hands—or as tall as a miniature man could stand. He poked out his chest and put his hands on his hips, smiling with his chin up.

"No need for applause, gentlemen," Vidogo said, deflating a little but keeping his chin up. "I'm sure your lives are saved all the time."

"In this dimension, they pretty much are," Sergeant Bethune said with a grim look. "But please, accept our gratitude. There's no telling how many shades of hell we would be in right now if you had taken a few moments longer."

"Pfft," Grodin said, waving the sarge off. "I don't know about you, but I had my *Midomo* right where I wanted him."

Vidogo laughed. "You *were* asleep, after all, so I suppose the fight had been boring you."

"See, he gets it," Grodin said.

"Enough. Can we get on with it?" the sergeant said, his voice hinting how nervous he still was, his eyes telling the same story every time he glanced at the dark opening.

"We should leave before they come back," Ruth said to Vidogo.

"Well that's the fastest way out of this place," Vidogo said, nodding to the dark opening.

"No, no, we do not want to leave the cave completely. We are here for research, and we are yet to complete that. We need to go back across *al Pango Maji* and study the plants and creatures on the island."

"Ah, you're still rowing with only one oar in the water," Vidogo said with a giggle. "Well, if it's potential death and mayhem in the name of science that you seek, it is in fact this a-way."

Vidogo hopped down and started walking, almost marching, back the way he'd come. Bethune glanced at Ruth for a while, using his eyes to ask if Vidogo was trustworthy. Ruth ignored him, grabbed her knife and followed happily after her old friend. The rest of the mercenaries fell into line behind her.

"I thought you were dead," Ruth said after a few minutes of walking. "How did you survive that sea creature?"

Vidogo looked over his shoulder but kept going. "It was the craziest, most difficult, and harrowing experience anyone alive could have ever undergone, but I'm pleased to say that it was picking fruit from a shrub for me—easy, you see."

They made a turn and continued on.

"After I bravely leapt from my glass prison, I sprinted away, which I'm sure you saw."

"Mmhmm, but after that your light faded."

"Well, after that I had to sprint for miles. The beast was hot on my heels the entire time, and if I slowed down a hair it would have gobbled me down in half a gulp. I zigged and zagged through the glow forest and eventually managed to confuse it by hiding among the other glow creatures living there."

"Oh wow, that must have been scary."

"Perhaps for any other, but danger and I are close friends."

Ruth started grinning at the grandiose tale. "Again, I am glad you are alive." Then, after a long pause and a few more turns. "Did you decide to live on the island? So many others like you. It seems like it would be a perfect fit."

"I thought of that, but no, I've made my home in a nook in a random corridor."

"Why? Is that safe?"

"Absolutely. Why else would I do it? Well, it's also because I'm so used to being alone, all the other things would eventually get under my skin. I meant to visit so many times, but this will actually be the first time since I fled from there."

"Getting across the water must have stunk."

"Nah. I have legs and arms akin to Poseidon! Magnificent swimmer, you see. Though, I decided it would be better to make a boat and drift to the other side."

Ruth recalled her own experience and how traumatizing it was. At least he had light to see his way around.

"How did you know we were in trouble anyway?" the sergeant said, walking a little faster and joining Ruth directly behind Vidogo.

"Since much of the cave was inhabited at one point, a number of peepholes were drilled and litter the caverns. Your company made a ruckus, and I looked through one of the holes. I saw an orange glow and grew curious. When I came closer I saw your peril, retrieved the noisemaker—which was a gift left from Ruth, so I suppose you all also owe a life to her—and came rattling back."

"Peepholes? Where? I don't see any."

"You need to know where to look first, before you start looking."

Sergeant Bethune wrinkled his brow and stared at Vidogo as if he would ask for an example of the holes, but he remained quiet and eventually fell back behind Ruth. They changed direction a few more times before turning down another passage that opened into the *al Pango Maji* cavern.

CHAPTER 36

Ruth marveled at the vast open space again, stopping on the rocky beach and staring out over the water stained green from Vidogo's light.

"Do you bring news of outside? I thought of leaving but realized the open world is too big for me to tackle alone," Vidogo said.

"I am afraid we only saw a few things before coming here. I have heard nothing of the Red Mage, or Koñél, but the Gray Lord's fortress was under siege when we were there."

Vidogo grunted. "A move Master Mage has planned for some time. I believe fate is no longer a pawn in the hands of the Lords of Luck. I fear master has put a plan into motion that will unravel us all." Vidogo rubbed his chin. "Which reminds me," Vidogo said, looking up at Ruth with a serious look on his face. "Master Mage is gone."

"Gone?" Ruth said, knitting together her brows. "What do you mean? He was attacking the fortress."

Vidogo shook his head. "The link I was forced into with him, the one that he could use to end my life whenever he so desired, is gone. It's possible he willingly released me, but I've known him a long time and that is unlikely. I believe he has left this side and crossed to yours."

Ruth's heart picked up pace and she felt like someone was sucking all the oxygen away from in front of her face before she could breathe it in.

"How? We had the parts at the fortress. How long has it been since you noticed the link was broken?"

"Hard to say, but I've gone to sleep over thirty times since I've felt the break."

Ruth considered the implications of Vidogo's words. If the Red Mage had already crossed over, he could very well be on his way to destroying their home. How long would it be before he succeeded? Did he lose his memory when he first went over, and how long would it be before he regained it? With no way to communicate there was no way to warn home, assuming there was still a home to warn.

"What happens if he succeeds at his mission? How will we know if he destroys our side?" Ruth said, still finding it hard to catch her breath.

Vidogo shrugged. "As far as I'm aware, it would be the first time someone committed genocide against an entire dimension. It could mean nothing changes, or maybe it'll wipe out everyone in the multi-verse. Only way to know is to wait and see."

"That is comforting," Ruth said, frustrated that Vidogo was less help than she'd hoped.

"Excuse me," the sergeant said, folding his arms. "But if I'm hearing you two correctly, and Mr. Big Bad and Evil is back on home territory, we need to abandon the mission and prepare our defenses."

Ruth thought for a moment. The sergeant was right, but how could they be sure the Red Mage had gone to *their* home?

"Is there anywhere else the Red Mage could have gone?" Ruth asked Vidogo.

"Sure. Anywhere he deemed fit. He was bent on destroying your side, but it's possible he simply took a vacation somewhere else. I'd say he needed one."

"See, greenie's got a point," Grodin said.

The scientific side of Ruth started pushing against her gut and she faltered. "Perhaps, but we're already here, and our mission is vital to our nations continued existence. We should at the very least collect a few samples before heading back to the fortress and leaving. Even if we left, there would be little we could do to stop him if he's already started destroying people."

"So help me," the sergeant started, patting his pockets before pulling out his pack of gum and popping another stick in his mouth. "If home is all smoke and rubble when we get back." The sergeant ended his sentence as if he had more to say but felt it improper to voice so he kept quiet. "How are we getting across this thing, anyways? You know Grodes can't swim."

Ruth sighed and looked around. Swimming was far too dangerous. Movement would attract the sea dragon to the surface.

"Vidogo," Ruth said, kneeling down as she continued. "Do you know if the boat I used to get back over here is still intact?"

"Yes, that way," Vidogo said, pointing.

Ruth sheathed her knife and headed down the rock beach. They walked for fifteen minutes or so before Vidogo's light revealed the leaf boat and Ruth nearly squealed. It was only big enough for one normal-sized person and Vidogo.

"No way," she said, in disbelief that the boat was still there. "I swore I had left it in the water."

"You did, but I took it out. Figured it might have some use one day. Guess I was right," Vidogo said, smiling proudly.

Ruth felt the urge to pet his head as if he were a dog, but she remembered he was a person and the action might offend him.

A brief argument broke out about whether the leaf boat could carry more than one person, but Ruth finally convinced them by citing her experience.

"I will cross over with Vidogo and bring back boats for everyone."

"So we have to wait over here in the dark while you take our only light source," the sergeant said, his voice taking on the nervousness he had at the beginning.

"What other options do we have?"

"We could abandon the mission instead of endangering the three of us and our entire dimension."

Ruth felt a flash of anger but she composed herself before responding.

"It is quite possible that the answer to many of our environmental problems lies hidden on that island. Returning home without at least some samples, when we are so close, could spell disaster for our dimension either way." She grabbed the boat that had been fashioned out of a giant, bendable leaf and eased it into the water.

"Don't even think about it," the sergeant roared, lunging at Ruth to stop her from leaving.

She grabbed Vidogo and jumped onto the boat, nearly capsizing it in the process, but casting off before the sergeant could nab her.

"Just keep quiet and stay still. And whatever you do, stay out of the water."

Sergeant Bethune yelled a number of pseudo-curses and scowled at her. Grodin yelled and threw a rock at her that plunked into the water a few feet short. Brooks remained mute.

Further from the shore, she used a slow, steady stroke to propel them forward. The water burned the cut on her hand a little, and she hoped it didn't get infected. She thought of Abram and of losing her hand, and how romantic it would be for them to have matching prosthetics. The urgency of their mission pulled her back to the present and she kept paddling.

CHAPTER 37

"**J**ust as cold and daunting as I remember," she said, glaring at the dark surface after they could no longer see the shore. "Though I am glad to be dry this time around."

"Dry is better," Vidogo said, sitting with his back pressed against the inside of the bow.

In the silence Ruth thought of all the questions she had the first time she was with Vidogo, and how he was unable to answer them because of the link with the Red Mage. Lacking anything better to do, she decided to ask them again.

"The first time we were in the cave I asked you how you were able to enter but nothing else from this dimension could. You had no answer then, but before you ran from the sea dragon, you said you were from 'Two' and that others had crossed over as well. I had all but forgotten what you had said until now, and my curiosity is through the roof." Ruth lifted an eyebrow before continuing. "I think 'Two' is my dimension, but how is that possible? How did others cross over?"

Vidogo smiled as broadly as she'd ever seen him smile. His face warped into a pleasantry that made Ruth think he'd been dying to tell her since they were first introduced, and now that he was finally able to do so he could barely contain himself.

"That's a topic I've yearned to discuss with you since we first met. I kind of blurted it out before I ran since I figured Master Mage could kill me if he wanted, but I was probably going to get eaten by the sea dragon anyway. I was prepared to die, but I wanted you to know before I did." Vidogo sighed and looked at her with his bright, green eyes. "I need you to understand that if it were possible, I would have told you sooner."

Ruth nodded quickly, the anticipation sending butterflies to flutter in her chest. "I understand completely."

"Okay. Promise you won't get angry or do anything stupid." Vidogo looked at the side of the leaf-boat. "Like get all excited or upset and capsize the boat."

"Yes, I promise," Ruth said. "Just spit it out."

"Okay, okay, geez, calm down." He looked at her with a smirk, intentionally drawing out the words until she started making him shiver with her icy gaze. He held up his hands in surrender. "Sorry, but I couldn't help myself."

Ruth tilted her head to the side and folded her arms, using her body language to say she was still waiting and growing tired of his games. After a few more seconds he finally spilled the beans and she continued paddling.

"Okay, so as you've already deduced, I'm from your dimension." Vidogo leaned forward and nodded slowly.

"Great, but I want to know how this is possible?"

"There's more caught up in this dimension than I'm sure you've been told or have been able to guess. The White Lord has been bringing people here for years. Well, he's stopped now since he's on indefinite hiatus, but before that he was in the business of preparation."

"Preparation?" Ruth said, leaning to the side and rocking the boat a little. Noticing her error, she sat up straight. "For what?"

"Redemption. I don't know how the White Lord has been able to sample visions of the future, but he was convinced that our worlds were in grave danger. He has foretold of a single character with enough power to snuff every breath from every lung of every living thing in every dimension. If this character were to realize and act on their potential, we will all die."

Ruth swallowed, wondering if the Red Mage was that character. "Has this, this evil character been born? Is it the Red Mage?"

Vidogo chuckled. "Yes, or at least we are convinced this character has been born, but she is not an evil entity, simply a powerful one."

Ruth thought to her encounters, and only one woman stood out. She whispered the name as she thought it. "Koñél."

"Exactly! Koñél is this character, and as of now, this character is heading down the wrong path."

"So why are you here? Why was he bringing others over?"

"We were the forerunners: preparers of the way for the saviors. Though Koñél was the most powerful, the White Lord foretold of others that would help guide and mold her into being the savior of all the dimensions. She was brought here before her appointed time, and only some of the forerunners from some of the sides were brought before her. It was apparently not enough."

"But I don't get it. If the White Lord knew Koñél had all this power, why wouldn't he just teach her to do good? Or, if he had to, prevent her from being born."

"Ah, but the White Lord has. He was a wise man, and a good man. He knew that he had no right to eliminate a life simply because it was powerful, so he intended to nurture this life."

"Let me guess. The Red Mage somehow intervened and now she is on his side."

They bumped into the shore of the island and they both jumped. They started drifting back so Ruth paddled until they were flush again. She let him hop out first before she stepped onto the shore and pulled the boat out after her. She set it on the beach and sighed.

"So, am I right?"

They both started walking deeper into the island where the plants with the durable, bendable leaves grew.

"Yes, you are right. It's a long story, but it is one that reveals why the White Lord left and how the Red Mage was able to sway Koñél."

"Can you tell me the story?"

"Another time."

"Well that stinks." They walked for a while in silence until the glow creatures appeared in the distance. "So if Koñél is here, and bad, what hope do we have?"

"Embers of hope will continue to smolder until Koñél has reached her full potential. Until then, it's possible she can be reclaimed from the darkness."

They reached one of the trees that had evolved to grow in the relative darkness of the cave. Vidogo outshone the other glow creatures that flew and moved around them, and Ruth yanked one of the bendable, large leaves free. As she started forming it into the shape of a boat, she realized they could take enough leaves for everyone if she held off on forming the boat and instead folded the leaves small enough to carry with her. They could take them back across and make the boats on the other side. Vidogo agreed to her plan and she pulled down two more leaves, folding all three to the size of laptops and carrying them back to the boat with Vidogo.

Back at the shore, Ruth put their leaves in the boat and placed it in the water, hopping on after Vidogo.

"If Koñél is more powerful than any other living thing, why is she a servant of the Red Mage?"

"Back home, on the Second, I once read the words of an old circus clown—from back when circuses were still legally allowed to keep living animals for their shows. He marveled at how circus elephants, though animals prided for their intelligence, were usually kept in place by constraints that could barely contain a pony. But, memory has power over even the animal kingdom, and elephants were slaves to their memories."

The boat rocked a little more than it did before, and Ruth wondered if the sea dragon was swimming below them. Escaping on land might have been doable, but trying to get away from it while in the water would be impossible.

"The baby elephants were tied to stakes from the time they were old enough to walk," Vidogo said, closing his eyes as if trying to remember the story. "When they were that small, they were unable to break free, no matter how hard they tried. Eventually they gave up. They got bigger and stronger, but the memory of their failure prevented them from trying again, and so they were able to be contained with constraints that were laughably easy for them to break."

"Okay, so the Red Mage trained Koñél from birth?"

Vidogo laughed. "No. I guess I'm bad at analogies, but bear with me. Koñél met the Red Mage before she had any training, and as such she was weak. When she started training she was weaker, and through the years this remained true, so she has stopped trying to be stronger than him, assuming he would always best her if they ever fought. She could very well be stronger than him now, but she continues to serve because her memory tells her she is weak, you see?"

Ruth sighed and grinned. "You could have just said that."

He shrugged and they continued on in silence for a long time.

"But if this life was so powerful, was it worth the risk?" Ruth said, wondering how much longer they would float before reaching the shore.

"Yes, and possibly no. Though he was yet to foresee it, he spoke of balance. For every iota of power in this universe, there is an equal opposite. Koñél's opposite is there, somewhere, and if Koñél is destroyed there will be no one to stop her equal, should said equal turn out to be evil."

"How did the White Lord know the equal wasn't the good, and Koñél was always intended to be bad?"

"Such is the way of existence. No way to know but to experience it."

A few minutes later they bumped into the shore.

"About time you two came back," Sergeant Bethune said, his hands betraying the fear and anger that his voice was able to conceal. "You ever pull a stunt like that again and I'll make sure Brooks put's a bullet through your spine."

"Do you have any idea of what it's like to be in the dark after dealing with those crazy freaks from earlier?" Grodin said, his face wrinkled in unhappiness.

Ruth thought back to her own experience and almost laughed at them. She had been alone, but at least they had each other. Plus, they were armed with knives, while she had nothing but her hands to defend herself. She thought of verbalizing what she had thought but decided it would only hurt their egos and make them angrier.

They unfolded the leaves and fashioned boats out of them that matched her own. They put the crafts in the water and traveled in close proximity, heeding Ruth's warning to paddle slowly so as not to awaken the sea dragon.

CHAPTER 38

At first no one spoke. Only the soft gurgling sound of hands rowing through water kept them company. Ruth was at the center of their four-boat fleet, and Vidogo's light stretched and cast shadows against the water.

Having the only weapon that had fired in this dimension, Brooks had taken care to prevent it from getting wet again. He still clutched his knife in a defensive position. She wondered how his voice sounded and what it was like to have a conversation with him.

"I felt like an arrow with no target when you were gone," Vidogo started, smiling at her. She kept rowing and he continued. "Missed you, you see?"

"I missed you too, Vidogo, but for more than just your light when it was dark and I was afraid." She smiled back and kept rowing. "You never got a chance to meet Abram, my fiancé, but I bet you two would get along." Ruth dropped her voice to a secretive whisper and grinned. "You're funnier than him, but you both are loaded with corny jokes."

Vidogo chuckled. Ruth sighed and pondered her relationship with Abram. She thought about what he still had to tell her and hoped it was something good. In her heart she knew it wasn't, but something bad coming from him just didn't fit. He had changed since his first trip to the Third, and even on this second trip he seemed off, like something was constantly bothering him. Her thoughts drifted to their wedding but the unfinished items on her to-do list started stressing her out so she refocused on the task at hand.

"What were you like?" Ruth said, studying Vidogo's glowing green skin. "Before the Red Mage cursed you."

Vidogo almost laughed and looked away, his face indicating that humor was how he coped with his loss of self. After a quick sigh he turned back to her and displayed a fake smile.

"Well for starters I was a decent height. No giant or anything, but I was who women have in mind when they say they want someone *tall, dark, and handsome.*"

Ruth chuckled and then felt bad, noticing the concealed pain in

Vidogo's eyes. "You said you were one of the forerunners? Abram said everyone told him he was the savior of the dimension. Does that mean you were his forerunner?"

Vidogo shrugged. "It never got explained to me. The White Lord told me my purpose, but never went into detail about who the savior was. Just that when the time came I would fit into my destiny without flaw. When he left, everything got discombobulated. The Red Mage foretold of things, but there were reports of others doing the same." Vidogo frowned. "But in the end none of it really matters if we can't get Koñél back to our side."

"Or find her equal and convince them to be good."

Vidogo huffed a laugh through his nose. "Yeah, good luck to us on that one."

Vidogo's light was blocked a little due to the sides of her leaf boat, but she remembered that they may be visible from below if he went uncovered. She picked him up and he allowed her to place him in her front shirt pocket.

They were quiet again for a while, and Grodin complained to the sergeant about seeing something swimming around in the water. No one else saw it, and the sarge called Grodin a whimpering pansy before they fell silent again. Brooks usually kept his eyes to the blackness in the distance, occasionally dropping his gaze to the water.

"I used to be an artist, you know?"

"Really? What happened?"

Vidogo held up his arms. "This happened. Well, I lost to the Red Mage in a fight and became his captive. He made me this way."

"Oh, sorry. Maybe you will be able to be an artist again since he's gone."

"Na, I don't think it works that way." Vidogo shrugged. "Though, if you can believe it, Master Mage is from the Second as well."

"What!" Ruth's jaw dropped and she felt her pulse quicken. "How? Why does he want to kill us all if he's from there?"

Vidogo chuckled but his face hinted he was angry as well. "We actually came over around the same time. I didn't know him back home, but he's taken a dark turn since we first met. The dark arts have consumed him."

"Wait, then why did he make me come to the cave the first time? That sniveling coward!" Anger and frustration built inside Ruth as she thought of her close encounters in the darkness.

"Well, inhabitants of this dimension were banned, but the White Lord also banned artists. That's why he can't enter but I can. I'm not an artist anymore."

Ruth still fumed, but did so quietly, and the remainder of the voyage was spent in silence.

CHAPTER 39

They reached the other side and Grodin hurried out of his boat, nearly tripping and falling back into the water.

"You need that to go back," Ruth said, pointing to Grodin's boat that still floated.

Grodin mumbled something under his breath but grabbed his leaf boat and tossed it onto the shore. For someone who hated being on the water as much as he did, he was far too nonchalant with his vessel. Ruth placed hers on the shore along with the others.

"What's a random jar doing in this place?" Grodin said, picking up the glass item and turning it over. "Ew, it's filthy."

"Well it is in a cave, genius," Sergeant Bethune said, shaking his head. "Everything's dirty."

"That's actually where I used to live," Vidogo said, again masking his pain with a smile.

"Keep it. May come in handy later," Ruth said, and Grodin shrugged, screwing the lid back on and holding it.

Ruth took Vidogo out her pocket and set him on the ground. She held out her arm for Vidogo to lead the way and he complied. They meandered up the lifeless, rocky beach until grass and vegetation started to coat the ground.

Upon seeing the plant life, the mercenaries showed the same fascination she had on her first visit. They'd had the same assumption she had about cave life being restricted to a select few mammals, amphibians, insects, and bacteria. But when the glow creatures came into view they started chuckling in wonder. The same assortment of butterflies and bats and tadpole-like rodents were present, and she wondered how many species that she was yet to see.

The lily pad creatures were just as lazy as she remembered and she figured they'd make the perfect first specimen. She only had a few tiny cages and test tubes in her pockets, and she pulled out one of the tubes and a cotton swab. She rolled the swab against the lily pad creature's side and it just stared at her, lazily lifting its head in slight curiosity before returning to doing nothing.

"What do you call those things?" Sergeant Bethune said, nodding to the creature she had just swabbed. She sealed the test tube.

She shrugged and pocketed the specimen, asking Grodin for Vidogo's old jar before trying to catch one of the butterflies. "Haven't decided on any names yet. What do you think?" Ruth continued to fail and huffed a frustrated breath out. The creatures had come to her on her first visit, but this time it was as if they knew she meant to catch them.

"For a name?" the sarge said, watching her and smiling at her failure. "Maybe brighticus flyicus."

"Sounds awful," Ruth said with a grin, giving up on a live specimen and settling on gathering dust shed by the glow bats.

"Yeah, well so do most scientific animal names."

She was happy to see that Bethune's anger had subsided. She guessed it was either the calm ride over or the fact that nothing bad happened to them after she had abandoned them.

After gathering half a jar of the dust, she handed it back to Grodin and pulled out a small vial, harvesting more dust until it too was full. Then she took some vegetation samples and drew a few sketches, wishing she had a camera. She debated gathering a soil sample, but before she could decide, she saw a glowworm feeding on one of the plant leaves.

This glow worm was much brighter than the others she had encountered, and as of yet it was the only one separated from a colony. Its body bore a striking similarity to a caterpillar, but the head was crustacean-like. Like a crab, it had a pair of stalked dichoptic eyes, but this creature's eyes glowed brighter than the rest of its body. The stalks were a deep, baby blue, and a navy blue halo surrounded the tips.

"What a cutie," Ruth said to herself, smiling as she pulled out the largest vial she had.

Slowly lowering her hands toward the creature proved successful, and she snagged it in the vial. She secured the lid and held it up. The worm writhed as if in pain for a few seconds. Then, its light simply winked out. Ruth brought her head back on her neck and grinned, surprised to see that the lights were controllable. The creature's body was a dull, cerulean blue when not glowing, and she detected spiracles for oxygen intake on each side along the length of its abdomen and thorax.

A few seconds later the worm's lights came back on and it crawled its way to the top of the vial, studying the enclosure with a pair of slender, furry antennae. A bubble of excitement over studying the creature upon their return welled up in Ruth, and she snagged a handful of leaves, stuffing them into the vial for the worm to eat.

After marveling at the glow ecosystem for a few more minutes, she said it was time to see what they could uncover in the castle. Grodin made more comments about how odd it was to have the creatures in the cave, and how it was even stranger to have a castle that looked exactly like the Walt Disney logo in a cave. Ruth ignored him and they found the entrance. They went inside and started their search

CHAPTER 40

The castle was as familiar and foreboding as Ruth remembered. In Vidogo's light, the vast hall that greeted them danced with their eschewed shadows. Paintings lined the walls, and although details were impossible to distinguish at their distance, she imagined horrid, twisted faces mocking their arrival.

"We hunting for anything in particular?" Sergeant Bethune said, scuffing his foot against the polished stone floor.

"General Alvarez wants to see if any of their old technology could be a potential energy source back home. We're to flag anything of interest for future recon teams, and if something is small enough for us to carry, we're to take it back with us."

The sergeant looked unhappy with the answer, but he remained mute, looking around.

"We need to hurry," Ruth finally said, trying her best to ignore the mercenary's glares. "We can split up, since this place is abandoned." Ruth glanced down at Vidogo. "Right?"

Vidogo shrugged. "Everything that once lived here should be long since gone. Doubt the *Midomo* would risk a swim across *al Pango Maji*."

"Spread out and document anything of interest. Here," Ruth said to Bethune, holding out her spare notepad.

She'd hoped to save it and fill as many of the pages as she could, but now that they planned to leave early, it would go to waste unless someone else used it. She produced her spare pen from her pocket and clicked the end after Bethune took the notepad.

"Please go with Vidogo to where the parts for the crude portal we made during my first visit are located. Catalogue every item you see." She looked at Vidogo as she finished her sentence. "Vidogo can translate the inscriptions. Give each item in the room the best description you can. Draw if necessary."

Bethune snatched the pen and eyed her for a moment in perturbed silence. She turned to the other two mercenaries. She waited until Vidogo's light began to fade as he and Bethune went to accomplish their task.

The light continued to fade and darkness closed in around them as she handed the smaller vial of dust to Brooks. The glow dust she had harvested made for makeshift flashlights, but Vidogo's light was much brighter.

She instructed Brooks to explore as he saw fit. If he saw anything interesting, he was to report to her. She said the same to Grodin, hoping he refrained from complaining about anything since his jar held more dust and was thus brighter than Brooks's. Thankfully, her hope came into fruition and the two moseyed off. They stuck close together at first, their lights two eyes in a sea of darkness. After a few moments, one light disappeared and Ruth assumed they had entered one of the rooms.

The darkness was unsettling, even with her glow caterpillar to keep her company. The vial fit in one hand, and she held it up like she held her cellphone whenever she lost something in the dark and only used the screen for light. The worm was brighter than her phone display, but it paled in comparison to Vidogo's light.

She trekked for a while and her boots clonked against the stone floor, sending hollow echoes. She tried to recall the layout from when Vidogo still illuminated much of it, and she was able to locate the steps that led to the second level. She headed up and continued holding her light, examining the paintings on the walls at first but losing interest after a few moments.

The stairs had a smooth wooden banister and she wondered if it had been carved from the trees growing outside. At the top of the stairs, the banister's post was carved into a replica of the top of the snake staffs wielded by the artists. The craftsmanship was stunning. To recreate the serpents inside the glass, the wood had been carved in such a way so that tiny holes provided a foggy window inside, where the silhouette of a snake could be seen.

"Simply beautiful," Ruth said, holding the worm up and examining the wood from all angles.

She moved around the second level. Paintings and murals beautified the walls. Though she could only see portions of the murals at a time, after seeing the care that went into the post for the banister, she imagined the murals were gorgeous when seen in full light.

Exploring room after room on the floor, she discovered that it was rather ordinary. She found a supplemental set of stairs along the wall toward one end of the second floor.

The third floor was narrow and had nothing but more empty and bland rooms. A final set of stairs was along the back wall of the third floor, and at the top she only found one interesting room.

She stood at the threshold of the room and looked inside. A bad feeling rotted in her gut and she was too afraid to enter, but from where she stood she could tell the room was built into one of the cone spires toward the top of the castle. The spire had windows throughout it. Glow bats fluttered past sporadically, sending rays of light bouncing magnificently around the chamber, making her gasp.

The brief moments of illumination allowed her to see that there were symbols etched into every space of the wall and floor, but she was unsure what they meant or said. At the far wall there was a rack of glass staffs like the ones the artists wielded, but these staffs were empty. She wondered if snakes were yet to be inserted, or if they had been removed.

"This place gives me the creeps," Ruth whispered to her glow caterpillar, still staring into the room.

She thought about grabbing one of the staffs and using it as a weapon, but she listened to her gut and stayed out of the room. She sketched the interior as best as she could, giving careful attention to the variety of symbols.

When she was done she returned to the castle entrance, where Brooks and Grodin were waiting for her in silence. They saw her approaching and Grodin called out before she reached them, waving as if they were in a crowded room and she needed help finding them.

"Anything?" she said as she walked up.

"Nada," Grodin said.

Brooks shook his head and she sighed. She thought about waiting for Bethune to return, but since waiting meant more time for Grodin to talk, she headed in the direction of the parts room, and the two mercenaries followed.

Bethune was about halfway finished when they arrived, and the scowl on his face indicated how much fun he was having.

"I can help," Ruth said, stopping halfway to the back of the room and yelling out the inscription for Vidogo to translate. He did without hesitation.

Vidogo went to stand between Bethune and Ruth. They took turns reading off inscriptions, proceeding slowly through the room. Bethune continued sporting his moue, and Ruth hoped the information they were gathering would somehow be useful to saving their dimension.

CHAPTER 41

"That took all day!" Bethune said, slamming the notepad shut and chucking it back to her after they reached the last item in the back of the room.

"Doubt it," Ruth said, pocketing the two notepads and following the mercenaries out of the room. "Probably only a few hours."

"Long enough for our dimension to be destroyed."

Ruth wanted to respond but felt they would enter a never-ending loop of speculation and likelihoods, so she kept quiet. They marched back to the front of the castle and exited in silence. Ruth had snagged a few of the smaller items that did not seem to have a direct correlation to something on their side, and they lay like lead in her pockets. Both items were light, but they made her feel guilty. What if Bethune was right, and they'd sacrificed the entire dimension for a couple of items and specimens that might prove to be useless?

As they walked toward the rocky beach, Ruth pulled out the items and examined them. The larger of the items was a flat container the size of a traditional mace spray bottle. The inscription called it *Nishati Unga*, which Vidogo said roughly translated into energy powder. Vidogo said to keep it sealed, simply because the container was difficult to close, and the powder inside was virtually priceless. A single grain could power the entire castle, back when it had electricity, for an entire month. This was the exact type of thing the general was hoping to find, though there was no way of knowing whether it would be compatible with things back home.

She shuddered at the idea of the general finding a way to weaponize the powder, though she knew he would try. If it contained the energy Vidogo said it did, finding a way to detonate it would be appealing to the military, though she hoped the use for energy prevailed. It was inert in its natural state, but when paired with water it activated. Vidogo said he had no clue how it worked, just that it did in water. Ruth was excited to study it back home.

The second item was the size of a gumball. It was a light, black sphere with a node on either side. Vidogo said it was another energy device, though instead of fuel it was more like a battery. He lacked knowledge about the chemicals locked within the sphere, but there were a few larger devices inside the room that he said were powered by it. The size of the sphere and the size of the things it powered was like having a watch battery powering a car, and the idea of compact, mobile energy like that was impressive. Again, there was a chance that there would be no way to charge or use the device when they returned, but the potential was present.

"Is that the last adventure we're having?" Bethune said to Ruth when they reached the beach.

"Yes, time to head home and warn them of the impending danger."

"Good. I'm on my last stick of gum and you're stressing me out."

On cue with the end of his sentence, a splash pulled everyone's attention to the water and Ruth's heart dropped. The sea dragon was back with its whip-like tentacles, bearing down on them with a guttural roar.

CHAPTER 42

Attempting to flee from his feelings of guilt and depression, Abram slept as much as he could for the journey. They stopped every so often and he ate whatever the Shaman or the Gray Lord handed to him, but he retreated into his thoughts and remained quiet. Every so often thoughts of Stribling suffering or dying popped into his head. He tried to shake the images, but they plagued his every waking and sleeping thought. Feldman crept into his mind every so often as well, but Stribling took prominence.

The days blended together and Abram lost track of time, but he did notice the land around them grow more mountainous than where the Red Mage took up residence. The Red Mage lived in a mountain range, but from what Abram could tell the range was linear, almost creating a dividing wall across the land. Here, the mountains were everywhere.

The *wam-baika* flew with their usual grace, but every so often they floated above the peaks. At least for those moments Abram was granted serenity and he took in the sights with a smile on his face.

Most of the peaks were crowned in snow and haloed with wispy clouds. The group soared above other, wild *wam-baika*, and every so often one or two would join their company for a few moments, flying and squawking before veering off and heading away.

It was rare to see anything crawling on the peaks, but occasionally one or two *baika* caught his eye, their white wings blending perfectly with the snow until they decided to move.

Below the peaks Abram witnessed whole colonies of *baika* roosting on ledges and clinging to rocks. The Shaman caught him marveling at them and said groups like that were called *makundi*. The creatures migrated but their homes were usually made near or in volcanos. Some of the mountains in this range were likely still active volcanos, but most of the *baika* had probably relocated from elsewhere.

He finally saw the angelic creatures' young, and they looked exactly like smaller versions of the adults except for the wings. Instead of white, stone-like wings, their wings glistened as if wet. They glowed a light blue that would have looked like white had the parents' white wings not been all around to offset the colors. None of the babies were flying, but instead sat around with their wings outstretched.

As they passed *makundi* after *makundi*, he wondered how many similarities the *fleigh* and the *wam-baika* shared.

When the Shaman finally announced their arrival at their destination, Abram was happy to see that it was a *Magnum* village. Instead of being on the ground, this village had been built atop a volcanic crater that now overflowed with life. The crater was miles around, and the village was at the center, offset from the rest of the environment with a large wall created from loosely stacked boulders. The size of the crater made Abram think half the mountain had been blown off in the last eruption.

Winding around the ancient volcano were steps that had been carved out of the rock. There were no guardrails. Every 200 feet or so was a crook that held a smooth, triangular boulder. The boulders were turned so that they rested on one of the points, and from what Abram could tell, they would be used as blockades. If an enemy were to ascend the steps, the triangular rock could be tipped over easily and would land on one of the flat sides, sealing off the steps and preventing easy access. The triangle boulders even had a black coating covering them that Abram assumed was oil or grease to prevent climbing over top.

The path leading to the village was bordered by boulders and the occasional tree, and the ground was flattened from years of use.

The outside rock of the crater was a dark brown with gray streaks throughout. Inside the crater, along the rim, various layers of orange and yellow and black stone could be seen. The lowest ring was all black, as was most of the ground.

Though the ground could be seen clearly in some areas, other spots were shielded with either thick jungle or large puddles of deep blue water. Trees were bursting with large pink flowers that had curled petals and foot-long pistils. Buzzing around many of the flowers were pink, hummingbird-like creatures. The only deviation from hummingbirds back home was that these birds had thin legs that dangled loosely below, wiggling whenever they moved to the next flower.

The *wam-baika* set them down and flapped away, disappearing over the lip of the crater. Abram stared for a while, wondering about the amazing things to explore in the jungle. A few high pitched screeches reported from within the trees and made him think of monkeys.

"Those things alive?" Abram said to the Shaman, pointing to a number of pink vines that were strung between the green trees. The vines moved, but he was unable to see any heads or determine if the vines were moving independently or from a breeze.

"Possibly. I am unfamiliar with most of the life in this crater." The Shaman looked at the jungle briefly before turning back to the gate in the *Magnum* wall. "This place is unique and the peoples relatively reclusive. Their place in history has remained hidden from most."

"How do you know about them?" Abram asked, finally turning from the jungle and facing the gate with him.

"My ability to locate the pure of heart stretches to even here."

Abram shrugged and walked with the Gray Lord and the Shaman as they passed beneath the giant archway.

The absence of *Magnums* was a bit jarring, and it was a while before they encountered their first one. The *Magnum* stooped down until her face was relatively level with his. When the Shaman and the *Magnum* spoke, the Gray Lord was the one to interpret for Abram, and he soon understood why there were so few *Magnums* tromping about. His thoughts of depression and failure returned.

The *Magnum* was a woman, though instead of wearing a covering on her nose, she had a shawl that was almost identical to the pink nose-cloths the Great River *Magnums* had sported from his first visit. She also had a groin and chest covering, though instead of tattered, ripped fabric, hers was tight and tanned-leather-like in appearance.

"He has just informed her that they were unsuccessful. That *we* were unsuccessful," the Gray Lord said, his head hanging as he finished his sentence. "She just asked about Mume. A person of romantic interest to her, I think."

Abram played with his engagement ring. He glared at the two as they talked and felt a lump forming in the back of his throat. The Gray Lord spoke no further about who or what Mume was, but when the *Magnum* woman's face warped in pain and she roared a long, anguished cry, he could tell Mume was someone of importance. At the sound of the cry a few other *Magnums* stomped over, shaking the ground a little with their weight.

The Gray Lord went on to explain that this village was once hundreds thick, and steadily growing. Most of the able-bodied men had left to help vanquish the siege. Abram had just left them all for dead. He turned from the sadness and walked back toward the entrance, unable to bear the guilt and the woman's grief.

CHAPTER 43

Abram passed the threshold and kept going, heading for the jungle. The closer he went, the louder it became. When he entered the trees, the strident blend of buzzes and screeches and bellows was thick in the air.

After passing a few trees he stopped and realized he was out of breath. He had only walked, so fatigue was out of the question, but the guilt pressed against his chest and he was unable to bring in air. He took a number of deep breaths and realized the pressure was in his head. Still, it lingered and he squatted down to sit.

But before touching down with his bottom, he saw the movement of crawling insects and decided to stay standing. He wanted to lean against a tree, but tiny insects crawled against it as well and he sighed. He stared off into the thick vegetation and tried to distract himself with all the sights and aromas.

The whole place smelled like a botanical garden in full bloom. He could see fruit hanging from some of the trees, and the ground was covered with rotting assortments of the same. The sickly sweet smell of the rotting fruit commingled in his nostrils after he saw it. The fragrances were thick enough to taste, and his stomach rumbled.

Movement caught his eye, and he confirmed that the pink vines were indeed snakes. Their heads had been hard to see before because they were stuck to the trunks of the trees. Abram went in for a closer look, allowing his face to get to within a few feet of the side of the creature.

Protruding like the incisors of a saber toothed tiger, the snake's fangs were embedded in the trunk though the mouth was still shut. Perhaps it was a sap sucker. Its body matched the flowers on the trees, and he wondered if the sap was pink as well.

"You feel guilty?"

Abram spun around at the voice. He had been startled, but relaxed when he saw it was the Shaman. The Shaman's pure white stood out brightly against the assortment of other colors, and it soothed Abram a little. He sighed and looked at the ground.

"I understand, but guilt is a great destroyer. Rarely, even when fault is accurate, can this emotion be used constructively."

Abram looked up at him and held his gaze for a few moments before looking back at the ground. For a while they stood in silence, with just the surrounding orchestra of animal and insect sounds.

"What we did was wrong," Abram started, playing with the ring on his finger. "We left all those people to die."

"No. We left in the hopes of saving the world. Our way is grim, and remaining with them would only end in disaster."

"But there were hundreds, if not thousands of people. They were dying, and we had the power to save them!"

"No, or that is what we would have done." The Shaman looked away and his face was drawn down with pain. He rubbed his knuckle a few times before continuing. "If we had tarried then the hundreds that died would be but a grain of sand in the desert of death the Red Mage and his forces would create."

"But I don't get it. I thought he just wanted to cross sides and kill everyone back at my home, to stop the destruction we were bringing down on everyone else."

The Shaman looked humored, but was silent for a minute. "Evil rarely works in the way it claims to. It is a poison. It takes but a single drop to ruin a glass full of purity. Even if the Red Mage currently wants to stop at destroying you, he will not. He cannot. He will continue until we are all undone to chaos."

But Abram couldn't shake the feeling of guilt. He sighed again and watched one of the hummingbirds buzz for a moment near them. It disappeared between two trunks.

"I still think leaving was wrong. Even if it took us a week to beat every last one of those *Ghafarians* into submission, we should have stayed and done it."

This time the Shaman did laugh. "Such brave talk for one who has only now experienced his second battle. Fate chose you to act as savior for that very reason. Your heart is in the right place, even when misguided and on the path to destruction."

Abram huffed a laugh through his nose that was meant to be sarcastic. "Thanks, I guess."

"There will be ceremonial arrangements to mourn the dead of this village at dusk. It would be a great dishonor to neglect attending."

Abram tried to find the sun through the canopy of trees. Though he could see light breaking through the leaves, he was unable to tell how high or low the sun was in the sky. He figured that since they were in a crater, when the sun dipped below the lip it would be close to the time of the funeral.

"Don't you feel even just a little bad, for leaving like we did?" Abram said as the Shaman turned.

"Of course, but I did what I could to save them, and am doing what I can now to continue saving others. I will grieve with the others for the loss, and continue on with our mission. We must keep the embers of hope smoldering within, and guilt only battles to douse those embers."

Abram continued playing with his ring while a nearby sap snake removed its face from the bark. Its movements were sluggish, and it slithered around to the other side before reinserting its fangs.

"Won't these *Magnums* be a little upset that you took the men from the village and let them die?"

"Perhaps, but they see that our actions bear a valuable reason, and they will understand. What is done was done because of the impossibility of any other action."

"Yeah, I guess I'm just beating a dead horse with a stick."

The Shaman looked at him confused, but decided against giving a response. He sauntered off and headed back to the gate, and Abram watched for a moment before turning back to the jungle. Going back into the village and seeing all the grief would only make him feel worse, so he decided to stay in the jungle until the last minute.

He walked a little further into the trees but was careful to keep his exit in sight. Though the Shaman or the Gray Lord would undoubtedly be able to find him if he was lost, it might be after the funeral service and that would be dreadful to explain. It would also make for a good excuse to avoid attending, though.

A tree blocked his path that he at first thought had strange, twitching bark. As he neared he realized the tree was covered from canopy to root with flying insects. The bugs had black bodies, orange blob eyes, translucent wings with orange veins, and orange legs. They were huddled together densely enough that he was unable to see the bark, and he was reminded of pictures of honeybees on honeycomb—though that was the only similarity between the two.

They created a chirping sound that rose and fell in waves as if the insects in the canopy were calling to their respective partners, who then called to their respective partners all the way down the tree and back up again. He stared at the phenomenon for a long time, wondering why this particular tree was cursed with the creatures, and why no other birds or insects went near them.

His imagination went wild and he thought of all the insects leaving the tree and attaching to him. He shuddered and kept his distance in case they did leave the tree. He guessed he'd be able to outrun them.

As he was about to leave, when the light was weakening and fading to blue, all the insects *did* leave the tree and he almost had a heart attack. The sound of hundreds of flapping wings was more frightening than he had anticipated, and his skin crawled. He felt as if the creatures were buzzing right beside his ears and he ducked, trying to flee but keep his eyes on them at the same time.

The swarm remained in a tree-like formation for a while before meshing into an oval of black and orange. Their flight was only temporary, and Abram stopped running when he realized they made no movement toward him. Instead, they went to the next closest tree and latched on, resuming their wave chirp as if nothing new had happened.

Circumspectly, Abram moved back toward them. They continued to ignore him and he focused on the tree they had been on and gasped. The tree had been completely stripped of bark. The leaves were still green for the moment, though he figured the tree would soon die with no outer layer. It was odd seeing the pale brown of the tree's flesh surrounded by the other trees, and Abram felt bad. The flying insects were a swarm of death.

Out of curiosity, he looked around the area and saw that other trees were indeed stripped of their bark as well. Some of the leaves of the trees were already starting to wilt, and Abram was certain that there were others, further in the jungle, that were completely dead.

It seemed as if death was pursuing him, and he turned back to the way he came with his head hung and his shoulders slouched. Even the forest started to make him feel guilty, and he wondered if every tree would succumb to the swarm. It looked like every other living thing avoided them, and he wondered what would become of the sap snakes when a swarm attacked a tree they were attached to.

He shook off the thoughts and continued on until he broke the tree line. The sun was still as high as it was before in the sky, and he realized he'd forgotten the sun didn't set and rise like it did back home, but the moon did. The sun's light was almost drowned out by the blue moon as it toyed with the horizon, and a part of him hoped he would make the ceremony with plenty of time. He hated being the last person to go to anything, and felt like everyone stared and judged that person for arriving after everyone else.

On the other hand, if he was late he could just skip the event and say it would have been rude to come after it had started. Maybe the Shaman would get mad, but at least he would avoid hearing the sobs and cries of anguish from all the remaining *Magnums*.

"Come, Abram, the ceremony will start soon," the Gray Lord said, exiting one of the massive structures and jogging to meet him. He no longer held the parchments from his fortress, and Abram assumed he had sequestered them somewhere safe.

Abram sighed and they walked toward the ceremony together.

CHAPTER 44

The residential structures were similar to the Great River *Magnus* buildings. Large stones had been abraded to form cone shapes and semicircles. Some had windows with no glass, and the pulse of fire could be seen glowing from within many.

They moved through the center of town, and a few *Magnums* periodically stomped past. Abram and the Gray Lord passed all the buildings and entered a clearing that was nestled against the back border wall. Some of the ground in town had grass and other vegetation sprouting up between discarded rocks and stones, but in this clearing there was only the black of aged volcanic rock.

Offsetting all the black were candles that glowed with a thin, pink light. They were situated on the ground beside a circle of rocks that most of the *Magnums* were squatted on with their hands on their knees.

The Gray Lord and Abram found the Shaman, and all three were able to fit on one of the rocks with room to spare. The Shaman had grabbed them both a candle, motioning to it when they sat down but remaining mute. The Gray Lord also said nothing and Abram refrained from asking questions, assuming silence was appropriate.

As the last few *Magnums* came over and sat, Abram realized there was no breeze. The air was as still and dead as a skeleton.

After a few minutes of listening to just the breathing of the thirty or so *Magnums*, a final *Magnum* marched over. Like the others, the last *Magnum* was a woman. She was thicker than the other *Magnums*, and Abram was reminded of King *Magnus*. Abram wondered if they had elected a queen as leader, or if the king had gone to battle and was assumed dead.

A stone had been placed in the middle of the clearing, and a tight circle of candles surrounded it. The queen sat down and raised her arms. The other *Magnums* remained quiet, but sat up straighter or leaned forward.

She began speaking in *Megamu*, and Abram wished he could understand. The Shaman stayed quiet, and Abram wondered if the words would ever be translated.

As the night deepened, the pink color of the candles became more pronounced, casting a beautiful glow around the stone.

When the queen finished her monologue, she stood. The other *Magnums* stood as well, and Abram noticed a few *Magnum* youths. He was unsure of their gender, but they were a few feet shorter than the adults.

Bending over, the queen picked up one of the candles from the circle and removed her shawl covering. The inside was the same pink as the candle and the nose coverings from the Great River *Magnus*.

Holding the candle on its side in one hand, she brought the shawl to it. Instead of freezing the fire like at the Great River *Magnus* ceremony, this fire caught onto the cloth. Abram expected the cloth to burn in silence, but it was loud, crackling like firecrackers.

The queen continued to hold the cloth as it sizzled, and instead of dropping it, she turned her hand over and placed the smoldering cloth in her palm. A few seconds later the cloth was burned out, and a small pile of dust was left behind.

Keeping her palm upright, she squatted down and put the candle in its place. Still keeping the dust in hand, she moved the candles surrounding her chair into a triangle in front of her. When the triangle was complete, she sat back down and divvied the pink dust between each hand. Then, she flung the dust into her face and rubbed it into her eyes.

Abram's face wrinkled in confusion and curiosity as she continued to rub her eyes. When she stopped, she calmly rested her hands on her knees. She cried, and pink tears streamed from her face. The tears streaked and branched across her cheeks and dripped down her chin onto her chest, and she let them.

Seconds passed before the group acted, beginning with the person directly across from the queen. This *Magnum* woman stood, walked with purpose over to the queen, and removed her shawl. She paused once it was off as if remembering someone special, but soon she draped the covering across the middle of the candles and it crackled and popped.

She turned and headed back to her place, and the female beside her went next. They passed each other in the middle. When the new *Magnum* reached the triangle, she laid down her cloth and walked away.

The process started a pink bonfire, and the *Magnums* continued laying down their cloths until it was the trio's turn. The Shaman was on the leftmost side of the rock, so he went first, but with no cloth to lay down he simply paused at the growing fire and headed back. The Gray Lord did the same and Abram went to the fire and stood when it was his time.

He realized heat was all but absent from the fire that now burned up to his waist with a pink flame. Though the heat was mild, the sound of the cloths was boisterous. During his pause he found it fitting to think of someone he'd lost. Though he had lost her long ago, he thought of his mother. There were families that were much closer than his had been, but the bond he shared with his mother grew after his father passed. Since Dad was a cheater, Mom had no love for him in the end, and his abandoning of the family caused Abram to despise the man as well.

As he stood there and thought, the pent up emotions of loss and heartbreak bubbled up and stuck in his throat. He usually felt pain from his mother's absence around Christmas—when his memories of her were the fondest and strongest—but as he stood there he felt it and felt it hard.

When he finally returned to his place, he knew he had taken too long, but the mood around the clearing put him at ease. Though the emotions were still wedged in his throat, he felt a little better and took his seat.

After the entire group had gone, they maintained their silence. The *Magnum* female who had first lit her cloth after the queen stood up again, bearing a long cloth that Abram had failed to notice before. Curious about the origin of the cloth, he looked around and saw that cloths were folded on the ground in front of everyone's stone. They were black on one side and blended in, but on the other side they were an opaque white. The female moved to the queen as deliberately as she had the first time around.

The fire was smoldering now, crackling loudly and popping pink embers in every direction. When the female reached the queen she spread the long cloth and wrapped it around the queen's face. The queen barely moved from the contact. The cloth wrapped around the queen's head once. The female pressed the cloth firmly against the queen, and after a few seconds removed it.

After the cloth was unwrapped, the design of the queen's tears was stained in it. The female took a slow bow and draped the cloth across the queen's back. The imprinted portion was facing out. The queen's eyes were open but still stained pink, as was her face, though the pink on her face was a little smudged and faded after the imprinting.

With the imprinting completed, the queen stooped over and dug into the embers. The large pile of dust had covered and extinguished most of the candles, though a few still burned cloths that crackled. The female that had imprinted her was still standing, and the queen threw dust into the female's face like she had done to herself. The female returned to her place in the clearing with pink streaking down her cheeks.

The process again continued in order and Abram's heart started to pound. Like back in the Great River *Magnus*, he again thought of how the cloths had been used as a body covering. Last time the remnant had gone into his mouth. This time they expected him to put it in his eyes.

His thoughts drifted to his amputated arm and he held up the prostatic, examining it. What if he got an infection from the dust and he lost his eyes? They had ocular prosthetics, but they worked best when one eye was still functional, and the prosthetic was more of a support system.

The Shaman went up, came back with pink eye and face, and the Gray Lord did the same. As the Gray Lord returned, Abram folded his arms and shook his head.

It took him a few seconds to realize the two were unable to see, so he vocalized what he was thinking.

"Nope, I'm not going to rub that junk in my eyes."

"It would be a great dishonor to skip any part of the ritual," the Shaman said. His eyes were open and pink, but he looked off into nothingness.

"Don't talk to me about dishonor. Dishonor is the reason we're here anyway. If we'd done the honorable thing we wouldn't be in this mess."

"Participation is not optional."

"Oh yeah, and what happens if I refuse?"

The Shaman was silent, but Abram felt a tug on his wrist. The *Magnum* that had been seated beside him was in front of him, using two fingers to pull against his arm.

"No, I'm not doing it," Abram said, trying to sound as polite as possible. "You can skip me."

The *Magnum* either did not understand or did not care, but she pulled him up until he was standing. When he made no motion toward the queen she dragged him along. He protested at first, demanding she release him, but the longer she ignored him the sillier he felt.

She used her index finger to push his head down, and before he could object he felt the thick, hard finger of the queen pushing into his face. It hurt, and Abram yelped in opposition, but she rubbed for a few seconds and he was released.

He turned and the world was a pink haze. The pink candles in the distance were distorted lines and the figures of the rocks and *Magnums* were dark blobs. The backdrop of the village was more pronounced, but he still felt lost.

He was grateful that the only pain came from having a large finger rubbed across his face, but thoughts of infection and blindness still reeled through his mind.

A gentle shove pushed him forward and he stumbled as straight as he could, hoping he was heading in the right direction. If he was going the wrong way, there was little he could do to correct it.

He stubbed his toe against the rock that the Gray Lord and Shaman sat on, but he patted the empty place to make sure it was still empty before sinking onto it and folding his arms.

During the walk back he had felt dazed, but as he sat on the rock the world seemed to sharpen. The pink lines meshed together and overlapped into a bright pink blanket, and he relaxed. He relaxed until images of his mother came into focus.

The pink dust must have acted as a grief amplifier, and he felt the lodged emotions spread from his throat throughout his whole body. His eyes had been leaking from the irritation of the dust in them, but now they started to well with sadness and he felt his heart sink. His face wrinkled and he wanted to sob, but did his best to hold it together. Whispers of things his mom used to say tickled his ears and added to the depression.

Icy, sharp sadness surrounded him and filled every crevice of his being. The tears continued to flow freely, and he hiccupped a few times. The urge to wipe his face was ever present, but his hands weren't clean and adding more germs was the last thing he wanted to do.

He felt the pressure of the cloth wrap around his face and at first he objected, knowing the fabric had been on the ground before being placed onto his face, but before he could produce a sound of protest, a soothing warmth soaked in. The warmth spread and melted all feelings of depression, and all the memories of his mother warped to happy ones. He heard her laughter and smiled, hugging himself before the pressure and warmth of the cloth was released.

With the cloth down, Abram could see again, though a pink tint overlaid his vision. Before he could see the imprint of the cloth he felt it across his back and he wondered if the placement was meant to symbolize keeping all the grief and pain behind him. He thought again of how the experience had been forced upon him, and though he felt a little salty about it, the splendor of the experience eased his mind.

The ceremony concluded after every eye was pink. The same silence stuck to every lip. Even as they stood and started to leave the clearing—abandoning the candles to burn out on their own—no one said a word.

As they headed back toward the village, a number of *Magnums* went before the Gray Lord, the Shaman, and Abram. The variety of patterns displayed on the cloths were beautifully unique. Since the trio of non-*Magnums* were smaller, their cloths dragged the ground like capes, and the Gray Lord's gray robe was concealed.

The group trudged back into town and split off toward their respective dwellings. Abram followed the Shaman, even after the Gray Lord walked away by himself. The Shaman was staying on the floor of one of the residential dwellings. The emptied-out boulder was a single room home with little more than a stone bed.

Grass and leaves had been piled together on the ground to form a thin mattress for the Shaman and him, and Abram sighed.

He removed the cloth from his back and held it up so he could see. The strip of fabric was too wide for him to hold taut at full length with both hands. The perimeter had a mild adhesive that allowed it to stay in place on his back. The ends dangled over his hands but he was able to get a clear view of the imprint. His looked like a pink tree that was dipping into a pink stream and he smiled.

Miss you, ma, he thought, rolling up the fabric and placing it on the ground as a pillow. With thoughts of his last Christmas with his mother he closed his eyes and went to sleep.

CHAPTER 45

"Come," said the Shaman, using a nudge to aid his words in rousing Abram. "We must attend to the matter of your training."

Abram was still groggy, but the words clicked and he blinked. He had almost forgotten how long it had been since he bathed, raising his hand to just in front of his eye before pausing and frowning. He felt like his entire body was covered in a layer of grime, and even if he used some of the sanitizer in his pocket he would still be rubbing dirt—if dirt was still called dirt after it has been cleaned—in his eye.

He sat up and kept blinking until the blur was gone.

"About time. I've been itching to learn since I first saw Koñél use the dust to dissolve my chains way back when."

The Shaman remained mute but moved to the front opening. He had used his cloth as a pillow through the night as well, but now it was discarded by the door.

The *Magnum* whose floor they had borrowed was still slumbering loudly. She was sprawled out on her stone mattress with no covering and no pillow. She was still as a statue, and were it not for the loud breathing he would have thought she were made of rock.

The *Magnum* wasn't snoring, but she breathed deep and loud. Abram had no clue how he had slept through the ruckus, but shrugged it off and assumed he had just been exhausted.

As Abram's senses came into focus he detected a subtle musk that reminded him of a locker room. He folded the cloth with his imprint and hoped he would one day return to claim it. Though it had been a traumatic experience, he still felt a warmth in his soul from the good memories of his mother.

Folding the cloth with care, he held it in his hands and thought of his mother for a while longer before leaving it on the floor where he'd slept. He touched it and sighed before finally standing.

Once on his feet, Abram followed the Shaman as he exited the structure and headed toward the front of the village. Abram looked around to see if the Gray Lord was heading out as well, but all was quiet in the village.

They made it to the front of the village and passed the threshold. The Shaman started whispering something into the air that echoed after his lips were still.

"Where's the Gray Lord?" Abram said, glancing back at the village but still seeing no one.

The sun was already shining with no blue in sight, but the jungle was just beginning to come to life. Colorful birds flapped from one tree top to another in flocks of four or five. Chirps and screeches grew louder, as if every animal in the jungle could sense them nearing and was demanding that they turn back and reenter the village.

"His presence is unnecessary. You will only train with me. He shall do what he wishes."

Abram shrugged as the Shaman's voice continued to grow louder, yet more distant. As he listened to the background chorus of the jungle, he thought of the strange swarm that had killed the tree the day before.

"Do you know anything about a swarm of bugs that eat trees? Yesterday in the jungle I saw some that pretty much devoured a whole tree before moving on."

"Perhaps. I only know of one species that fits that description: the *misimu dudu*. This creature devours tree bark."

"Yeah, that's the one then. I forgot they only ate the bark. Stripped the poor tree of its clothing and left it naked and vulnerable."

"Not all things are as they appear at first glance. The *misimu dudu* does not kill a tree, but instead strips it of its old bark to allow rebirth."

"Rebirth, ha," Abram said as two *wam-baika* appeared over the lip of the crater in the distance and flapped toward them.

"Yes. The saliva of the creature forces the trees to go dormant, and during the dormancy their vitality is renewed. The trees only appear to be left defenseless. *Misimu dudu* leave behind a bitter saliva, and it repels other lifeforms, which allows the trees to remain alive. Their leaves will wilt and their fruit will fall but their roots will remain grounded. They will thrive again when the time is right."

"Still a little crazy in my book," Abram said, thinking back to how dead the trees looked. "Though, these bugs seem to do something similar to seasons back on my side. In fact, we could probably use them because our seasons are starting to vanish. Pretty much all we have now is scorching summers and hot winters. At least where I live."

The *wam-baika* alighted and plucked them up into the sky. It was odd to leave again, and Abram was reminded of how they'd left the Gray fortress. He sighed and tried to shove the thoughts from his mind. What was done was done, and now he needed to focus on the future. He had to save Koñél, defeat the Red Mage, and save the world.

They put some distance between them and the crater and Abram's thoughts drifted to Koñél. Where in the world was she now, and why was she in hiding? If she was the sword that Zanda had mentioned, how long would it be before she came swinging down to strike them and the hopes of the aggregate worlds? And why had the Red Mage stayed in hiding when Zanda had confronted them? As good as Red was at foreseeing things, he should have known the ally would lose.

Mountains and valleys passed beneath Abram and the Shaman, and Abram thought of Ruth. He almost felt guilty for thinking of her hours after he had thought of Koñél, but he was still confused. Even if he and Koñél remained a non-item, he questioned if he should keep things going with Ruth. In the end, he knew it wasn't right to string her along, and he still needed to tell her about how he felt for Koñél. Even if it turned out to be nothing, she deserved to know the truth.

He resolved to tell his fiancé that he had kissed another woman before he remembered he was engaged, but also that he was in love with this same woman. It was possible that the kiss had forced Koñél to replace Ruth in his heart. Potential outcomes flashed through his head.

Finding the right time to tell her was proving problematic, and whenever they reunited again, the mercenaries would undoubtedly be nearby. Still, he felt waiting the remainder of the month until their return home seemed too far in the future.

And how was the group doing in the cave? If their experience was anything like her first, they were in trouble and the thought worried Abram. Though he loved Koñél, he still cared for Ruth like a best friend.

They flew on through the day and landed once near a small river that Abram was more than happy to jump into. He stripped off his clothes first so he didn't have to worry about them drying off, but once he was in the buff he hopped in and grabbed the cleanest stone he could find, rubbing the rock around on his body like a bar of soap.

The water was less than crystal clear, but it was good to get wet. Still, when he exited the river he used half his bottle of sanitizer on his skin, hoping to kill any lingering bacteria. The Shaman laughed at him and said he was the first sentient he had seen to use a rock as a cleanser, but Abram ignored him.

Since the water was quick flowing, they dubbed it safe to drink and had their fill. The river ran down from the mountain but very few trees were in the area. The Shaman journeyed to a couple but reported back that there was no fruit growing.

They tried standing in the water and catching fish, but none swam by and they gave up after an hour without seeing so much as an insect. Abram tried to persuade the Shaman to sprinkle some powder into the river and whisper a fish death utterance, but the Shaman refused and said they could survive for a while longer before they decided to kill every fish in a river just to eat one or two.

So they were hungry. The *wam-baika* picked them up again and flew them off under the Shaman's guidance. Abram repressed more depressive thoughts of Stribling and the others, allowing fantasies of Koñél to spice up the otherwise boring journey.

CHAPTER 46

They landed again in the middle of the night and Abram woke up with a start. The *wam-baika* had just set him down on his feet when he opened his eyes, and he woke up as he was falling. He caught himself from landing too hard, but still plopped onto the rocky ground.

"Maybe a few squawks to wake me up next time, guys," Abram said as the *wam-baika* set down again a few feet away.

The one that had been carrying him screeched and he shook his head. He had no injuries so he stood up and looked around.

Mountains could still be seen in the distance, though they were shrouded in a blue fog and barely discernible. A few bushes and short trees dotted the area around them. None of the vegetation was straight. Branches and trunks zigged and zagged at a variety of angles, and short circular leaves went in every direction. The ground was plates of rock, though some soil could be seen between cracks in the surface.

A relatively narrow canyon cut through the ground to his right, and he peered across to the other side. More of the same vegetation and rocks could be seen. He could probably jump across the ravine if he got a running start, though the canyon widened going in either direction.

Rapt with thoughts of attempting to jump across the canyon but falling, Abram neglected to see a giant body that lay sprawled along the precipice. When he noticed it, he took a step back, and his jaw hung open.

"What the—what is that?" Abram said, taking another step back and gawking at the body.

The Shaman had been walking toward a small hut but stopped and turned, glancing at the body before making eye contact with Abram.

"One of my biggest regrets."

The creature had translucent skin that made it appear fragile. Its head was ovular, though instead of eyes it had two furry nobs that could have been shut eyelids. The head led to a long neck that was at least ten feet. The neck was connected to a slender torso that was barely two feet around, but seven spindly arms sprouted from it and hung limp to the side. One dangled over the canyon's cliff out of sight. Though the arms were at least fifty feet each, the torso was longer and stretched beyond where he could see.

"Is it alive?" Abram said, dropping his voice to a whisper and thinking of all the horrible things the behemoth could do to him if it chose.

The Shaman hung his head and swallowed hard before responding. "No."

"Where are we by the way?"

"The dwelling I consider home."

"Okay, great, welcome home and all. I'm sure there's a perfectly sane reason why you keep the corpse of a monster on your porch, but can you please get rid of it? Maybe whisper and have it fall into the canyon or something."

"No. It is an intentional reminder of an atrocity."

"Great, but it's also prime real estate for a butt-ton of bacteria." Abram sniffed the air for a second. "It may not stink, but if it didn't just die then it's got to be rotting."

The Shaman walked over to a portion of the monster and squatted down. If they had been anywhere aside from the head, Abram would have been unable to tell the body once belonged to a living entity. The arms and torso would just appear to be odd vines.

The Shaman sighed and dropped to the ground in front of the corpse, rubbing his knuckle and glaring at it. Abram walked over with his face wrinkled in confusion.

"Unfortunately, decomposition is not a part of this creature's destiny."

"It was alive, and now it's dead. Whether it decomposes fast or slow, it's going to harbor the types of things that like death. That means they're all over the place. What if they decide to hop on over to your hut and make themselves at home?" Abram glanced at his arm. "You're going to end up like me—matter fact, we're both going to end up without *any* body parts if you keep this thing displayed like it's a trophy. All it takes is a scratch."

The Shaman scoffed. "Trophy? Nay, Outsider, it is my greatest affliction."

Abram thought about joining the Shaman on the ground but opted to stand.

"Affliction? What happened? What is this thing?"

The Shaman stood and walked around the head. Abram followed, but they soon moved to the precipice. They looked over for a few seconds in silence, save for the occasional *wam-baika* squawk.

"Long ago, following my transition from apprenticeship to mastery, I experienced my first altercation in this valley, very near here." The Shaman pointed as if he could see through the fog that veiled the bottom of the canyon. "Because I was new, I was wild, uncontrolled, raw."

"Hard to imagine a you that wasn't in complete control," Abram said, watching the shifting fog below. He could see a black substance leaking from the behemoth and down the canyon wall. It coated the whole surface like an oil blanket.

"Yes, my life's expedition is much further along now. But, at that time, I saw only two things: an enemy that needed defeated, and a simple way to defeat it. I acted, whispering an utterance that obliterated the entire valley of opposition, blasting them with so swift a force that their bodies are still embedded in the wall below. But I neglected to take mind of innocents. My vision saw only my enemy and how to end them."

Abram tried to picture the Shaman, blasting a whole army back and into the walls by whispering a single word. The Shaman sighed loudly before he continued, taking some time to look at the creature again.

"My negligence led to this innocent's death," the Shaman said, nodding to the giant corpse. "An innocent so rare that sightings of them are often thought to be hallucinations. I murdered a *Maisha Moa*, and it may very well have been the last of its kind."

"But it was an accident. It's not like you knew it was up here, right?"

"Accidental or purposeful, intention matters little for the victim."

Abram glared at the corpse. He wanted to contradict the Shaman again but thought of his own feelings toward much of what had happened to him. If their roles had been switched, Abram would undoubtedly have felt the same way as the Shaman.

"I'm sorry."

"As am I. The body never decomposes, and the scavengers never eat it. It will be a testimony to my recklessness even after I have transitioned from this life into the next."

They sat in silence for a long time, just peering over the edge and glancing at the corpse. Abram tried to imagine what the beast looked like alive. It was so scrawny and gangly and tall, it would have been unique to behold.

"Many say this creature was able to grant life to the lifeless. Even more believe the *Magnum* race, the *wam-baika*, the *fleigh*, and the *ma-laika* were created from boulders that were graced with the touch of a *Maisha Moa*."

Abram remained mute, but his heart ached for his friend. It was a wound the Shaman refused to let heal, and though Abram somewhat understood, he wished he could do something to help.

After more time, Abram finally said, "So how did you know you killed it? Since it never fell down into the valley, and you were down there, what made you come up here?"

"As I relished the totality of my victory, the blue plasma of this creature's life force cascaded down the canyon like a vile curtain. Curious, I traveled up and found it here. Its life force has since turned black."

Again they were quiet for a long time, gazing down into the shifting fog tinted blue by the moon. Finally, the Shaman turned and headed toward his dwelling and Abram followed. The *wam-baika* were huddled together nearby, sleeping soundly.

The Shaman's home was a meager mud hut about the size and shape of a shipping crate. The entrance was shielded with a boulder and the Shaman whispered into the air. A few seconds later the boulder slid back a foot and he squeezed inside.

Abram stuck to his heels. Inside was pitch black, save for a sliver of blue that was let in by the opening. The Shaman moved into the darkness but Abram stayed put, fearful of tripping over something.

A dim light flickered in the corner as the Shaman lit a candle. Abram had suspected the Shaman lived on very little, but even that was an understatement. A cloth bed was on the rock ground in the corner near the light. At the head of the bed was a sack that leaked browning leaves, and Abram assumed it was a pillow. Across from the bed was a chest with a flat top, and atop the chest were a trio of tomes.

The ancient books had glossy finishes that had been dulled by time, but in the light they still glistened with a mild luster.

"So why did we come to your home? What are we learning here?"

"I will review the history of the utterances."

A smirk slid across Abram's face and he thought of all the crazy things he would learn to do by just whispering. He walked over to the books and reached out, but the Shaman snagged his hand, quick as a cobra strike.

"In the morning. Now we will rest."

Abram looked around. There was just the one bed, and the Shaman was already moving to get onto it.

"Why do I feel like my sleeping arrangements keep getting worse? Don't you people find mattresses to be comfortable?"

"Comfort is a poison that saps the strong of their potency. Learn to overcome discomfort or suffer a slow death."

Abram almost laughed but held it in, grinning instead. He thought of responding about how comfort, at least when relating to sleep, could only lead to more strength in the morning. It was tough to be strong when fatigue was around. Though, Abram thought, perhaps that's what the Shaman meant.

"Why did you pick this place to call home?" Abram said, trying to distract himself as he sat on the hard floor. He leaned against the wall and did his best to ignore how dirty it probably was.

"We are near the Mubaya mountain range, where the Red Mage's lair is, or was. I settled here hoping to spot him at random, but the opportunity never arose until you arrived in this dimension."

"And you kicked his butt!"

The Shaman rubbed his knuckle again. "I remember the event disparately, but a victory is a victory."

Abram glanced at the opening. "Will we be safe?"

"Yes. The predators native to this area mainly stick to the canyon, and the others are either too large to enter or too small to wish to attack us."

"I'll take your word for it, but if I wake up missing a toe or two, I'm burning this place to the ground and kicking you with my nubs."

They both laughed and Abram was pleased to hear the Shaman in better spirits. After all the depression Abram had harbored through the past few days, he needed the Shaman to help balance things for him.

He closed his eyes. After a while the Shaman snuffed out the candle, and the place was cast in darkness. The wind snuck through the slit at the front and whistled every so often. Abram thought the sound was an animal, and he kept waking up, but eventually fell asleep with thoughts of his own transition from apprenticeship into mastery of the arts.

CHAPTER 47

The sound of the *wam-baika* awoke Abram from a night's sleep that had been riddled with interruptions and bad dreams. He sat up exhausted and yearning for a comfortable mattress.

Already awake and seemingly full of energy, the Shaman greeted Abram with a pleasant grin. Abram was excited to see his good mood still lingering in the morning.

"So what's first? Can you teach me that 'rewound' curse you used to save me in our first battle together?" Abram said, swallowing his pill and envisioning the fate of that *Ghafarian*.

The Shaman replied with a polite smile before speaking: "No, I apologize, but learning the utterances is only possible through the *Infernites*, in *Volcanu*."

Abram's spirits drooped a little, but he stretched and looked at the tomes atop the chest. Their dull glamour had vanished in the natural light, but there was something uncanny about them. He stepped toward them and could almost hear his name being whispered. The room seemed to squeeze down to nothing but he and the texts, and he longed to open them.

"I will, however, distill the importance and danger of your impending journey," the Shaman said, snapping Abram from the trance he'd slipped into. "The arts bear the burden of a history punctuated with disaster and foolish decisions."

The two made eye contact, and Abram could see that the Shaman still harbored guilt about his own foolish choices.

"How long have you been an artist?" Abram asked, hoping he didn't reopen more old wounds.

"Longer than the years I have counted."

"You know—and don't take this the wrong way or anything—but I've been meaning to ask you. You seem so, well, so good at what you do. I imagine you've been doing it for," Abram started, struggling with finding the right words to avoid offense. "For longer than you can remember, like you said. The Red Mage probably has been too, but he seemed on a different level, like he knew he was in the major leagues and you were still playing tee ball." The Shaman's response was more confused looks. "Sorry, it's another reference to something back home. A sport, one that has been around forever." Abram sighed. "What I'm trying to say is how come the Red Mage was able to beat you so easily? Shouldn't all of your experience have helped you?"

Hearing the words out loud sounded harsh, and Abram wanted to take them back, but the Shaman's face remained neutral.

"It is impossible to accurately judge one's skill against another's until a challenge arises." The Shaman rubbed his knuckle as he continued. "Experience only aids when dealing with similarities. One can breathe on dry land until experience grays hair and brittles bone, but submerge this same person in water and all their experience will be for naught. For experience to aid in a challenge, the challenge must tie into the experience."

"But he's an artist, like you. Isn't that similar enough?"

"Ah, but that is the greatest factor of all. An artist's creativity only knows the bounds of his imagination. Only dueling with the Red Mage would properly prepare me for a dual with the Red Mage."

"Maybe, but I feel like he got into your head."

"Enough. My time with him has elapsed for a period. Until it comes again, we shall focus on you."

The Shaman led Abram outside. The sun was bright but mild, and a steady east breeze cooled the area. The trees scattered around them barely rustled, but the *baika* played together, nipping and jumping atop each other.

Heading back to the edge of the canyon, Abram saw that the fog had cleared. He tried to avoid looking at the massive corpse on the precipice, but it was too glaringly obvious to avoid. It looked as it did the day before, but the black life force paradoxically appeared darker in the sunlight.

"It is every artist's duty to only practice against other artists, or against those that stand to destroy the lives of innocents."

"Got it, so no casting spells on people that cut me off in traffic."

The Shaman ignored Abram and continued.

"Artistry dates back centuries. Long before the White Lord and long before any of the ancients were born. The mages and lords of old were a curious force, and it is difficult to say if they were good or evil. In more sensible terms, they just were. They did what they thought was best, and the morals we have today have stemmed from their varying viewpoints."

Abram looked down the canyon. The walls dropped down for hundreds of feet, and long pools of green water splashed variety into the miles of orange-brown rock.

"So if those guys just were, but they never really said what's good and what's bad, how do we know we're fighting for the right side?" Abram said, following two small birds that drifted through the air below.

"Simply put: life. Reckless destruction of life, when taken to its finality, would mean the end of existence everywhere. Because I am living, I believe the preservation of all things living is good, and its opposite bad."

Abram shrugged. "Fair enough. I'm all for living, so you've sold me."

"There are ancient texts that dictate laws and good and similar things, and the same is true for evil, but I stick to simplicity. Your path is your choice. I can only bestow you with what I think is best and allow you to decide for yourself."

They were quiet for some time before Abram felt it right to speak again.

"So what's with those big books sitting on your chest? What are they for? Why didn't you want me to touch them?"

"They are sacred. When your time has arrived, they will speak to you and tell you what to say."

Abram thought back to the whispers and smiled. "I heard them, they were calling me back in there!"

"As I have foreseen, your time is primed. You have only to endure the trials."

The sound of that sent a chill through Abram and he gulped. "What exactly am I going to have to do? I'm not the best talker, though I do it too much sometimes. I feel like having a trial for learning the utterances, since they're a form of talking, would be bad."

"The trials are decided in *Volcanu*. No one can foresee the decision, even the artists. It is the way it has always been, and the way it will always be."

"Great, I can't wait," Abram said, rolling his eyes and taking a final look down the canyon. "Can we go? Not to rush you or anything, but I'm getting kind of anxious."

The Shaman remained mute but turned from the canyon and headed back to his dwelling. Abram jogged after him and watched as the artist carefully wrapped two of the books in a cloth that had handles. The cloth was the same fabric as the powder sacks, and the Shaman tied the books to his waistband. They were snug but still bounced a tad as he moved.

After the two books were secure, he gingerly moved the third book to the ground before opening the chest. Blue and green light shone from within, bathing the Shaman's face and causing his eyes to sparkle like gemstones. He reached inside and did something with his hands, soon pulling two bags of powder out and affixing them alongside a solitary powder bag that was already on his hip.

Having everything else in place, the Shaman closed the chest and placed the book back. The front cover had a symbol etched into it that made Abram's skin crawl. He was unsure why, but something about the symbol said evil. It was very much like the letter S, though the bends were sharpened and triangular. Each point seemed to angle back toward the middle, and if they were any longer it would create the infinity symbol.

"What's that book?" Abram said, spinning the ring on this finger.

"*Harumu Nakala*. The forbidden text."

Abram shot the Shaman a look. "Then why do you have it? Shouldn't you only have good things?"

"Perhaps. There are only two *Harumu Nakala* known to still tarry in this dimension, and the Red Mage possesses the other. I intend to keep both sequestered and safe after I retrieve it from his hand."

"What's forbidden about them? What do they say?"

"They illustrate evil in written form."

"Not as descriptive as I'd hoped for, but I assume you don't exactly peruse through it for light reading."

"You must never read from it. You must never approach it with an open heart."

Abram brought his hand to his chest and mimed locking a door and throwing away the key. "Heart closed and locked."

The Shaman seemed satisfied with this, and they headed for the exit. Abram turned back. Though he had no intention of reading it with an open heart, he wondered what would happen if he did read just a few pages. What would it teach?

Once they were outside, the Shaman whispered and the stone sealed the opening. Abram questioned how safe the dwelling really was, even with the stone in front of it. It was only crafted from mud, after all, so all it would take was a few strong hits to the side and a person could break right in without having to move the stone. He shrugged off the notion. It was possible the Shaman protected the hovel by other means, and so far it had worked.

The pair walked over to the *wam-baika* and the *baika* instantly hopped into the air, grabbed them by the arms, and flapped until they were soaring among the clouds.

The Shaman's words drifted back into his head and he wondered what trials he would encounter. He'd found success so far in the things he'd tried, and he looked at his arm. At least if they tested his physical strength he'd pass with all the flying colors imaginable.

When the moon reached its peak height, Abram glanced over his shoulder in its brilliance. He could barely see the *Mubaya* mountain range in the distance, and he pondered where the Red Mage was. It was odd to him that their nemesis had been all but silent.

CHAPTER 48

The sea dragon huffed a gust of air and water from its mouth as it neared them. Its lips were pulled back like an open flower and its mouth dripped with water and saliva.

"I see your friend is back for another round," Sergeant Bethune said, chewing his gum vigorously enough to hear.

Bracing themselves for an attack from the creature, the mercenaries raised their weapons and tensed their muscles. The pulsing semicircular membrane was pumping faster than she remembered it beating before, and the whiskers wriggling from its neck seemed longer as well. Even the fins seemed more powerful, more able to overtake them if they ran.

"I'm not trying to say you all are a few pawns short of a chess set—stupid, you see—but standing around while that thing gets closer seems like a bad idea," Vidogo said, taking a step back that drew the attention of the beast.

"Is there a chance it will back off? I'd rather conserve ammo if we can," Bethune said, still looking at the creature but talking to Ruth. She shrugged.

"I say you act as bait again, while we escape. You were living in here fine enough before we showed up," Grodin said, holding up his combat knife.

"Whoa, now, just hold on a minute," Vidogo said, holding up his hands but keeping his eyes on the creature. "There's no way I'm staying behind again. I want out of this cave and you bunch are my ticket."

"Plus, we need his light," Ruth said.

"Exactly! Though I hope that's not all you think I'm good for. I'm a pretty stellar human being in general too."

As the whiskers wriggled and neared his bright light, they paused, and the creature's head pulled back a little on its neck. The guttural growl it was producing lowered to little more than a purr.

Without further warning the sea beast exploded forward, the whiskers reaching and the mouth unrolling to form a slender snout. The tail had been splashing in the water, but it exploded upward and snapped forward, poising above the creature in the air.

In its fervor the beast ignored the others and knocked them over. Ruth landed hard on her backside and felt a jolting pain shoot up her spine. She cried out in agony. Bethune was crushed as the creature waddled over him. Grodin was knocked down but landed on his side, and Brooks was the only one to dodge, whipping his rifle around and firing into the creature's side. The bullet disappeared into the creature's flesh, but the wound leaked no blood as if the creature was made of jelly

Vidogo broke into a sprint as if he'd been expecting the attack, and his light began to fade, drawing the creature after it. Brooks dropped to one knee and glared down the scope, keeping the weapon trained on the back of the beast's head.

Just as the light winked out, Brooks fired and the area flashed as the round discharged. The cave echoed the gunshot back a few times and Ruth's ears rang a little from the noise. Then all fell quiet. The sound of the disturbed water lapping against the rock beach was in the background, and Ruth held her breath, trying to see if she could detect any distant roars or grunts from the sea creature.

"This is giving me the creeps, guys. I feel like its standing right in front of me with its mouth open," Grodin said, his voice quailing.

"Quiet!" Ruth said, her voice a loud whisper, and she went back to straining to hear.

"I can't, man. Freaking Brooks! Why did you take so long to shoot? You couldn't have just fired when there was still plenty of light?"

Ruth decided to ignore him and hope he lost interest in speaking. She was wrong, and he continued to complain until the green glow of Vidogo started to lighten the area. She smiled. When he was back in front of them he was smirking.

"I'm pretty sure I ran so fast the creature couldn't handle it and his head exploded."

Ruth laughed and the others chuckled, nervously looking around.

"Did you see it? Are you sure it's dead and not coming back?"

"I was moving too fast to see," Vidogo said, shrugging.

Sergeant Bethune walked up to Brooks and grabbed him on the shoulder. "Did you hit it? Is it dead?"

Brooks nodded, tapping his scope lightly before slinging the gun over his shoulder.

"If Brooks says it's done, it's done. Let's get out of here before it does something freaky and comes back to life." Sergeant Bethune spit his gum on the ground and started limping toward the water.

"Rude!" Vidogo said, stepping over the glob. "You know there are people down here? And don't forget there's a whole community of glow things back there. Could you please be kind and spit your gum in the trash?"

The sergeant stopped and looked down at Vidogo as if he was going to start yelling, but instead he just patted his pockets. He pulled out the pack of gum and opened it, pseudo-cursing loudly and chucking the empty container at Vidogo. It slapped into the little green man and knocked him over.

"Of all the things in all the world!" Vidogo's eyes were wide and his mouth loose. He pushed the empty container off of himself, and Ruth squatted down and scooped him up. "I'm guessing an apology is out of the question?" Vidogo yelled.

"I'm sick and tired of this stupid cave, and this stupid dimension," Bethune said as they reached the beach. He picked up his boat forcefully and shoved it into the water. The others put theirs in as well and cast off for the other side. "I just want to go home."

"Keep polluting this cave and you'll have to sleep with one eye open. I'll crawl into your ear when you're dreaming and lobotomize your no-care-for-anyone-but-himself brain, you see."

"Try me! I'll yank you in half and chew *you* up for gum!"

"Could you two put a sock in it?" Ruth said, almost laughing with how childish they were being. Vidogo was always a bit childish, but the sergeant was usually more composed. She guessed the stress was starting to get under his skin again.

The two listened and the group boarded their makeshift boats. They made it to the other side without event, and Ruth was reminded of Koah the heat leach that had helped her escape the first time she was stranded. Thankfully, they docked at a spot very close to where they had started, and with Vidogo's light they would be able to retrace their steps without incident. They left their boats in a pile in front of the exit path, though Ruth had no intention of ever returning to the cave, even if she was granted a full research team with proper equipment.

"Keep that thing locked and loaded," Ruth said to Brooks as they entered the first corridor, and he nodded.

Though Vidogo's light was bright, the group huddled close to him and Ruth as if danger could only harm them in the darkness. The mercenaries moved with their knives out again, and Grodin complained a few times about hearing the hyena-like laughs of the *Midomo*. Even when they re-entered the room where they had almost been killed, they saw nothing but what they had left behind.

Before they reached the entrance, they encountered a strange creature that was very much like a beaver. It had a flat tail and a chubby head, but instead of ears it had furry protrusions that curled around and around and dragged the ground.

When they encountered the cave beaver it was standing in their path, resembling a wet rock in its inertia and pelt color. They paused, but after seeing that it had no visible, threatening body parts they tried walking around it. As they neared, it turned and banged its tail down on Grodin's foot and he howled in pain. His boot, though reinforced for durability, was dented. He crumpled to the ground and clutched at his leg as the cave beaver slammed the ground a few more times before shuffling off.

Ruth checked Grodin's foot, which was only bruised, but he whimpered and complained about hardly being able to walk for the rest of their exodus.

CHAPTER 49

When they broke through the dankness of the cave and made it to the entrance, Ruth breathed deeply and smiled. It was good to have fresh air again. She was happy to see the open sky and feel ground that yielded beneath her feet.

Clouds streaked across the sky in thin lines as if some heavenly *Magnum* had raked a hand through them. Night was coming. The horizon was stained purple, and for a while the group was content to just sit and admire the beauty of creation.

But admiration transformed into anxiety as they remembered the urgency of their mission. Free from the bonds of research, Ruth knew that getting home and warning General Alvarez was imperative. If the Red Mage had figured out a way to cross over, he could wreak all shades of havoc across the dimension, and there was even a chance he would start fulfilling his desire to eliminate all life.

The *wam-baika* read their minds, swooping down and grabbing them by the arms before taking them back toward the Gray fortress. Ruth acted quickly before her *baika* grabbed her, wedging Vidogo in her biggest pocket and telling him to hold on tight. He may have been good at escaping death at the hands of sea monsters, but falling from the sky would surely kill him.

As Ruth thought about the Red Mage ruining the world and the aggregate universes, she thought of the things in her life that he would ruin. Her wedding was the first thing to pop into her mind. There were still things that needed to be completed, and it stressed her out thinking about having to rush and do things before the date arrived.

Thinking of the wedding made her think of Abram, and she hoped he was doing okay. Images of his prosthetic arm flickered in her mind, and she wondered if she would ever get used to it. It was as lifelike as she could have hoped for, but there was still something jarring about it. It could be the slightly off temperature of it, or the fact that when she held his hand tightly there was no pulse. The skin was rather natural, but the infinitesimal differences between artificial and authentic niggled her.

Even if he mastered using it and was able to give her two handed hugs that didn't crack her back uncomfortably, or was able to squeeze her hand without it hurting, she questioned if she could ever get over the fact that it was fake. Having no arm at all seemed better to her. At least he would be fully human. But it was his body and if he was happy she could find some happiness in that.

All the thoughts of change triggered a new worry in her heart. Abram was to become an artist, and accomplishing the task would mean he would wield an even greater amount of power. Would he accidentally blow things up with magic? What if he abused the power or turned evil? Could she live with a husband that was no longer good natured and pure of heart? She shuddered at the thought of an evil Abram and hoped the power stayed in his arm and away from his head.

Now that they intended to leave early, it was possible Abram would have to stop his task before completion, and the thought of never having to find out if an evil Abram was a possibility made her smile.

The *wam-baika* sped on through the night and Ruth focused on a bright future with Abram by her side. She even fantasized about their dimension abandoning their destructive habits and rejuvenating the Earth. Everyone said it was impossible, and only preventing further damage was a doable task, but she kept hope alive.

"If there's a dimension that can use magic, which no one thought was possible," Ruth muttered to herself, "then by golly there's a way for us to do whatever we put our minds to."

CHAPTER 50

Usually when Ruth was on a return trip somewhere, time seemed to pass quicker. Now, with thoughts of Abram, saving the world from the Red Mage, and her wedding plans plaguing her, the return trip seemed to take ages. The *wam-baika* stopped at every sighting of fruit dangling from a tree and at every clear stream that gurgled below. Vidogo noticed how down she seemed when they stopped the first time, but she feigned happiness until they were airborne again and he left her alone.

"Finally," Sergeant Bethune said while they were flying, staring into the distance.

Ruth followed his line of sight and saw the edge of the black mass sieging the Gray fortress. A wispy white haze hung over the *Ghafarians*, like a fresh morning mist upon a black swamp.

"We should go above the clouds to pass them," Ruth started, willing her *wam-baika* to climb higher, "We can sneak above them without having to worry about getting shot out the sky."

The others willed their *baika* to do the same and the aerial creatures rose until they coasted a few feet above the clouds. A feeling of darkness took hold of her and squeezed her chest until she felt short of breath. Her hair stood on end and her skin tightened. They were supposed to be safe, but something was horribly wrong.

She scanned the top of the clouds, searching for an answer, but saw nothing except the swirling white.

Then, a winged shadow. The shadow came from something above and behind her, and as her eyes widened as she realized it was growing. Whatever it was, it was closing in on them.

Willing the *wam-baika* to turn so she could see, the creature gave a great flap and folded its wings before spinning.

By then the creature that had been stalking her was already within grabbing distance, and time slowed down as it opened its terrible talons wide.

It was all black, like the description of the *fleigh* that Abram had given, but this creature went against every description he had listed regarding the frailty of the *fleigh*. This new beast was right on them, and it gave a flap to slow its momentum so it could dig its claws into their flesh.

Her *baika* turned but was too late. It squawked in pain and was answered by a shrill cry that curdled her blood. The evil beast was twice the size of the *wam-baika*. It sank a snout full of daggers into her *baika's* neck. As the connection between her and her *baika* was severed, she felt a jolt of pain an instant before the attacking beast twisted. The *snap* of bone scratched a chilled finger up her spine.

Dead, her *baika* fell limp and its claws slackened. She fell toward the ground and started screaming, but her voice was choked off in her throat. She swung her arms and time continued to crawl forward. She looked over her shoulder and saw the evil creature toss her *wam-baika* to the side. Its red eyes locked onto her and its powerful wings narrowed again, swooping down to kill her before gravity could steal the pleasure.

It was upon her in an instant, and it stretched all five of its talons toward her. Its powerful jaw was splayed, and a red tongue as sharp as its teeth could be seen on the bed of its mouth. Everything about this beast was deadly. As it came to snatch her from the air and the land of the living, she could tell how it meant to end her. It would grab her body with its talons and then clamp down on her head with its jaws.

Inches from contact, something slammed into her side. A single talon from the evil beast snagged the edge of her uniform and pulled her back a little before ripping a patch atop her ribs free. If she had been free from peril she would have been grateful.

The whole world seemed to tumble, but she finally caught her bearings and realized she was beneath a *wam-baika*. Her heart was trying to pound a hole in her chest, and she still felt short of breath. Beside her was a wide-eyed Brooks. The *wam-baika* was forced to hold them each with one of its talons, and they now had a free arm.

Looking down, Ruth realized they were sinking. Their combined weight was dragging them to the ground, and they dipped below the clouds. The nightmarish creature broke through the white blanket and soared after them, and the *baika* tucked its wings to fall faster. Danger was above and below, but the ground seemed like the safer bet so they fell. They managed to stay ahead of the creature and it veered off for some reason as they pierced the mist covering the *Ghafarian* army.

The *baika* remained airborne, but slammed them into a group of

Ghafarians. The last thing the soldiers had expected was for their enemy to come barreling through the mist, and they were caught off guard. No attacks came at first, but as the *wam-baika* continued to struggle to make it back into the safety of the sky, the enemy started to act.

Soldiers started running after them, and one blew a horn. The *Ghafarians* in front now started to turn. Brooks and Ruth shared a look, and then Ruth was on the ground. The *baika* had dropped her!

She groaned for a second before pushing up from the hard dirt. She froze. A circle of *Ghafarians* brandishing swords began to close in. Vidogo pressed out of her pocket and his gulp was loud enough for her to hear.

One charged her and her eyes spread in fear. She stepped back.

Before the *Ghafarian* reached her, the evil beast from above landed atop him, smashing his torso and spearing his head into the ground with a talon before shrieking a long scream at her. When the scream was stopped she could see the bright blood of the *wam-baika* staining the edges of its mouth.

The other *Ghafarians* backed off, and though they appeared to be on the same side they yielded to the beast. It was as if it was telling them it wanted the pleasure of killing her. Another shriek pulled her attention from behind, and a second creature landed.

Both creatures screeched at one another, and as they screeched she heard more screeches in the distance. Ruth turned so she could keep an eye on each of them. Her heart pounded even faster and she almost hoped she had a heart attack before they could kill her.

The first beast lunged toward her, but the second beast lunged as well, cutting off the other with its wings. It curled its long neck around at her as it held off its companion. It hissed and took a bite toward her, but a bang rang out.

A hole appeared on the top of the creature's head, between its eyes. The hole was the size of a quarter, but no blood leaked from it, and a formation of tiny cracks angled out from the wound. The beast seemed confused but unhurt.

It lunged at her again but Ruth jumped back, and its jaws clamped shut onto air. She felt an arm latch onto her and she turned. A *Ghafarian* was bringing her closer to the beast.

Another bang echoed through the area and the soldier fell down dead.

The first creature shoved its companion aside and lunged at its neck. It gnawed for a while but stopped and jumped into the air, flapping once to get over its companion before landing on the ground closer to Ruth. It hissed and reared its head as if it was going to strike, but the second flapped around and slammed into it. The two creatures snapped and bit and bumped into one another.

Ruth started running and she felt another grip lock onto her arm. She tried to fight but when she felt herself go airborne she looked up and saw it was Brooks's *baika* again. He had only one arm to hold his rifle, but he still managed to aim down the scope and fire again, though she was unable to see the target.

The *baika* continued to struggle, but they made it a little higher and Ruth could see the fortress.

Just a little further, she thought, hoping the *baika* could feel her will as much as it felt Brooks's. If reading her thoughts without a previous bond was possible, the *baika* did it and they flapped higher. Its face was distraught with the struggle, and it wheezed each breath. But each flap took them higher and they cleared the mist.

Arrows flew through but missed. Multiple shrieks came from behind and Ruth's heart started to sink. If the flying agents of death caught up to them again, there would be no escaping.

After breaking through the rim of the mist they neared the fortress wall. They flapped higher and higher, though each flap was a painful process for the *baika*.

The others were already at the fortress, standing on the walkway that was on the highest wall and screaming for them to hurry. Grodin waved both hands, but suddenly started pointing.

The Lords of Luck frowned upon Ruth and Brooks, and the two beasts that had attacked Ruth were joined by two more that appeared equally menacing and bent on their deaths. The creatures were faster than the *wam-baika* and closed in on them as they neared the top of the wall.

With a final flap their *wam-baika* cleared the top, but jaws sank into its back as it did. Ruth's eyes widened and she almost cried as their evil attacker yanked them downward.

CHAPTER 51

Ruth's eyes splayed wildly and she reached out instinctively as if the others were close enough to grab her hand. As they were pulled downward, the *wam-baika* brought its legs up and released her and Brooks in a final heave. They soared up and over the wall, and landed on the walkway.

Instantly Ruth was on her feet. The split second of grief over the lost *baika* dissolved. She knew the malevolent beasts pursuing them would keep coming until the group was dead.

"How do you get inside!" Ruth yelled to her pocket.

"I think I broke every bone in my body," Vidogo said, groaning.

"Just tell me how to get inside!"

"I don't even know where we are!" Vidogo said, moving around in her pocket as Ruth continued to run. The others trailed behind and ducked every time a screech pierced the air. Vidogo poked a head out. "I think you just keep going down this path and it'll lead to a way in."

They pressed on and Vidogo's insight was right. As they reached the door a beast landed on the wall to their rear and shrieked, blood dripping from its jaws. Ruth was the first to the door and flung it open, falling inside and crawling back on her hands and knees.

The hallway she had fallen into was dark, and all she could see was what was happening outside. Bethune and Brooks made it in, but Grodin had lagged behind. The beast hopped down onto the path and lunged after him, missing and coming again. He reached the door and fell inside as well, the creature lunging after him. Its mouth was wide and ready to snag Grodin's foot, but before it could, its face crumpled into an invisible wall and it grunted. It pulled back and lunged again, again ramming into something. It postured up and tried clawing at the blockade, but to no avail.

Wailing in defeat, it leapt, took two flaps and was gone.

"Well, that was exciting," Grodin said, breaking the minute-long silence and pulling everyone's stare away from the doorway.

Danger had passed, but everyone's shoulders heaved as they breathed deeply. Ruth felt dizzy and fought to retain consciousness; all the falling and being thrown and near-death encounters caused her to feel faint.

Everyone was still in shock. They had survived, somehow, but stared at the opening as if the moment they turned away the threat would return and succeed in breaking through this time.

"Shall we?" Ruth finally said after a few more minutes, standing and turning toward the darkness.

A hallway opened before them, and they walked down it until they came to a door. Ruth eased it open—remaining cautious in case the fortress had been breached.

The hallway opened into a stone stairwell. Every third step had a candle burning atop it, but only a centimeter or two of wax remained. Solidified wax tears were suspended from the lips of each candle step.

They descended until they reached the ground floor, and, again exercising discretion, Ruth pressed the door open just enough to look through before opening it all the way.

A thick, putrid wave punched her in the nostrils and she blinked a few times. She tasted bile and dry heaved, closing the door and turning back to the group. The mercenaries all jumped back as she continued to dry heave, but nothing came. She coughed a few times and gulped.

"It smells like a million corpses in there," she said, frowning and drawing her eyebrows together.

"Well, if the siege has been as successful as it seems, there's a good chance that's exactly what's waiting for us," the sergeant said.

Ruth glared at the door and swallowed hard again. She knew they had to go through, just in case there were survivors, but the thought of the smell forced her to hesitate.

"Get out of the way," Grodin started, walking up to the door and forcing Ruth to step back. "It can't be that bad."

Ruth raised her eyebrows as if to send him a word of caution, but instead she lifted her collar up to cover her nose.

He opened the door and took a step before pausing. She looked at him as he bent over a little but forced himself to stand. He started breathing deeply in an effort to remain in control, but that only made the situation worse. He soon doubled over and started dry heaving as well.

Bethune and Brooks looked at Ruth and mimicked her, and they all went through the door. They were in the courtyard, and a few bodies were strewn about. Some barely breathed, others were motionless.

Since a chunk of her shirt was missing, the smell was still rank even when she held it over her nose. Body odor, feces, rancid food, and decomposing flesh created a macabre mix of smell that seemed to coat her entire throat. Every so often she coughed, forcing her to constantly, consciously prevent her stomach juice from spewing out.

"You think they're still alive?" Grodin said, heeding everyone's makeshift mask example but still jerking a little whenever his body attempted to vomit.

"Looks like some of them are still alive, but barely. Maybe—" Ruth paused and looked down at her pocket as a warm-wet sensation reached her skin. "—Aww, come on. Please tell me you didn't do what it feels like you did."

A muffled response came from her pocket. "Correct! I did not soil my pants. I did however, vomit. Being so small, my stomach is weak, you see."

Ruth rolled her eyes and hoped the pocket at least prevented the smell of Vidogo's vomit from joining the other horrific scents. "Let us just see if we can find Abram and the artists."

A standing gray soldier spotted them and ambled over. He had removed his armor and only a thin chainmail vest covered a ragged fabric shirt. A pair of trousers matching the fabric of the shirt covered his lower half. His brow was furrowed and his lips a solid line.

"*Jinsi kana kuinji?*" he said. "*Nia ya vichugu.*"

"I am sorry, but we do not speak your language," Ruth said, speaking through her shirt. "We are searching for the Gray Lord and the Shaman, and another person that is dressed like us."

"*Kigeni,*" the soldier said, before turning abruptly and limp-running off to another room.

"Hey, that's where they're holding Stribling," Grodin said, jogging after the soldier.

Ruth took off after them, as did Brooks and Bethune. They entered the room and Ruth regretted moving fast, as she had to inhale deeper for a moment and could taste the smell of death permeating the air.

Bed after bed was draped with white sheets that covered the deceased. Some had blood stains but most were just a sordid white. Only a handful of soldiers were moving, transferring bodies from beds to stacks on the ground in the corner. They stacked corpses three or four high, draping sheets over top of the completed stacks.

Instinctively, Ruth covered her mouth as a wave of sadness squeezed her gut. They had turned the sickbay into a morgue. The nurses were gone, and she feared the worst for Stribling. His wounds had been severe, and with the ongoing siege there was no way they would have continued to waste resources on people unlikely to survive.

The soldier that had seen them outside was talking to one of the soldiers stacking bodies. The stacker dropped the dead legs he was holding and walked over to the group.

"Outsiders?" the soldier started, tapping his side like Ruth had seen them do sometimes as a salute. "Why did you return? Only the dead reside within these walls."

Ruth decided it was appropriate for her to speak: "We actually came—"

"Where's Stribling?" Grodin said, stepping forward with a scowl. "He was in this room when we left. Where is he?"

The gray soldier tilted his head to the side and wrinkled his forehead. "Stribling? I do not understand this Stribling?"

"The other Outsider." Grodin pulled up the shoulder of his shirt. "He wears what we wear."

A flash of anger turned the soldier's face but he collected himself and spoke calmly. "Other Outsider leave. Go with master and Shaman. Abandon us here."

"Wait," Ruth said, holding up a hand to Grodin before he could respond again. "The Gray Lord and the Shaman and Abram are all gone?"

The soldier nodded his head. "Gone. No hope." He held up his hands. "Now, walls our tomb." He motioned to the dead bodies. "Few remain. More few can walk like me."

"There has to be some mistake. When did they leave? When are they coming back?"

"No know they coming back. Leaved before *malaika* come to feast on the bodies outside."

Ruth felt like a brick wall fell on top of her. Even with the smell, she started breathing deeper and her heart pounded faster. The world started spinning and everything felt distant as if she were listening through a glass window.

"No, no, no. Not that outsider, the other one! Where is Stribling?"

Grodin's yelling snapped her back to the present and she tried to focus.

"I no understand. Stribling?"

"The other guy! The hurt one! He was in this room!"

"Dead in this room."

Grodin started getting frustrated, refusing to believe that Stribling had died and was simply buried beneath another corpse and a sheet. He started rubbing his head and pacing back and forth, but was quiet.

"I apologize," Ruth said, turning. "Our home is in grave danger. I know you all are in pretty bad shape too, but we have to go."

"You don't owe him an explanation," Bethune said as they all turned and headed for the door. "Your allegiance and only concern are to the stars and stripes, and we should focus on that."

"I still feel bad."

Bethune shook his head and they all followed her to the room that housed the transportation device. It looked exactly as it did when she first crossed over, but the floor was stained with faded red and black streaks.

"But what about Stribling?" Grodin said, folding his arms. "We can't just leave him"

"We still don't know where he is. If we stay, he's likely to die. If we go over, we can bring him back some help. For now we cross over, warn everyone, and then we can come back and get Stribling," Bethune started, turning to Ruth and holding his arms akimbo as he looked at the mess of makeshift wires strewn across the floor. "How does this thing work?"

"It is far more rudimentary than the portal back home, but it is simple to operate. We activate it. The power source, assuming it is charged, will create the energy necessary to project a doorway."

"And if it's not charged?"

"We will have to charge it, and the process takes thirty days."

"Great! Just great!" Bethune said, chewing on the inside of his lip.

Vidogo popped up through the pocket. "No use putting the meat in the pot before we have a fire burning, you see?"

"No, I don't see. What does that even mean?" Bethune's voice was elevated and he continued to chew on the inside of his lip.

"It means wait and get all the facts first before you get disappointed," Ruth said checking the battery. With a deep breath she activated it.

CHAPTER 52

The device was in fact charged, and the whole group cheered as the black doorway opened.

"High time something went right for a change," Bethune said with a grin.

"Looks like we can throw that meat in the pot now!" Grodin chimed.

Everyone agreed, but Vidogo pushed his way to the top of the pocket.

"Wait," came Vidogo's voice from Ruth's pocket. "I don't know if I should go."

Ruth lowered her head, bunching up the skin on her chin and neck as she tried to look at him as she spoke. "Why not? Your family is through that portal."

"Exactly." Vidogo climbed up and hopped to the ground. He held up his arms. "I can't go back looking like this. What if they don't accept me?"

Vidogo's light shone brightly in the room and Ruth thought of what she would do if Abram returned home one day a tenth of his size and glowing. "But if you stay here, you will always wonder what could have been."

"But what if my wife," Vidogo choked on the words for a moment before taking a deep breath. "What if she assumed I was dead and got remarried?" Ruth opened her mouth to respond but the words stuck to her tongue. "Plus, my entire existence here is pain and remorse. What's adding a little more to it going to do? If I go there, it'll be a whole different level of anguish, and I don't think I could handle that."

The acrid smell of something burning pulled Ruth's attention and she looked at the main part of the device. It was smoking and shook a little. The mercenaries saw the smoke as well and they all glanced to the doorway. The black portal flickered as if it were only an image projected before them.

Grodin's eyes widened and he screamed in protest, lunging toward the doorway. Bethune jumped and knocked him down before he could make it through, and a second later the doorway vanished.

"No! That was our only shot!" Grodin said, staring at where the doorway had been.

Bethune released him and they both stood. "There's no telling what would have happened to you if you went through and the device shut down the way it did." Bethune put a comforting hand on Grodin and Ruth was surprised he was the one to keep it together now.

Ruth ran over to the battery. She yanked the plug out the battery and the machine stopped vibrating, though it continued leaking tendrils of smoke. She inhaled and exhaled deeply before walking over to the main part of the device. She opened the side and her heart sank.

"The coolant fluid has been removed." Ruth examined the tubing that fed the coolant into the rest of the device. "I imagine it briefly operated before the device overheated."

"Great! Just great! Why would the coolant have been removed?" Grodin bellowed.

Ruth shrugged. "Someone with knowledge of the device wanted it to be inoperable."

Grodin marched over to Vidogo, anger rippling through his features. "This is all your fault. If you were more of a man we would have been through already, but no, we had to listen to your sniveling, emotional diarrhea and now we're all up crap creek without so much as a boat, much less a paddle."

Vidogo's shoulders were still slumped from before, and Grodin's tirade appeared to have no impact on the tiny man, but Ruth still jumped to his defense.

"You should be thanking him! If he had kept his thoughts to himself, we could all be floating through sub-dimensional plasma. Who knows what would have happened if we were crossing sides and the device malfunctioned."

Ruth's voice was louder than she remembered it ever being around the group. She always tried to retain some level of calm, but after the loss of their way home and Grodin's outrageous claims, she had lost her cool. The anger burned hot against her face and her fists clenched. When she realized how she must have looked, she relaxed a little.

"Look at it however you want," Grodin said with a cold, calm voice. "And I'll look at it how I want. Either way, what now?"

Ruth gulped and glared at the machine. She thought of workarounds or possible alternate liquids that could act as a coolant, but every idea fell apart. Even if she thought of one that was potentially usable, the chance of something else going wrong was still high, and risking death would only be justifiable in the last case scenario. Regardless, none of the solutions she could think of were in the fortress as far as she knew, and venturing elsewhere was problematic at the moment. Equally troubling was the siege's threat of a painful and slow death.

"I can honestly say I have no clue."

Grodin threw up his hands and let them fall to his sides in defeat. Without another word he headed for the exit. With nowhere else to go, the others followed him to the morgue. Being absent from the room for so long had allowed their noses to adjust to cleaner air, and so the smells were just as potent as when they first entered the room. The soldiers that had been stacking bodies before were on a break, leaning against the uncovered pile of bodies in the corner as if it were nothing more than a mound of dirt.

"Hey, guy who speaks English," Grodin said, pointing at the soldier that had spoken to them before. "Where can I get food around here?"

The soldier sighed and stood up, walking over to them before speaking. "None left. Unless you like taste of dead," he said, a sadistic smile dancing across his lips as he gestured to the bodies.

Grodin's face wrinkled in disgust, but before he could respond, another soldier rose to his feet and walked over. He was a little scrawny for a soldier, but he had a long scar running the length of his neck that gave his thin frame an air of savagery.

"*Maji?*" the new soldier said in a raspy voice.

"What's his deal?" Grodin said, glaring at the new guy as if *Maji* meant 'let's fight.'

The soldier that had been talking to them remained quiet and stared at Grodin. It was obvious the soldier disliked him.

"He's asking if you want any water?" Vidogo said from Ruth's pocket, popping his head out and pinching his nose.

"Son of a gun." Grodin started, stepping toward the soldier that spoke English. "He's holding out on us."

Vidogo looked at the scrawny soldier and said, "*Sisi ni ki.*" The scrawny soldier nodded and Vidogo continued. "*Je una maji?*"

"*Uni kwenda kwa nia ya vichugu. Kama wengine.*"

"What'd he say? Where's the water?" Grodin said, impatience hanging to his every word.

"He says we can go through the tunnels. Like the others." Vidogo paused and said a brief word of confirmation to the scrawny soldier. "There were others going through the tunnels, but they stopped returning."

"Why? What happened?"

Vidogo translated the question and the scrawny soldier shrugged, spouting off several brief sentences.

"Anything could have happened to them," Vidogo started, motioning for Ruth to scoop him up. "The *malaika* could have found them, the *Ghafarians*, a cave in, or simple desertion."

There was a pause as the words sank in, and the weight of the situation dug hooks into everyone's shoulders and pulled down.

"Staying here is certain death. I vote we take our chances in the tunnel," Ruth said, securing Vidogo in her pocket.

The rest of the group agreed, and Vidogo informed the scrawny soldier what they had decided. The bigger soldier said something in *Tatu* and went back to relax against the pile of corpses. The scrawny soldier spoke up next and joined his companions.

"He wishes us good luck. Said the tunnel starts behind the stairs leading to the Gray Lord's overlook."

"They aren't coming?"

"No. They say they have lost the will to live. With no master and no purpose, they will happily die in the fortress."

"Ain't nothing happy about that. Just plain stupid," Bethune said.

Ruth agreed, but the gray soldiers had made their decision. There was no telling if the decision her group was making was much better, and only time would tell if the Lords of Luck would smile upon them.

They made their way to the tunnel and Ruth was surprised. She had envisioned a formally constructed opening. Instead, the stone on the ground had been broken apart down to the soil, and a crude tunnel with no light had been carved into the earth. If Vidogo abandoned them, there would be no way to see.

One by one they hopped down. The tunnel was just wide enough for two to walk side by side, but the group still went single file. Vidogo was persuaded to lead the way, but Bethune trailed him with his knife drawn and Ruth followed them both. Brooks had his rifle primed and ready for action, but he took up the rear. The plan was for everyone to duck if something was ahead. That way, nothing could surprise them from the front and snag the only firearm they had before Brooks could make use of it.

"We didn't even go looking for Stribling," Grodin said.

"We will. We're going to fill our canteens with water, maybe find some food, then go back and find him."

Grodin remained mute but his face softened a little. The tunnel progressed in a crooked line with no forks or additional routes. They walked for what felt like hours, and she wondered how many *Ghafarians* were atop them at any given time. What would happen if the tunnel collapsed?

But no danger presented itself, and they reached the end. The tunnel's exit was carved soil steps that opened up into an expanse the size of a football field.

The grass on the expanse was trampled down with use, and at the end was a pond that appeared to have been filled with *muva* water. There was no apparent inlet or outlet, making the body of water foreboding. Bacteria loved stagnant water, and the discolored film coating the surface put an unsettling rock in Ruth's core.

"If this tunnel leads to open ground, why didn't the soldiers just lead everyone out?" Bethune said, looking over the pond.

"The gray soldiers mentioned it briefly. The tunnel route was deemed unsafe after the soldiers stopped returning," Vidogo started. "In case the tunnel soldiers had merely deserted, a scout was sent out but he reported unsettling sounds reverberating through the tunnel and they ultimately decided against leaving."

"Well, if the enemy discovered the tunnel, why wasn't it destroyed or at least guarded?

"The inside of the fortress is protected, even if a *Ghafarian* were to try and enter from below he would fail."

They turned their attention back to the water. The pond seemed devoid of life, though a constant clucking sound could be heard in the distance. A few trees bowed over the water, but they had all lost their leaves.

A distant screech froze everyone's bones and they turned. A flock of *malaika* was speeding toward them.

CHAPTER 53

"**Q**uick, get as much water as you can!" Ruth screamed, moving to the muddy shore of the pond and unscrewing her canteen lid.

She submerged her canteen in the stagnant water and the others did the same. The water covered the wound she'd received from the *Midomo*, and infection jumped into her mind again.

"It will only be potable after we boil it," Ruth checked her shoulder.

No arguments came from the group. Another shriek tore through the air and Ruth decided she had enough water. She stood, but before she turned she noticed a number of *Ghafarians* jogging toward them from the left, curious about what the *malaika* had spotted.

Seeing the group, the *Ghafarians* broke into a full sprint after them. . Ruth was the first to leave the pond, knowing the others would catch on when they saw her.

There were only a couple of *Ghafarians* pursuing them, but there had to be more nearby. The back of her mind told her that if they intended to live they would have to leave the fortress, but if the only known escape was watched by *Ghafarians* and *malaika*, there was a good chance they would be trapped forever.

Ruth glanced back to make sure the group was keeping up, and thankfully they were.

"Shoot the hell bats!" Grodin yelled to Brooks, but Brooks made no motion of readying his weapon.

"He's already seen that bullets aren't able to kill *malaika*. They're an immortal species, like the *fleigh*," Vidogo yelled from her pocket. "You can punch as many holes in them as you want, but they will live on indefinitely."

Reaching the tunnel, Ruth hopped down and started sprinting back the way they'd come. The mercenaries dropped in and Brooks was last. They ran a few paces before they heard the sound of the *Ghafarians* dropping in, their armor echoing and their grunts booming. The screech of a *malaika* also reverberated down the tunnel, but there was no way the creature could fit so it must have cried out from the opening, lusting to participate in the hunt.

A bang resounded from behind Ruth and she knew Brooks was covering their rear. There was no light behind him, but the tunnel was relatively straight and the *Ghafarians* were loud.

After another two shots the clanking and grunting ceased. As if to put a period on all the noise, a barely audible *malaika* shriek ripped through the tunnel and then all that they could hear was the sound of their own footfalls and breathing.

Even though Ruth was convinced the *Ghafarians* had been killed, she kept running as best she could. By the time they made it back she was wheezing and barely able to stand, but she heaved herself out of the tunnel and collapsed on the ground.

She heard the others come out as well and the whole group was all inhales and exhales for a solid five minutes. Brooks kept his weapon pointed at the opening for most of it, even though Vidogo had said the *Ghafarians* would be unable to enter.

"I can't keep doing this," Ruth said, still a little out of breath but able to talk normally.

"Doing what?" Bethune said. He was the first to stand and he unscrewed the lid on his canteen, taking a sniff.

Ruth sat up. For a few seconds she just sat and glared down. When she eventually stood she groaned her way to her feet. "This—this whole thing. I want to go home. I want to go home and never return to this dreadful place."

"*Now* you want to go home?" Bethune said in a mocking tone. "Maybe if we had headed back when I originally said we should have, instead of tromping through a cave, we would be back already."

Guilt exploded into Ruth's heart and she wanted to respond but the words fled her tongue. He was right. If she had cared less about her research and finding a savior for their sides crisis, it was possible they would have made it back before Abram left. If she had done that, she could be relaxing at home planning which flower worked best in the bouquet she would have on her table at the wedding.

"Maybe now you'll listen to me," Bethune added, walking away.

The rest of the group followed and Ruth fell in line. They headed to the courtyard and Bethune found a large black pot that was relatively clean. It was already resting over a bed of half burnt wood. He jogged back to the stairwell that had the candles and grabbed one, carefully shielding the flames with his hand as he brought it back.

CHAPTER 54

A few minutes passed before Bethune was able to get a fire roaring big enough to heat the whole pot, but once it was ready they all overturned their canteens into it and waited. Everyone looked at the ground except Bethune. Ruth had voiced what they all felt.

"I apologize," Ruth said, twiddling her thumbs.

She wanted to say what she was sorry for, that it had been idiotic to think it was worth risking not only their lives, but the lives of their entire dimension in the name of research, even if their mission could also save their side. But it hurt too much, and she let the words hang just the way they were.

"I have no clue what to do now," Ruth said, fighting back tears and talking over the lump in her throat.

No one responded and she slowly shook her head, closing her eyes and pinching her nose. She knew if she started crying she would lose control, and even though it barely mattered, she felt the need to try to keep herself composed.

"I want to die of old age. Not trapped in some stupid castle a million miles from home."

Her words came out as half-whimpers and the group continued staring at the ground.

The water started boiling and steam rose from the pot. The aroma of the previous food cooked inside danced playfully in the air and made her mouth water. Her stomach grumbled and she thought of how horrid it would be to starve to death. They would have a little water, but so what. It would be impossible to go back and get more, and water would only sustain them for a few days. She questioned if it would even be worth drinking. At least if she died of thirst it would be quicker. But the run over had dehydrated her, and she desperately wanted to ease the pain. Her whole face felt parched and cracked, and the sinister thought of stealing everyone's water to wash her face crossed her mind.

After three minutes she nodded to Bethune and he removed the pot from the heat. He set it on the ground with a plunk and the water sloshed around.

Grodin held up his canteen, hinting he wanted to go first. They had left their canteens turned upside down to let any of the lingering dirty water drip out, but the more Ruth thought about it the more she thought they should abandon the canisters all together until they could clean them.

"Don't bother," Ruth said to Grodin before Bethune could pour some inside. "When the pot is cool enough, we can just drink straight from it."

Bethune had the pleasure of the first sip. He *ahhed* loudly and passed it around to Ruth. She took a gulp and let Vidogo do the same, though she had to hold it for him to allow him to partake from the pot's rim. She passed it down the line and sighed.

"I'm imagining one of those old charcoal grills that had been sitting outside after a rain storm," Grodin said, smacking his mouth together a few times. "Or perhaps the scrapings off an old stove that's fallen into a mop bucket."

Brooks chuckled and took his turn before setting it down between the four of them.

Footsteps drew their attention and they saw three gray soldiers heading toward them. The scrawny soldier with the neck scar walked alongside the bigger soldier that spoke English. One other gray soldier was with them, and Ruth thought she recognized him from the morgue, but it was hard to be sure.

"You return? We took bets on you be eaten, or maybe butchered," the bigger soldier said with a smirk.

"Takes more than a screaming demon and some body builder bums to do me in," Bethune said with a straight face.

"You have water? You make to tunnel end?"

"Obviously," Bethune said, folding his arms. "Look, pal, if you don't have another way for us to get out, then keep walking. There's nothing for you here."

"Another? Tunnel has many way. You try each?"

Bethune wrinkled his brow. "You smoking the grass outside? That stupid thing had one entrance and one exit. No others."

"No. Builders no clue where water. Open to surface many time. Close hole when no water."

Bethune looked between Ruth and the gray soldier. "How do we find them?"

The gray soldier shrugged. "Holes closed. Dirt maybe loose. Maybe less dirt."

Ruth stood up, a hope kindling in her heart like the embers beneath the pot. "Will they be watched? *Malaika* spotted us almost the moment we popped out."

The gray soldier shrugged again. "We take bet either way. How long you live in here. Or how quick you die out there."

Ruth rolled her eyes and turned to Bethune. "I vote we take our chances through another exit in the tunnel."

Bethune shrugged and started smiling. He took another gulp of the water and brought it down hard, making splashing sounds.

"Beats waiting around here to die."

Ruth nodded and took another drink of the water as well. Grodin and Brooks finished it off, and she hoped the soldiers had their own supply that they had hidden somewhere.

CHAPTER 55

"Our bottles are no longer safe," Ruth started as the gray soldiers headed back in the direction they'd come. "We should see if there are any viable containers here to store food or water."

"You really think we're going to get far enough to be concerned with food?" Bethune said matter-of-factly.

"Not really, but thinking keeps me occupied."

Bethune shrugged. "Fair enough."

So they searched. Most of the rooms were empty. Ruth half-expected to see trash accumulating in the rooms for some reason, but there was barely even any dust. If they had never seen the siege outside or the junk in the courtyard, she would have thought the inhabitants were simply in another part of the fortress going about their business.

They came to a room that was filled with cookware. She was hungry enough to get excited at the idea of finding some old food scrapings at the bottom of a pan or pot, but there was nothing. All the storage containers for food had been broken as if someone had searched them all and, and upon finding no food, smashed them in a fit of rage. They did however find a single bottle with a screw lid. It appeared to once have been used for storing oil, and some still coated the insides. They snagged the treasure and moved on, hunting for more.

When they came to the dining hall, Ruth paused and almost refused to go in. The smell was exponentially worse than the general aroma in the fortress, and the room was humid, almost dripping with the hot odors of unwashed bodies. The smell was bad enough that it burned her eyes and caught in her throat. The sensation one gets right before heaving was ever-present, but she kept it together and fought through the blur in her eyes to comb the gaps in bodies and junk for anything useful. Though, even if they did find something, it dawned on her that the item might be in worse condition than their canteens. The sounds of coughing and groaning provided a constant background. She questioned why they all huddled together instead of spreading out throughout the fortress, unable to formulate any good working theories.

"Stribling? Stribling!"

Grodin's excited cries surprised Ruth and she jumped, turning in time to see Grodin hopping over a few limp bodies and stopping at their big friend's side. Stribling was propped up against a wall with his head slouched to the side. He was shirtless, and tufts of thick brown hair peeked out and around the gauze that wound around his abdomen and arms.

"Come on, Stribbles, wake up," Grodin said, grabbing his friend by the chin and moving his head so they were facing one another.

Stribling remained inert. His hands were face up on the ground. His face was sordid and his lips were chapped and cracked.

The rest of the group joined Grodin by Stribling's side and Ruth checked his pulse. She slid a finger under his nose and sighed.

"He has a weak pulse and shallow breaths."

"Don't even think about saying we should leave him behind," Grodin said, checking Stribling's body as if there were more to discover. "Come on Brooks, give me a hand."

"There are too many bodies covering the floor to drag him," Ruth said, feeling a twang of guilt for referring to the others as if they weren't people. Some were alive and some were dead, but it somehow felt disrespectful to just call them bodies. "It will be better to carry him."

They each grabbed a limb and eased out of the room. Since there were so many people strewn across the floor, it was impossible to avoid them all, and they stepped on a couple, but no one so much as grunted in pain. The people barely even noticed their presence, and Ruth wished there was something their group could do to help.

When they made it back outside the dining hall, they set Stribling on his bottom and dragged him by his arms. The pulls re-opened healing wounds, and crimson stains started appearing across his body before Ruth halted them.

She hurried over to the morgue and briefly spoke with the bigger soldier, explaining the situation and asking him to borrow an extra sheet, and, if he had one, a slab of wood or a stretcher. He balked at the first part of the request, but resolved that the dead only needed covering for the sake of the living. She had a greater need than him, so he complied. The second part of the request made him laugh, and the most he could offer was helping them break one of the booths in the courtyard and using that wood.

He accompanied her and helped them retrieve the wood. Ruth wanted to make a sled, and thought about trying to use one of the discarded shields as a metal runner on the bottom, but there was no way to fasten the wood and the metal together. Instead, they laid Stribling on the wood and wrapped the sheet around him and the wooden plank.

Ruth decided to take one of the shields along in case they needed it. There were a number of weapons scattered on the ground with the shields, but wielding a sword seemed unrealistic. She could barely swing her knife the right way. Bethune took two swords and said one was for Grodin if they came across more of the *Ghafarians*. Brooks stuck to his gun. Ruth scribbled a note and left it in the portal room for Abram in case he returned, and she told him they would wander until they found shelter or food.

CHAPTER 56

Grodin volunteered to do the pulling, and they headed for the tunnel. He complained and made jokes the whole way about Stribling weighing a ton and still eating too much even during the siege.

They reached the tunnel and Brooks helped Grodin ease their injured friend inside.

"If you don't make it," Vidogo started, deciding to hop down out of Ruth's pocket and lead the way from the ground. "I just want you guys to know that I forgive you for not repaying the life debt you owed to me."

Ruth chuckled. "You talk like we will die and you will live."

"Well, if we encounter any danger in the dark, I think the best thing for me to do is run so the enemy can't see. Surviving will be a toss-up at that point, which is good since the *Ghafarians* are bred for battle."

Ruth shook her head. If he ran she would run with him. She had a knife, and bringing it to a sword fight was just plain stupid.

"And I don't owe you nothing," Grodin said, turning to their *mantern*. "I could have handled that situation back in the cave if you hadn't showed up. You just made it easier."

Vidogo chuckled and they walked a long ways in silence. Ruth tried to remember how long it had taken them the first time, hoping to start checking the ceiling away from the army but also a good distance from the pond.

Eventually Grodin got winded from dragging Stribling, and Brooks switched off with him. Bethune handed Grodin the sword, and Grodin played with it a little, jabbing the air and swinging at the walls.

When Ruth thought they'd gone a good enough distance she had everyone check the roof for signs of previous openings. It took them a long time before they found one, and she realized the walls and the ceiling had actually been fortified with a clear, gel-like substance. She only noticed after digging at the dirt for a while and finding that the dirt was sticky and stayed in large clumps instead of crumbling. It made her think of the mucus secreted from a worm, and she was reminded of the tunnel worms from the desert. She relaxed a little but the thought of one barreling down and attacking them still niggled her mind.

After digging for fifteen minutes they cleared the gel sealant and the dirt fell through and on top of them, shooting up a cloud of dust. When it settled, a beam of sunlight warmed the group's spirits and Ruth smiled. Grodin helped hoist Bethune up and he climbed out the hole. The group eagerly looked on from below, and at first he told them to hold off on coming up.

When he gave the thumbs up, they tried to push Stribling up first, but failed. It took them almost an hour to accomplish the task, as the wooden plank didn't fit through the circular hole. To get him up, they had to send Grodin up first with one end of the sheet. Once he was up, they discarded the plank and looped the blanket under Stribling's arms. Bethune and Grodin were able to pull him up after that. Vidogo was put back into Ruth's pocket before the sheet was lowered and she was pulled out. Brooks was last.

Outside the tunnel, the smell of fresh air went unnoticed. Their daunting situation loitered in the forefront of their minds and brought down everyone's spirits. Bethune helped Grodin wrap the sheet around Stribling again, ensuring things were loose enough for him to remain comfortable. They were still on the plains, but they could see the edge of a mountain range in the distance. Herds of amphibious yaks were grazing nearby, and when Ruth squinted, she was able to see the dark army on the horizon, and above it were a number of black dots that she assumed were the *malaika*. They could only hope the beasts' vision was limited.

"We all set then?" Bethune said as Grodin hooked the sheet around his chest for an easier time pulling Stribling.

As ready as we'll ever be, Ruth thought, imagining all the fresh horrors they might encounter. With thoughts of Abram and a sigh that she felt with her whole body, Ruth hiked with the mercenaries in the direction of the mountains.

CHAPTER 57

The prairie was cooler than the desert, but trekking for hours caused them all to drip sweat. Grodin and Brooks continued to alternate lugging Stribling. Sometimes *muva* popped up and rolled around in the distance. Thankfully, none neared them. A few times Grodin joked about wanting to hop into the water storms and cool off, but he complained about having a headache more than anything.

The group was still antsy from the encounter with the *malaika* from the pond, and even though the tunnel was far behind them, every rustle of grass and every shadow of a bird passing overhead caused them to pause and search for danger. By the time they reached the mountain range, the sun was starting to lose its radiance.

"We need to find a good spot to make camp," Bethune said, staring in the direction they had come from.

"Agreed."

Ruth studied their surroundings. Though they had recently entered the outskirts of the range, they ultimately decided against climbing any of the mountains. Lugging Stribling would only get harder if they were constantly going uphill, and there was no real reason to climb. With no imminent danger and nothing specific they knew of on any of the mountains, they opted to stay on the ground. Still, the ground presented its own slew of difficulties: rocks were everywhere, both big and small, and the area was pocked with craters like it was one big stretch of pumice.

"What about in the trees?" Bethune said, squinting his eyes, trying to get a better look at the trunks to the west.

Ruth took a deep breath. "It would provide the greatest shelter from being spotted by enemies."

"Exactly!" Bethune noticed the distress drawing her features down. "So, why the long face?"

"We would be protected from enemies living *outside* the forest, but any dangerous inhabitants *of* the forest would likely have little trouble locating and devouring us."

"I think our chances are better in there than out here."

Ruth took another deep breath and they all headed toward the cover of the trees, which were still a good ways from them. They reached the trunks a little after the sun had completely vanished, and the sky was clothed in its usual cerulean robes.

Upon entering the trees they realized hauling Stribling very far would prove impossible. The forest floor was blanketed in dead leaves that camouflaged the tangle of roots and fallen branches. Virtually every step was a near disaster, but they didn't halt until Grodin tripped and scraped his face on a branch. The branch was wedged into the ground and pointed straight up like a spear. An inch to the left and he would have been seriously, possibly mortally, wounded. They made camp and hoped they were deep enough into the forest to remain hidden from outside eyes.

The trees were different from any other she had seen so far in the dimension. They had medium sized trunks with a dull, auburn bark that flaked off in pockets to reveal the trees' ripe-grapefruit-colored flesh. The flakey bark reminded her of certain types of birch trees. The part of the tree exposed by the flaking bark had a slight gloss to it and reflected glints from the moon—a crowd of old women showing off their best jewelry at a fancy night party.

At first glance she had thought the trees were simply dense, but upon closer inspection she realized that each tree was a tripod. It really had three trunks, or pronounced roots, that grew upward and joined together into a main trunk that supported the branches and leaves. If there was ever a species of plant that naturally demonstrated a perfect shelter, they had found it in this forest. The platform that the trio of roots formed once they met in the middle was roughly the size of a small car, though much taller and shaped more like a head. The leaves sprouting from the top were thin and constantly shed from the tree.

The head-shaped trunk was the perfect covering, and if they intended to live for very long in the forest, they could potentially climb the trees and carve out cubbies to hide in should danger ever present itself on the forest floor.

The visit had been riddled with disaster, but in the midst of the gorgeously colored and unique trees, she found herself falling for the dimension again. It was filled with so much wonder, and she knew she had barely scratched the surface. There was so much more to see. She pulled out her notepad and jotted down a few notes, examining the trunk closest to her and noting the tiny insects that crawled around on the bark. She wrote down guesses about the forest's ecosystem and how the trees fit into that.

"Ruth?" Grodin said, pulling her from her thoughts.

They were far enough apart that they would have to yell unless they walked over to talk to one another. She let her notepad flop into her lap and looked up at him, hoping she could convey how much she wanted to be left alone.

"Yes?"

"It's Stribling. I'm no doctor, but he doesn't seem to be alright."

Ruth pocketed her pen and pad, using the trunk she had been leaning against to push herself up. Standing again, she realized how sore she was and she paused to stretch her legs and back. Grodin stared at her impatiently, waiting for her to finish before leading her over to their fallen companion.

They had unwound the sheet from him and propped him against one of the trunks. Brooks and Bethune both faced outward. Brooks stood across from Stribling holding his rifle. Bethune was to their left.

Stribling's bandages had dark red blotches covering them where they had accidentally reopened some of the wounds. His skin was pale and his head was slouched to the side.

She grabbed his wrist to check his pulse and was taken aback by how cold he was. It was always cooler at night, and the cover of the trees was even cooler than the open ground. It was a solid sixty degrees, but his skin felt like he'd been sleeping in a refrigerator.

She glanced up at Grodin. He had his arms folded and a worried look across his face. He started pacing as she placed two fingers on his wrist to check Stribling for signs of life.

There was no pulse and she was unable to see or feel him breathing. She tried putting an ear to his chest and beneath his nostrils, but both came back negative and she felt a dark weight press against her. She turned and sat on her butt and processed the information for a second.

When she looked up at Grodin again and shook her head, he turned away and brought his hands up to cradle the back of his head. He just stood there like that for a few moments before bending over. She could tell he was breathing deeply, trying to prevent crying. He dropped to his knees and pounded the ground a few times, which disturbed the leaves and created a rustling sound. After a few more seconds he simply dropped his face to the ground and yelled.

CHAPTER 58

Hearing the cry sent a sharp jolt through her body that settled into her breast, like a clawed hand had reached inside her and squeezed her heart. Brooks and Bethune jogged over. Ruth made eye contact with each of them and they looked at Stribling. She shook her head and they each dropped to one knee near Grodin.

Ruth felt like an outsider and she squinted her eyes. She barely knew Stribling, as she had barely known Feldman, but it still felt just as wrong. It was true that the men knew the dangers when they'd signed up—they used to be soldiers for crying out loud—but it still felt wrong. Something about dying so far from home irked her.

Grodin continued to release long, heavy cries, and she felt the urge to comfort him. She moved over and put a hand on him.

"Don't you dare touch me!" Grodin said, startling her as he whipped around.

His turn didn't actually strike her, but she fell back on her butt and her heart pounded in her chest. He pointed a cruel finger in her face, his shoulders heaving, his eyes wild and bloodshot. He roared a curse at her, spewing globs of spittle as he spoke. He glared at her for a beat longer before his features softened and he turned back, pressing his face into the ground again.

The words never manifested on his lips, but his eyes screamed the message: he blamed her for Stribling's death. Whether because she had been the reason they had stayed in the cave a little longer, or because she was one of the main reasons they were on the mission in the first place, she was unsure, but it hurt her either way. She swallowed the knot that caught in her throat, backing herself up to the cover of the tree Stribling was under.

Grodin's laments carried on for a while longer. Ruth could feel Brooks and Bethune staring at her, but she persisted in avoiding eye contact with them. Vidogo pressed his head out through her pocket and looked up at her. "You okay?"

Ruth slowly nodded but avoided eye contact with him as well, and Vidogo left her alone, disappearing back into her pocket and remaining still. She had assumed he had been asleep all along, but now she wondered why he'd been so quiet for the latter part of their day.

Footsteps crunching over dried leaves and twigs lifted her chin. She made eye contact out of habit before catching herself and turning away. Bethune towered over her with his arms folded.

"We're giving him a proper grave." She sensed him looking out into the forest. "But not in this crap. Out on clear land, where we can put up a tombstone or a memorial or something."

Moving felt wrong, so she remained still until he reached down and grabbed Stribling by the torso, pulling him away from the tree. He made it a few paces before pausing and looking around. Grodin was still on his knees, but he had pulled his face from the ground and simply stared off into the distance. Brooks was propped up against one of the trees, glaring out among the trunks with his rifle at his side. Bethune brought his attention back to her.

"You're helping."

Rejecting the command was out of the question, but she took her time standing. She walked over to Stribling's legs and grabbed them, her stiff joints and sore muscles protesting with a shot of pain. They carried him to the edge of the forest and stopped a few feet outside the line of trees, setting him down with care and respect. Bethune scanned the ground for a second before grabbing an old, flat branch and snapping it across his knee. He handed one end to her and they started digging.

Digging a grave with a stick was merciless on her muscles. She scraped for five or ten minutes at a time before enough dirt was loose. Then she scooped the loose soil up and tossed it to the side before repeating the process. Her hands throbbed, especially the one that had been bit, and her muscles fatigued, but she kept going, praying for the pain to numb her heart's feelings. And it worked. It worked the whole time they were digging and only stopped when Grodin finally walked out holding the sheet. He also held a large branch that he'd stripped of bark and sharpened on one end.

The grave was as deep as they cared to make it. Grodin insisted that they use some dead leaves as a bed for Stribling, so they piled a layer of leaves into the pit before putting the dead mercenary's body in. They covered him with another layer, except for his face, and then scooped the dirt back into the hole.

Grodin laid the sheet overtop of the grave and impaled the sharpened branch into the ground just above where Stribling's head would have been. The top of the sheet was impaled as well. She had been too preoccupied with swallowing her guilt and completing the burial tasks to notice at first, but as Grodin knelt down at Stribling's grave and silence settled in, she saw that he had carved *Big Stribbles*, into the wood.

Brooks finally came stepping through the line of trees. His rifle was still shouldered and a solemn, sad look turned his lips into a hyphen. Ruth remained on the verge of tears, her guilt tearing at the strings in her heart. Still kneeling, Grodin was the first to say something.

"We'll miss you, big guy," he said, looking at the white sheet for a moment longer before standing.

"We carry on," Bethune started, his features set. "We carry on and we get out of this place with life and limb intact. For Feldman and for Stribling." He paused a beat before, "Hooah?"

"Hooah," Grodin answered.

Brooks went over and touched the makeshift tombstone.

"Hooah," the silent man said, shocking Ruth.

Hearing him speak was a surprise, but it also felt right. If he never said another word she would be okay with that, but if they ever had a conversation she could tell it would be meaningful. He had a baritone voice that fit well with the way he looked.

They headed back to where they made camp and kept the same distance as before. Grodin took first watch for the night, and Ruth observed him from afar. He kept his eyes on the ground and broke down a branch twig by twig until there was nothing left but a few patches of bark. When he finished the first branch he found another and repeated the process, never taking his eyes off the ground for more than the couple seconds needed to find the next piece of branch.

Ruth eventually closed her eyes, and thoughts of their own deaths tormented her. She dreaded the idea of dying alone in the wild with no one to bury her, and it made her shiver. Their bodies would probably get desecrated by wild beasts. Even if their remains were found, they would be unrecognizable. What if Abram also died, and no one was around to tell their families? Telling people about where they were and what they had experienced was a thought that only came to her as she thought of death, but she was convinced the Army would lie about how they died. For now, the project was top secret, and they were destined to die in a way their families would never fully understand. If the world was even around long enough for it to matter.

CHAPTER 59

*V*olcanu was a smoldering wasteland filled with active volcanos, lava geysers, and pools of bubbling magma. The uncountable plumes of smoke merged and formed a thick blanket of black that covered the land like swirling storm clouds.

Abram had thought the desert was bad, but the heat in this wasteland made the desert laughable in comparison. There were spots where the sun's radiation snuck through gaps in the blanket of smoke, allowing in heat that failed to exit. Further, heat was produced from all the volcanic activity, and the whole place exemplified his idea of hell in every way, lacking only the screaming, tormented people.

"I can't imagine how anyone lives in this," Abram said, coughing every few words, wheezing when he wasn't speaking. "I swear I have lung cancer now."

"Count yourself in the Lords of Luck's favor. Most artists must endure this environment alone and on foot. Some are lucky enough to have a steed." Then, after a beat, "I was alone and on foot."

Abram thought of how the Shaman was always barefoot, and his feet were miraculously immaculate, and he wondered if they would at least have a few specks of soot on them after trudging through *Volcanu*.

"I don't know how you do it," Abram said, examining the harsh terrain below. "Barefoot all the time without so much as a dirty toe to show."

The Shaman chuckled. "My feet have been blessed by the White Lord with an utterance that has continually lingered."

"Why would he care if your feet were clean all the time? I mean, no disrespect, but just put some shoes on and save the utterance."

"Perhaps that would have been an option as well, but the White Lord accepted me as his messenger." The *wam-baika* banked hard to the left and descended to the foot of a volcano that appeared dormant. They had been below the clouds of smoke the whole time, and Abram wondered how the *baika* would handle flying through the clouds above. "As a bearer of news, my feet were of the utmost importance, and his utterance was to preserve them in their natural state, so I could continue to carry his good news even when shoe and sandal wore out. I have never seen the need to waste shoes since my feet are protected, so I go without."

Abram shrugged. "I feel like blessing you with wings would have made more sense, but what do I know?"

After they were released from the *baika*'s grip, the Shaman led Abram around the volcano to a cave. The entrance overlooked a geyser field, and the sound of gas expulsion could barely be heard. No magma and only a little water came through the holes in the ground, and most of the liquid evaporated before it landed. The ground rumbled every so often, most likely the distant eruptions of volcanos.

The cave opened into a medium-sized room. There were a number of symbols etched into the walls, and the symbols were activated by proximity, glowing a warm orange when they passed nearby. At the center stood a stalactite and stalagmite formation. The stalagmite supported a stone cup that caught drops of water that accumulated every few seconds and fell from the tip of the stalactite. The entrance to a dark tunnel was set in the back of the room.

"Is this where I train?" Abram said, glancing around the room a bit more.

"No. You will begin your training by reading from the sacred texts," the Shaman started, patting the sack that held the two tomes. "But that will start elsewhere."

"So why are we here?"

"We must wait to be escorted into the *Infernite* village."

"Let me guess. The words all around the room are warnings for intruders?"

"Yes, but not against entering the village. They warn of drinking from the sacred cup." The Shaman nodded to the cup at the center of the room. "The *Infernite*s are a fickle people that care little of the happenings of others. Their rules are to be respected, or the offender will be subjected to severe consequences."

"Great," Abram started, his nerves getting to him a little at the thought of another group of people whom would potentially harm him if he did any number of unknown things. "Which reminds me. Are you ever going to knowledge share with me so that I know what people from this side say about or to me?"

Abram recalled how easy the knowledge share had been when he had partaken with the Shaman. The Shaman had literally gone into his mind and extracted memories about the transportation device so that they could build it, and he said the ritual worked both ways. Being able to go into someone's mind and implant information was the fastest way to learn something new, and if the people back home ever found a way to do it the world would be free from ignorance in no time.

"Yes, you will be bestowed with the languages of the Third when there is no doubt it is the proper time."

Abram mumbled about being tired of waiting, but the Shaman didn't hear him or simply decided to ignore. After some time standing in silence, Abram's patience wore thin and he spoke.

"So how long do we have to wait for an escort?"

"Uncertain. *Infernites* remain near their village for most of their lives. Only this room is monitored, but there is little information about how often."

Abram took a deep breath and sat on the ground toward the edge of the cave. The Shaman joined him. The *baika* lingered near the entrance and squawked every so often but generally remained quiet.

Looking out at the geyser explosions became a game for Abram, and he tried to predict where the next one would erupt. He was terrible at the game, but it helped pass the time.

He had never seen a geyser back home, but Old Faithful of Yellowstone National Park popped into his head. Few people cared, but the geyser had apparently lost its timeliness and now exploded sporadically. Since hardly anyone cared about the change, the name remained the same.

The sun eventually set and no escort came. Nighttime in *Volcanu* was far more pleasant than the burning day, and some of the smoke clouds even cleared up. The distant orange glow of exploding volcanoes offset the vivid blue of the night, the geysers took on a new beauty, and even the earthquakes were soothing.

With no need to stay up, Abram folded his hands behind his head, lay back and went to sleep shortly after nightfall.

CHAPTER 60

Morning came but the escort did not. The heat and bleakness of *Volcanu* came back with a vengeance, and Abram woke up feeling like someone had dumped a bucket of sweat on him. Waking up also caused him to notice how high the humidity was, and even though there was little smoke in the cave, he still found it hard to breath. He popped in one of the vibration pills and rattled the bottle, checking how many were left.

"You know," Abram started, speaking slowly to allow himself time to take deep breaths. "You guys had a lot of prophecies about me, or at least someone like me, the first time I came. Shouldn't all those prophets have been able to foresee all the disasters that happened?"

"Perhaps, but only a small fraction of truth was revealed to you."

Abram lowered his chin a tad and wrinkled his face. "What? Are you telling me you guys have been holding out on me this whole time? There's more than what you've said?"

"Indeed."

Abram let out a frustrated sigh and felt his heart pick up pace as a nervousness about the unknown settled into his heart. He had felt bad about the idea of spying on them, mainly because of the dishonesty involved. But now, knowing that they had been just as dishonest, the trust he felt toward them was flash cotton in a fire.

"Great. Next you'll tell me the Gray Lord meant to cross over to take control of my side instead of to try and convince us to save the environment."

The Shaman shrugged. "It was always a possibility, but in the end his heart proved clear. I have seen visions of him turning to evil as much as I have seen visions of him remaining true to the cause."

"And you don't think that maybe that would have been good to tell me!" Abram said, almost yelling now. "We're talking about endangering everything I consider to be home. Lives were—*are* in jeopardy!"

"Lives are always in jeopardy. Revealing this to you could have altered your course and caused an unfavorable outcome. I did what I thought was best."

"Who gives you the right to decide what is best! I'm the one who was supposed to save the whole world." Abram bit his lip and shook his head. The sentence sounded odd to say out loud, selfish even. He stood up and folded his arms as he looked out at the geysers.

The Shaman remained calm and glanced at him. "You are only a solitary piece to the puzzle. One part of the prophecy. The importance attached to you existed because of your ability to cross over."

"Well, what else is there to the stupid prophecy?"

The Shaman stood next to Abram as if trying to reconnect the bond they once shared. He put a hand on Abram's shoulder, and Abram wanted to shake it off but let it stay. After a pause the Shaman finally started talking.

"You must understand that clairvoyant visions are never guarantees. Choice is tricky, and the visions merely give one aspect of one choice. In some instances, multiple visions are granted, but even then none can be definite. A single action can alter a course and ripple through the actions of a million others."

"Everyone's heard that before. Still didn't stop you guys from knowing the person coming over would be in the Army."

"There are, in actuality, seven saviors. The White Lord predicted all seven would unite and keep the dimensions safe, overseen by the purest savior from the First. The pathway for each of the seven would be prepared by a forerunner from their side. The forerunners would act as—I believe a similar word from your home is teacher, or, some may say, sensei."

Abram stared out at the geysers. The Shaman had mentioned his importance, and knowing that he was only one of seven was a bit of a shot to his ego.

"Wait," Abram started, turning to the Shaman. "Does that mean you're from my side? Since you're training me?"

The Shaman chuckled and cracked a smile, the first he'd made in a while. "No. The perfect order of things was disrupted long ago." The Shaman paused as if the next words would bring him pain. "A good man named Vidogo was to be one of your sensei. He was defeated some time ago, and his abilities as an artist were stripped away. The Red Mage was to be your other sensei."

Abram's jaw dropped and he lowered his head but kept his eyes on the Shaman. "Shut the front door! No way that evil prick is from my side." But even as Abram said the words he thought of all the bad people that had lived and died from back home. If anything, the Red Mage fit in perfectly. "Why does he want to destroy his—our home?"

The Shaman shrugged his shoulders. "Motive is irrelevant. He lusts for power and finds pleasure in destruction. Obliterating your home would only be his initiation. We are the only limitation to his vileness."

Abram soaked up the words and his desire to learn the arts renewed within him. He envisioned epic ways of destroying the mage and he balled up his fists. He thought of the power in his prosthetic and a dark thought of choking the Red Mage popped into his mind.

"So what happens after we beat Red? What about all the other saviors and such? What will we need to be saved from then?"

"If we defeat him, the saviors are to protect against all evils, big and small."

"Seems like overkill for your everyday common criminal." An image of a pickpocket getting blown away by an energy blast from a staff came to mind.

"Perhaps. The threat of opposition is always present. For every good thing, there is a bad. With all the power the saviors possess…" The Shaman paused a beat. "Will possess. There will be an equally powerful force to oppose them."

Koñél popped into his head and he started biting his lip.

"And what of Koñél? Is she that evil force?"

"Her place in this mess is still muddied in my mind. She was originally thought to be the pure savior from the First, the one to oversee all other saviors."

Abram's heart started beating faster as he started putting the pieces together. He thought back to words others had spoken about her, and how the Gray Lord said she had been deceived. Being the most powerful of the saviors, Koñél's loyalty would prove fatally detrimental to the opposing side. All doubt cleared from Abram's mind, and he knew she was the blade Zanda had spoken of. She had to be.

"Is there still a chance to bring her back to the good side?" Abram said, his face distorting in worry.

"Hope always burns, Outsider, even if now it is but an ember buried in a pit."

"No, that's not what I mean!" Abram realized he was talking too loud and softened his tone a bit. "I mean, like have you seen her come back or have you seen her stay evil?"

The Shaman shook his head. "I have seen neither. Visions of her are rare, and I am yet to be granted anything new of her."

Abram sighed and turned back to the geysers. Though no positive visions had occurred yet, at least the same was true for the negative ones. Abram held onto that ember of hope and fantasized about seeing her again. He thought of all that the Shaman had said about the saviors and started to feel like he and Koñél were destined to be together. All they had done was kiss, but there was something special about it that he knew she had felt as well.

Grandiose visions of ruling and protecting the aggregate dimensions made him smile, and he wondered what it would be like to be that awesome.

A hissing sound came from behind Abram and he jump turned, raising his fist and preparing to fight. The Shaman turned as well, albeit a little slower and less defensively.

Standing in front of them were two creatures. One looked like a sentient piece of volcanic ground: cracked, black skin covered the entirety of its body. A faint orange glow emanated from within the cracks, and its eyes were orange globules that glowed as well. Steam puffed out its nostrils with each breath and shrouded its face, giving it a sinister appearance.

Its companion was a black blob that looked like a snail with no shell. It too had orange orbs for eyes, though they didn't glow. It rested close to the volcanic-ground-looking one, but only the volcanic-ground-looking one was hissing. As Abram listened, he realized the raspy voice was speaking *Tatu*.

The Shaman responded and Abram stared at the creature. The smoke that came out every time it breathed made Abram think it had to have a high internal temperature. When considering the environment was scorching hot, yet was still cool enough to condense its breath, the creature very well could have had magma for blood.

"Come," the Shaman said as the magma creature and the slug turned and headed toward the opening in the back. "The *Infernite* has granted us passage."

"That was an *Infernite*?" Abram said. "I feel like if we made it mad it would erupt."

"Were you expecting something different from a people that reside here?"

Abram shrugged. "You know, I guess I wasn't really thinking much about what they would be like. I knew they would like heat, but I didn't expect them to pretty much embody the terrain."

The Shaman gave no response and they headed into the darkness after the *Infernite*. The *Infernite* did glow in the darkness, but the illumination was only enough for Abram to barely see the surrounding rock.

A slight tilt told Abram they were heading downhill, and the further they went the cooler it became.

Finally, Abram thought, *some relief for a change.*

CHAPTER 61

The Shaman pulled back his robe and loosed a bag of powder as they walked. He dumped it atop his own head, and whispered something quick before loosing another bag and dumping it on Abram's head, whispering the same.

A cooling sensation cascaded down Abram's skin, even beneath his clothing, and he felt a little better.

"What was that for?" Abram started.

"A cooling utterance to prevent you from being baked alive in these passageways. The temperature is scorching, and it will intensify the deeper we traverse."

"Will the utterance last? Is it strong enough to withstand the temperature? I can still feel the heat"

"You will survive. The utterance will keep your skin and internal temperature normal, but the heat still reaches you. It will be milder, but it will remain uncomfortable."

They barely traveled a full five minutes further before magma started cascading down the walls and heat grew near-unbearable. No danger was present, as the molten rock was trapped in irrigation-like canals that funneled the orange-hot liquid alongside their path. No danger, but the heat made Abram want to shout at the so-called Lords of Luck, demanding that they treat him better. Instead of yelling, he simply complained internally, wishing he could have at least had a full sixty minutes of milder temperature.

Sweat beaded on Abram's forehead and neck and he wished the utterance worked better. The wet spots on his ACU had actually been pleasant before the magma arrived, but they now transmogrified into rivers of warmth that exacerbated his constant discomfort. It was a little easier to breath, since the smoke was relatively light, but the humidity level was still high.

They trudged on for what felt like an hour before the descent transitioned to more level ground. He knew they were still walking downhill, as the magma continued to flow, but he could no longer feel the slope. A little while further they entered an open cavern that made

Abram gawk.

Their walkway continued straight, but the walls dropped off and the irrigation ditches ended. The magma flowed over the sides behind them like two thin, orange-red waterfalls. Spanning the room, various other walkways had similar entrances, and the magma-falls were everywhere. The magma's hue tinged the entire room. It was a bit smokier in the cavern than in the tunnels, but still thinner than outside.

Looking down, Abram noticed a burbling pool of magma that the falls emptied into. Immediately he wondered how long it usually took for the room to fill. Did they have a failsafe to prevent its destruction, or did they just wing it? He spotted holes spanning the perimeter of the cavern, and he guessed they were outlets to prevent the magma from rising too high. A small circle of white, the open summit, was hundreds of feet above them.

The walkways were just wide enough to support a single *Infernite* and potentially a slug on either side. Each of the paths was suspended above the pool of magma below, and Abram hoped to never find out what the weight limit was.

The upper reaches of the room seemed to convulse, as if alive, and Abram strained to see what was causing the movement. After a few seconds, four beings swooped down and he received his answer. Two *fleigh* and two *wam-baika* zipped passed them, swirling to avoid the platforms, then flapping to perches lower down. The four creatures landed one after the other, and Abram wrinkled his brow. They didn't appear to be fighting or pursuing one another.

He reverted his attention to the juddering cave walls above, straining to see as many details as possible. He was reminded of bees buzzing over honeycomb. The *baika* wings were darker than usual, and Abram wondered if it was simply because the smoke and soot of the area stained them, or if they were a sub-species with differently colored wings.

Other *Infernites* moseyed about on the various platforms mazing throughout the cavern. Their escort acknowledged no one and never slackened his brisk pace. Questions toyed with the tip of Abram's tongue, but he held them in, unsure if speaking was appropriate.

Their path branched off a few times, but the main part wound about and dipped, taking them to an even hotter, lower level.

Down a level, the humidity was so thick he had to take long, deep breaths just to get any oxygen. It took a few moments before openings appeared and allowed the magma to cascade again. Seeing the molten rock in the new passageway made him think the irrigation ditches had holes along the floor that also continually let magma down to the level below.

His skin tingled and he felt lightheaded, and he hoped whatever challenges he had to complete took place up higher. They traveled deeper and the vibrations of seismic activity intensified. A few times he stumbled, but thoughts of slipping and falling into the ditches kept him as close to the center of the path as possible.

They finally reached a stone impasse and halted. The Shaman pulled out one of the books from his waistband and glanced back at Abram but remained silent. Abram checked his six, but the grinding sound of stone against stone pulled his attention back to the front. The stone blockade slid up into the ceiling and boomed to a stop. Once it was finished, the *Infernite* led them inside, turning and hissing something before moving behind the Shaman.

"So, I suppose something's going to happen in here, huh?" Abram said, taking in the room around him.

It was about the size of a baseball diamond, but instead of angled it was circular. The room retained the irrigation ditches, and the glow from the magma provided the only illumination. The same drably colored rock was everywhere.

"Indeed. You will learn the utterances in this chamber, and your retention ability will be tested," the Shaman said, handing the tome over to Abram.

"Sounds simple enough." Abram took the book and looked around the room again. "There isn't a desk in here, is there? Knowing my luck, I'll have to do wall sits above those ditches while I read."

"There is a stool at the center of the room. You may rest upon it until the challenge begins." The Shaman's face was serious and firm, ending Abram's occasional grins. "It is imperative you clear your mind and remember your purpose. You are currently still the only savior fighting for this side. The obliteration of the aggregate sides rests upon your success."

"Unless you're going to start giving out massages, you've got to stop putting so much pressure on these shoulders," Abram said, unable to stop himself from joking around to help ease the stress he felt.

The Shaman followed the escort out of the room. The stone door grinded back into its place on the floor with a punctuating boom that echoed in the otherwise silent room. Abram sighed and took a few steps forward, squinting in the darkness and trying to find the stool. When he finally found it, he sighed and sat down.

It was a relief to be able to sit, as uncomfortable as sitting on rock was, and he held the book for a few moments without opening it. It felt warm in his hands, as if it were alive, and his heart started racing. It was a moment he had looked forward to since first witnessing the dust in action, and though he was currently only learning to speak the spells it was enthralling.

When he did finally build up the courage to open the book, all else around him was whisked away. Despite the darkness of the room, each letter inked into the pages was vivid and clear. He scanned the first page and whispered each word as his eyes came across it, only finding it odd that he could understand after he realized the letters were a foreign language. Each page also contained an illustration for each of the words.

He continued on and a grin toyed with the corner of his lips. With each turn of the page he could feel the information sinking in and taking hold in every nook of his brain. It was unlike any other reading experience, as if he had opened his mind to the book, and the words were living entities taking residence inside. They moved on their own and found their own homes, connecting with him at the core of his being in a place that held his most valuable memories, where he hid both small triumphs and aching regrets.

As he read, nothing else mattered. Every burden he bore and every worry that pained him became distant, and all that was important was the next letter, the next word. He turned page after page, but halfway through the book a strong vibration shook his chair and roused him from the trance.

He looked up and around, confused, until another vibration shook the room. Pebbles and dust fell from above and he glanced up, wondering if the ceiling would collapse. Another vibration rumbled through and he tilted his head, listening and timing the booms. When the next vibration came he was certain they were footsteps.

The tell-tale sound of a stone door grinding open echoed in the room, and he saw a panel across from him opening. Where he had entered was at his back, so whatever was causing the vibrations was through the door ahead. Smoke seeped from the opening, tainted orange from the magma in the ditches.

After a few seconds and one additional boom, a massive head was revealed with the light from the trenches. The head was attached to a body that filled the entirety of the doorway, and it had to squeeze through. The trench light allowed him to lock gazes with a pair of pitch black eyes that sent a shiver up his spine, but it was the creature's stomach that made his heart pick up pace.

The creature was blocky, and there was little to differentiate the belly from the rest of the body except it was made from a different material. Instead of opaque stone, the stomach was glossy and see through. A white and orange and black liquid bubbled and churned within. The beast took a loping step forward and opened its mouth. The belly glowed and the liquid swirled, and a fluid fire spewed from its lips, heading straight for Abram.

CHAPTER 62

Time virtually stood still. The liquid fire would slam into Abram's entire body and consume him, but the fear he would have normally felt seemed distant. His heart had started beating faster, though now he barely noticed its existence. He stared at the fluid fire and his lips moved on their own, manifesting his will before his conscious mind could register what was occurring. The words left his mouth, followed by a shockwave.

Once the shockwave had blasted through the room, time returned to normal and Abram looked around. He vaguely remembered the page in the tome that contained the ice utterance, but as he witnessed all that his mere voice had accomplished, he shuddered. The power made him short of breath, and he smirked.

The spew of fluid fire had been split into sections from the middle and curled back before being frozen solid. It dangled in mid-air like a giant, jagged fishhook. The beast had been turned to ice mid-vomit, and the trail of frozen liquid fire was still attached to its throat. Even the magma on the walls had been turned to sheets of ice. The only source of illumination was now the creature's stomach. Though frozen over, Abram could still detect slight movement within the belly.

He closed the distance to the beast and examined it. It had already started melting, but the idea of it being free again barely registered as something that should strike fear into him. If nothing else, he could simply refreeze it. If that failed to work, his mind reeled through potential other utterances and he smiled, continuing to watch as the creature's ice-glazed body started to glisten and then drip water. The face and nostrils returned to their usual, rocky selves, and steam started puffing through the nose before anything else. The creature's breathing was fast and angry, and the idea of it being frustrated but powerless brought a sick satisfaction to Abram.

The connection between the throat and the frozen fluid fire melted next, and the object broke free, shattering against the ground. With each second that passed, the belly glowed brighter, hotter, and Abram wondered if the beast would die if the belly's light was extinguished. He toyed with the idea of killing it, but ultimately decided against it. The beast was powerless against him.

Another grinding sound pulled his attention to the other side of the room, and the door opened. Abram walked over, grabbing the tome along the way and stopping in front of an ecstatic Shaman.

"Well done. Even my first utterance was not as complete as the one which you have released."

Abram bowed his head, thinking the action odd halfway through but finishing it out anyway. He glanced over his shoulder. The beast was making noises, and its head was completely thawed. It moved its head back and forth as if rocking would free it. It roared and continued to melt, but the Shaman led Abram back through the opening and the door shut.

"So what would have happened if my utterance failed?" Abram paused and thought of being unable to whisper the words. "Though, now, it seems impossible."

"The sacred texts effect different artists in different ways, and there are some rare occasions when the potential artist is incompatible with the text. Death is definite in such situations."

Abram laughed with relief, thanking the Lords of Luck that he was compatible with the text. "So, what now?" He glanced at the tome. "Will I have time to finish this?"

"Perhaps, when your initiation is complete. You must now learn to use the blessed dust. To accomplish this, a consecration of sorts must occur."

"Then consecrate away." Abram stared at the sacred text, excited to finish and see what new powers his tongue could unleash.

"The consecrator is one other than myself. Normally more time is taken between trials, but I have stressed the severity of our situation, and the *Infernites* have agreed to expedite the process."

Abram shrugged. Though the Shaman said no more on the subject, Abram knew he had no option but success. After the victory over the utterances, his confidence was higher, but a little doubt lingered in his heart.

Their escort rejoined them and led them down more passageways. They journeyed for a while longer before again arriving at a stone door that lifted similarly to the utterance chamber door. When he walked through he was welcomed by the sweet smell of flowers and streams of sunlight.

The cavern they had entered was a garden. Plants covered the floor. Vines crawled up the walls like spider veins. A few insects buzzed and flew from flower to flower, and pollen drifted about like a light yellow fog. He sneezed after a few seconds, his whole body clenching from the force.

"These are the *fim*. They are the plants which we use to create the blessed dust. Tread lightly, for they are sacred."

Abram looked at the ground and lifted an eyebrow, wondering how he was to *tread lightly* when the entire floor was made up of the things. He sneezed again.

"I guess I'll do my best. Would you happen to have a tissue?" Abram grinned as the Shaman gave an annoyed look. "I don't have allergies, but whew would this place be a nightmare for someone who did."

Abram thought back to when he was a kid and some of his friends had pollen allergies. Now, with barely any flowers remaining in existence, seasonal allergies were all but a thing of the past. Since pollen was never in the air back home anymore, he attributed his nose's reaction to his current low exposure.

"It is the time of reproduction for the plants. A time when their pollen is needed most."

Abram shrugged. "So what do I do in here?" Abram started, his voice trailing off at the end as the Shaman spun and headed for the exit with the *Infernite*. "Guess I'll just figure it out on my own," Abram said, half yelling at their backs.

With a sigh he turned back to the expanse of vegetation. He pondered plucking a few plants and saving them for whenever he had to make the blessed dust, but ultimately decided to leave them in place. The Shaman had mentioned treading carefully, so he figured he had to go somewhere. He started walking.

The ceiling was riddled with holes that allowed sunlight from above to filter down. The plants themselves were fernlike with flowers curling outward from the tops of many of the stalks. Most of the stalks were short enough for him to step over, but every so often he encountered tall clusters that he had to go around or push aside in order to pass. All were colored orange with black veins, but Abram detected a variety of subtle colors tainting many of the leaves. When caught in rays of light, the undertones became more apparent, and he figured it was where the different colors in the dust originated.

The bugs that buzzed around the place landed on him and he

waved them away, careful to avoid killing any against his skin so as to prevent their germy guts from getting on him.

So on and on he walked, stepping as lightly as possible, excited and mildly apprehensive to see what his next challenge would be.

CHAPTER 63

He came to a spring that created a creek, and seeing the water reminded him of how thirsty he was. Despite continually moving downward since he had arrived at the *Infernite* volcano, this room seemed near the surface. Having adequate ventilation made it cooler than the underground portions, but it was still hot.

Almost dipping a cupped palm in for a drink, he paused and glanced at his hands. Dirt was embedded in his fingernails, and the wrinkles zigzagging through his hand had dirt caked into them. Instead of using his hand he dipped his face to the creek and took a sip. He immediately withdrew.

"Give me a break!" Abram yelled, almost shaking his fist at the water.

Even though there were no bubbles, the spring was scalding hot and his lips throbbed. He licked them a few times and debated taking another sip. Hot water meant less chance of germs, and he was thirsty. He darted his mouth beneath the surface and sucked in a gulp that burned his tongue and singed his throat on the way down. It simmered in his gut and he decided his thirst was quenched. He sat down on his butt next to the creek.

Further down from where he was, a number of amphibians peeked out from the surface. Their tiny orange heads could easily have been mistaken for pieces of leaves floating on the water except they made *kerplunks* when they snatched their heads back beneath the surface. A burble also arose from somewhere hidden and he figured it was the song of the amphibians.

"*Ni kupatikana kwa urahisi,*" came a soft, female voice behind him.

He was on his feet in a moment, his pulse pounding and his defenses raised. The beginnings of an utterance started on his lips, but upon seeing that the newcomer was in a neutral pose and bore no weapons, his mind relaxed.

"What? What are you?"

A brief moment of silence was shared between Abram and the female sounding creature before him. It was more plant than humanoid but oddly alluring. Her torso was plain and thin, complimented by lithe limbs that bent and wavered beside her body. Her face was really the most humanoid part of her, yet, also the most terrifying. A set of black marbles acted as eyes that offset the orange color of her skin, making her appear perpetually angry. A smirk pulled up the corner of her thin, black lips, eerier still since she had no nose. Instead of hair she had vines. The vines swirled and curled around her face and he was instantly reminded of Koñél.

"Ah, English," the female started, propelled forward by a tangle of vines beneath her that were like a moving throne. "A language of the Second. Most intriguing."

Her voice had its own echo, as soft as it was, and Abram gulped.

"That's right. Who are you?"

"Beyond your comprehension."

Abram blinked and a nervous grin found its way into his face.

"I control what I will. My opposition bends beneath my power like a single blade of grass in the north wind."

"Good to hear," Abram said, wondering what to make of the creature.

Its vines propelled it further until it was close to him. The ground became alive with her vines, and one slithered around his waist. The contact was smooth but still made him uneasy. If she intended him harm, he was unable to run now. The tangle at her feet sprouted two vines that grabbed her arms and lifted her up. The bottoms of her legs had been inside the tangle, but she was brought fully out and down to the ground, closing the gap between their faces. She huffed a sickly alluring, honey-like scent into his face.

"Tell me, Abram Jacobson of the Second, what is it that you desire?"

Abram stumbled over the first few syllables that came out of his mouth, feeling an odd passion burn in his chest. The woman was starting to terrify him, yet somehow he felt drawn to her. It was as if she were releasing pheromones that he was unable to refuse.

"I don't know. How did you know my name?"

"I know much that is only revealed to my darlings." As she finished her sentence a vine reached down and lifted up the end of one of the orange ferns for a moment. "Now, tell me, what is it that you desire?"

Koñél's face popped into his mind but he pushed it aside. "You know so much, you tell me."

The creature produced a "Hmm," drawing it out like a moan. "You desire to help, but you desire to be seen as the one who helped, to be viewed as strong in the eyes of the weak. Mmm, and in the eyes of the one with which you wish to mate."

Abram swallowed. "Look, lady, I appreciate all that you're doing here, but I was told I need to find a blessing of some sort so that I can learn to use the dust." Abram glanced at the plants. "I think it's made out of your darlings though."

The female laughed a cruel laugh and set him down. "Why should I help you? The Second is the most destructive of the Seven."

"That's exactly why," Abram said with a cool confidence that sprouted from going unharmed for so long. "If you don't help me, the Second will destroy everyone eventually. Or, someone else will destroy the Second and then destroy everyone else." Abram locked eyes with the creature. "If for nothing else, help me to help yourself."

The creature laughed again. "You are by far the weakest of those that have entered my sanctuary. How will *you* help me?"

Abram frowned and drew his eyebrows together. The blow stung his ego, but in the back of his mind he'd known that already.

"I don't care if I'm the weakest man to ever walk the face of the Earth. I've been told that I can help, and I'm going to do whatever I can to accomplish just that."

The female laughed again, and being berated started to make him angry. "A laughable quest at best." Her vines lifted her higher and she looked down on him. "But, I've seen your desires, and, however selfish they remain, purity is at their core."

"Then you'll help," Abram said, wanting to be rid of the female as soon as possible.

"Though failure looms on the horizon in every direction you seek, I will grant you blessing. Your path has been predicted, and though the way is dark, you will bring light."

"Does that mean I'll win?"

"It means you will bring light. Stars are brightest upon their death."

"What—what do you mean death?" Abram said, his pulse quickening again, moving after the female as she propelled herself away from him. "Am I going to die?"

"Come, Abram Jacobson of the Second. Your last task in my sanctuary is to create your first of the blessed dust."

Abram trailed after her but kept asking about his death. She ignored him, but the idea weighed down his shoulders and made him feel short of breath. In the heat of battle, when he had been faced with dying, there was little thought involved and it bothered him a lot less. Dying was always a possibility, but so was living, and life had always found a way to overshadow the specter of death. But now, she had all but said he would die, and that was scary. She hadn't said when or how or why, which meant it could happen at any moment. They trekked on and Abram eventually gave up asking about his death, but the notion plagued him the rest of their travels.

CHAPTER 64

They trekked through the garden until the blue moon morphed the yellowish tint of the pollen fog to green. When the female creature finally allotted a time to rest, Abram tried to lie down but was stopped. She informed him that his bodyweight would crush her *darlings* and that if he wished to rest, he would have to rely on her support. He would have rather slept without her embrace, but she gave him no other options so he allowed her vines to prepare a bed for him.

It was a perturbed, on-again off-again sleep that left him fatigued when he awoke. Lying on his back allowed the pollen to settle in his nostrils, and for the remainder of their journey, the constant tingle of an oncoming sneeze niggled his nose. In addition, his eyes felt thick and full of pollen, but he persevered until they arrived.

Finally stopping in front of an artificial fountain that spouted a stream of water straight up and onto artfully arranged, flat, black stones, the female spoke again.

"Drink, if you thirst," she said, motioning to the water.

The water crackled against the stacked stones and Abram stepped toward it. He let it strike the back of his hand to test the temperature, and after confirming it was mild enough to drink, he took a sip. He spit the first drink out before swallowing, staring at her as if she were playing a joke. The water was disgusting and reminded him of skunked beer, but when she gave no indication that he was meant to do anything but drink, he felt the need to do so. He drank a few more gulps and fought through the taste, eventually finishing and wiping his mouth.

"Was that water the blessing?" Abram said before noticing a stone table a few feet behind the fountain. Vines and a few ferns wound around the legs. "Or is it that? Cause the water was more like a curse."

The female nodded to him and they moved over to the table. It was no bigger than one side of a ping pong table, and two circular divots were carved into the stone. A small stone club was inside each of the divots, and seeing orange stains against the inside of the divot and bottom of the club told him the two were used in conjunction like a pestle and mortar.

While Abram examined the table, the female plucked a small fern and placed it inside the divot.

"The blessed dust can only be created with stone against stone. Using another substance will yield unusable chaff. To inspire the dust, you must utter *watabarikiwa*."

Abram thought he would understand the word, having understood the text in the ancient tome, but hearing the word from her meant nothing to him.

He tried it out but the stress on his syllables was a little off. She corrected him and he tried again and she nodded. He tried a few more times after that, just to be sure.

She started grinding up the fern, whispering *watabarikiwa* into the divot a few times as she crushed and ground. Eventually, the leaf was pulverized and an orange glow emanated from within.

She plucked another fern leaf and handed it to him. He took it and placed it in the divot, mimicking her actions and whispering *watabarikiwa*. He smiled from ear to ear when his dust started glowing an orange-green color.

"Splendid," the female started. "Green is the rarest of hues. Only the special receive such favor. Grind a while longer to purify the color."

Abram smiled and stared as he ground, happiness tingling his arms as the green sharpened and the orange faded. When he felt the product was finished, he set the pestle down and reached in to touch the powder.

A vine snapped up and stopped him.

"You must never waste it! Each of my darlings sacrifice so much to provide this. Cherish it!"

Abram felt a flush of regret. The female reached two vines into the brush that grew everywhere but the way they'd come. She pulled out a square, burlap-like fabric with each vine and placed them atop each divot. Another, thicker vine shot out and wrapped around the middle of the table. While the two vines held the fabric in place, the thick vine overturned the stone table. The smaller vines lowered a little and turned quickly, securing the dust and twisting the fabric closed. The table was put back in place and the bags set atop it.

"Take and prosper."

The female snapped two slender vines from her own cluster and offered them to Abram. He took them and tied the sacks closed. He moved to put them in his pocket, but the female stopped him and pulled off another slender vine, giving it to him as a belt. He thanked her and tied it around his waist, using the remaining length of vine on the bags to secure them to his waistband.

"So how do I get more of the dust?" Abram said, looking around at all the plants ready to be ground.

"You must find the *fim* where it grows."

"I can't just take a few of these for the road?"

"No, my darlings have dealt with enough. You will leave and find your own way."

Abram suddenly felt like he was being rushed.

"Okay," he said, drawing out the word in his confusion.

She ignored him and spread her arms. Her legs were still absorbed in the cluster of vines that propelled her, but when she spread her arms, more vines wriggled free and wrapped around her whole body. Soon, the vines eased her inward until she was almost covered, camouflaged and motionless.

"Don't worry, I know my way back," Abram said sarcastically to the inert female.

It was almost as if she were turned into a plant, and Abram detected no movement from anywhere around him. It was still night, and blue light filtered down through the holes in the ceiling. All was quiet aside from the occasional chirping of distant, nocturnal insects.

With a sigh he decided to take a quick nap before powering back. As he tried to fall asleep at the foot of the black stone fountain, the fact that he was almost a full-fledged artist started to sink in. He tapped the bags of blessed powder on his waist and smiled until his face hurt. It had almost been too easy. Even thinking back to the magma monster, defeating it barely took any effort. He grew excited with how much easier life would be for him.

Thoughts of his artificial arm joined his thoughts of artistry. How could anyone defeat him? He had the strength of a hundred men in one hand, and blessed dust in the other. Even the Red Mage would shake at his feet. Thinking Earth was all but saved, he smiled himself to sleep.

CHAPTER 65

How much time passed eluded Abram when he awoke, and the moon still cast its blue. He felt a little refreshed and stood, checking the female and confirming she was still stationary. He tried saying goodbye but felt silly when she remained quiet.

Originally he thought he would get lost, but once he realized the cavern was essentially straight—save a few minor bends—he found his way back with ease. Evening loomed by the time he reached the entrance, and as if they could see him the whole time, the doorway opened upon his arrival. The Shaman and the *Infernite* escort greeted him.

"Congratulations. You have reached the final stage without issue."

"Thanks. So, what's next?"

"The only challenge left is *al mafimdu nafsi.*"

"Not to be a squeaky wheel, but if you did the knowledge share with me I'd understand what you were saying."

"In due time."

The Shaman turned in unison with the *Infernite* and they marched back through the opening. They both ignored Abram's occasional questions. They retraced their steps until their excursion ended back at the cave entrance, above ground.

"Thought I had one more challenge?"

"*Al mafimdu nafsi* is the soul bond with the *nokofimbo.* These serpents sustain every artist, acting as the keeper of his power."

"Okay, great, but why did we come back up here?"

"The serpents are only found in *al nyasi nyisu*: the black fields."

"Sounds foreboding," Abram said, chewing on his lip. He turned to glance at the *Infernite* but the escort had disappeared back into the tunnel.

"Truly. You must venture there, alone, and bond with your other. Then, your journey will be complete."

"You're going to give me a GPS right? Or at least a map?"

They walked outside and Abram was reminded how irritating the smoke was in his lungs. He gave a few hard coughs before clearing his throat and refocusing on the Shaman.

Before he could ask another question, one of the *wam-baika* that had transported them flew over and nabbed Abram in the usual way.

The *wam-baika* felt differently and sounded annoyed as they progressed, squawking loudly and repeatedly throughout most of the trip. Abram expected the trip to be days long, but he was pleasantly surprised to find that it was only a few hours. They had taken off at the beginning of the night, and he slept through most of the trip. It was late morning when they arrived.

The *wam-baika* swirled down and landed on the outskirts of an expansive swath of tall, black grass. If they had kept flying, Abram would have assumed the swath to be a slab of volcanic rock, or perhaps even smoke if he'd perceived the blades moving in the wind that whipped in from the west.

Failing to goad the creature to enter the black expanse with him, Abram left the *wam-baika* at the perimeter and pushed through. He found it was a few degrees cooler, but where the heat had been obstructed, other annoyances prevailed.

Stalks constantly smacked against his face and arms. Insects decided he was a tasty treat, and when he was in between brushing off the stalks, he was slapping at his neck or face to kill the invasive species. They buzzed around his ears like gnats, sucked his blood like mosquitoes, and bugged him worse than Grodin's voice ever could.

Aside from the heat, the only other positive aspect of the black fields was the fact that the smoke had thinned enough for him to take deep, clear, easy breaths without the repercussive cough that usually followed.

Hours into the fields he encountered a clearing that appeared intentional instead of a naturally occurring depression. At the center of the clearing was a tent that had been woven out of the black grass. He searched the interior but nothing was present aside from more bugs. He stepped in and realized it was cooler still.

After a short debate about spending his daytime in the tent and his nights searching for his soul's match, he decided waiting would only waste time. It was true that it would probably be a little cooler at night, but he was growing accustomed to the current temperature since it was much lighter than the rest of *Volcanu*. Plus, there was a chance he would find his *nokofimbo* before night fell and he would be able to leave once it was accomplished.

As he continued his adventure, a troubling thought dawned on him: when he did find the *nokofimbo*, how would he catch it?

With no cage or glass staff to house the serpent, he wondered if his journey toward artistry would grind to a halt because of something silly like a lack of preparation. And what would he do if the creature was hostile? Would a bite be fatal?

He shrugged and kept moving, shoving aside his concerns. All he could do was his best. Still, worrying about the task had granted him relief from the thought of all the bugs and how their endless bites could eventually lead to something far worse than an arm infection.

CHAPTER 66

The remainder of the day dragged but finally came to a close. The clearing Abram originally saw was the only one of its kind. When the blue of the moon stained the black grass, a species of lightning bug clung to the tops of the stalks. He tried catching one for fun but they floated higher than he was able to jump. A hummingbird-like creature hovered through the flickering swarm, gobbling down the bugs. The bird ate the bugs whole, and the bugs' lights flickered from within the thin lining of the bird's belly.

After struggling for a few hours, he took a power nap to try and recharge.

Upon awakening, he was no more refreshed and started to feel defeated until he remembered the utterances floating around in his mind. He whispered an energy utterance and kept going. The words gave him strength, but it was an odd feeling. He had the energy he needed to move forward, but he could tell his body was off. His eyes felt grainy, but he was easily able to keep them open. His legs felt heavy, but he was easily able to take the next step.

He kept going and daylight eventually encouraged him. The biting bugs came back and he rethought sleeping at night, but pushed on.

"What was that?" Abram said, meaning to think the words but saying them out loud.

Something had glided underneath his hand. At first he assumed it was a *nokofimbo*, but whatever it was had been off of the ground. It was possible the serpents climbed the stalks, but he had an inkling that something else had moved past him.

He proceeded with caution but his skin tightened and the hair on the nape of his neck stood on end. Shaking the *being-watched* feeling proved impossible, and he looked over his shoulder almost the same amount that he looked ahead.

The grass to his left rustled and he froze. Nothing came charging through at him, but he still opted to turn a little to the right. Another noise came from ahead, so he turned ninety degrees and kept going, clenching and unclenching his artificial hand, ready to fight whatever threat was making the noises.

Then the world was upside down and he was falling.

Thudding against soft soil, he groaned and looked up, trying to coax his heart from his throat and back down into his chest. A circle of light above him revealed that he had fallen into a pit and he sighed. He looked around and saw that the pit was either manmade or dug by a large burrowing animal. Dark tunnels branched off in every direction, the light from the partially shielded sun only revealing the first few steps into each.

A corpse was near one of the tunnels. Half the skin had either decomposed or been melted off. There were no apparent bites or breaks on the skin the corpse still had, so the cause of death remained unknown.

Balling up his fist, he whispered a glowing utterance on his artificial arm. He was unable to recall an utterance that would make his entire body glow, but artificial objects could always be inspired. He planned no particular color, but like the dust on his waist his arm glowed a deep green.

Except the corpse tunnel, all of them appeared the same so he walked into the closest one. The black grass had provided some relief from the heat, but underground he almost felt chilly. The temperature encouraged him a little and a renewed vigor joined him as he progressed.

The walls were moist and cool to the touch. He expected to see earth worms or pill bugs, but the place was barren.

As he trudged onward, the tunnels started to decrease in size and he questioned how long he would be able to press forward before the size halted him.

An answer came just as he was starting to have to lower his head to progress without scraping it against the ceiling. The tunnel dead-ended and he smiled. Pockets were dug into the dirt wall, and inside each of the pockets was a sleeping *nokofimbo*. The serpents were curled up with their faces beneath part of their body. They varied in colors that had no apparent consistency, though only a few were bright and vivid. Even fewer were solid colors, and most were dappled with complementary colored shapes.

One *nokofimbo* seemed to draw him to it. The creature had a black body with green stripes that went from head to tail.

Furtively, he raised his real hand toward the creature, smiling as the last leg of his journey could finally be met.

But tendrils of smoke started to swirl around him. It took him a few seconds to realize the smoke was an anomaly. He'd spent enough time in *Volcanu* to be desensitized to seeing smoke, but when he caught on that the tunnel should be devoid of smoke he whipped around.

The smoke swirling around him withdrew as if startled, rejoining with another plume of smoke and taking on a green tint from the light of his inspired arm. The mass swirled and moved around itself, taking no definite shape. Still, he was certain it was alive. He glared at it for a moment, debating if it was a friendly.

Seconds later a thick tendril exploded forward and rammed into his face. His eyes and nose burned, and he gagged as the smoke forced its way into his nose and mouth. It tasted like dirt.

He dropped to one knee as the smoke kept ramming into his mouth and nose. He coughed, but the smoke kept coming and he started to feel lightheaded. He rose back to his feet and lunged at the smoke, but his blows passed harmlessly through the main mass and it surrounded him. His skin felt like it was on fire, and it felt like the creature was attempting to enter his every pore.

Panicking, he started swatting wildly around his body and face, trying to get the smoke away, but it only worsened his situation. The oxygen in his lungs was replaced with the smoke, and the oxygen in his blood was getting used up the more he moved.

Then his lips were moving and a gust of wind exploded forward. The smoke was blown back and dispersed. What was in his lungs shot out like an eel through water. His skin continued to burn, but after a moment smoke seeped out of it and sped down the tunnel as well, joining the tendrils that had been inside his lungs.

He gasped, finally able to breathe, and fell to both knees. His inhales and exhales were loud as he tried to catch his breath. His eyes darted around and he strained to see down the tunnel. He held up his arms, but nothing moved for a while.

Then the smoke beast started to amass before him. He lowered his eyes and started moving his lips, but before the utterance was complete the creature dissipated, spreading out and dissolving into the walls without a sound.

CHAPTER 67

Finally catching his breath, he inhaled deeply a final time and turned around. All the *nokofimbo* had been disturbed during his altercation. All had burrowed into the soil through small tunnels and his shoulders slumped. Coming the distance he had to have it ruined by a creature he had failed to kill angered him. He balled up a fist and punched the soil wall.

His arm sank in up to the middle of his forearm, but the dirt was soft and he easily removed it. He thought about punching it again but decided he wanted nothing more to do with the tunnels. He gritted his teeth.

A hissing sound spun him around. A smirk walked across his face as he locked eyes with the black and green snake he had seen before. As before, he was drawn to the creature, and it seemed the creature was drawn to him.

The serpent reared up like a cobra, though it had no hood, and Abram took a few steps forward. He held his hands out to signify he meant no harm, but after a few seconds he lowered them and realized the serpent probably only understood snake signals.

With each step he took, the environment darkened. His arm had still been glowing, casting green on the walls and a shadow behind the serpent, but soon everything faded away until he stood on a black plane with the *nokofimbo*. The light from his arm was gone, and no other light was present, but the *nokofimbo* in front of him was somehow clear and vivid.

Its green eyes were like jade gemstones flecked with bits of black. An uncanny desire to walk around the snake possessed him. He started but a barrier stopped him and he resorted to walking forward. The serpent stayed in place, wavering a little and flicking out its tongue every so often.

Abram closed the gap to touching distance, and reached out his real hand. Before he could react, the snake sprung forward and coiled around his wrist. A moment later its fangs were embedded in the meat between his thumb and index finger.

Before the pain could register in his brain and he could react by shaking off the creature, his eyes widened and he froze. A deep, perpetual nothingness surrounded him. He saw the vastness and comprehended its infiniteness, but he had no eyes. In an instant every sensation he had ever experienced, and every sensation he would ever experience coursed through him, but he had no body.

Every memory from his childhood to the present zoomed into his consciousness, and every memory from his death back to the present flashed by as well. He tried making sense of it all. He blinked and realized he was still standing in the tunnel.

He vomited and heaved a few more times and started to breathe deeply. Though he vomited, the nausea passed in an instant and he felt better. His body tingled and the hair on his arms and neck erected.

Still attached to his wrist, the *nokofimbo* tightened its grip. Mild pain registered in his mind, but it was distant enough to bear and he took a deep breath.

"What did you do to me?" Abram said, exuberance filling his heart.

The serpent remained in place and Abram headed toward the exit. Things had returned to normal, and the glow of his arm led the way back to the entrance.

He daydreamed the whole way back, trying to reconnect with the experience he had undergone but failing to fully grasp it. However, he was able to grasp a single item from the experience and it gave him chills.

A man stood at the precipice of a rocky ledge and looked out toward the horizon. Purples and blues stained the bottom of the sky and clouds, and distant birds or aerial beasts flew around. The valley below him was vast. Gardenias were in full bloom and their white petals blanketed the ground.

But atop the gardenias were bodies. Thousands of corpses of sentient beings of different races were scattered in a macabre menagerie. The shadow from the cliff he was on covered one third of the corpses, despite the fact that the sun appeared to be setting from in front.

At first he was uncertain if it was a memory from someone else, or the future for himself, but as he thought he soon realized he was the man in the vision. Why he was on the cliff or where the cliff was eluded him. How the thousands had died also remained a mystery, but it unsettled him just the same. Was it a premonition or something else? A cauldron of intense emotions bubbled in his chest.

Back at the exit for the pit, he was shaken from his thoughts. It only took a moment to whisper an utterance that granted him the ability to jump out of the hole, and when he did he felt an odd sense of displacement. The sun seemed to be at relatively the same height, but he thought it had been in a different location in the sky when he had fallen into the pit. It was impossible for him to be certain, but the feeling that something was off persisted to niggle him.

Though starting to rise to its usual position, the black grass he had trampled to progress was still bent enough that he could tell which direction to go. The utterance on his arm expired after a few more moments.

Again, as he walked he felt he was being watched. After seeing the smoke creature he started to imagine that was what spied on him. He knew how to defeat it now and fear never trickled into his brain. He wondered how the *nokofimbo* attached to him would react to the smoke creature. If the creature was his claim to artistry, he would defend it with his life. He had only been an artist for a brief time, but he still felt his newfound abilities were how he would now save the world.

The *baika* was waiting for him when he exited and it took him back to *Volcanu*. Even with the temperature change there was no movement from the *nokofimbo*.

Just like the journey to the black grass, the journey home ended quickly and without altercation. Once he heard the high pitched shriek of something terrible, but it graciously stayed out of sight.

The *wam-baika* took him to the same cave and the Shaman was resting against his staff when they arrived. Abram started smiling and couldn't stop as he walked up to the Shaman, displaying the serpent on his arm with pride.

"Congratulations on your completion!" the Shaman said. "Though it took you longer than most, you have reigned successful."

"Really? I was only gone a couple days, and most of that was the journey. How quick do most people take?"

"A couple days? My friend, your excursion was at least seven."

Abram's jaw dropped. "No way!" His mind flashed to the experience. "This *thing* happened to me. I saw a vision or something."

"When the *nokofimbo* first bit? That is usual."

"Yeah, well," Abram thought of how to convey what he was thinking. "I guess that was what took so long."

"The reasoning is irrelevant. And do not speak of what you saw."

The Shaman turned and Abram saw that their escort and his slug companion were back. "Come. It is time."

Abram's heart beat faster and his mouth started to hurt from all the smiling. He followed the Shaman and the escort back into the tunnel and was even able to ignore the heat.

CHAPTER 68

They started on the same path but used a different walkway once they reached the subterranean city. The *wam-baika* and *fleigh* were a little noisier the second time he came through, and the idea of the two species living in harmony was still jarring.

They finally reached a room and the grin on Abram's face refused to leave. Inside were two other *Infernites*, and they both held long tongs. The two stood around a staff Abram knew would become his companion. His mind flashed to the hammer he had left behind, and though he wished he could have used that, the staff would be adequate.

Currently empty, the staff was secured between two thin pillars. The ends were open, and the top pillar poured lava through the staff into the bottom pillar. The staff glowed a bright yellow and the magma passing through it flowed quickly. Cut around the floor of the bottom pillar, a trench spiraled out and wound around the room, disappearing into the wall.

Their escort stopped in front of the empty staff and the pillars and nodded to each of the *Infernites*. They nodded back and the one on the right lifted his tongs up to the staff. He yanked the weapon free and the magma leaked out. Ensuring all the molten rock was removed, the *Infernite* spun the rod, spewing the cooling remnants onto the ground. The escort exited quietly.

The pillar continued to stream magma toward the bottom, but without the staff to funnel the liquid into the proper hole, most of it missed and cascaded down to the trench, increasing the intensity of the heat in the room and causing the sweat beading against Abram's forehead to begin dripping down his face and from his chin.

Now clear and truly empty of anything but air, the staff was placed on its side against the ground. Keeping the tongs attached, the second *Infernite* whispered an utterance and one end was sealed. The process was too fast for him to see. One minute it was open, the next it was closed.

As they progressed, the cascading magma reached the base of the stalagmite and crawled through the spiraling trench, adding more heat but also adding light to the room. Abram constantly glanced at his feet as if the lava would overflow from the trenches and singe his toes. The trench was deep and thin enough to house the magma safely below his boots, but it still freaked him out a little.

The second *Infernite* approached Abram with the tongs and Abram figured he came to remove the *nokofimbo* so he held up his arm. He guessed correctly and the *Infernite* grabbed the serpent at the base of the neck. The serpent released and went limp, and the first *Infernite* held up the empty rod. The second *Infernite* lowered the serpent into the rod, whispering an utterance as he did. When his lips fell still the bulbous end of the staff appeared as quickly as the bottom end. One second nothing was there, the next second the staff was complete. The serpent was still and Abram was compelled to step forward.

He grabbed the staff with his real arm and held it up. The glass emanated enough heat onto his face to tell him it was scalding hot, but in his hand it barely felt warm.

"Before the bond is complete, you must verbalize your commitment," The Shaman said, taking a step toward Abram.

Abram couldn't take his eyes off the staff, but the words registered and he said what the Shaman wanted him to say.

"Then it is finished," the Shaman said, appearing solemn.

Abram barely noticed and took a deep breath, putting the bottom of the staff on the ground and leaning on the bulbous portion. He grinned and again thought of all the good he could do with the power he now wielded.

"We must remain vigilant," the Shaman started, turning and heading toward the exit. The escort was still gone and the two *Infernites* in the cave stayed put. "Even with you as a newly initiated ally, the Red Mage's forces retain the upper hand."

"How? We already killed Zanda. All he's got left is Koñél, a few *Fleigh*, some *Magnums*, and the *Ghafarian* army." As Abram spoke he realized how great their challenge would be. "Oh, right."

"Time wanes and our potential allies are already spread thin."

"Don't get me wrong or anything," Abram said, feeling old as he walked with his staff. "But you're starting to convince me that there isn't much hope."

"I apologize if this causes distress. It is the truth."

Abram sighed. They were quiet for the remainder of their exodus. No one stopped them or said goodbye. Uneasy, Abram rested his staff across the back of his shoulders and neck like he had seen Koñél do, and the action made him think more of her. She was still mysteriously absent, as was the Red Mage.

Outside, their *wam-baika* were waiting for them. The *baika* picked them up and took them away from *Volcanu*. The smoke made it difficult to determine exactly which direction they had originally flown and if they were now retracing their steps, but Abram had a hunch that they were doing just that.

It was dusk when they left, and Abram slept through most of the ride back. He briefly woke up after they cleared the smoky skies of *Volcanu*, and breathing in near perfectly clear air tickled his spirits until he fell back asleep.

He was unsure how much time had passed when they took a break. They were on the outskirts of a moderately wooded area, and the trees gave off a sappy smell. The place was devoid of insects and any apparent life. The trees had leaves and healthy bark, but no fruit was produced and hunger pains squeezed Abram's stomach.

"So where are we going?" Abram said, after nodding off a few times.

The Shaman was staring at the horizon opposite the line of trees with his hands behind his back. He held his staff horizontally and remained in the direction he was facing for his response.

"We return to the Mountain *Magnus*. Our only hope for survival seems to be retaliation or hiding." The Shaman turned to Abram.

"Great," Abram started, using the staff to aid him in standing as the Shaman walked over. "We retaliate then. Hiding fixes nothing. At best it saves our lives, but when the aggregate lives of the dimensions of the universe are at stake, there's only so much hiding we could do anyway."

"Oh, how your newfound powers grant you confidence!"

Abram shrugged. "Don't know if it's confidence or just common sense. If we don't strike back we're all dead, so we might as well give it our best shot."

The Shaman made no expression of agreement, but Abram knew that if the Shaman had not dictated that they were going to hide as they did when they fled the fortress, they were going to fight. The idea of testing out his powers against the forces of evil made his skin tingle.

An image of the gentle giant the Shaman had killed during his first major battle flashed into Abram's mind's eye, but he suppressed the thought and focused on good things.

The *wam-baika* picked them up again and soared toward their destination. As they flew, Abram's thoughts turned to Ruth and the other men. He wondered if they had made it back to the fortress yet, and if they had, he questioned whether they were able to sneak past the *Ghafarians*. If they had returned to the fortress, he hoped they had decided to turn away without entering. He doubted anyone in the fortress would still be alive.

Still, an inexplicable feeling of assurance settled into his shoulders and he knew they were alive. Though he was unsure where they were or if they had even accomplished their mission to the *Giza Sana*, he could sense them. The feeling was subtle, like the sense of being watched, but the more he focused on the sensation the more he knew what it was.

Clouding the back of his mind was a dark spot that brought uncertainty. His heart told him it was Koñél's presence, but his inexperience with the sensations made him question if it was really the Red Mage. Whatever or whoever it was, it made his heart sink and his stomach turn.

CHAPTER 69

The closer they flew to their destination, the brighter another spot in his head became. Putting two and two together, he figured the new spot he sensed was the Gray Lord, and when they finally arrived at the crater he was confident he had guessed correctly.

Landing, the *wam-baika* released their load in front of the *Magnus* entrance and flew toward the trees. The ground rumbled with the footsteps of the remaining *Magnums*, and leading their pack was the Gray Lord.

There were less than twenty *Magnum* females, but they were all armed.

"So it has been decided," the Gray Lord started, stopping in front of the Shaman and grabbing his shoulders. The *nokofimbo* in their staffs wriggled to life as usual. "We three artists will lead the way."

"What hope have we three in this hour?" the Shaman said, worry wrinkling his features.

Abram scrunched up the skin between his eyebrows and frowned. "What hope? Weren't you the one who told me that hope is all we have? That hope is all we need?"

The Shaman sighed deep.

"The Outsider is right. However dim, and however pathetic, we must grasp this hope to persevere."

A pause elapsed, and Abram wondered if the Shaman was debating if he would actually fight. What had caused the change was beyond Abram. The Shaman was clairvoyant, but until now he had seemed hopeful. What had he seen? As if reading Abram's mind, the Shaman glanced at him with a sad face.

"So be it," he said, turning back to the Gray Lord.

"Indeed. I have been busy in your absence. The remaining of this *Magnus* will journey with us. All of *Electrode* has also answered my call and will meet us in the Far North." Abram wondered how they had communicated about where to go. It was as if they could project messages telepathically. "Also, the *Slithe* have been beckoned and are expected to meet us there before battle."

Abram had never heard of the *Slithe*, but whoever they were he hoped they were strong enough to fight against the evils that awaited them.

"Should we go back to the fortress and see if any of your soldiers can fight?" Abram said, his face steady.

"No. Our time dwindles. Our enemy has taken refuge in the Far North. We attack now, while we retain surprise as an ally."

Abram shrugged. The decision had already been made. He was only along for the ride, and he was as nervous as he was excited. They were finally back on the offensive, but the Shaman seemed more depressed than he had ever been. What faced them in the Far North that he was so afraid of?

***

The journey was longer than Abram had expected, but he managed to retain a good mood for the first few days. They stopped every so often and he napped when they did. They rarely stopped just for food, so he ate whatever he saw the Shaman or the Gray Lord eat. Abram noticed his memory pills were almost gone, and he wondered what would happen when he ran out.

For their other journeys the environment had changed, but usually remained hot. But the further they traveled north, the lower the temperature fell. The temperature drop made sense, as he lived above the equator back home and going north meant decreasing temperatures. Still, he was surprised when blankets of snow started coating the ground.

Shivering became a constant soon after, and he had to whisper a warming utterance every so often to keep his appendages from going numb.

When the *wam-baika* set them down for the first time in the snow he reminisced of the heat from *Volcanu*. The Shaman and the Gray Lord shivered alongside him, whispering their own warmth. The *Magnums* had been walking and were still out of sight, but he imagined their thick skin would insulate them from the cold.

"Is it really a good idea to have the only *Magnums* left from that village come with us?" Abram started, his voice stuttering occasionally from the cold. "Haven't we taken enough from them?"

"We have," the Shaman said, his voice steady despite his quaking limbs. "But we need their assistance. Failure equals their destruction either way. At least they have a fighting chance if they are with us."

Abram sighed. "Well, could we at least have grabbed some warmer clothes? I'm freezing!" He smiled as he finished his sentence, and his two companions allowed slight grins to turn up their lips.

"A creature dwells here that will warm us from the inside," the Gray Lord started. "But I have not seen any."

Abram looked out over the horizon. The temperature made him feel as though it should be snowing, and he wondered if a snow *muva* would pop up at some point.

The clouds were heavy blankets that cast a bleak gray around the land. A regular breeze sent wisps of snow curling through the air.

"Ah, there!" the Gray Lord said, reaching out a hand and snagging something.

When Abram saw what the Gray Lord had grabbed, he jumped a little. It was like an albino scorpion, but things were backwards. Instead of a stinger it had a claw, and instead of front claws it had two stingers. The venom sacks in the stinger hands glowed a faint red. The creature squeaked in the Gray Lord's grip, jabbing at him with both stingers. Avoiding the stings, he carefully held the creature by its claw and looked at it.

"These will be what keep us alive for the duration of the journey. For each that we can consume, another day of warmth shall be ours!"

The Gray Lord whispered something that made the scorpion fall limp, and he held it up before dropping it into his mouth. Abram's eyes widened.

"Are you crazy? Dropping it in like that. Won't those stingers get you?"

The Gray Lord laughed this time and scanned the ground for more. The Shaman was doing the same. He spotted one first and crunched it down.

"Their toxin only provides warmth. Being stung is good, though ingesting is better, for it will be digested and better move through the entire blood stream."

"What type of nonsense—what would be the point of a predator that gives its prey warmth?" Abram looked for his own backward scorpion, wondering if the sting hurt.

"Here, creatures thrive in the cold. Warmth slows them down. The *nawiba* sting and then are able to eat without the fear of their food running away."

Abram almost laughed at the idea. It countered his idea of what cold did back home, and he wondered what type of blood these creatures had.

But even as he thought of the oddity of the backward scorpions, more and more started to pop out of the snow and scurry toward them. Abram finally caught one of his own and he glared at it. The idea of eating a dirty, disgusting looking bug made him gag, and without cooking it no less.

"Can't we at least cook these things first?"

The Shaman shrugged, biting half of one of the creatures and talking with the other half in his hands. "Cooking only makes the toxin viscous, which in turn slows down its effect."

Abram bit his lip and stared at the squeaking creature. It continually and fruitlessly tried to sting him. The cold was powerfully persuasive, but the tangible disgustingness of the backward scorpion was stronger. He whispered a fire utterance on the ground, and a ball of flame burned blue against the snow. The snow melted until the flame was six inches down and atop dirt. The circle of melted ice flickered and he lowered the scorpion into the pit. It screeched and he felt bad. He felt worse by the fact that he was unable to lower his hand too far or he would be burned, so the scorpion had to be slow roasted.

When the fire finally did its job, Abram brought the scorpion to his mouth. He paused, but closed his eyes and plugged his nose with his free hand. Holding his nose blocked less of the taste than he had hoped, but this fact pleasantly surprised him.

"This freaking thing tastes like ice cream!" Abram almost yelled. "I don't know if this cold has stolen my sanity, but I swear if you threw this in a bowl and refroze it I would believe it was Breyers."

"Why would you ice your cream? What is Breyers?" the Shaman said, finishing off another scorpion.

"Remind me to expose you guys to the wonders of ice cream one day." Abram snagged another and brought it to the fire, excitedly lowering his hand as far as it could go to try and expedite the process.

A rhythmic rumble put Abram on edge, but no one else changed their demeanor or stance. He looked around until he found the source of the rumbles, and realized it was what was causing all the backward scorpions to exit their homes beneath the snow and flee in the direction of the party.

Massive beasts stomped through the land. They had furry ears that dangled down to the snow, dragging lines beside their bodies. Their bodies were humped but their faces were flat, and Abram wondered what they ate. They were roughly the size of elephants, but with no trunk and no vegetation nearby, eating from the ground would be difficult. They took slow, determined steps like elephants, and their legs didn't appear to bend any more than an elephant's might. Unless all they ate was snow, they would have trouble catching any live animals.

The snow beasts continued their stroll toward them, and by the time they were close the *Magnums* stomped over too. They had apparently been running, and though out of breath they seemed excited and headed toward the herd of beasts. The beasts appeared equally as excited, and changed direction. A few made sharp, trumpeting sounds in quick bursts that were echoed back to the rear of the pack. They appeared afraid of the three artists, but when they neared the *Magnums* they were set at ease. The *Magnums* stroked the creatures' backs, and the creatures bleated. The herd was about forty strong. After a few minutes, they eventually moved on.

Once the herd was gone the scorpions stopped appearing, but by then everyone had eaten enough to keep them warm for a long time. The *Magnums* apparently were okay without eating for the time being, and after briefly talking with the Shaman and the Gray Lord, they continued running toward their destination, the ground quaking with their strides.

It took some time for Abram to feel the heat from the scorpions, but when it did, he felt like he was sitting above the fire that burned a few inches away from him. The Shaman and the Gray Lord had eaten enough that their veins took on a reddish tint, and they contrasted with the white snow.

Day slipped away. The thick covering of clouds hindered the blue light from shining through, and a black darkness similar to night at home covered the area. Though it was normal at home, here the blackness reminded him of evil. They slept when it was darkest.

CHAPTER 70

Abram awoke with a start, pulse pounding, breathing elevated, but once he realized he was safe, he relaxed. With the clouds gone the sun appeared without hindrance, and soon after the rest of the troop was awake. He took his vibration pill.

The *wam-baika* came over and picked the trio up, and on they flew. They overtook the *Magnums*. They moved through the snow without difficulty and left a cloud of white in their wake. Their body heat melted much of the snow they ran over, allowing patches of brown to peak through. They had run all night, and Abram wondered how long they could go without sleeping or eating.

Stopping once more, they found no food but Abram melted some snow and drank it. It was bitter and tasted nothing like water, but he was parched half to death. The idea of how germ-infested the snow was made him cringe, but he convinced himself no one had traveled the snow in ages so there probably weren't many germs.

The *Magnums* beat them to their destination, and were in the company of a small army of *Elecki* when the trio arrived.

Abram noticed that the light from the sun was a bit off. He felt like they still had a number of hours of daylight, but the sun seemed trapped behind a black curtain that filtered out most of the light.

The *Elecki* were as Abram remembered, but instead of just the fur pants, they now had fur garments covering their entire upper halves. A few also had fur caps. The fluffy material they wore was perfect camouflage, and if the *Magnums* weren't scattered throughout to break up the white, Abram might have overlooked them.

The Gray Lord went to speak to three of the *Elecki*, and Abram assumed they were in charge of the tribe. The Shaman stayed with Abram, though there were *Elecki* and *Magnums* all around them.

"So, how far are we from the fight?" Abram said, trying to detect any evil artists lurking nearby.

The Shaman still seemed bothered, as if he had seen a future that was filled with death and suffering.

"I sense a large gathering of evil forces less than a day's journey from our position," the Shaman said.

"Does that mean they can sense us too? Does it work both ways?"

"Most likely. I have concealed my presence, and partially concealed yours and the Gray Lord's, but the others remain in the open. What will come, will come."

"Why only a partial concealment for us?"

"I am attempting to save my strength. The artist among the nearby evil forces is powerful. Arrogance has prevented them from even attempting to mask themselves."

"*Karibu, mgeni*," came a voice from behind Abram.

He turned and faced an *Elecki* with a crooked nose. He glanced between the Shaman and the *Elecki*, wrinkling his forehead.

"When are you going to knowledge share with me so I can learn how to speak to people?"

"In due time," the Shaman said, nodding to the *Elecki*.

"*Sisi mara moja tu kumjali kwa wenyewe, lakini sasa, na wewe kwa upande wetu, sisi kupambana na kifo kutetea njia yetu ya maisha na giza.*"

"He welcomes you and says that the *Elecki* once cared only for themselves, but now that you fight by their side, they will fight to the death to defend their way of life from the darkness," the Shaman finished.

"Tell him I'm glad to hear it, I guess."

The Shaman spoke, and the *Elecki* saluted in the way of the gray soldiers before falling back in among his kin.

"So where are those *Slithe* the Gray Lord mentioned before?"

"They are here. What you know as *Elecki* are descendants of the *Slithe* people."

"But they're all dressed alike. I thought only the *Elecki* needed the furry clothes to protect them from their homeland."

"The *Elecki* do need the apparel for that reason, but their people have long been weavers of various fabrics." The Shaman took a seat on a lone rock that was half buried in the snow. "The *Slithe* may dwell outside of Electrode, but they too skillfully grasp the ways of a weaver. This environment demands protection, and they have yielded to that demand in the same fashion as their brethren."

Abram slowly nodded and looked out over his allies. To him, there was no noticeable difference between *Slithe* and *Elecki*, so he decided to call them all *Elecki* in his mind. They all had the same large noses that covered a third of their faces, and they were all the same short height that most inhabitants were.

"I'm ready to get this show on the road," Abram said, straightening up and looking at his *nokofimbo*. He was eager to test out his power against something vile.

"First, we gather our strength for the night. We face an obstacle like this side, or any other side, has never seen before."

Abram caught a glimpse of doubt in the Shaman's features, but he stoked the fires of hope burning in his chest.

"Maybe, but I'm ready to give it my best shot."

The Shaman merely sighed, and Abram turned his attention to the army surrounding him. The *Magnums* and the *Elecki* conversed, speaking in the main language of the dimension as if they were old friends catching up.

Another *Elecki* walked over, and the Shaman perked up when the newcomer started talking. "*Asante kwa kuja,*" the *Elecki* said, glancing at the Shaman.

"He says, 'thank you for coming'."

Abram nodded and verbalized a *you're welcome* before the *Elecki* continued.

"*Mbali kaskazini ni kujazwa na maovu roho,*" the *Elecki* said, his face animated and his hands moving as he continued. "*Maovu inatisha, na bila wewe najua tunatarajia kufa.*"

"He speaks of the Far North and how it is filled with evil spirits, shadow evils, and without you, he knows we would all be doomed."

"Gee, that's encouraging," Abram said. "I'm the least experienced of the bunch, and this guy looks to me as the savior."

"Is that not what you have always experienced since your arrival?"

Abram sighed. "Yeah. Thanks for reminding me. I guess it's just a little disheartening to hear someone so sold out to the idea that I'm the answer."

"Before now you have always gone with this."

"True. I guess it's just finally hitting home. Too much time to sit around and think."

"I suppose. Would you like me to convey all of that?" the Shaman said.

"No, just tell him thanks."

The Shaman did and fell silent again. Abram eyed the *Elecki* as he walked back and went to talk to another person. They glanced over at Abram every so often and smiled, nodding as if they were saying things that were so true no one could deny them with a straight face.

When night fell Abram was convinced the light of the area was off. The pseudo darkness had lingered for hours, but soon fell to a complete blackness that sent shivers up his spine. No howls or spooky sounds echoed around them, just the breathing of hundreds of *Elecki* and *Magnums*, but he felt afraid all the same. The lighting made him think of the parts of the north back home that went whole months without so much as a sunrise. He wondered if this place was similar.

Reminiscing about all the time he'd spent in the Third, he pondered why his role suddenly began to give him doubt. The Shaman was right, and he had been sold out to the idea of being the savior this entire time, even relishing in the thought of it, but doubt now squeezed around his heart. Despite his pondering, he was unable to nail down exactly what caused the switch to sprout, though the Shaman's shift in demeanor seemed the most likely root. The Shaman had always been the one to encourage victory and hope until they fled from the Gray Lord's fortress.

Abram's thoughts drifted to Ruth and the mercenaries, and he hoped they were okay. He wondered what the consequence would be if he returned alone, but shook off the thought. He sensed they were alive, and though he was unsure where they were, he knew he would link up with them again.

Unless he died.

CHAPTER 71

The next morning the sun glowed faintly on the horizon, shielded behind the clouds. The land was hardly brighter than it was at night, confirming his suspicions of the area being plagued by a season of perpetual darkness.

The small army moved out about an hour after he woke up, and the darkness only thickened the further they walked. Soon, many lit torches. The lack of lighting carried with it a vileness that weighed down the air and seemed to clog his lungs.

Everyone was on edge, scanning around them as if there was something lurking where the light was yet to touch. The wind howled every so often, and each time it did Abram saw at least a few people whip their heads around as if something was attacking.

Abram's skin prickled and his hair stood on end. The reverse scorpions still warmed him to the core, but a subtle shiver set in and he was unable to shake it.

As they continued, Abram realized no one had any armor. For weapons, the *Magnums* had an assortment of clubs and spears. The *Elecki* all held spears. No one had a shield. No one had a bow or an arrow.

The Gray Lord was ahead, leading the procession, but Abram and the Shaman mingled with the front of the army. Snow remained on the ground, but it felt harder, more compact. Drifts and wind-swept mounds of snow started popping up. They were small at first, but as they trekked deeper into the Far North, the mounds turned to jagged boulders of ice that hindered their range of vision.

The boulders only increased as they progressed, and the army was often forced to move in single file lines through the blockades.

Wanting his own light, the Shaman overturned a bag of powder over his staff and whispered a staying utterance. His *nokofimbo*'s eyes glowed, casting dual beams through the darkness in front of him, and the powder would allow the radiance to remain for longer than if he had just whispered the words. Abram followed suit, only whispering instead of using powder.

Then Abram saw a torch ahead and to the right wink out. The *Elecki* holding the illumination brought it down and tried to light it again, setting it on the ground and striking two black rocks together that he pulled from a pouch inside his fur clothing.

A distant scream made Abram's pulse pound and he glanced at the Shaman. Everyone stopped moving. They waited a beat, straining to hear. Abram swallowed and gripped his rod tighter.

More screams came from the distance and everyone ducked even though nothing appeared to be in the air. Abram pointed his rod in different directions, trying to control his breathing and spot what was causing the screams.

An *Elecki* sprinted out from around an ice boulder in front of them, eyes wide, arms out in front. He tripped and hit the ground hard, releasing a bellow. He tried to crawl. The Shaman was closer and shone his light on the fellow. A second later the *Elecki* was dragged behind the boulder and his fading screams were cut off in an instant.

Now Abram's pulse thumped in his ears and his eyes spread in terror.

"*Vivuli!*" came a cry that echoed through the ranks.

"What! What is it!" Abram screamed, still turning his staff in every direction but seeing nothing.

"The shadow!" the Shaman responded, also turning in different directions but appearing far calmer than Abram.

Something cold wrapped around Abram's ankle and pulled. He almost fell but caught himself, shining his light at his leg and beginning an utterance before he saw what was attacking him.

The light from his *nokofimbo* illuminated the threat before he finished the utterance. He assumed it was 'the shadow' that the Shaman mentioned. It had a thin, translucent upper body with long, slender limbs that were sharpened at the joints. Its face, or where a face would usually be, was instead an emptiness that seemed to suck in the surrounding air. The look was very much like seeing heat drifting off of the blacktop on a summer day, but instead of coming off it was going in.

A split second after Abram witnessed the creature, he felt it release its grip from his leg. It made no sound, but it vibrated violently in the beam of his *nokofimbo* light. A clock's tick later, tumors started bulging out, growing from and covering the joints first before spreading across the torso.

The utterance forming on Abram's lips ceased, and he lowered his eyes as he realized what was happening. Soon, the creature was covered in tumors that solidified into ice. Before long, the whole creature was a block of ice, resembling the boulders that surrounded them. Abram stared at the frozen creature, panting, his heart still pounding. A warm confidence glazed over his heart. If this was the worst the Far North could toss his way, things would be a cake walk.

More screams honed his attention and he looked around. The Shaman was no longer within eyesight, and mayhem had erupted everywhere else. Every so often an *Elecki* would run past, fleeing from the shadow creatures.

Abram tossed his staff into the air and whispered a rotation utterance. His rod turned into a disc that rained light around the area. In the brightness of his staff, the boulders became translucent, and inside were a variety of twisted figures. After whispering for the rod to spin for a while, Abram finally stopped and caught his staff when it fell back to Earth. The Shaman walked around an ice boulder a few seconds later with a smile on his face.

"Grand thinking, Abram," he said, tapping his staff against the ground. "Absolutely grand."

Abram smiled as his ego swelled. The screams had stopped, and the sound of shattering ice started ringing out.

When the group started moving again, the *Elecki* were more hesitant than before. A few still had their torches lit, but the ones that had their lights snuffed by the shadows were unable to rekindle. The group was darker than before, and despite the boost to his ego, the doubt squeezing his heart grew stronger.

They walked over a few *Elecki* corpses, and Abram realized the dead had been taken by frostbite. He thought back to the faces of the *vivuli* and wondered if they could suck all the heat away from a person.

Another hour into the land and a massive *vivuli* appeared above them. It was ten times the size of the others, but instead of attacking it simply hovered. Abram only noticed a small part of it first as torchlight reflected off of its belly. Even with the recent victory, seeing the size of the creature made his heart quicken. When the *Elecki* saw it they fled in terror, though some were bold enough to chuck their spears at it. The weapons drifted right through the creature with no effect.

Abram glared at the face of the creature. Defiant of its very presence, he held up his staff and started whispering a brightening utterance. The beam coming from his *nokofimbo*'s eyes widened and brightened until it tore into the creature's entire front half. The vibrations started and the beast soon fell, cracking but not shattering against the ground. Abram hoped none of his allies had remained beneath it.

Abram thought of making a joke about the size of the creature and whether the darkness had anything bigger for him to destroy, but movement atop the solidified shadow drew his attention. Something small slid down the frozen face of the beast, and about halfway to the bottom kicked off and sailed through the air. The newcomer landed on bended knee with a thud.

Abram's heart skipped a beat and he stepped back. Recognition sent his mind reeling and he felt his mouth go dry from surprise. He gulped and struggled to find words.

"I have longed for this moment for what seems an eon," the newcomer said, smirking as she fully erected herself and locked eyes with Abram.

Abram started playing with his engagement ring. "Koñél?"

CHAPTER 72

"**A**s impossible as it seems, you appear more surprised at my presence than I of yours," Koñél said.

"State your intent!" the Shaman said, assuming a combat stance and pointing his rod at Koñél.

She barely glanced at him before focusing on Abram again. She stared at him for a bit in silence before taking another step forward. The last time they'd been together, he'd been tricked into believing she was on the good side. Still, a persuasiveness clung to her presence, and he felt compelled to trust her. Her hair swirled gently in the air, casting shadows against her face and the ground.

"That scar," Koñél said, reaching out a hand and stroking the remnant from Abram's first battle. She looked like she would mention it some more, but instead changed the topic. "I sensed your arrival, and though I have other matters to attend to, I had to see you for myself."

Even in the darkness Koñél looked the same. She had the same tan skin with the same raspberry beryl, almond-shaped eyes. Abram spun his engagement ring around his finger a bit more as he glanced at her mouth, remembering their single kiss and yearning to feel the grace of her lips against his again. The low lighting made the situation worse. The pendent around her neck glinted in the light from his staff.

But with all the similarities, something about Koñél was different. Same height and apparent age, but she seemed more mature, as if she'd undergone something that had transformed her to her core.

It took Abram a few moments to notice it, but the metal rod she once carried had been replaced with a *nokofimbo* staff. She was a full-fledged artist now. The reasons she took so long to receive a *nokofimbo* remained a mystery to him.

"I am pleased to see you have become an initiate of the arts," Koñél said. "Have you—"

Koñél's sentence was cut short by the Shaman's swing toward her head. In an instant she raised her staff and blocked, countering with her own staff. The blow was an uppercut and a sharp crack echoed as the Shaman's head snapped back on his neck. His body slackened and he dropped over backward toward the ground.

"No!" Abram screamed, dropping his staff and attempting to catch his friend before he hit the ground.

He succeeded, but the Shaman's body was limp. Abram held the Shaman in his arms and fought back tears. He shook his friend and gingerly placed his body on the ground. He tried shaking a bit more, but to no avail. He checked the Shaman's pulse at the wrist and the neck. No response.

Abram's eyes went wide and he felt like he'd been punched in the gut.

"You can't be dead," Abram said, his emotions clouding his mind. "You can't be dead!"

Koñél's counter attack was almost effortless, and she moved with such speed Abram had barely been able to track her. The surrounding army of *Magnums* and *Elecki* closed in around the three artists. Many had spears raised, but no one made a move.

A few seconds later the Gray Lord pushed through the crowd and fell to his knees when he saw the Shaman. Tears welled in his eyes and spilled over, and he swiped at his eyes with his forearm and free hand. Wailing, the Gray Lord hung his head and dropped his staff, supporting his upper body with his palms against the ground.

Abram rocked for a few seconds, the sadness burning his whole face and twisting his gut. But the sadness turned to rage and he clenched his teeth. He balled up his fists and rose to his feet, glaring at Koñél, embracing the rage as it boiled inside him.

"I apologize," Koñél said, her face still steady. "He attacked and I defended."

Abram was at a loss for words. His breathing elevated and he lowered his head and eyelids, each second adding to his rage. Though it had been still before, his *nokofimbo* started to wriggle, as did Koñél's. She glanced between the two.

"I mean you no harm, Abram of the Second."

Abram reached to his side and pulled out his bag of powder, wishing the Shaman had done the same before even thinking of attacking her. He whispered a protection utterance on the dust and poured it atop his head. The powder showered around him and twinkled green in the light of his *nokofimbo*. He felt a cooling sensation cover his body for a moment and he bent down, gripping his staff in his real arm, balling up the fist on his prosthetic.

"You killed my friend and want to help the Red Mage kill everyone and everything I know. Koñél," Abram started, his rage bubbling to a point it had never reached before. "I mean you all the harm in the world—in all the worlds."

Koñél laughed as he finished his sentence. "You may mean ill, but harm will only come to those that attack me."

On queue with her words, a spear pierced through the darkness. It sailed straight for her temple. At the last second she turned her head and her hair caught it. The strands tossed it harmlessly into the snow. The army didn't give up after one failed spear attack. Hundreds of spears came next, and Abram took a few steps back, wondering if any strays would strike him by accident.

Koñél locked eyes with him and smirked. She whispered something quick. Again, moving so fast Abram could barely detect her, she stooped down and grabbed two handfuls of snow, throwing the powder into the air. The snow melted and formed an umbrella of water that shielded ten square feet around her, but instead of falling back to the ground it hovered. The spears struck the liquid and plunked into it. Instead of passing through, nothing came out the other end.

When the last spear had entered she winked at Abram. The water rained down toward her, returning to snow and forming a white cloud around her before dissipating. Some stuck to her shoulders, and her hair brushed the residue off and onto the ground.

Abram's eyes widened in surprise, but as he looked at the Shaman's body his rage returned. Seeing her display of power made him nervous, but he knew there were no other options. He cared about her, but she stood as the greatest threat humanity—and the aggregate life forms of every dimension—had ever known. He had to attack, but a mix of shock and fear kept him still.

An *Elecki* came barreling toward her, lunging at her with his fists. She easily dodged, turned him around, and kicked him back behind the boulder he had come from. After another charged and was defeated, she threw back her cloak, overturned a bag of *fim* powder onto her staff and slammed it into the ground.

An orange shockwave shattered every ice boulder and knocked Abram off his feet. He landed on his backside with a groan and blinked a few times before being able to focus again. He had dropped his staff when the shockwave hit, and its light cast an arch of brightness in one direction. Ice shards were mixed in with unmoving *Elecki* and

Magnums alike. The darkness concealed whether they were alive, but Abram sensed they had been killed.

"They too attacked and suffered the consequences. Still, I have spared the artists. I have spared you."

Koñél smiled and held out a hand for Abram. He scowled at her, rejecting her hand and scooting back a few paces before grabbing his rod and pushing up to his feet. He glared at her for a long time, his anger compounding in his veins.

"Join me, Abram, for I have missed you. I long to spend every moment with you at my side."

A shutter of desire jolted through him and for a moment his features softened. He missed her too, and wanted to be with her. He almost croaked, *I can't*, but knew his voice would crack and betray his emotions. Even without speaking, Koñél lifted her chin and smiled, detecting his true feelings.

After taking a second to collect himself, he slowly exhaled a long breath. He closed his eyes and tried to think of all the good he had experienced around her. He knew she had a good heart, and good hearts always came around eventually. The Gray Lord's words popped into his head, of how Koñél was merely a deceived character, like he had been. Being the victim of deception meant she had acted in ignorance and could only be held partially responsible for her actions.

But then he thought of all the death she had caused, and, even in ignorance, the deaths she intended to cause.

"I'm sorry, Koñél, I really am," Abram said, pausing and squinting his eyes. A well of sadness rose within him even as he thought the words. "I can never be with you as long as you're on the wrong side." He glanced at the ground. A smidgen of hope still smoldered in his heart. "*You* need to join us. Let us open your eyes and show you what evils the Red Mage has tricked you into believing."

Koñél giggled. "I have witnessed all that I needed to in order to know the truth."

Movement to Koñél's right caught Abram's attention. The Gray Lord, also being an artist, had recovered from the orange blast. He had inspired his staff and was swinging it toward Koñél's head.

CHAPTER 73

Things slowed to a crawl as Abram watched the Gray Lord take a swing. Koñél continued to look at Abram, but at the last moment she bent her head and the rod missed. The Gray Lord spun the rod around. The light utterance was gone, but the glow of the inspired weapon created an arc of light as he swung for a second strike.

Koñél ducked, wedged her feet between his legs, and rammed her shoulder into his torso. He flew back six feet and thudded into the snow. He slid another foot or so before stopping. Visions of the Shaman's defeat plagued Abram's mind, and he narrowed his eyes, yelling and charging Koñél. The Gray Lord hopped back to his feet.

The two artists headed for Koñél from opposing directions: Abram at her front, the Gray Lord at her back. Abram led with his staff. Glints of light caught on the Gray Lord's face, turning his eyes into angry thunderstorm clouds. Koñél faced Abram but lowered into a fighting stance as the two approached her.

Abram reached her first and couldn't bring himself to swing for her face. He jabbed at her midsection and she jumped back just as the Gray Lord reached her. He had started a swing, but since she moved back it hindered his blow. He pushed her forward and swung again. She turned and somersaulted over him this time.

Landing behind him so their backs faced, she leaned forward and kicked back. He flew into Abram and they both fell to the ground.

Koñél had kept her stance after the kick, and as they recovered she finally lowered her leg, rotating until they were facing. She smirked again and Abram realized her eyes were glowing orange. He had only seen her inspire her rod, which also glowed orange, but she must have poured dust atop her body at some point.

With a growl the Gray Lord was back on his feet and charging toward Koñél. Abram struggled to stand but joined the lord, running behind him and whispering a speed utterance as he went.

The light utterance on his rod faded. Only the colored glows from Koñél's rod and eyes, and the Gray Lord's rod remained for illumination. The glows pierced the darkness a few inches around wherever they traveled.

The Gray Lord was the first to take another swing at Koñél, but she ducked and Abram heard a thump. Her rod swung next, but the Gray Lord blocked, and the shockwave almost knocked Abram over. He kept coming and took his own swing at Koñél. Her rod was still locked with the Gray Lord's but Abram's rod stopped before hitting the mark. She had caught his attack with her free hand, even with his speed elevated from the utterance.

Something rammed into his stomach and pressed the oxygen from his lungs. He bent over and coughed as he recovered, but before he was finished a foot slammed into his face.

Pain rocked through his skull. He landed on his back. Blackness was all he saw and he thought he was unconscious until he heard the crack of the staffs slamming together again. Another shockwave blew over him and he found it even harder to breathe.

His head throbbed but the time on his back allowed his diaphragm to recover. He groaned and switched his staff to his prosthetic arm. He sat up, turned over, and pushed off the ground with his real hand, feeling something soft and cold.

He nullified his speed utterance and whispered the glow utterance again. Bringing his glowing rod around revealed it was the Shaman's body. Abram swallowed the lump that formed in his throat and he embraced the pain. He embraced the feeling of regret and grief and anger.

"I won't let you die in vain," Abram said, a renewed vigor pulsing alongside the adrenaline in his veins.

The Gray Lord and Koñél were still dueling. Though barely visible in the low lighting, Abram could make out that Koñél appeared to be playing with him. His strikes would fly harmlessly through the air, revealing portions of her body at a time as she dodged. Weak blows intended to merely knock him off balance were used as retaliation. Abram was unable to see the lord's face, but he assumed frustration rippled across it.

Back on his feet, Abram charged and took his own swing at Koñél. He put all the force he could muster behind the blow, hoping his prosthetic was strong enough.

Abram's blow was blocked by Koñél's staff, but this time she was rocketed backward. The crack echoed and deafened Abram, and the force of the shockwave put him on his butt again.

His eyes darted around but all he saw was darkness and the Gray

Lord. Moments later the lord walked over to him and put a hand on his shoulder. Abram stood and smiled, glancing at his arm. For the first time in his life he was thankful for germs.

But a distant orange glow appeared in the darkness and Abram's joy began to fade. He focused and assumed the fighting stance he had seen the Shaman assume many times before. The orange glow turned into an orange streak, reaching them faster than Abram anticipated. The Gray Lord saw it too, and tried cutting it off.

Koñél spun as he swung, catching his rod with her free hand. Still moving toward Abram, she continued her spin, holding onto the Gray Lord's staff until she was facing forward again. She released, and the lord flew in Abram's direction. The throw was strong enough that the Gray Lord sailed over top of Abram.

As Koñél neared, the glow from her eyes showed that her nose was leaking orange powder from both nostrils. Rage was etched into her features and accentuated by the shadows. Trying to time his attack to adequately counter, Abram jumped forward and swung.

But she was too fast. His swing sailed down but she sidestepped, sending her rod into his spine. A crack that he felt through his whole body rang out and he felt his limbs go limp. The pain was brief, and then he felt nothing. He was airborne and heading toward the ground face first. He willed his limbs to break his fall, but nothing moved.

He landed in the snow and thought he would suffocate. Unable to breathe or move, terror settled in. But before he felt lightheaded from the lack of oxygen, something turned him so his face was to the sky. Koñél's orange-tainted face consumed his view as she bore down on him.

Her smirk had faded, and a deadly seriousness was across her features. Dust still leaked from her nostrils, and some sprinkled against his face, but after a few seconds it stopped and she wiped away the remnants.

"I think, I think you broke my back," Abram said, his voice trembling with the implications of what that meant. "I can't," Abram started, willing anything aside from his lips to take action. "I can't move!"

"You will be fine," Koñél spat, lifting his torso up so that he was sitting upright. She straightened his legs out in front of his body.

"I'll be fine! I'll be fine! You broke my back! Not my finger! Not my toe! But my back! I kind of need that unbroken and intact to be freaking fine!"

Koñél put both hands on his shoulders and lifted him so that only his heels remained on the ground. She whispered something before lifting him quickly and forcefully off the ground. He felt a pop.

In line with the pop, pain seared through his every molecule and he cried out, falling over to the ground and hugging himself. Again Koñél's face consumed his line of sight and he whimpered as the agony continued.

"See. Fine."

Abram was in too much pain to provide a verbal response, but he frowned, breathing deeply as he tried to manage the suffering. She stroked his head in a tender manner, confusing him. After a few more seconds the pain subsided enough for him to speak.

"Where's the Red Mage?"

She smiled at him as if all it took to abate her anger was his vulnerability.

"He is completing his mission. Were you unable to feel him in your world? I know you went back, as did he."

"What? He's back home?" Abram moved to stand as if there were a portal nearby for him to use, but once he was sitting up he stopped. "How?"

"Irrelevant, but I am sure that he will complete the mission momentarily."

Fear tightened Abram's chest and he stood up. The darkness pressed in around him, and he felt the remaining embers of hope suffocate in his heart. He thought of the Shaman.

"Now do you understand? There is but one choice left. Join *us*."

"Never!" Abram said, almost screaming at the top of his lungs. "I'll never join a group that thought it was a good idea to murder billions of innocent people."

Koñél shrugged. "You will join us eventually."

"Never," Abram whispered this time.

Koñél turned and scanned the darkness as if something were waiting for her. "When the opportune time arrives, we will meet again. I hope then you will be willing to remain at my side."

With that she walked off into the darkness. Abram glared at her orange glow until he could no longer see it. His shoulders heaved as he breathed deep and he stood.

"Take heart, Outsider, there is still hope."

Abram turned and saw the glow of the Gray Lord's staff. He had caused it to cast a beam of light again, and walked over with no apparent damages.

"Don't be so naïve. The Red Mage is already back home. If he's been there all this time…" Abram couldn't bring himself to finish the sentence.

"We can still go and stop him."

"How? Your fortress is under siege, Koñél just kicked our butts without breaking a sweat, and we're stranded in the middle of the shadow realm with no army."

"Come, we will do what we must."

The Gray Lord turned and walked back through the darkness. Abram sighed and found the Shaman's body. He said a final goodbye and realized the Shaman had attacked without using his dust because he had no more bags. Abram snagged the coolant for the transportation device. He also picked up the Shaman's staff, finding the *kumiza* had been attached to one end. He removed the sacred spearhead. As the only thing able to penetrate the blessing of the *fim* powder, it was the best weapon to use against an artist.

Even with the weapon, he knew all hope was lost. Images of the small army they had taken with them to the Far North appeared in his mind and despair darkened his spirits further. He followed the Gray Lord through the darkness in silence, wishing Koñél had left him paralyzed on the ground. Left him there to die.

CHAPTER 74

They retraced their steps and Abram was too distracted with thoughts of doom and failure to pay much attention to the deceased *Elecki* and *Magnums*. He crunched over ice shards from the shadows and ice boulders. The Gray Lord was equally quiet, though he somehow still moved with purpose.

More light filtered through the clouds as they continued to move, and when it was bright enough to see a few hundred feet in any direction, the *wam-baika* swooped in and grabbed them. Only when he was airborne again did Abram realize how cold he had grown. Adrenaline had lingered in his veins for a while during their journey out, but even when it faded and his senses should have normalized, he was numb to it all. Now, with the change of travel, his senses heightened for a while and he shivered.

They stopped every so often, as usual, but he refused to eat or drink, even when they made it back to fertile ground and the Gray Lord tossed a fruit at him. He simply moped and remained secluded in his head.

Almost at the end of their return journey, Abram ran out of vibration pills and his memory became blotchy. The Gray Lord knowledge shared with him and retrieved Abram's recent memories, but he also shared the various languages of the dimension. After Abram's memories were made clear again, he regretted receiving them.

It was bad enough that his mission had been an utter failure. He had allowed people to get hurt and die under his watch, and now Koñél was too powerful to defeat and the Red Mage was back home murdering everyone. The Shaman was dead, any hopes of an army had been cut down by Koñél in a flash, and Ruth and the mercenaries were MIA.

Close to the Gray fortress, the army of blackness appeared, stretching in every direction and smothering the grass. The *wam-baika* had taken them high, and they had a clear view of the battlefield. Large winged creatures Abram had never seen floated above the soldiers in certain places, but none seemed to notice them.

"The soldiers are still here," Abram started, looking at them with disgust. "What are those flying things?"

"*Malaika.*" After a pause. "The blessing on the *Ghafarians* has faded. We can defeat them with the arts."

"How can you tell?" Abram said.

"You will learn," The Gray Lord replied.

Before they reached the fortress, a pair of *Malaika* noticed them and gave chase. The Gray Lord whispered something and the two creatures' wings tied together like a bowtie. The beasts dropped to the ground, shrieking.

That caused the *Ghafarians* to notice, and they started shooting arrows. Abram assumed they would just dodge or block the arrows before entering the castle, but the Gray Lord willed the *baika* to set down a few feet from the front door.

Ghafarians charged, and Abram narrowed his eyes, lowering his head and clutching his staff. Anger hammered adrenaline nails through his veins and he started to shake.

"We will smite this scourge from my land once and for all," the Gray Lord said through gritted teeth.

For the first time in a while Abram agreed wholeheartedly. He was less concerned with clearing the land than he was with releasing his frustration and indignation. Fury hummed in his heart and he switched his staff to his prosthetic.

The *Ghafarians* came in waves of six or seven, so the Gray Lord and Abram spread out a little so friendly interference was kept to a minimum. Abram swung and struck gold almost every time, the rapidity of his prosthetic too much for the strong, but still relatively slow *Ghafarians*. The *Ghafarians* adapted as they did in previous battles he had witnessed, but Abram did as well.

When they changed their attack plan to surround him and move in from all angles, he whispered the utterance of fiery follicles. When new attackers came, he whispered the utterance of oil blood. When new attackers came he whispered the utterance of magnified sickle cell.

Eventually he grew bored of whispering utterances, noticing mere words robbed him of the satisfaction in smashing into flesh and bone. So he danced a ballet of torment with the *Ghafarians*. In his rage he slew hundreds of *Ghafarians* without falling out of rhythm. He swung his rod and twirled his body. He punched his prosthetic and smashed through armor. A *malaika* decided to try and attack him, but he sent the creature into the ground before beating one of its wings to goo.

The attackers eventually thinned as their numbers dwindled, and Abram took his time with each enemy. Instead of a single, fatal hit, he opted for three or four injuring strikes before dealing the death blow.

His dance brought him pleasure. He embraced the anger and pain of the past month and relished each connection he made with an enemy body part. He smirked at every crack and grinned at every crunch. The screams of flying *Ghafarians* made a warm sensation drip through his veins, and his passions were only quenched by their deaths.

All the suffering he had endured surfaced and egged him on. All the death he had seen told him he was justified in his brutality. All the lives that would be lost told him the *Ghafarians* deserved no mercy.

With each spin of his rod and strike of his fist, Abram could feel his power increasing. Instead of tiring, somehow he grew more energized, his movements accelerating and his strength rallying.

Soon, the *Ghafarian* army realized there was no beating an angry artist, and the remaining troops turned to retreat. Abram almost laughed as he whispered an utterance to his staff before slamming it down, using a modified version Koñél's utterance that had killed all but the artists.

Instead of killing, Abram merely crippled them all. *Malaika* fell from the sky with broken wings and *Ghafarians* stumbled to the ground with broken legs and backs. Cries of anguish and torment filled the air and Abram smiled.

One by one, Abram stomped through the field of battle, dealing death blows to the crawling enemies until a tug on his arm stopped him. It was the Gray Lord. A troubled look wrinkled his countenance, and Abram felt his heart sink a little as he recognized what he was doing—what he was allowing his heart to enjoy.

"Even the barbaric deserve mercy," the Gray Lord said before whispering an utterance and slamming down his staff.

A white light shone and flew through the battlefield and Abram squinted. When the light faded, the black army had been turned to piles of dust. A breeze carried much of the remains away, and Abram calmed the racing horse within his chest. His breathing normalized and he turned from the Gray Lord, angry he was forced to stop the killing.

The Gray Lord walked the distance back to the fortress. Abram followed, and in front of the gate, the *wam-baika* came and picked them up, ferrying them over the wall and through the opening in the courtyard.

It hit Abram all at once, and he wondered if the Gray Lord felt it as well. Exhaustion like he had never felt dragged his whole spirit downward, and all the times the Shaman and Gray Lord had spoken of conserving their energy finally made sense. In the heat of the battle the sensation had gone unnoticed, but now that he was drained he realized that an artist's power, while renewable, was finite. His physical strength remained, but it felt as if his soul was diminished.

Smells of death and decay were thick within the fortress. A few bodies lay scattered throughout the courtyard, and Abram started to wonder if he would see the mercenaries and Ruth.

The Gray Lord led him toward the transportation room and Abram paused, lifting a questioning eyebrow. It took the Gray Lord a few seconds to realize he was walking alone, and he turned.

"Aren't you going to see if there's anyone alive in there?" Abram said, thumbing over his shoulder, allowing the faulty actions of another to bandage his guilt.

"They are all dead. I can sense nothing but emptiness."

The Gray Lord's face was haggard as if he felt the grief of losing each and every one of the soldiers. Abram remembered how he could sense certain people and wondered if it were possible for the Gray Lord to sense all of his men. Could he feel their pain?

In the room, they saw that things had been tampered with, and Abram knew it was the mercenaries or Ruth.

Abram found the note left from Ruth and read it. A ping of anxiety ricocheted through his ribcage as he thought of the group out in the wild, but he would have to hunt for them later. He told the Gray Lord of their decision while he helped put things back in order.

The Gray Lord remained mute and Abram fished around in his pocket until he pulled out the coolant the Shaman had taken. Thinking of his friend produced a bubble of sadness, but he swallowed it.

After inserting things in their proper place, the Gray Lord activated the machine and joined Abram in front of the doorway.

Abram thought of Ruth and the mercenaries and strained to see if he could determine how close they were. He was unable, but he still knew they were alive. Now he was leaving them, and it made him feel worse, but he knew they had to see if there was anything to be done back home to stop the Red Mage.

With a sigh, Abram followed the Gray Lord into the portal and sent up a silent prayer.

CHAPTER 75

Abram slowly opened his eyes and blinked the blur away. At first he thought he was dreaming. Fires smoldered everywhere. Trees had been blown over—all in the same direction. All the vehicles on the road had been burned out and overturned. Debris of all kinds littered the ground. Surprisingly, aside from a few charred forms still inside the cars, there were very few corpses.

Smoke and ash blotted out most of the sun, and he was instantly reminded of *Volcanu*. He coughed hard a few times and had to fight the urge to wipe his eyes as they grew watery from ash.

A burning smell clung to the air. At first it smelled like burning rubber, but then he thought it was wood. Soon he realized it was a combination of the entire area. Everything was either burning or burnt.

He was on his stomach when he came to, his staff on the ground beside him, and he pushed up but kept his lower half flat on the ground. With wide eyes he scanned the area. No birds chirped or glided overhead. No distant car horns or screams. Nothing moved. Nothing made a sound except for fire as it constantly crackled.

It took a lick of flame catching on his pant leg to really believe that what he was seeing was real. The Red Mage had to have succeeded in his mission and fled the scene.

Groaning from behind him pulled his attention. The Gray Lord was waking up, pushing off the ground and blinking. Confusion and fear rippled through his features and Abram pushed all the way to his feet. The Gray Lord jumped up and brought his staff around to a striking pose, but Abram held up both hands to placate his friend.

He explained the situation to the Gray Lord, and clued him in on his thoughts.

"I believe you are mistaken," the Gray Lord started, examining the environment for signs of life. "It is true that the Red Mage appears to have obliterated all living things in this land, but he has not left. I sense his darkness."

Abram all but ignored the Gray Lord, thinking of his loved ones and wondering if they suffered. He dropped down to his knees and glared at the ground.

"What's the point? If he's here or if he's gone. The deed is done. We're too late."

The Gray Lord fell to one knee in front of Abram and glared at him with determination until Abram glanced into his eyes.

"Regardless of the outcome here, the Red Mage will not stop. His thirst for destruction will only be quenched when nothing is left."

Abram shrugged. "I'm done trying. I just want to die with the rest of my world."

"Then die," the Gray Lord said, standing to his feet and turning away from Abram.

Agreement was the last thing Abram expected, and it jarred him. He looked at the Gray Lord's back for a beat before returning to staring at the ground.

"Die, but die with the knowledge that you are only truly defeated when you yield to difficulty. The ones for which you mourn would be ashamed. Your company stranded back on my home would be ashamed. Safi would be ashamed." The Gray Lord turned back to Abram, refusing to coddle him. "I, more than the others, am ashamed. Ashamed to have taken the prophecies for truth. Ashamed at your weakness."

Anger and embarrassment scorched through Abram's veins and he started breathing harder. He stood to his feet and charged the Gray Lord, furious that the lord was bold enough to say what he said, but madder over the fact that it was all true.

The Gray Lord easily dodged Abram's attempt at a tackle and Abram didn't try to attack again. He simple dropped to his knees again and let the tears flow. He cried for a moment before the Gray Lord placed a hand on his shoulder. Thoughts of every failure the past month had brought came rushing over his body. He had failed at everything, and nothing he could do could fix that. More tears pushed from his eyes until they dripped against the concrete.

"Arise, Abram. There is still time to act in a manner worthy of honor."

Abram's breathing remained elevated but he swiped his forearm across his face. He looked out at the destruction around him and his scowl deepened. He clenched his teeth and punched the ground with his prosthetic, leaving a crater.

"You win. Let's go find Red and end him. I want revenge."

The Gray Lord nodded. "This is your home. Where do we go?"

Abram shrugged. "I don't even know where we are." Abram bit his lip and thought for a moment. "We need to find the military base where the portal is. You say you can still sense Red, but he won't want to stay here much longer if he's already killed everyone. He'll have to head there to leave."

The Gray Lord nodded again and waited for Abram to lead the way.

"But I still don't know where we are or how to get to the base."

Abram looked around but nothing looked familiar. Picking a random direction, he started walking.

They walked for what felt like hours before Abram found a half destroyed street sign. He cleared off some soot and dirt and smiled.

"The base isn't right around the corner, but it's less than a day away." Abram looked at the sky but was still unable to determine the time of day. "Guess we can walk until it gets too dark to see."

So that's what they did. Abram led the way. He was able to navigate using the road. The street sign he had recognized told him they were near the highway, and when he saw the damaged ramp they took it. From the highway the base was a straight shot.

Walking with vigor allowed them to get within a few miles when night fell. The environment turned blacker than the Gray Lord was used to, and it was a challenge for Abram to try and explain the differences between their moons.

The darkness was broken up by car fires and burning debris. Being the highway, there were far more cars and a lot less other debris.

The Gray Lord said it was best that they rest. His sense for the Red Mage had been continually growing, and now that they were close to the base he guessed the Red Mage was already at their destination. It was true that they would reach him sooner if they walked through the night, but if they confronted him with anything less than full strength they would be defeated. They had to risk the time and take a break.

CHAPTER 76

Grief, nervousness, anger, and the memories of previous defeats slashed at Abram through the night. The cries and agony twisted faces of the *Ghafarians* he had killed in battle haunted his mind and he was unable to sleep more than a few minutes at a time.

He thought of his family and friends and everything he knew being gone in the blink of an eye. It felt like he had just been home on the base the week before. He found some comfort in knowing that Ruth was still alive, and he began to doubt if he should tell her about Koñél. Now, if he told her she might leave him and he would truly be alone. Before, it was what he wanted, but now the thought was terrifying.

Dawn came and Abram was saddened by the absence of morning bird songs. But he felt refreshed despite barely getting any sleep, and a renewed vigor for the Red Mage's demise overtook him. He shook the Gray Lord awake.

"Can you still sense him? Is he still here?"

"Yes, there is still time."

So the two set out for the base, walking the remaining distance to their destination. Surprisingly, it was in relatively good shape. There were a few buildings that had caved in roofs, but most structures were still standing.

Abram led the way to the proper building and they walked through the halls toward the room that held the device. Bodies were everywhere. Some were twisted in unnatural positions as if they had been hooked and tied together by a giant, invisible chain. Others were missing limbs, though there was little blood, as if their appendages had simply been sucked back into their bodies.

"He is close," the Gray Lord said, pulling out a bag of powder and dumping it atop his body. When the dust settled he whispered an utterance on his staff.

Abram did the same, adrenaline hammering through his body and making his veins shake. Things were quiet in an unsettling way. It was the first time Abram had experienced the halls so silent since he had snuck to the portal when he first crossed over. Even then the occasional clomp of the patrolmen's boots had sent him scampering to find cover. Now, nothing.

They passed through the door to the portal room and fresh waves of anger and adrenaline broke into Abram's system. The Red Mage was indeed inside, tampering with one of the consoles. He looked up non-chalantly before returning his attention to the console.

The Gray Lord dropped to his fighting stance. He opened his mouth to speak, but Abram beat him to it.

"You killed everyone," Abram said, his voice laden with grief and his mind reeling from the thought of facing the man that had murdered everyone he had ever known. An overwhelming black weight pressed against his chest and he found it hard to breathe. The staff in his hand almost fell, but he forced in a deep breath and narrowed his eyes.

"Well, not everyone. That's actually why I'm here. So far only one-third of this diseased dimension has been absolved, and this device is proving to be more difficult than I expected." Then, under his breath, "I knew I should have kept at least one alive."

Abram realized a million phrases of contempt and hate were running through his mind, but he was unable to produce any on his tongue. His breathing elevated and he made a fist. How dare the Red Mage speak of this destruction as if it were no more important than making a mistake on an etch-a-sketch and shaking things up to fix it.

"I knew it was a risk coming over and leaving the Third—if you haven't figured it out, I came over when you did, barely sneaking through the fortress using a disguise utterance—but I thought the lot of you would be dead." Surprise flashed across the Gray Lords face after the Red Mage said he had infiltrated the fortress. "I'm surprised Koñél and Zanda neglected to kill you two. I would have expected her forces were able to overrun you with no trouble. I suppose it was a mistake for me to have them attack in my absence."

"Zanda has been vanquished, as has your army. After we defeat you, we will destroy your apprentice and restore peace to all sides."

The Red Mage looked up, his face indicating annoyance with the Gray Lord. A little shock weaved through his features, but he quickly steadied his face and tinkered for a few more moments before turning to Abram.

"Your leader, Alvarez as he said his name was, was very helpful in explaining that you people have been busy." He smiled wickedly. "Ap-parently, they've devised a way to not only move from side to side, but also from place to place on the same side." He looked back to the console and sighed. "But, it seems I absolved him too quickly. I neglected to ask how the traveling works, and these controls are different than ones I am familiar with."

"I tire of your voice," Abram finally said, closing his eyes, shaking his head as if someone had asked him a question. When he opened his eyes again he continued. "This ends today. No one will suffer your presence ever again."

The Red Mage broke into a cackle, hunching over to finish his laugh and supporting his weight on the console's desk. Abram didn't flinch or change his features. Images of his mother flashed in front of his eyes, even though the Red Mage hadn't killed her.

"You dare challenge me?" The Red Mage said, walking out from behind the console and limping down to stand in front of them by the door. He noticed Abram's glance at his thigh and smirked. "You think that just because you dealt a lucky injury the last time we met that you can defeat me? Your skills have barely been conceived. At best you remain in infancy."

Abram pulled out the *kumiza* and flipped over his staff, fitting the piece atop it and whispering the sealing utterance. "This will taste your flesh again today."

The Red Mage stepped back and dumped a bag of black powder atop his head. Like before he almost disappeared in the cloud of blackness, but this time when it faded Abram noticed the dust was discoloring his veins. His eyes were blackened and the veins in his hands and arms, up to where Abram could see, were streaked with black.

"I found little enjoyment in absolving the inhabitants of this place," the Red Mage started, looking around. "But I will find the highest of pleasures in dismembering you."

Without another word the Red Mage swiped his staff upward toward Abram's chin. Abram blocked with his own staff, but the power from the blow nearly knocked him over. A crack clapped through the air but he remained on his feet, pulling a shocked look from the Red Mage. Abram smirked and shoved the staff down, swinging his rod for the Mage's side faster than he could block.

The blow was softened by the Red Mage's lifting of his arm, but the power behind Abram's swing sent the Mage flying into and through the wall to their left. Blasting through the wall created a loud boom, and when the Red Mage tore through two more walls, two more booms sounded off, though they were muffled.

Refusing to let the Red Mage recover, Abram and the Gray Lord darted through the hole in the wall, passing through the hallway and through the second and third holes as well. The Red Mage had been blasted into one of the indoor plasma rifle ranges. He struggled to his feet, coddling the arm that had been hit. It was broken in the middle of his forearm, pointing his wrist and half his forearm outward. He'd held his rod until he'd stood, but let it rest against him while he straightened his damaged arm, gritting his teeth and tilting his head to the side as cracks and pops filled the air.

The Red Mage only had a few seconds as Abram and the Gray Lord continued their charge. Abram swung again, but the Red Mage ducked and sent a foot into Abram's gut. The adrenaline in Abram's veins allowed him to all but ignore the pain, but the force still created some separation between them. The Gray Lord swung and the Red Mage blocked, dodging the Gray Lord's follow-up punch.

Using his good leg to back flip, the Red Mage landed and hopped forward, slamming his shoulder into Abram's stomach and knocking him to the ground. Mounted, Abram bucked but the Red Mage postured up, raising his staff over his head and bringing it down toward Abram's face. Unable to block, he cringed and prepared for the pain.

The Gray Lord clipped the Red Mage's head before he connected, causing him to miss and crack the linoleum floor beside Abram's head. Abram grabbed the Red Mage with his prosthetic and flung him to the right, jumping to his feet and sprinting after his target.

The Red Mage landed on his feet, the momentum of the throw causing him to skid backward a bit before stopping. He started whispering the reverse joints utterance, and the counter utterance automatically formed on Abram's lips. The two met and slammed together, cracking their rods with a boom that they both struggled to withstand. Their *nokofimbo* slithered and pressed against the confines of their rods.

Lending another helping hand, the Gray Lord struck the Red Mage's back. The Mage started whispering a freeze utterance on the Gray Lord but the lord countered while Abram whispered a blinding light utterance. Abram's utterance succeeded, though the light was visible only to the Red Mage. Abram kneed the mage, and after the knee strike created some distance, spun and swung his rod. He struck his mark, the Red Mage's face, and his enemy sailed up toward the ceiling.

Abram tossed up his staff, caught it in the middle, and chucked it with all the force he could muster from his prosthetic. It caught the Red Mage midair during his descent and pinned him to the wall with the firing range targets.

Still breathing faster than usual, Abram ran over to where the Red Mage was pinned, balling up a fist, preparing to deal the finishing blow. But the Red Mage was slumped over the staff. The *kumiza* had pierced his heart, and black dust sprinkled from the wound. His face was caved in from the original blow, and dust poured from his eyes and nose and mouth. His arms were limp and Abram grabbed his staff. He whispered the release utterance for the *kumiza* so that it remained in the Mage's heart, preventing the dust from healing him. The Red Mage dropped to the floor when Abram removed his staff, and the black dust continued to pour out of the hole in his chest.

A bit in shock, Abram glared at the Red Mage's corpse and swallowed.

"You have succeeded," the Gray Lord said, walking over and putting a hand on Abram's shoulder.

Abram didn't feel like talking. He had indeed succeeded. He had completed the mission he had been tasked with after learning the truth, and it had been a long time coming, but he had won. He had avenged the deaths of billions, the deaths of his family, the deaths of his friends.

But even with all their lives avenged, he still felt a gaping hole in his own chest. None of the dead were brought back. He would still have to live the rest of his life without ever hearing their voices again. He tried to swallow the bulge of agony that welled up in his throat, but it came back up and his jaw fell open. His eyes were forced shut and his whole body heaved in sorrow. Dropping to his knees, he let the pain spill from his eyes and he cried out as loud as his lungs allowed. The Gray Lord tried to console him, but all Abram felt was despair.

CHAPTER 77

Abram sobbed until his eyes, face, and lungs hurt. Then he whimpered and sniffled on the ground for a while. When the grief had softened a little, he briefly thought of what the Gray Lord would think of him. He was supposed to be strong in his moment of victory, and instead he had broken down like a little baby.

"I heard the cries and came to investigate," came a voice from behind them. Abram and the Gray Lord both whipped around, their staffs raised in preparation. The newcomer held up his hands. "Take it easy guys." He glanced down at the Red Mage's body. "Didn't figure the bad guy to be one that cried, so I figured he had left." When Abram and the Gray Lord relaxed, the newcomer lowered his hands. "Never would have thought he would be dead."

Abram swiped a forearm across his cheeks and tried to compose himself. He recognized the newcomer as Ronald Sundback, the lead engineer that had done their final preparations. It was also the same engineer that had given them their pills.

"It feels like forever since I've seen a familiar face."

"How did you survive?" Abram said, the awe finally wearing off. "Is there anyone else?"

The engineer sucked his teeth. "Doubt it. When he first attacked everyone ran to defend this installment. I ran the other way." Sundback glanced down, ashamed of what he had done. "I was in a custodian closet in the next room over. He didn't think to look in there." There was a pause and the three looked at one another. "What happens now?"

All the negativity Abram felt weighed down on him, and he knew he needed something that would make him feel better.

"Do the showers work? It's been forever since I've taken one," Abram said. He knew it was an odd thing to think about with all that had happening and still needed to happen, but cleanliness calmed him.

"I didn't want to say anything, but you guys reek," Sundback said. Abram looked at him, the possibility of finally getting clean exciting him. "But no, there is no running water. Only still power so the bad guy could do whatever it was he wanted to do before you showed up."

Abram's shoulder sank. "Is there any food then, or has it all been eaten or destroyed?"

"Come to think of it, there is food actually. And a few hundred gallons of water. But it's probably better if we use it solely for drinking. No telling how long we'll be stranded without potable water."

"I'll take my chances," Abram said. "Where's that water?"

Sundback led them to the mess hall and opened the walk-in fridge, presenting the contents with an open arm. Abram grabbed two gallon jugs and found the bathrooms with the showers. He disrobed and stepped inside a shower stall, thanking God the soap in the dispensers was still available. He poured a little water on his body and lathered up with his hands, scrubbing every nook and cranny with glee. He even allowed himself the pleasure of humming a familiar tune.

He poured both gallons over his body and wished he had grabbed a third. He found the towels, picked one up, and took a deep sniff. The smell of fresh linen still lingered in the fabric and he took another hit. He had missed the smell.

Pausing when he picked up the sordid and torn ACU he had been in for the entirety of his visit in the Second, he decided to find a fresh one. He knew where the spares were kept, and even though it was against protocol to take from the supply without written permission, he did so anyway. As a formality, he took off his name strip and applied it to his fresh ACU before rejoining the Gray Lord and Sundback in the mess hall.

They had already gone through a number of canned beans, both green and baked, when Abram walked up.

"What'll it be," Sundback started with a grin. "Le crème of corn or le bake of beans?"

Abram shook his head at the bad go at a French accent. He opted for the baked beans. Creamed corn never sat right in his stomach. Abram picked up the can opener, opened his can and selected a utensil.

"These spoons clean?" Abram said, examining one.

"Probably not to your standards, but as far as I know."

Abram ignored the comment and debated going to heat up the spoon. His worried side won and he excused himself, using the stove's fire to disinfect before rejoining them again. He dug in and smiled. Baked beans had never tasted so good.

"So what is our next course of action? There's a good amount of food and water here, but it won't last forever."

Abram shrugged. "We look for other survivors. There have got to be some around here, right?"

"Doubt it. Whatever he did to obliterate the continent was pretty thorough. When he came to the base, he mentioned something about being drained, and having to kill everyone one by one because his power wasn't replenished enough to just wipe out the life without also destroying the electricity." Sundback looked at the table, a pained look on his face. "He was pretty confident everyone on the continent, except inside the base, was dead."

"The evil one mentioned only succeeding in killing one third, that means the remaining population is still alive." Abram nodded and downed a couple of spoons of beans as the Gray Lord continued. "Our first priority is to defeat Koñél. Her rage seems yet to be awakened, but who knows how long that will be."

"Stop her?" Abram said, his words broken up by his chews. "She barely even tried and was able to beat us in less than five minutes."

"Perhaps, but there is a way." The Gray Lord paused as if they would ask another question. When they were both quiet, he continued. "Koñél wears a pendant of purity, but because of the nature of her arrival in the Third, the pendant is incomplete. The other half, still rumored to be on the First, is the key to reclaiming her to the light."

"Rumored?" Abram started. "Sounds like a stretch. Even if the rumors are true, we've never been to the First. It's not like we can just Google Maps some directions."

"But you have the device necessary for crossing sides. We can use that."

Abram looked to Sundback. "That true? Can we modify that thing to go to another dimension we've never been to?"

Sundback perked up, as if he had been waiting to be called upon in class, and now, finally having the opportunity, was overjoyed to give his answer. "Theoretically, absolutely. The device is currently calibrated to carry any number of persons or items from this dimension to the one running parallel to it. If the way you guys are talking about it makes sense, and we're the Second, and have been traveling to the Third," Sundback held up his hands and moved his right hand parallel to his stationary left. "We should be able to recalibrate to go to the other side of us." He moved his right hand to the other side of his left. "Probably take some time before we can figure out how to get to the Fourth or however many other dimensions there are, but the First should be possible."

The Gray Lord nodded. "Then we shall try."

"Wait, wait, hold on," Abram said, setting down his can, the spoon clinking against the metal edges. "Are we sure it's safe? Theoretical and practical are not the same."

Sundback shrugged. "There's always a margin of error. You'll either end up floating through space, or, I don't know where, or you'll end up on target."

"Comforting," Abram said with a sigh, looking to the Gray Lord. "But what choice do we have?"

"Failure equals destruction either way. We try and we try soon."

"I appreciate your zest," Sundback said, smiling. "But, the reason the evil guy couldn't cross to the next continent was because there are fail-safes in place to prevent erroneously traveling to the wrong location. I need to bypass that, but new code and calculations need to be formulated before we can make the portal work right."

"So, get it done."

"Problem is, I'm not the guy that writes the code. That was Mike." Sundback looked down but said no more. "I know all the equations, but translating that into something the computer will understand is harder than it sounds.

"You were the one that got us all set up to go. You have to know something." Abram brought his eyebrows together, feeling a surge in urgency.

"True, I know something, but I don't know everything. Do you really want to risk the fate of the world on *something*?"

"Look around, Sundback, you're all we have. Give it your best and get it done. Like he said," Abram started, thumbing to the Gray Lord. "If we don't do this, we all die."

Sundback sighed. "Fine. But it won't be a thirty-second process. I could review Mike's code and figure something out, but I need time."

"How long?" the Gray Lord said.

"No clue. Three days. Thirty?" Abram and the Gray Lord shot him a look and Sundback held up his hands. "I've never done it before! Give me a break."

"Then get started!"

Sundback complied with a few more grumbles, and Abram and the Gray Lord followed him. He continually reminded them that their presence would only hinder his progress. He convinced them to go away, and the two went outside. Abram grabbed a few rations along the way.

Everything was still smoldering, but it seemed the fires were dying down a little. The world was quiet and Abram played with his engagement ring. He sat on a pile of rubble and ignored the discomfort. The pleasantness he felt from the shower wore off, and the turmoil of the past events returned to the forefront of his mind.

Thoughts of Ruth and the mercenaries and Koñél and the end of the world started to drag chilled fingers down the nape of his neck. Images of the *Ghafarians* he'd beaten to death flashed in front of his mind and he felt a darkness settle into his chest. He imagined he could still hear the Shaman's voice and thought of how senselessly his friend had died. A black mass settled into his heart and he wanted to scream but just sat there and glared at the destruction around him.

He wanted to keep the hope in his chest burning, but a thick oil smothered it out. Even if Sundback was successful, so what. Everyone in the dimension he cared about was dead. Ruth and the mercenaries were lost and might die at any moment. They stood as the last connection he had to home, but even if they made it back safely, then what? The world was dying before they left, and now their part of it was all but dead.

Picking up some rubble he chucked it as far as he could with his prosthetic but closed his eyes instead of watching where it went. The images of *Ghafarian* corpses and the Shaman and the dead bodies of his family and friends plagued him. He looked at the rations he'd grabbed and tossed them on the ground.

He wasn't hungry and didn't know if he ever would be again.

---End---

INHABITANTS AND HABITATS

Anga [*Ahn – Gah*] = Term used to describe an environment where grass is more abundant than anything else. Terrain can be hilly or flat. The area is always undeveloped with no sentient beings taking up residence. Can still include hunting grounds for civilizations taking up residence nearby.

Bu [*Boo*] = Blood sucking insect similar to mosquitos. Uses its feet to drain blood, and thus leave six itchy bumps after biting. The bite is painless. Enjoy sucking blood around the ear and mouth. The males are larger than the females, but unlike mosquitos both sexes need blood to reproduce. Usually do not travel in swarms, but on rare occasions they have been seen in swarms thousands strong. There have only been three recorded incidents when a swarm killed a sentient being, and in all three instances the victims were children who were asleep outside when a swarm overtook them.

Chawa [*Chah - Wah*] = Small colony insects that are found everywhere. Thousands of different species exist, and they are critical to most eco-systems. In almost every environment, some other creature eats them. Some species are also known to eat rotting flesh, helping in the decomposition process. In some environments, they are known to eat fabric, and in yet others they are known to eat wood. Considered pests when they enter a dwelling.

Craw [*Craw*] = Small bird with wings colored for camouflage. No other defenses. Eats insects and grubs. Sometimes roost on *kondor* and slurps the parasites off the cattle.

Elamu [*Ih - Lah - Moo*] = Language spoken by *Elecki* natives. Fluid and quick.

Elecki [*Eh - Leh - Kihy*] = Natives of *Electrode*. Created a wool-like lower garment to protect them from electricity. Hunter-gatherer society. Utilize the resources of the river for food. Also eat the reeds that grow along the water in select areas. The women do most of the cooking, while the men go hunting. Hostile to outsiders of all kinds.

Electrode [*Ih - Lek - Trohd*] = Land where an inorganic liquid-metal compound mixed with the soil. Constant electrical storms electrify the ground at night. The voltage in the ground is strong enough to fry higher functions and cause brain damage, but victims usually survive. The listless survivors found in the land are harmless, but serve as warnings to visitors.

Fim [Fihm] = Plant species used to create the blessed dust. A variety of colors exist among the plants, but they are all the same species. Some believe the plants are sentient and able to communicate and sense like any mobile creature, but evidence of this is lacking. Grow only in hot and humid environments, though can also only grow in soil. Once thought to grow out of lava and/or rock, this rumor was dispelled when researches attempted to start a *fim* field by scattering seeds inside a lava pool. Any *fim* growing on rock have actually grown through the rock, and their roots are still absorbing nutrients from the soil. One of the only plant species that can actively burrow in search of heat. Can either use photosynthesis for sustenance, or they can absorb nutrients through the soil exclusively. Have been known to grow in volcanic caverns underground, their roots stretching miles from the soil source.

Fleigh [*Flay*] = Species of singed creatures with black, oily skin. Native to caves next to the center of the Earth. Weak, but invincible. Most dangerous when they are able to swarm in flocks. One on one they are more terrifying to look at than to fight. Eats whatever fits into their mouths. When underground and food is scarce, their bodies can adapt to process rocks for nutrients. In rare occasions they have been known to be trained and kept as pets.

Ghafaria [*Gah - Fahr - Ee - Ah*] = Beach city. One of the only cities with the creation of true glass in the Third dimension. Also one of the largest. At one point in history they were a main hub for buying and transporting goods across to the other continents.

Ghafarians [*Gah - Fahr - Ee - An s*] = Natives of *Ghafaria*. Men respect strength and disrespect women because, physically, they are weaker. Women attend to the children, do most of the cooking, and make most of the clothing. Men hunt and relax. Main diet is fish and aquatic mammals. Eat the occasional shellfish as well. Seaweed is their only form of vegetation but they rarely eat it. The weakest *Ghafarian* still possesses double the strength of most sentient beings of non-*Ghafarian* descent.

Giza Sana [*Gee - Zah* ● *Sah - Nah*] = The cave where the White Lord once reigned. Also home to the *Midomo* tribe and a variety of glow species. Largely unexplored and most people fear it. Very few that enter have the privilege of exiting.

Gome [*Goh - Mee*] = Ancient trees that can cause un-healable harm to anyone practicing the arts. One of the only trees able to survive any temperature ranges and any form of weather, save for firestorms. The trees were blessed by artists at the beginning of time. Unlike the art practitioners of the current time, the artists of old were able to cast lasting spells without using the blessed dust. The first *gome* was blessed and bore fruit while still under the blessing, and thus every *gome* after has been blessed. In an effort to become invincible, hundreds of years after the initial blessing, ancient evil art practitioners banded together and cast a curse onto the trees that caused them to become fruitless. They couldn't kill the trees with the arts, but they were able to cut off their reproduction. The trees gradually died out, and only one is known to remain. The one is said to be the original *gome*, and is under the protection of the tribe that live within its branches. It is unusually large. Some say there are *gome* growing again, but this rumor has remained hearsay.

Haraka [*Ha - Rah - Kah*] = Large, slender, fast lizard. Most species are found near mountains. Some species are found on plains. Eats grubs and insects. Have been known to catch craws and eat them, but that is abnormal behavior. They have flaps on their bellies that assist them in descending heights that would otherwise cause death upon impact. They aren't capable of true flight, but someone people call them flying lizards. Used by many people for transportation. *Haraka* are easily tamed and mild mannered, and they make wonderful companions.

Haroka [*Hah -Roh - Kah*] = Large, hump-stomach lizard found in deserts. Flat feet for walking on sand. Eats smaller lizards, other reptiles, cacti, and dessert shrubs. Can go months without drinking water, but fills up hump when water is present.

Horako [*Hoh - Rah - Koh*] = Large, thick, slow lizards. Found near large bodies of water. Eat small fish and amphibians. Powerful, wide jaws allow for easy catching and sealing. Also used for transportation. Due to their girth and size, these lizards are often used for hauling heavy materials, and their strength is unmatched among other creatures of their size.

Infernites [*In - Fur - Nights*] = Volcanic dwelling people. Their internal body temperature is hotter than lava, but their external bodies can only remain intact if cooled. As such, they formed a symbiotic relationship with the *jojani*, who are able to leach the heat away from their bodies to prevent the *Infernites* from melting apart. Known as the keepers of the ancient ways, most new artists must interact with them to become initiates. Many of their tribal customs and rituals remain a mystery.

Jojani [*Joh - Jah - Nee*] = Heat leeches found inside of caves. Sap heat from prey, but keep prey alive. Can immobilize with the slime they secrete. Extremely strong but lack bones or formal body parts. Can form any appendage they need with their gel-like body. Dine on anything that is warm-blooded, but find the heat of beings from the Second most pleasing. Some tribes have been said to trap *jojani* and use them as torture tools.

Jusi Magamba [*Joo - See* ● *Mah - Gahm - Bah*] = Large scaly mammal that many confuse for a reptile. Scaly skin only covers the top of their body, and their bellies are as soft as the skin of any normal mammal (in females, the nipples for feeding their young are located toward the front of their abdomen). Though large and imposing, the species is peaceful by nature, and rarely attacks or charges. Easily tamed. Though peaceful, a bold species that is rarely spooked or startled. Natural environment is in the plains, but is also sometimes found at the base of mountains. Usually only *Magnums* use the creatures for meat or milk, but some other tribes have been known to also farm the creatures. The horn on their head is sometimes harvested as a weapon for *Magnum* soldiers.

Kondar [*Kon - Dar*] = Species of amphibious cattle. Native to valleys. Eats vegetation and small insects. Its three heads can move individually, but it thinks in unison. Hunters used to put two moving objects in front of the creature, sneaking up behind it while it tried to focus on the distraction. Its pelt is said to be good luck for reproduction when worn around the waist.

Kondor [*Kon - Door*] = Species of amphibious cattle. Native to plains. Exclusively eats grass found in prairies. Only drinks water while engulfed in water storms. Its meat is considered a delicacy by some.

Kubeba [*Koo - Bay - Bah*] = Large pets of *Ghafarians*. They are vicious looking but their bark and snarl has much more fight in it than they do. The entire species used to be wild, but through years of captivity and capture, the *kubeba* are almost exclusively tame and serve as glorified guard dogs. Main diet is dead fish hand-fed to them. Some species still exist in the wild, but they are endangered.

Kutisha [*Koo - Tish - Ah*] = Protects the *Giza Sana* island from intruders. Mainly feeds on blind seals native to the *Pango Maji*. No eyes, but sense movement to hunt. Normally avoids light, but there have been reports of the creature hopping onto land and eating the bioluminescent creatures of the island.

Magamu [*Mag - Ah - Moo*] = Language of the natives of *Magnus*.

Magnums [*Mag - Nuhms*] = Natives to *Magnus*. Giant humanoids with unparalleled strength. Mainly vegetarian, but sometimes eat small to medium-sized birds and cattle for snacks. Grow their own crops and harvest. Men are the cookers and warriors, while the women usually gather. Some women have been known to go into battle, but often are allowed to stay at home. They are not prevented from fighting because of a lack of strength or valor, or even any lack of respect on the part of the men, but they are kept at home because their value is held in the highest esteem.

Magnus [*Mag - Nuhss*] = Land of the giants. The land is similar to any other, but the structures are massive due to the natives.

Maisha Moa [*Mah - Ee - Shah* • *Moh - Ah*] = Long thought to be the originators of life. The giant beings are thought to be extinct, but sightings of the creature have been so rare throughout history, they are thought to have never existed in the first place. Most recent sightings are considered hoaxes. Said to exist across the seven dimensions, and many believe they are not extinct but have simply moved on to new dimensions (created by them). No information about their mating processes, language or behavior has ever been documented, though many theories and rumors exist about them. The ancients wrote extensively about them, though none of the ancient text illustrate or specify interaction between the ancients and the creatures. Considered sacred by everyone. Various literature illustrates sighting the creatures as good luck, and many fortunate events have been attributed to sightings.

Malaika [*Mah - Lay - Kah*] = Species of large, powerful, winged creatures. Eat whatever fits into their mouths. Will play with prey before killing it. Thrive in darkness. Unknown origins. Some say they can only be summoned by the arts, others say they can be trained by anyone skillful enough to best them, but none have been reported to be skillful enough. Though believed to be a naturally occurring species, they are seen as evil.

Mamba [*Mahm – Bah*] = Predatory species of mammal. Hunt in packs. Powerful hind legs allow the creatures to jump great heights. Skin flaps that run from their front paws to their back paws allow for gliding after jumps, and is the fastest way they can move forward. Known to attack anything small enough for them to take down as a pack. Usually hunt at night, but have been documented hunting during the day if hunger drives them to do so. Rumored to have been used as guard animals for the ancients, whom were able to tame them.

Midomo [*Mih - Doh - Moh*] = Native to the *Giza Sana*. Torturous, masochistic tribe. Women and men have the same bodily features, mate by standing back to back and exchanging sperm or egg depending on the need of the partner. Thought to be extinct but thrive in the absence of the White Lord. Mainly eat the blind creatures of the cave, but sometimes dine on glowworms. Use echolocation to see in the dark. Rumors speak of the tribe being the guardians for the White Lord during and after his reign, but this rumor contradicts what is known of the

White Lord, since he is said to have a pure heart.

Misimu Dudu [*Mih - See - Moo* ● *Doo Doo*] = Flying insect that synchronizes with its colony through sound. Nomadic in nature, the colony is always moving from one forest to the next in search of food. They constantly mate and are able to produce young every six days. Young reach maturity every seven years, but because they reproduce so often, a constant stream of them are usually being born. The newly born young form colonies with other newly born young, and the cycle continues. They have no natural defense mechanism and make easy meals for predators. Some people groups have been known to eat them. The only way to prepare them is to boil them alive for ten minutes, and they create a horrible raucous while cooking. Once done their exoskeleton is left crispy and the inside left fluid. They have a taste similar to peanut butter and a crunch similar to potato chips.

Moshi [*Moh - Shee*] = Rare species of intelligent, molecule-sized creatures that exclusively feed on the cell nuclei of mammals. Though the creatures usually travel in communities about the size of *paka*, there are some reported accounts of seeing the creatures form a mass as large as *Theluji Tembo*. When sighted they often appear as a cloud of smoke. Defense against the colony is impossible for all but artists. If sighted, fleeing is the best course of action, but the creatures are quick. Because they are so small, they seem to achieve levitation but are in fact hopping or moving over molecules of water that float in the air (so they can only move in humid environments). They are small enough to penetrate the pores. Little is known of how they reproduce, or if they ever attack as individuals. Ancients confused the creatures with evil spirits, and many myths about spirit-based attacks were really *moshi* attacks.

Mubaya [*Moo - Bi - Yah*] = Mountain range taken over by the Red Mage. A natural land barrier, as most of the mountains in the mountain range are purely vertical surfaces. The base is often sloped, but at the middle and higher they are exclusively vertical, and very few passes naturally exist. Before becoming the lair of the red Mage, it was an avoided range. Most people went around the range, and traveling through by foot was often fatally impossible.

Muva [*Moo - Vah*] = Main source of water-based nutrients in the dimension. Instead of falling from the sky, the water droplets accumulate in the air due to wind currents, temperature, and atmospheric pressure. As the currents grow stronger and more droplets condense and are trapped, the aggregate droplets begin to roll across the land. The giant water oval (or wall, depending on how the currents go) grows until the wind and pressure can no longer contain the droplets, then it gradually gives off its water to the land. Can be dangerous for anything without gills, but most structures in the dimension have been built to withstand the pressure from the water. Any structures that can't withstand the pressure are usually built with porous walls that allow the water to pass through. The homes are then outfitted with drainage systems and dry rooms.

Nawiba [*Nah - Wee - Bah*] = Cold scorpions whose sting provides heat. Their venom is sometimes used as a salve to remedy frost bite. Only found in cold regions, but most abundant in the Far North. Possible to harvest their venom without killing them, but they are so abundant in the Far North, safe harvesting is rarely practiced. No natural predators aside from sentient beings seeking warmth.

Nokofimbo [*Noh - Koh - Fihm - Boh*] = Species of snake that is used inside the staffs for the arts. Little is known about the elusive serpents, but legend has it that art practitioners have one *nokofimbo* that is linked to their soul. When they begin to practice, the two come together and the *nokofimbo* bonds with its counter-soul forever. Some say whenever an artist dies his staff dissolves and his spirit enters the snake where he will live on. If he is powerful enough, he may be able to resurrect himself when a new host body is found. Records of this process have never been documented, and artists are forbidden to speak of their ways to any other than those versed in the arts. It is also said that the *nokofimbo* lie in peace inside an artist's staff until another *nokofimbo* is near, and when the spirits disagree, the serpents try to fight. One story tells of two supremely powerful artists who released their *nokofimbo* and let the creatures fight when the arts failed to yield a winner. The result was a destroyed continent and poisoned waters that remained tainted for a decade. Others say the first crossing was done when a *nokofimbo* and an artist's spirit were destroyed and the released energy ripped open a portal. This theory was perpetrated by many who were leery of the White Lord's rule, saying that he crossed dimensions through murder.

Nokotomvu [*Noh - Koh - Tohm - Voo*] = Species of snake that drinks sap by tapping directly into a tree's bark. Sloth-like and rarely known to attack, they usually only move when traveling to a new spot to drink sap. Their bite is not venomous, but they are rarely eaten as they secrete their excrement through their skin instead of anus. Excrement is also used as a defense mechanism when threatened.

Nyasi Nyisu [*Ni - Ah - See* ● *Ni - Ee - Soo*] = Land with exclusively black grass. A few unique species live among the stalks, though why the grass has turned black is unknown. The separation in the black grass and the surrounding grass is only the color. Known to be a sacred ground for the arts, it is the only location where *nokofimbo* can be found, though this is also a mystery. Rumors are that in an attempt to lure *nokofimbo* to his property, an artists harvested seed pods from the black grass and attempted to grow it away from *Nyasi Nyisu*, but the grass grew green instead of black.

Paka [*Pak - Ah*] = Feline species found in plains. Rarely spotted any-where else. Eats *kondor* and occasionally other birds when able. Though a relatively small creature, it is able to bear more than twice its weight. Its jaws are powerful and it's claws quick, but it rarely attacks anything but *kondors*, unless in self-defense.

Pango Maji [*Pahn - Goh* ● *Mah - Jee*] = Body of water inside of the *Giza Sana*. Separates the island of technology from the rest of the cave. 777 feet deep. The water slowly swirls without a current. Thus, the water never stagnates or festers. It drains through a small funnel at the bottom, and is rerouted up to the apex of the chamber where it filters back down through cracks and small holes.

Pangoyoka [*Pan - Goh - Yoh - Kah*] = Blind cave snake. The antenna on its head act as sensors that pick up scents and sounds. Non-venomous. Catches prey by wrapping around and swallowing hole while prey is still alive. Eats anything smaller than itself. Only moves with speed when it senses food. It has been known to sit motionless for years, wait-ing for prey to come along.

Panyorofa [*Pan - Yoh - Roh - Fah*] = Cave mammal. Has eyes but rarely utilizes them. Amphibious and prefers cold water. Antenna used to sense vibrations in water, and smells on dry land. Main diet is salamanders and algae.

Panzi [*Pan – Zee*] = Small hopping insects that exclusively feed on grass seed pods. They do not bite and are not poisonous, but their feet have tiny hairs that can cause irritation on the skin of people. Build colonies on grass stalks but lay their eggs on the ground amidst the roots of grass. When the eggs hatch the young are born in adult form (though smaller for a few days until they mature).

Slithe [*Slihth*] = Tribe of people that are relatively peaceful. Long since thought to be the most artistic and skilled weavers. Their main trade is fabric creation, and they create every imaginable fabric for any imaginable need. Their trade skills are a secret passed down through the generations. The clothing they hand create is often expensive to purchase and seen as premium.

Sodarma [*Soh - Dahr - Mah*] = Acidic drink of the *Ghafarians*. So acidic, it eventually puts holes in the drinker's mouth, throat, or stomach. *Ghafarians* drink it to display their strength. Also has enrichment properties that act similar to adrenaline. The recipe isn't a secret, but none but the *Ghafarians* desire to prepare it.

Tatu [*Tah - Too*] = Common language of the dimension. Has different dialects, but most usages are the same in all territories. Some say the White Lord created it, nullifying most of the native languages in the process to help unite the land.

Theluji Tembo [*They - Loo - Jee* • *Tehm - Boh*] = Only found in the Far North. Passive creatures that are hunted by tribes native to the Far North. Because the creatures only defense is their size, they are easily overtaken and once faced extinction. To prevent their main food source from vanishing, the tribes banded together and only hunted the more mature of the creatures, leaving families and young alive to continue to reproduce. The more mature creatures do have a tougher meat, but consumption is also said to bring wisdom to the consumer. All of their body parts are used. Bones are used to create and fortify dwellings as well as for weapons, the skin and fur is used for clothing and insulation, and the organs are used for medicinal purposes (when not eaten with the flesh). The creatures feed through their feet, drinking snow and crushing rodents until an absorbable paste is created.

Tumbili [*Tuhm - Bee - Lee*] = Small but intelligent mammals that live in forests and jungles. Howl and screech to communicate, but have no vocal chords in their throats. The vocal chords are instead located in their prehensile tails. Though prehensile, the tails are only used to communicate and do not aid in their tree climbing. The tails have been documented grabbing some small objects, but sightings of this are rare. Territorial but passive toward most other species of mammals and reptiles. Often fatally fight with birds for nesting grounds.

Vivuli [*Vih - Voo - Lee*] = Creatures that thrive in darkness. They are allergic to light and are able to devour it in small amounts. If exposed to light for too long, their bodies crystalize as a defense mechanism that is known to last for six to ten months. Feared by all inhabitants of the Far North, these creatures eat heat and hunt anything that moves. Their crystals are often mistaken for ice, as they are usually found in cold regions that only experience seasonal sunlight.

Volcanu [*Vol - Kay - Noo*] = *Infernite* homeland that is rife with volcanic activity. Covered by a veil of ash during the day, very few life forms are seen. Though cooler and more hospitable at night, the only creatures that survive in this environment usually do so by remaining underground all the time. *Volcanu* is also the language of the *Infernite*.

Wam-Baika (Baika) [*Wahm - Bay - Kah*] = Species of winged creatures with hard, scaly skin. Native to mountains and volcanoes. Strong, but susceptible to attacks under the wing. Eat birds and some vegetation. Its clear stomach provides onlookers with a show of its digestion. It has been long believed that they are the most intelligent of the winged life forms, and what they lack in brutality they make up for in wits.

Wanake Kupanda [*Wahn - Ah - Kee • Koo - Pahn - Dah*] = Mysterious and unpredictable. Though sentient, the creature is equal parts humanoid and equal parts plant. Possess the ability to control certain species of plants, including the *fim*, and is known to be telepathically linked to the plants (though there is no evidence the plants are able to sense pain and talk, this creature has reported feeling the pain of plants).

Known to be vengeful toward people that intentionally harm any plant life, though also an individual that can be reasoned with. Understands morality, but is said to ignore socially constructed viewpoints. Considered by some to be of a higher intelligence than other sentient beings, but many simply fear the creature because of its ability to control the environment. Is never found away from vegetation. Uncertainty exists about whether the creature can take control of all plants or just certain species.

Wangapanyo [*Wahn - Gah - Pahn - Yo*] = Hairless rodents that glow from their feathery antenna. The antenna are used to sense movement, so they can escape danger. Blind. Their noses are their main source for finding food, and they exclusively eat a fruit that grows on the *Giza Sana* island.

Wangapepeo [*Wahn - Gah - Pee - Pee - Oh*] = Glowing insects native to the *Giza Sana* island. Pollinate the flowers of the island. Diet consists of nectar and pollen found in the flowers. They are a-sexual, though two genders still exist. Only males produce more males, and females more females. The insects must work in unison to pollinate. Because of the stiff nature of most of the flowers, the males must stand on the female's backs until the flower opens enough for them both to insert their proboscis. The males are two ounces heavier than females. The males will fight to the death if another male lands on its back.

Wangapopo [*Wahn - Gah - Poh - Poh*] = Dust bats that eat the *wangapepeo*. Surrounds prey in dust that coats its wing. Utilizes light-location to track prey, and can only eat bioluminescent creatures because that is all it can see. If a person were to put a *wangapopo* in a room with other illumination, the creature may go crazy trying to eat the light fixtures.

Wangayoka [*Wahn - Gah - Yoh - Kah*] = Flat reptiles that eat energy. Their bodies have adapted to process the energy given off by other creatures, and their flat bodies are absorption panels for the energy. Unlike *jojani*, they live like scavengers, soaking up energy released or produced by other life instead of hunting and sucking the energy.